'Breathtaking and heartrending, by turns hilarious and devastating and surprising and wild ... Mensah's prose makes the intangible deft and tremendous – from the balm of friendship, to the beauty of queerness, and the all-encompassing elixir of community. Tender, thrilling, and honest; *Small Joys* is a beam of light' **Bryan Washington, author of *Memorial***

'A largehearted look at the importance of found family, Mensah's first novel focuses on the lifesaving friendship between a cast-off son ... and the easygoing new roommate whose affection becomes a balm. *Small Joys* dwells in the sometimes-fleeting moments of pleasure and happiness that stave off the iniquities of the world' **Michelle Hart, *Electric Literature***

'I adored *Small Joys* – a sweet, moving, funny, strikingly open story. I don't know if I've ever rooted so much for a protagonist as I did for Harley. What a gorgeous novel' **Jennifer Saint, author of *Ariadne***

'I loved it. *Small Joys* is a wonderful book full of music, life and a great deal of heart. An extremely BIG joy!' **Matson Taylor, author of *The Miseducation of Evie Epworth***

'This heart-warming, witty, and moving debut is one of the most charming books you'll read this year. Exploring love, friendship, grief, and the bittersweet joy of being young, *Small Joys* is utterly beautiful' **Louise O'Neill, author of *Idol***

'A captivatingly tender novel ... it's beautiful' ***The Bookseller***

'Kind, careful, beautiful, and profound ... Elvin James Mensah has an uncanny ability to give voice to the most delicate nuances of the human experience. His characters will stay in your heart forever' **Alison Larkin, author of *The People We Keep***

SMALL JOYS

ELVIN JAMES MENSAH

SCRIBNER

LONDON NEW YORK SYDNEY TORONTO NEW DELHI

SCRIBNER

First published in Great Britain by Scribner,
an imprint of Simon & Schuster UK Ltd, 2023

1 3 5 7 9 10 8 6 4 2

Simon & Schuster UK Ltd
1st Floor
222 Gray's Inn Road
London WC1X 8HB

Simon & Schuster Australia, Sydney
Simon & Schuster India, New Delhi

www.simonandschuster.co.uk
www.simonandschuster.com.au
www.simonandschuster.co.in

A CIP catalogue record for this book
is available from the British Library

Hardback ISBN: 978-1-3985-1488-1
Trade Paperback ISBN: 978-1-3985-1489-8
eBook ISBN: 978-1-3985-1490-4

Typeset in Palatino by M Rules
Printed and Bound in the UK using 100% Renewable
Electricity at CPI Group (UK) Ltd

To Terry Miller,
In friendship; with love.

'Friendship marks a life even more deeply than love. Love risks degenerating into obsession, friendship is never anything but sharing'

ELIE WIESEL, *The Gates of the Forest*

PART ONE

One

I had never thought much about birds before I met Muddy. Any interest that I had in them, and the various species that inhabited Britain, was because of him. There were a lot of things I hadn't considered before I met him.

I'd often thought of life as something to be bargained with, to be battled with. It was an entity to which you repeatedly justified your existence, to which you made your case for why it deserved to be embellished with happiness and love and friendship. There was something almost mythical about people for whom it hadn't been this way, people who were simply entitled to happiness by virtue of being alive.

Muddy often made me feel as if I deserved to be one of these people. His enthusiasm for his own life made mine feel better by association. It was an enthusiasm that seeped into quotidian things like swimming, various kinds of rock music, karaoke, and, yeah, birds.

The first time I saw him was on a warm afternoon in July. I'd just returned home to Dartford from university, and I had no intention of going back. I stood in the woods by my flat, staring at a small X-ACTO knife cradled in my palm. I thought I'd submerged myself somewhere that felt thickly wooded enough that nobody would see me. It was so quiet. From the trees to the dirt to the wildflowers, it felt as if the woods were closing in on themselves. The quiet hadn't brought with it any peace; in fact, it had amplified my ominous thoughts. I pressed my eyes shut and begged life for something it had refused me, desperately hoping that once I opened them up again, amongst the leaves and branches, there it would be, some glorious manifestation of happiness. But when I opened my eyes, the world seemed darker somehow, crueller, as if it had collected in its palms my every failure, my every inadequacy, and presented them to me, instructing me to behold the beauty around me and deem my presence here inappropriate.

I closed my eyes again.

A hand suddenly landed on my shoulder and I squeezed the knife tight, gasping in pain, dropping it into the ferns. I turned around and there he was: a tall husky guy holding a pair of binoculars, with brown hair down to his neck and a concerned expression on his stubbled, dimpled face.

'Oh, pal,' he said. He was wearing cargo shorts, brown safety boots and a plaid shirt with the sleeves rolled up. 'What've you done to yourself?' He had a distinctive Mancunian accent. I looked up at him, panicked, trying to catch the blood dripping with my other palm. I was so embarrassed and desperately wanted to be alone, so much that I wanted to cry. But it had been my father's teaching that I shouldn't cry in front of other people, some 'wisdom' from childhood that'd been implanted like a chip in my brain. 'Ah, you're bleeding, mate ...' he continued. He fished out a handkerchief from one of the pockets on his shorts, waved out the crumbs and began to wrap it around my hand. 'Had my sandwiches in this but it should be all right.'

'I'm fine,' I said curtly, yanking my hand away and unravelling it from the blood-soaked fabric.

'Ah, come on, mate,' he said. 'Don't be like that. You're bleeding. Here, look—'

'I said I'm okay.'

'Oh, pal, you can't just—'

I walked away from him before he could finish, holding my shirt over the cut, all the way back to the flat. Crossing the road, I realized I hadn't brought my keys with me. I also realized that he had been following me. When I got to the front door, I sat on the bench just outside the building and kept my head down as he walked towards me.

'Is your name Harley by any chance?' he asked, looking down at me. I nodded, still not looking up. 'Thought it might be. I'm Muddy. I suppose I'm your new flatmate, then.' He went to shake my hand but then stopped. 'Shit, yeah, sorry.' He took his keys out of another pocket on his shorts. 'Let's get you inside, then.'

Muddy and I had a mutual friend, Chelsea, whose dad owned the flat. Before I came back from university, I'd asked her if I could have my old room back, but she'd already let it out to somebody else, so I had to take the smaller third one instead. It turned out that somebody was Muddy.

I spent the afternoon avoiding him. I locked myself in the bathroom for a few minutes, running some cold water over my hand and then looked through the first aid kit for something to bandage it with. I couldn't bear the thought of throwing my bloody shirt in the kitchen bin where Chelsea might see it, or where Muddy might be reminded of this encounter, so I balled it up and stuffed it under my bed, later disposing of it in one of the bins outside. I stayed in my room with my headphones on, pretending to be asleep whenever Muddy knocked on my door and asked if I was all right.

Honestly, I didn't really know what I was doing in the woods. I had always assured myself that I wasn't suicidal because I didn't meet the criteria. It was usually like I was on autopilot or something, but only until I reached that pivotal moment before I shuddered back into consciousness. But I'd got so close this time.

I slept well into the evening. When I woke up, I heard loud voices outside. I didn't want to get out of bed: the thought of doing so terrified me. At university, hearing other people's voices in the communal area meant I wouldn't leave my room at all, not even for the bathroom, until it was pin-drop silent. But I couldn't do that now since Chelsea had texted from the living room, asking me to come out. And not wanting to irritate her, I did.

On the sofa, Muddy was sat beside a brawny guy with muscular arms and a cap on backwards. He was in a white polo shirt, navy workman trousers and had a full-sleeve tattoo down his left arm. They were playing a wrestling game on the PlayStation; they didn't look like each other exactly, but there was a certain brotherliness about them. Chelsea was sat on the single chair against the wall, fiddling with her phone, looking at them, annoyed. When she saw me, her face broke into a wide smile, which put one on mine. Her face was more bronzed than I remembered, and her ginger hair was shorter too, all glossy and swinging atop her shoulders.

'Oh, it's so good to see you, dropout,' she said.

I kept my bandaged hand in my pocket as we hugged. 'Come on,' I said. 'I don't want that to be a thing.'

'Too late,' she said, licking her thumb and dabbing away the sleep in the corners of my eyes. I batted her hand away, laughing. I took a step back to enjoy her outfit: a long-sleeved black top with a cut-out across the chest, fitted into a short leather skirt.

'Chelsea Taylor,' I said enthusiastically. 'I *love* everything about this. And you've finally done the hair. You've been talking about it for ages.'

'Oh, hun,' she said, 'I've done the hair. I've done the brows. I've done the nails ...' I looked down at them. 'I didn't think I'd like a neon green look on me. And I never used to like 'em this long either, to be fair. But I've been getting my jollies clackety-clacking away on everything.'

She drummed her nails gently on my forehead. 'They're cute,' I said. 'What made you finally change things up?'

For months, she'd been texting me about getting the chop, as well as rejuvenating her wardrobe, which up until recently had mostly been jeans and oversized belts with huge silver studs and colourful one-shoulder tops.

'Oh, it was all Nor's idea,' she said. 'She's coming over in a bit, so you might want to wear a hat or something.'

Noria, Chelsea's other black friend, was obsessed with my hair. I rarely went to the barber's, and she enjoyed how fast and long it grew. It was like a cosmetic playground for her. Whenever she'd come round to the flat or whenever I went over to hers, she liked to style it in various ways and put all these different products in it. Chelsea had been friends with her long before I was. They used to be colleagues at a shoe store in Bluewater, before Chelsea left to work at Regal Cinemas, where we first met and where she was now a supervisor.

I asked her where they were going and she said ATIK, a nightclub in town near Dartford station. Just then, the guy in the cap shouted: 'Chels, be a babe and get us a couple more beers, would you?'

Chelsea didn't answer and rolled her eyes. She took my arm and pulled me into the kitchen, removing my hand from my pocket. Startled, she brought it close to her face and inspected the gauze.

'What's this?' she asked.

'Oh,' I said, trying to be nonchalant. 'I was just out and about earlier, and I had a little accident. It isn't—'

'What kind of accident?'

I laughed. 'Chelsea,' I said. 'It's nothing.'

'Harles, you've got a bandage on—'

'Stop!' I said. 'I told you, it's nothing. Anyway, who's the guy next to Muddy?'

She looked at me curiously for a moment and then said: 'Oh, that's Finlay.'

'He's fit.'

'He's all right.'

'Is he your new fella?'

'I don't know if we wanna start calling him that, to be fair – my new *fella*,' she said matter-of-factly. 'So, are you still "not drinking" then?' she continued, gesturing air quotes at me.

'I don't know why you're doing that,' I said, 'I still really don't drink.'

'I dunno,' she said, pulling a few beers from the fridge. 'Uni could've changed you. I don't know everything you got up to there, do I?'

'Anxiety and depression.'

'Kinky.'

'Yeah,' I said. 'We were all doing it.'

For weeks now, I'd been texting Chelsea about how I hadn't been enjoying myself and how it had been the uni and the course and the people's fault. I felt uneasy about discussing things like sadness with her, so I couldn't bring myself to disclose the gravity of my despair. I'd hoped these texts would make me sound ironic and petulant, which was my preferred dynamic between us.

I followed Chelsea back into the living room with a glass of Coke. Muddy had just won a match against Finlay and had slung an arm around him, singing 'Dry Your Eyes' by The Streets very loudly. Finlay frowned, removing his hat, and ran a hand through his short dark-blonde hair. Muddy got up to turn off the PlayStation and saluted me with two fingers when he saw me sitting down; I smiled at him hesitantly.

Chelsea took his place next to Finlay, who slouched into the chair and put his arm around her, gently stroking her shoulder, while Muddy sat on the armrest of my chair.

'So, you two all acquainted then?' Chelsea asked.

'Yeah,' Muddy said, looking down at me. 'We had a bit of a run in this afternoon, didn't we, pal?'

Everyone else looked at me too. 'Yeah,' I said, trailing off. 'In the woods—'

'The woods?' Chelsea said. 'You're not outdoorsy, Harles. What were you doing in there, then? Is that how you did your hand?'

I was silent for a long time, aware of how tense I'd suddenly made things. I'd just thought of something to say when Muddy placed his hand on my back and said: 'We were out seeing the birds, weren't we, Harley?'

I smiled shyly at everyone. It was like he'd uncorked me and, for the time being, drained out all that anxious energy.

'Mud,' Chelsea said. 'You ain't even known him two minutes and you're already chewing his ear off about the bloody birds.'

'Well, you know me, Chels,' he said. 'Put a coin in, and you'll get the whole song, won't you?'

Finlay laughed. 'Mudzie,' he said. 'He don't wanna hear it, mate. How many times have I told you? No one fuckin' cares.'

'Eh,' Muddy snapped. 'Back off, Finn.' He put his large, hairy arm around me. He had a strong earthy scent that made me want to smell him. But without making things weird. 'He loves the birds, he does,' he said, winking at me. 'Or at least, he's gonna when I'm done with him.'

'Mate,' Finlay said to me, 'if he tries to push any of this bird bollocks on you, just let me know, and I'll sort him out. Send him back up north.'

'Oh, pack it in,' Muddy said, 'you're half-Scottish, pal.'

'Hardly the same thing, mate.'

'And anyway,' Muddy said, 'he won't need your help, will he? 'Cause we're gonna have a great time, me and him.'

I decided to join the conversation. 'What do you have against birds, Finlay?'

'Don't have anything against 'em, mate,' he said, crossing a leg over his knee. 'But you ain't gonna catch me in the middle of a fuckin' field with a pair of binoculars, jumpin' about like a dozy twat whenever I see one of 'em, are you?'

Muddy looked at me. 'You wouldn't think he were my best mate, would you?'

'Nah,' Finlay said. 'I'm not your best mate. Your best mate is that bloke you go in the woods with at all hours.' He started to laugh. 'They say they're out looking for birds, but you never really know what's going on, do you?'

'Mate,' Muddy said. 'Ian wouldn't be my first choice if I went dogging.'

Chelsea laughed now. 'Then who would be?'

'So, what d'ya say, pal?' Muddy said to me, tapping my chest. 'Fancy a bit of dogging later?'

There was protocol I followed around straight guys, or guys I perceived to be so. I made a conscious effort not to touch them whenever I was engaged in conversation, however playful. It was difficult to stay the course with Muddy, though, it was as if he were goading me.

'Mud, you perv,' Chelsea said, 'get off him.'

Muddy laughed. 'Nah, I'm only joking, pal.'

'Well, you better be,' Chelsea said. 'You don't want to piss Nor off.'

Finlay sat up, interlocking his fingers. 'So, what's this about you dropping out of uni, then?'

I didn't expect that I'd have to explain this to anyone but Chelsea. I was annoyed that he'd asked, but still I told him that I'd studied music journalism, but that the course hadn't been for me. I began the sentence as if it might lead to another thought, but I said nothing else. Finlay said that he'd lost a few mates to uni, holding up a bottle of beer as if they were dead, and that he didn't think it was worth going unless you knew exactly where you wanted to be at the end of it.

'How old are you? Twenty? Twenty-one? See, when I was your age, I got me a nice little NVQ in plumbing and heating. Bloody high life, mate.'

Returning from the bathroom later, I walked down the corridor and saw Muddy in the kitchen by the fridge. I was still apprehensive about talking to him; he'd witnessed me at my most broken, and I didn't know what this meant now. As I approached the kitchen door, I tried to take a bigger step past than usual so I wouldn't be in view for long, but still he saw me.

'Tryna get those lunges in, are you?' he said, taking a huge lunge himself and grunting with his fists on his hips. I laughed to mask the embarrassment. He stood back up and took out a bottle of Carling from the fridge, holding it up. 'Fancy one, pal?'

I shook my head and stepped inside. 'I'm sorry for being so short with you before,' I said.

'Oh, don't worry about it, mate,' he said. 'You were bleeding, weren't you? Try catching me in a good mood when I've been injured.' He closed the fridge, and leant on it, crossing his arms. He looked at me as if we were about to have a serious conversation. 'I'm glad you're all bandaged up now. But you owe me a new handkerchief. That was my favourite, that.'

'Really?'

'Yeah, pal,' he said. 'Used that one for everything, I did. My sandwiches, my sweaty forehead, shite that comes out my nose. Everything, mate.'

'Right.'

'So, whenever you're ready to settle up, give me a shout,' he said, tapping me on the back. 'I'm just across the hall from you.'

I stopped him before he left. 'Muddy,' I said, 'why did you tell Chelsea that we were out looking at birds earlier?'

He turned back to face me. 'Well,' he said, 'you just looked like you didn't really wanna talk about it, didn't you?' I smiled at him. 'Like I said, pal,' he continued, 'I am just across the hall from you. Not just about my handkerchief, but if you need anything or whatever. My door's always open.'

The longer he fixed his brown eyes on mine, the more I felt like crying. 'Thank you,' I replied.

'Yeah, well,' he said, 'my lock's fucked and Chels won't pay to have it done, you see.'

'Oh,' I said. 'I thought you were just being nice.'

'Me? Nice?' he said, giggling. 'Nah, mate, I'm a right nasty piece of work, me.'

Noria arrived later in a short black sheer dress, with her dark hair blown out, all soft and long and curly. She and Muddy kissed at the front door and I watched for a few seconds before I looked away. She lifted herself onto her toes and clung onto his broad shoulders, while he clasped her waist. When she saw me, she screamed and pointed at me. Despite packing my hair down tight, she still commented on how long and bushy it had got. I pretended to run in the other direction as she went through her little purse and retrieved a thin black comb. 'Eh, Harley,' she said, pointing it at me, 'where'd you think you're going?'

In Chelsea's room now, Noria sat on the bed, and I sat cross-legged on the carpet beside her glistening legs, while she combed out my hair and etched the back of that rat-tail comb through it, idly separating it out into large sections. We could hear Muddy and Finlay back in the living room shouting at the telly, but Chelsea looked less annoyed now; she was standing in front of the mirror, dancing seductively to Gwen Stefani's 'Luxurious' on the radio.

'Chels, I told you,' Noria was saying, twisted around to her. 'A nude nail with a neon tip is *it*. Maybe chill out a bit with the bronzer next time, yeah? But you look amazing, babes, I could cry.'

Chelsea turned back to us. 'Oh my god, Nor, stop,' she said. 'You're getting me gassed.'

'Well, get gassed,' Noria said. 'The cab will be here in ten. So, we can still do Tesco if we leave in five.'

'For what?'

'Literally anything that'll fit in my clutch, Chels,' she said. 'I'm sorry but I'm not tryna do club prices tonight.'

'Fair point.'

Noria looked back down at me, still gliding the comb through my hair. 'What do you think about cornrows, Harles?' she asked. 'You'll look like a four-foot, dark-skinned Ludacris.'

I laughed. 'Or someone actually dark-skinned, like D'Angelo.'

'You think you look like D'Angelo?'

'I wish,' I said. 'But I'm closer to him than Ludacris, surely?'

'Yeah, you're right.'

'You know, I'm all right with anything as long as you don't try and straighten it again.'

'Okay,' she said. 'Let's do it! Oh, and don't pack down your hair so much anymore. It's only gonna kill when I comb it out again.'

Muddy walked by then, stopping in the doorway. He started to mimic Chelsea, who had gone back to dancing in the mirror; seeing his reflection, she put her middle finger up at him, stifling a laugh. Muddy then asked what Noria was doing to my hair.

'Mud, mind your business, yeah?' she said. 'This is between me and my babe.'

'Oh,' he said. 'He's your babe now, is he?'

She stroked the side of my face. 'My one and only.'

Muddy laughed, looking down at me. 'Taken my missus now, have you, pal?'

I looked up at Noria. 'You heard her,' I said. 'I'm her one and only.'

'That's right,' Noria said, before looking at Muddy curiously. 'You haven't been using that skincare set I got you, have you?'

Muddy made a face. 'Nah, not for me, that.'

'Why not?'

'Because you want me smellin' like the bleedin' Body Shop or something, don't you? And I can't be arsed puttin' all that shite on my bastard face every morning. I think I look and smell pretty fuckin' great, me.'

'Your face is really dry.'

'Bollocks.'

'It's like kissing sandpaper.'

'Oi, Harley,' he said, stepping into the room. He got on all fours and held his face directly in front of mine. 'Do you think I have a dry face, pal?'

'Mud, I beg,' Noria said, tapping on his shoulder with the comb repeatedly. 'Please get your crusty face away from him. C'mon! Get!'

Muddy winked at me and started to lift himself up when Finlay came into the room too and straddled his back. He was pretending to be a cowboy, wielding a phantom lasso, and yelling: 'Yippee-ki-yay, motherfucker!' Muddy called him a prick but played along anyway, laughing and neighing and tottering out of the room. Chelsea rolled her eyes in the mirror as she applied some lip liner, then pulled down the hem of her skirt and asked Noria if she was ready to go. Noria got up and they faced each other, energetically feeling each other's hair and clothes. I hoisted myself up onto the bed and watched them.

All evening I expected to be reconciled with the sadness from earlier. The reunion came soon enough, emerging in the pit of my stomach as everyone crowded around the kitchen table and had a shot of vodka, before Chelsea and Noria hugged and kissed me goodbye. It remained as I went into my room, closing the door quietly as Muddy and Finlay bleated with laughter from the living room. Finally, I closed my eyes and forced myself to sleep.

Two

From my bedroom window, I could see our road, as well as the woods and the vast green meadows that lined it. Muddy liked to stand out there in the mornings before he went to work, looking up into the sky for a while. I'd started watching him, looking down with the curtains partly drawn. With his binoculars around his neck, he'd arch a hand across his forehead with either a confused or very happy expression, then he'd write something down in his little notebook and disappear into the woods.

One morning the following week, he offered me a lift to work. Chelsea had spoken to the deputy manager, Eddie, at Regal, who said he was happy to have me back. Chelsea told me afterwards that Muddy worked there too. My first shift was in the afternoon, and I planned on taking the bus, but as I left the flat and walked to the end of the road, I saw his little red Vauxhall Corsa coming the opposite way. He had an arm out of the window, a hand on the wheel, and he was smiling at me. 'Ey up,' he said, 'you off to work, pal?'

'Yeah.'

'Just getting back myself,' he said, 'fancy a lift?'

This must've been the first time I realized how much I liked his smile, how much I liked his cavernous dimples and how his eyes squinted, how the wider the smile got the more his cheeks puffed into ping-pong-sized balls. He was in his uniform, a black polo shirt, the sleeves of it only just hiding a colourful tattoo on his arm. I felt bad about letting him give me a lift, when he'd only just returned, so I held up my hand and told him that it was all right, that I was going to jump on the bus, aware of how unconvincing I sounded. I didn't even inch away as I said it to make it seem as if I was in a hurry. I wanted him to really insist, just to alleviate my guilt.

He lowered his eyes, as if he knew this. 'Come on,' he said. 'Hop in, pal. Let's get you to work.' I reached for the back door of his car, and he said, chuckling: 'Surely not . . .'

'You really didn't have to drop me off,' I said, sitting beside him and fastening my seat belt.

'Oh, it's nothing,' he said, 'you gotta make time for a mate, don't you?'

I looked up at him. 'A mate?'

'Yeah,' he said, 'what? We *are* mates!'

'If you say so,' I said. It sounded sarcastic but I meant it. At uni I became obsessed with how other people saw me. I'd wonder if people thought me mysterious because I was so quiet, thinking that I must hold so much wisdom that I tran-scended things like small talk. But really, I knew that wasn't the case. People saw my inability to speak at various socials as

simply weird. I was weird because I was weird. At least that
was the story, until I realized that I had anxiety, and that was
what made me feel weird. I decided then that the nature of
my anxiety was of the social kind, and I suppose it felt good
to tether these feelings to something real.

He drove to the end of our road, eventually arriving at the
interchange near the edge of Dartford, a web of roads unfold-
ing towards London, Essex and further into Kent.

'Are you looking for birds when you're out in the field in
the mornings?' I asked.

He smiled. 'Ah, you've been watching me, have you?'

'I can see you from my bedroom window.'

'Yeah, I am, pal,' he said. 'I gotta get out there, haven't I?
Get down as much as I can for the old life list.'

'For the what?'

'My bird book. I got a bit of a competition going with my
mate Ian. I'm trying to bury him.'

'That guy Finlay said you keep going out into the
woods with?'

'Yeah,' he said, chuckling, 'but it's nothing dodgy, mate.
You can't listen to Finn, he's a muppet.'

I laughed too. 'I've never heard of competitive birdwatching before.'

'Hold on,' he said. 'First off, pal, I'm a birder, me. Not a
birdwatcher. I'm looking *for* 'em, not *at* 'em. Very important
distinction, that.'

'Noted.'

'Mind if I put on some tunes?' he asked, already pressing
buttons on the dashboard.

'It's your car.'

'Supersonic' by Oasis started playing. He drummed both fingers on the wheel and made percussive noises with his mouth. He glanced down at me, nodding his head to the guitar riffs, pushing his bottom lip out, raising his shaggy eyebrows. I looked away. I'd already grown so used to avoiding eye contact with him. His pale brown shorts were taut across his thighs and he was fanning his knees in and out. There was a long silence when the song ended that made me nervous. I thought this meant he was wondering whether he could ask about what had happened in the woods. When I felt like he was about to say something, I asked him why he was in shorts and not the full Regal uniform. He said that he worked on deliveries mostly and spent most of the day waiting for the delivery trucks to come in and sorting out the stock on them, so he and the other guy he worked with were exempt.

'So,' he said now, 'you were doin' music at uni, were you?'

'Music journalism, yeah.'

'How was that then?'

'Well, I dropped out, so . . .'

He laughed. 'Well, you must've really liked yourself a bit of music to have gone to bloody university for it, mustn't you?'

'Yeah, I suppose.'

I had told a lot of lies about studying music journalism. My dad didn't even know I had chosen it as a subject. I'd told him that I'd gone to do mathematics or computer science (I couldn't remember which), something he could brag about to his church lot. There was a familial prestige, however illusory, about attending university in order to pursue an esteemed career that I'd felt compelled to preserve.

'Go on then,' Muddy said, 'what sort of stuff you into?'

I told him that I liked hip-hop, particularly female MCs, and whatever Noria suggested that I listen to. I asked him if, in addition to Oasis, he played the Stone Roses and the Smiths on rotation.

'Nah,' he said, smiling. 'They're all class, they are. But I got one of them open minds, me. I'll give anything a go.'

I started to get even more nervous when we got closer to the Regal building, so I asked him about his tattoo. He beamed, twisting his body around at a red light and pushing up his sleeve.

'It's a starling,' he said. 'It's my granddad's favourite bird.'

It was a beautiful tattoo, intricately coloured, with bright yellow on the starling's beak, and green and purple plumage that had an almost iridescent quality.

'It's stunning,' I said.

'Cheers, pal.'

Eventually, he pulled into the bus lane outside of the cinema and I got out. Before I closed the door, he said: 'Have a nice one, mate,' and then told me to take it easy, pointing at my bandaged hand. I thanked him, smiling timidly, and walked towards the automatic doors.

It was an awkward and mostly lonely shift. To get acquainted with the new tills they'd installed, Eddie made me shadow an enthusiastic girl on concessions named

Emily, who had bleached blonde hair and very dark make-up. She became less enthusiastic, however, the more I messed up on the tills, and I started to feel this debilitating sensation every time she apologized to customers on my behalf.

At lunch, I went to a small café down the road with Chelsea and sat outside in the sun. She was working a thirteen-hour shift that day, compared to my five. I wasn't very hungry, so she ordered a full English and let me eat bits from her plate. We'd started doing this after the first few times we'd gone out to eat, and I'd confessed that I was such a slow eater that I didn't feel comfortable eating in front of other people. She'd laughed and asked what that was all about, and I'd explained that I'd always felt this strange pressure to finish my plate or I'd be judged by the other person, that sometimes I'd even store food in my cheeks until I'd finished chewing the previous mouthful, just to create the illusion I was eating quicker than I actually was.

Moving the last piece of bacon back and forth in her baked beans, she asked what my plan was now that I was back.

'I don't know,' I said. 'But thank you for getting me my job back.'

'Oh, don't worry about it, hun,' she said, and then continued jestingly: 'I mean, you ditch me for a new life at uni, and then come back expecting everything to be the way it was, but you know, Harles, it's fine.'

I smiled at her and leaned back in my chair.

'Ah shit,' she said, pointing behind me.

I turned around and saw an elderly man at the table

behind ours reading a newspaper. On the front page, there was a picture of a double-decker bus with its roof torn off.

'Oh,' I said. 'I don't know if I want to keep looking at that. It was still on the news this morning.'

'Well, I think we better get used to it.'

'How do you mean?'

She shrugged. 'Just because it happened the once, don't mean it won't happen again.'

'Chelsea,' I said, 'are you fearmongering?'

'Well, aren't you scared?'

I shrugged at her, looking down, circling my thumbs around each other. The societal whiplash, with London's win to hold the Olympics being followed by a string of terror attacks, had made me uneasy. It'd roused in me so much anxiety that I had this insidious feeling of never being okay again, not until another bad thing had happened to give this swell of fear some validity.

I decided to change the subject. 'How've you found being a supervisor?'

'Oh, it's lush, Harles,' she said. 'I'm drunk on power and I love it. I'm hoping Eddie stops messing me about and just makes me deputy manager soon.'

I smiled proudly at her.

I had worked at Regal for three years before I left for uni. My dad had too, doing security. He'd been one of two guys on the rota. The other guy was a thickset Jamaican man called Benzo. He worked evenings and would joke around with the rest of the team and regularly slack off. My dad, who was the total opposite – a tall, tight-fisted

Ghanaian man who wore seriousness like a medal – had done mornings.

It had taken several weeks for my colleagues to realize that he was actually my dad. I bore quite a striking resemblance to him, but since I'd mostly worked with white people, no one dared point that out. But then Benzo had called in sick one day, so my dad had covered both shifts. I had been cleaning one of the screens that afternoon, while he manned the ticket point. When I was done, I'd radioed him on my walkie-talkie to let him know the customers lined up outside could come in and I'd accidently referred to him as Dad, instead of Kwame like everyone else did. I'd walked out with my dustpan and brush to a small huddle of colleagues with confused looks on their faces.

'So, Finlay,' I said now. 'Where did you meet him, then?'

She scrunched up a tissue and placed it in the centre of the plate. 'The little Mexican place in town,' she said. 'We had one of our staff dos in there and he was there with some of his rugby mates. We all had a bit of a dance afterwards and he got involved, and at the end of the night we had a little cheeky snog. So, the next morning, he comes up to the cinema and asks one of the cashiers if he can speak to the "fit ginger bird" he met last night. Ah, Harles, it was brilliant. I went, like, proper red though. I swear everyone was in stitches when he left.'

'Then why do you look so pissed off whenever he's around?'

She cackled. 'Do I?'

'You haven't noticed?' I asked. 'You look like you properly hate him.'

She sighed. 'I don't know. I mean, you saw him. He's twenty-six but he also acts like a big bloody child. You can't talk about anything serious with him. It's like he's allergic or something. Does my fuckin' head in.'

'How long have you been seeing him for?'

'Couple months now, I think,' she said. 'I'll admit that he's not too bad when you get him on his own. He mostly acts like that when he's around Mud. But you can't tear 'em apart usually. It's annoying.'

'I think they're cute.'

'Oh, give it a couple weeks, hun.'

I laughed. 'So, how did Noria and Muddy happen then?' I asked. 'I'm actually pretty surprised at that. Do you remember the night before I left for uni, and you guys got drunk and she gave us that speech about how she'd never date another white guy again?'

'Yeah,' Chelsea said, 'but then the week after she gave me the same speech about black guys, so I think it's best we just take it as it comes now. They've only been going out for a few weeks, but yeah, I think she's into him. I mean, he's lovely. When I went out with him, it was mostly about the hugs. Oh, he gives great ones, Harles. He's like a big bear. You sort of just sink into him like a pillow.'

'Wait a minute,' I said, surprised, sitting up. 'You went out with him?' She flinched at my enthusiasm, so I reined it in. 'I mean, you've had Finlay *and* Muddy?' I continued. 'I have, like, so many questions. There's conflicts of interest all over the place.'

'There's really not.'

'Oh, but there is,' I said. 'Let's lay them out, shall we? So, doesn't Muddy mind that you're going out with his best friend? And doesn't Finlay mind that you're still living with your ex? And didn't Eddie give you shit for going out with another member of staff? Especially since you're his supervisor! And, what's left? Oh, isn't it a bit awkward that Noria's going out with him now?'

'Stop shit-stirring,' she said, laughing, picking up the sauce-soaked tissue and throwing it at me. 'So, what do you think of Mud, then? Since, you know, you've been out seeing the birds with him and everything. I'm sorry about all that dogging stuff the other night, by the way. He can be a bit overly familiar.'

'Oh no, it's fine,' I said. 'He actually gave me a lift to work this morning. But if I say I *don't* like him, will you kick him out, so I can have my old room back?'

'Absolutely not, hun.'

'Then he's all right, I guess.'

As we walked back to the cinema, she asked about my hand and I said that it was fine, and then she told me that whatever I'd done to it, that I really needed to be more careful, and I told her to stop mummying me.

'You spoken to your dad yet?' she asked next. 'Have you told him that you dropped out?'

I shrugged. I didn't want to talk about my dad, and I wished there was something about my disposition that reflected this.

I spent the rest of the shift standing behind Emily on concessions again, watching her upsell to customers and hand out little feedback cards. I'd hoped that somehow I'd be able to accommodate my anxiety better, renegotiate my contract with it and let it inhabit me in ways that were convenient for us both. But still I feared being asked to pour drinks or prepare popcorn or hot dogs because I couldn't stop my hands from shaking. I pleaded with whichever cosmic energy had been facilitating this episode of mine to grant me some kind of reprieve, to not embarrass me completely. But pleading be damned. I spilled an order of rosé across the counter. Emily offered it to the customer for free and apologized, and I took a few steps back, desperate to do something to repair the last few moments.

Emily smiled at me and said: 'Don't worry about it, Harley. We all have our little moments, don't we?' And I just stared at her not saying anything. I suspected her warm expression concealed some irritation.

In my teenage years, I'd thought self-assurance would come with age. I'd staked so many of my future glories on my twenties signalling something, as if the ground beneath my feet would feel different somehow or that life would take on this beautiful, previously undiscovered shape, into which I'd slot with a sigh of relief; I'd made it, I'd say. Of course, it didn't signal a thing and all the anxieties simply evolved into new and fun shapes, and came at me from all these imaginative angles. At twenty-one, self-assurance hadn't come at all.

I had to walk through the foyer to leave the building at the end of my shift. A few of the other cashiers were disassembling some old standees that they'd put up to commemorate the latest *Star Wars* movie. Emily shouted goodbye to me on my way out, but I'd been so embarrassed with how the shift had gone that I couldn't bear to respond.

So, I just kept walking.

Three

The anniversary of my mum's death, which was also my birthday, had just gone, so I called my dad. I thought the occasion might give the call some meaning. When he answered the phone, I was surprised at how pleasant he sounded. He called me 'his boy', which he had never done, not even in childhood. I hadn't seen him in person for a few years and we'd left things quite badly. I willed myself not to think about this too much, since the recovery always demanded so much of me.

I asked him how he was. 'I'm okay,' he said. 'Getting on. Getting by. Are you visiting from university?'

Anxiety and queerness and failure only served to make me further unrecognizable as a black man to him, so I said yes, in a bid to protect myself. I often felt as if I was contorting myself into all these impossible positions for the sake of making sense to people. Handing over these little pieces of myself, taking them back, flipping them over and handing them to someone else.

'When are you going to come and see me?' he asked.

I paused. 'Really?' He asked what I meant by this, and I said: 'I haven't seen you in ages. It's literally just been these quick calls.'

'You don't want to come and see your own father?' he asked, laughing. 'Don't you know that I've missed you?'

Despite everything, I'd never dismissed the option of repairing our relationship. But pretending nothing had happened didn't feel particularly healthy.

'I'll come and see you whenever.'

'Good,' he said, 'How is university? Are you studying hard?'

'Yes.'

'My boy,' he said again. 'An engineer. We thank God for your life.'

Ah, I thought, *that's what I'd told him. A chemical engineer.* Noria's older brother had studied engineering at university. I guessed that's why it'd leapt to mind when my dad had asked me. I wasn't sure why he believed me though; I'd never shown an interest in such a thing. But, I supposed, if anything, it spoke to a fundamental truth that who I really was hadn't mattered to him.

'So, what have you been up to?' I asked. 'Do you have a new job now?'

'No,' he said. 'But by the grace of God . . .'

It sounded like an incomplete thought, but it was the whole thing; he was manifesting something. He had been let go from Regal for being homophobic. A gay Scottish guy called Darren used to work there and my dad used to roll his eyes and mutter to himself whenever Darren walked by, until one day

Darren had asked him to man the ticket point and my dad had kissed his teeth and told him that he felt sorry for his mother.

I'd come out to my dad three times between the ages of sixteen and eighteen, but he never took it seriously. In response to the second and third time, he'd assumed the role of matchmaker, and started selecting women that attended his Pentecostal church in Crayford for me to look over. On my eighteenth, we'd had dinner and he'd presented me with a picture of the church's choir director: Gloria, a recently divorced black woman who had two kids on her lap. He had been so excited about this birthday. I think he'd thought that at eighteen, I'd undergo some kind of transformative episode and, like a soft, expandable water toy, I'd grow into whatever he wanted to see when he looked at me. And the parts of myself that were at odds with that would simply fall away as I squeezed into his mould.

On the phone, I gave him some vague details about my time at uni, about the many friends I'd made and how insightful I was finding all the lectures and seminars, cringing every time he mentioned things like graduation and degrees and finding a job in the engineering field. When he asked how long I'd been back, I told him about a week.

'Ah,' he said, feigning offence. 'You've been here a whole week and you are only now just calling?' I apologized. 'So,' he continued. 'When can I expect my son to visit me?'

'Whenever.'

'When will you be going back?' he asked. I was silent. 'Do you not know? Do they not give you a timetable?'

'In a few weeks.'

After I ended the call, I wondered why he would extend to me what was surely a false white flag. I'd thought we were both relatively content living on the periphery of each other's lives. We agreed to meet the following Sunday in the end, and he said that he looked forward to seeing his son again after so long.

I went for a walk in town that afternoon, idly weaving through Dartford Farmers' Market. It was deceptively busy; the path was crowded but not too many people seemed to stop at any one stall. I'd hoped the walk might make me feel better after the call with my dad. But instead, thinking of Muddy did. There was a stall that had a selection of handkerchiefs suspended from a white ring and I wondered if Muddy had been serious about me replacing the one I'd ruined, if it had indeed been his favourite. It felt cruel not to do so even if he had been joking, so I bought one. Muddy was out with Finlay and a few of their friends in Central Park playing rugby, so when I got back, I sat in my room and listened to some music until he came home. I chose *The Miseducation of Lauryn Hill* and skipped the scholastic introduction track.

I'd decided that while I was biding my time at Regal, I'd still pursue music journalism in some form. Reviewing music had been my favourite aspect of the course, so I created an account on Blogspot and started looking through my CD collection for something to write a post about. But I felt so strangely excited about giving the handkerchief to Muddy that the elation itself became a distraction. He was so enthusiastic about everything that I couldn't wait to be ensnared in the warmth of his gratitude. A few days before, he'd shattered one of the eye cups on his binoculars. Finlay had brought over a replacement, and Muddy had hugged him, lifting him off the ground, spinning him around and calling him a 'top bloke', while Finlay begged him to let go.

I sat up when the front door opened and I heard his footsteps clanking on the floor, his bedroom door shutting shortly after. I thought it would be best to give it a few minutes; I ended up waiting an hour. There were large viscous mud tracks trailing up to his room. When I knocked, he said distractedly: 'Sorry about the mess in the hall, Chels. I'll clean it up, give me a sec. I'm restoring life, here!'

I cleared my throat. 'Um, Muddy, it's Harley,' I said. 'Chelsea's working late again.'

'Ey up, mate!' he said. 'Get in here, you!'

The room was immaculate, but he was filthy. There were patches of dirt on his face and legs and all over his white and navy rugby kit. It was strange seeing the room that'd been mine for several years look and smell so different. The bed had been moved from one end of the room to the other, near the window, the drapes had been changed from red to blue, and there was a new dresser by the door with a pair of dumb-bells and a stereo on it.

'Oh, thank god it's you, pal,' he said, turning to me. He was knelt by the window ledge looking inside a shoebox. 'Thought I was about to get a bollocking for the mess.'

'I know you were playing rugby,' I said, 'but why have you got so much mud on your face?'

'I've been kickin' my can all over the place, haven't I?'

he said and then laughed. 'No,' he continued. 'This is what trying to see the owls will do to you.'

'How do you mean?'

'Well, I was on the phone to my granddad the other night, right,' he said. 'And we're always talking about birds we've seen recently and stuff, and he was telling me about a tawny owl he'd seen in the owl box he has up in his garden. His mind's not what it used to be, bless him, he probably saw it centuries ago. Don't think the bleedin' box is even up there anymore. But, anyway, pal, it *did* remind me that I've barely seen any owls out in the wild myself. I've seen a shit-ton of barn owls up at the nature reserve in Elmley, but nowt else.'

'Well, how often do you go looking at night?'

He clicked his fingers and pointed at me. 'Well, that's it, pal,' he said. 'I don't, you see. So, I chucked my torch and my binoculars in my bag and after the training with the boys, I got myself in the woods. Mind you, I didn't see a bleedin' thing.' He turned back to the shoebox and muttered: 'Slippery fuckers.'

'Did you fall over?'

'Like lead, mate,' he said. 'I shone my light on something, tried to get closer to it and stacked it, didn't I? I'll get in the shower in a bit after I figure out what I'm gonna do with this little guy here.'

'Little guy?'

He waved me over. 'Come and have a look at this, pal.' I climbed onto his bed and asked him what it was. 'On my way out the woods, I shone my light on the ground and found this little lad just sittin' there.' There was a bird shifting around in the shoebox beside a bowl of water. It was only a little bigger than a pebble, with a white face, blue wings and yellow plumage. 'I thought he was injured, but I can't see anything wrong with his wings. He looked all right, to be fair, except he weren't movin' or nothing. Lucky I still had this shoebox in my trunk and no one had trod on him.' He went quiet for a moment and then said: 'Isn't he beautiful, mate?'

'Yeah, I guess.'

He looked at me. 'What do you mean: you guess?' he said. 'Look at that little bleedin' face and tell me that that don't make your heart swell.' He looked back into the box, and I asked him what kind of bird it was, and he said: 'That, pal, is a little blue tit.'

'It's cute.'

'You gotta stop callin' him an "it", mate.'

'Well, how do you know he's a him?'

'The stripe on his gut, for starters,' he said. 'It's bloody massive.'

'Right,' I said. 'So, what are you going to do with it – him, sorry.'

He sighed. 'I don't know,' he said. 'My plan was to chuck him in a box, keep him warm, give him a bit of water or something, then see what happens.'

'Isn't there somewhere you can take him?'

He said he'd thought about taking him to the local rescue centre, but because he'd had a bad experience there once, and because he'd wanted to give the little blue tit his best chance at survival, he'd consider venturing further into Kent. 'The one in Sheerness, maybe?' he suggested. 'I don't know, though. I do love him already, but I'm not sure if I really want to trek all that way on my own. He'd better blimmin' hope this water gets him back in the air, or he's out of here!' Muddy held his face really close to the bird, watching him writhe almost undetectably and told him he was only joking, that he wouldn't ever dream of doing that to him. 'Ah, come on little fella,' he said now, 'what's wrong with you, eh?'

There was a calm silence while he looked at the bird. I touched his arm. 'Muddy?'

'Yeah, pal ...' he answered absent-mindedly, before turning to face me. 'Shit – sorry, mate! You come into my abode with something on your mind and I'm here chewing your ear off about bleedin' birds.' He crawled to the edge of the bed and slapped the space beside him. 'Let's have you, then, Harley. What can I do for you?'

I sat beside him, feeling foolish suddenly. 'I got you a new handkerchief.'

He raised an eyebrow. 'You what?'

I repeated myself, taking the handkerchief out of my pocket and holding it out to him. 'Because I ruined your other one?' I said. 'You told me it was your favourite.'

He laughed. 'Christ!' he said, 'I feel like a right knobhead. I was only joking. No one ever takes me seriously, my apologies. I got loads, pal.' I clenched it and was about to put it back in my pocket when he, seemingly sensing a sadness or embarrassment in my expression, took it from me. 'But you know what, mate,' he said, 'this is gonna be my favourite now. I'm gonna use it for everything: my nose, my sandwiches, everything.'

I chuckled. 'Not in succession, surely.'

'Eh!' he said. 'I said it's my favourite. It's *all* going in there now, pal.'

I smiled at him. 'You know,' I said. 'If you don't want to go to that rescue place on your own, I could come with, if you'd like.'

'Really?' he said. 'Well, happy days, then. That'd be brilliant.' He put his hand on my knee and jostled me a bit. I was mortified by how wide a smile this drew from me and tried to stop it. I went to get up after and put my hand over his by accident. He looked at me, giggling, and said: 'You wanna hold my hand, do you?'

That evening, before Chelsea came home, we poured some warm water into a yellow bucket and Muddy brought out a terry cloth that he'd left in his room the last time he'd cleaned it. We wiped the mud off the floors while he played a new Oasis album from his stereo. It was called *Don't Believe the Truth*, and as he moved the cloth back and forth he said: 'This album's just all right, but it's miles better than their last one. That was total bobbins.'

I didn't think I cared about Oasis, but his enthusiasm made me feel like I did, or could.

'I think I only know "Wonderwall",' I said.

He gasped. 'You're not a bleedin' Blur fan, are you?'

I laughed. 'And what if I was?'

'Then we'd have big problems, me and you,' he said, laughing back. 'I can guarantee you though, pal, that you know a lot more than bloody "Wonderwall". And if you don't, you certainly will by the time I'm done with you.' He shook his head, smiling. 'No mate of mine only knows "Wonderwall".'

I didn't think I cared if the bird lived or died. But its survival suddenly meant something to me when Muddy came into my room the next morning, saying he'd called up the rescue centre in Sheerness, and that they were expecting us in an hour. He asked if I had a shift at Regal that day, and that if I did, he'd drive me down afterwards, and that I could use him as an excuse if we were late. He was in grey shorts and a white top with an unbuttoned blue shirt over it. There was an excitement in his eyes, an anticipation to not only do something good, but also something that probably aligned with his philosophy of what constituted a good time.

I held the bird in the shoebox as we drove out of Dartford. As we went down the M2, beneath that bright, empty sky, he told me he'd given the bird a name. I looked into the box and the bird's little white face was just barely twitching, but no other part of its body was moving. I looked back up and asked if he thought that was a good idea.

'You know what happens when you name something, don't you?' I asked.

'Well, I'm already quite attached to him, pal,' he replied. 'It's why I did it.' It got very quiet in the car after that, and then a discomfited look appeared on his face. 'Ah, you think I'm being silly, don't you?' I shook my head. 'Nah, it's all right, mate,' he said. 'I've got people laughing at me all the time, I do. I know sometimes people think I'm a bit of a joke, but, you know, as long as I'm happy, I'm not really too fussed.' I felt guilty and I think he could tell. He nudged me with his elbow and smiled. 'I love my birds, me,' he said, 'you can laugh at me, if you want, it's all right.'

Just as we were driving over the River Medway, 'Ocean Drive' by Lighthouse Family came on the radio. Muddy's back stiffened and he started nodding his head to the music and tapping his fingers on the wheel. 'Proper tune, this, mate,' he said, and started singing along. As I watched him, I wondered if I could ever love as much as he did, if there was anything for which I'd endure any judgement. What in my life had been worth defending so avidly? It became important to me that he wouldn't think I was one of those people that thought him a joke.

'Actually, Muddy, I don't think you're being silly,' I said. 'It's just . . .' I looked into the box and the bird wasn't doing anything now. 'I mean . . .'

'What, you don't think Mate's gonna make it?'

'Mate?'

'That's what I've called him.'

I laughed. 'Why?'

"Cause he's a mate, isn't he?' he said. 'Or I'm his, at least.'

Oh, it was such a gorgeous day. The song, as breezy and happy as it was, encapsulated how good I felt being beside him, how good I felt that someone who would drive thirty miles for an injured, dying bird considered *me* a friend. We had the windows rolled down on both sides and the wind was making his hair dance. Every time a lock of it fell over his eyes, he would bat it away and say: 'Get back, will you.' There was something pleasurable about looking at him: at his large, rough hands on the wheel; at his sleeves clumsily pulled up his forearms and the brown wavy hairs that swept around them; at his roundish stomach perched above his lap; at the way his stubble skirted around his dimples; at how he seemed to emanate happiness long after he'd stopped smiling.

We didn't make it to the rescue centre in the end. Mate died twenty or so minutes into the journey. We were parked on a narrow road in Chatham, flanked entirely by vast verdant countryside.

'Well, it's how it goes sometimes, isn't it, pal,' Muddy said, looking out onto the car bonnet. 'Can't say we didn't try, eh?'

'I'm sorry.'

He smiled at me. 'Ah, don't be, mate,' he said. 'I can be a right soppy old sod, me.' He looked out the window on his right, into the forest across the field. 'I think we should bury him.'

'Here?'

'Yeah,' he said, tapping my shoulder and opening the door. 'Come on, lad.'

I stood at the edge of the road and watched him climb over a narrow gap in the hedge covered in webs of branches. I nearly tripped as I followed him, so he held his hands out for me to hold and told me to be careful.

Once in the forest, the leaves above us seemed as if they were patterned across the sky, through which darted little streams of sunlight. We walked up to a tree; it was just an ordinary tree, but Muddy wore an expression that said this was *the* tree. After he buried Mate, on his hands and knees, dirt clumped beneath his nails, he stood up with his hands balled into fists on his hips and said: 'Well, that's that, then.'

As we walked back to the car, I asked him what it was about birds that made him so happy. He had his hands in his pockets and he was looking into the sky.

'It's because of my granddad, pal,' he said. 'He loves 'em. When I was a little'un, after my dad went away, my granddad used to tell me all about 'em, take me out birdwatching and to these sanctuaries and stuff. You know, sometimes you have these little memories that just pop into your head, and make you feel dead happy for a bit?' I nodded. 'Mine are usually about that, mate. My granddad knows his stuff, he does. Knows his blackbirds, sparrows, finches or what have you, without even lookin' at 'em – he just has to hear 'em. He's a bleedin' legend, him. He's the reason for when I'm not really keepin' up with the date or the month, and I hear a nightingale knockin' about, that I know spring's on its way in.'

I looked up at him. 'You have moments where you don't keep up with the date?'

'Well, you can't be on the ball all the time, can you?'

Before we drove back, after rooting around for it under his seat, Muddy inserted *Definitely Maybe* into the CD player and told me that this was my first lesson in expanding my knowledge about Oasis. I said that, actually, I *did* know more than just 'Wonderwall', and he said it was too late to back out now. But when he pressed play, the CD began to skip. He made a soft, wounded noise and ejected it. He held the CD and slowly turned to me with a sad face, and I put my hand on his shoulder to express my sympathies.

When we eventually got the journey underway, we listened to Radio 1 instead, and Muddy sang along to Crazy Frog's 'Axel F', accurately replicating all the gibberish in the song, thrashing his hair about, doing these insane shoulder movements, and then looking at me, making a fist and holding it at my lips like a microphone and me, despite myself, singing back.

Four

Over the next few days, I started bringing thoughts of Muddy with me everywhere, like a sort of intangible pet. He occupied my brain so frequently that I began to question his niceness, wondering if there was an element of sympathy entangled in it because of how we'd met. But then my mind would become flypaper whenever I'd see him, especially when he'd smile at me, and the adorable, scruffy images of him would stick onto its surface for as long as I needed them to. These thoughts felt like gifts to myself, and they allowed for some light amidst the anticipation of the meeting with my dad, who had called an additional two times by then, sounding joyous and interested in my life. He had me confirm that I was still coming over on Sunday, and even reminded me of his, my old, address.

After my shift on the preceding Friday, which had been another anxious and awkward couple of hours, I met up with Chelsea and Finlay at Bluewater Shopping Centre. Even though it was only a ten-minute journey out to Greenhithe,

Chelsea's comment about the attacks in London happening again had worked its way into my psyche. Normally, I liked sitting on the top deck of the bus and having an aerial view of all the trees and meadows and farm animals passing by. But, when I got on the bus that afternoon, I sat on the lower deck, on the closest seat to the exit.

In Bluewater, I browsed in HMV with the intention of replacing Muddy's broken CD. I ended up buying a copy of *(What's the Story) Morning Glory?* because it was one of only two Oasis albums that they had in stock. As I left the store and rode the escalators down to meet Chelsea and Finlay, I decided that I would listen to the album myself, and got very excited at the idea of telling Muddy that not only did I know the songs the band had released as singles, but also ones that they had not.

In the food court, Chelsea and Finlay were sitting at a table outside McDonald's, surrounded by lots of shopping bags. Chelsea was on her phone, with her chin in her palm, looking profoundly bored when Finlay pinched the sleeve of her grey hoodie and waved me over. He asked me what I had in the bag and when I told him, he said: 'First the birds. Now Oasis. You know what Mud's trying to do, don't you, mate? He's trying to mould you in his image.'

I laughed and asked what they had planned for the rest of the day. 'Well, I'm gonna go for a piss,' Chelsea said, 'and then we're gonna catch *War of the Worlds* after a couple more shops and some dinner. We've got about three hours to kill.'

I smiled at them. 'Ah, date night?'

'Only if you don't wanna tag along,' she said.

'Well, he's paying for his own ticket, then,' Finlay said, jovially.

Without looking at him, Chelsea replied: 'Yeah, no one's expecting you to actually pay for anything, Finn, so don't worry.'

Finlay looked away defeatedly. I tensed up and told her that it was all right, that I'd just accompany them to dinner and then head home. She got up and touched my arm, saying she'd be right back. I took her seat and when she was out of view, Finlay looked at me.

'Can I ask you something, mate?' he said.

'Sure.'

'You talk to Chels a lot, don't you?' he said. 'You're like best mates or whatever, so she probably tells you all sorts of stuff.'

'I guess so.'

He moved his chair closer to me. 'She said anything about me?' he asked. 'You know, recently?'

'How do you mean?'

'I don't know,' he said, 'she just seems a bit off, mate.'

'How so?'

He looked away from me and sighed. He was in a black gilet with a white T-shirt underneath that stretched over his large biceps. He kept idly hooking a finger in the silver chain around his neck and dragging it either way. 'She's just being a bit weird with me,' he said, 'she don't wanna do any of that couple shit anymore.'

'What, like hold your hand?'

'Exactly, mate.'

I liked Finlay and thought he was very handsome. But I

imagined that any friendliness he showed towards me was simply a result of him going out with Chelsea. As if liking me was a scent that he'd happened to get on his clothes. But I'd have certainly understood if Chelsea *had* been the only reason that he wanted anything to do with me. In secondary school, I'd become suspicious of the kindnesses of straight men. In these younger, less lonely years, I'd hung out with a small group of girls, which meant that other boys found me fascinating. They'd mostly assumed I was fucking all of them or that I could set it up so that they could. Either way, these days, it seemed as if a lot of my life was spent dissecting the kindnesses of other men, bringing them up to the light to inspect their authenticity.

I didn't know what to tell Finlay about Chelsea, so I asked if he'd spoken to her about it. I'd only known Chelsea to have three other boyfriends since I'd met her. And with all three, after she'd grown tired of the relationship, she simply let it rot, as if they had all been plants to which she was refusing sustenance; she'd grow cold and quiet and reply to texts only periodically, calls even less so. I wondered if the reason she'd been so disparaging about Finlay was because she was planning on breaking up with him, and didn't actually care about him maturing.

'So, there *is* something to talk about?' he asked. He kept looking at me as I stayed silent, his pale blue eyes going all soft. 'Ah, mate, you gotta tell me if there is—'

'Okay,' I said. 'I'm going to tell you something. And when I do, you can't, under any circumstances, ask me follow-up questions.'

'Right?'

'I'm serious,' I said, 'you'll have to drop it after.'

'Yeah, mate, I got it.'

I paused for a moment. 'Maturity.'

'You what?'

'That sounds a lot like a question.'

He laughed. 'So, she wants me to be more ... what? More serious? I can give her a bit of that. This is good. What else she say, mate?'

'Finlay, I feel like you're not really grasping the whole no follow-ups concept.'

'Oh, come on, mate,' he said. 'Help me out.'

I sighed. 'I mean, I don't think she's really ever been into the whole public display of affection thing. So, the fact that there was even some to begin with is pretty surprising.'

'That's bollocks, mate,' he said, 'she was all over you at the flat that time.'

'Well, that hardly counts, does it?'

He leaned back in the chair and drummed his fingers on the table. 'Well, if she wants serious,' he said, 'then that shouldn't be too hard, should it? I can do that easy, mate.'

I nodded. 'Good for you.'

I'd never been in a relationship. At least, not anything like Chelsea and Finlay. When I was seventeen, I'd started seeing a guy called Paul who was twice my age. He'd posted an ad online, in which he said he was looking for somebody young, obedient and, most importantly, black, and when I'd responded with the details of what I looked like, he'd replied with a badly lit photo of his flaccid cock. He lived a few towns over in Gravesend and, at the end of almost every weekday, I'd take a train over to his flat. He was a bald, stodgy guy who looked a little like Winston Churchill and always smelled like cigarettes. I imagined him having a pint in a pub somewhere, laughing at a racist comment someone else had made. But he did have a fetish for young black boys. In the pursuit to prove to myself that, after a lonely adolescence, I could in fact be wanted and valued by somebody, I was willing to submit to and feed that fetish.

I asked Finlay why he hadn't just asked Chelsea if anything was up.

"Cause then I'd know, wouldn't I?' he said.

'Isn't that what you want?'

'Well, yeah,' he said. 'And no. 'Cause then she'll wanna have it out or something. Or, you know, she might decide to piss off. And she hasn't yet, so probably best to stay away from that hornet's nest, mate.'

'I mean, it's bothering you so much that you even asked *me* about it, and you don't even know me.'

'Yeah, well,' he said, 'she'll tell you stuff she won't tell me, won't she? And Nor still thinks I'm a twat for some reason, so obviously I'm not gonna ask her. But I thought I could squeeze some information out of you. I know how you girls like to gossip and stuff.' He winked at me. 'Not saying you're a girl, obviously. But, you know, mate, close enough.'

I stared at him for a moment. 'It's going to be a chore trying to like you, isn't it?'

'You don't like me?' he said, shrugging. 'Eh, you'll come around, mate. They always do.'

'You sure?' I said. 'Word is Noria still thinks you're a twat.'

'Below the belt, that.'

'Well, can I ask *you* something now?' He nodded. 'I'm just curious how you and Muddy are okay with your arrangement?'

'How do you mean?'

'Well, you're going out with his ex,' I said. 'And Chelsea is still living with him. Isn't that awkward for you two?'

He chuckled. 'Hardly.' I raised an eyebrow. 'Look, I love Mudzie to bits, mate, but he is a bit weird when it comes to women. He needs a massive kick up the arse to get something going with a bird. But yeah, he and Chels went out for a bit, but Chels said he didn't even touch her, really. I didn't even know they'd gone out beforehand; he kept it pretty quiet. I just met her on a night out with some of the boys and thought she looked quite tasty, so I said: yeah, I'll have a bit of that.'

'Charming.'

He shook his head, still chuckling. 'We did have a chat about it, me and Mud, and he weren't fussed.'

'Really?'

'Yeah,' he said. 'I suppose it was pretty good for us, though. None of that awkwardness and we can still be mates. And he's seeing Nor now anyway, after I made him pull his fuckin' finger out.'

'You *made* him?'

'Yeah, he's just a big lazy sod, isn't he?' Finlay said. 'Chels made us all go and see that *Boogeyman* film a couple months ago, and we thought it might be good to bring Nor along, see what happens. He was a bit clueless about the whole thing, bless him. After the movie, I had to shake him and be like: "Mate, how are you not getting that this is a set up? Stop talking about bloody birds and tell her her hair looks nice or something, for god's sake!"'

'So, what you're saying is you've been his wingman ever since you stole his girlfriend?'

'I stole bugger all, mate,' he said, looking at me sternly. 'I don't know where he'd be without me, to be fair. The bloke thought he could just crawl out the mines, come down here in his little Flintstones car and take our women. Little did he know that you can't just bash 'em over the head with a club and drag 'em back to your cave around these parts.'

I looked at him curiously. 'Finlay, you *can* hear the things you say, can't you?'

'Yeah, why?'

'Just wanted to be sure.'

When Chelsea returned, Finlay offered to carry all the shopping, brutishly grabbing her hand when she reached for a bag. Chelsea yanked her arm away from him and asked what he thought he was doing, and he said, facetiously, that he was feeling mature today.

'What – like cheese?' Chelsea said, and when he didn't reply, she walked ahead of us.

I was about to join her when Finlay put his arm out in front of me and asked that I help him with the bags.

'Oh,' I said. 'I thought you were going to carry them on your own?'

'Don't be a smart-arse, mate,' he said. 'Get yourself a couple bags.'

Chelsea gestured that we should catch up. Finlay smiled at her and then, through gritted teeth, said: 'Ah, she fuckin' hates me, don't she? First time she smiled all day was when you rocked up.'

'I can have that effect on women.'

'Not fair though, is it?' he said. 'What do you need that for?'

'I'm literally only joking.'

'Not a joke, though, is it?'

I rolled my eyes. 'I feel like you'd be a lot less hostile if you stopped looking for some kind of magic trick and just talked to her.'

'Nah,' he said. 'I'm gonna go full pelt with this maturity bollocks. See what happens.'

'Finlay, that's stupid, why don't you just—'

'Now, that's enough out of you.'

'If you're not gonna talk to her then maybe you deserve to feel like she hates you.'

'You're a bit of a bitch, aren't you, mate?'

Before they went up to the second level of the shopping centre to see their movie, I asked Chelsea if she would accompany me to see my dad on Sunday because I was scared. She had been just as baffled as I was by the optimistic nature of the calls, and said she'd obviously come with, and joked that she would fight him if he tried anything. This made me laugh. My dad wasn't a violent man. In fact, a lot of my childhood could be characterized by him not touching me at all.

I often felt like a houseplant he'd never really wanted,

something a friend had given him in the early eighties that he'd taken in only because he'd owed them something.

The first time I'd started living with Chelsea was a few days after my eighteenth birthday. The story I'd told her was that my dad had kicked me out. But he hadn't really. It was more of a choice he'd given me. I'd been walking home with Scottish Darren from Regal one evening. I'd been so grateful that he'd remained friends with me given my dad's homophobia. Even weeks after the incident, I'd been so desperately apologetic, but he'd always say that he'd heard worse, and genuinely didn't seem as bothered about it as I was. He was the only openly gay person I knew. At that point, having already come out, I'd certainly felt as if I was gay, but idly so, as if I held the identity in my hands, but wasn't really doing anything with it.

Darren had been about to move back to Scotland; he'd been living a few roads down from my dad's house in Crayford with his aunt. It had been his last day at Regal and we were stood on my road that evening having a whimsical conversation about the future. He had routinely told me how he wanted to be an actor and a singer and a dancer and a playwright and a model; and I'd been saying how I wanted a review of mine – a review of anything – to be featured in a major British publication. He'd asked me if I'd considered studying journalism and I'd laughed and said that university hadn't really been an option for me. And when he'd asked why, I'd listed things like money and fear and a lack of talent, and then *he'd* started laughing. 'Those aren't even close to being valid reasons, Harley,' he'd said. Before I could argue that they were, he said I should think about it; I ended up thinking about it for two years. He'd hugged me good-bye then, for a long time and so tightly, nestling his nose into my neck.

I have always felt somewhat melancholic when I've thought about Darren. When we were on shift together, I'd sometimes look over at him, at his short, immaculately trimmed hair, at his faint beard, at his little pale-ish face, and imagine we were dating. How simple it would be, I'd think, to be with someone to whom you hadn't had to explain your anxieties or strug-gles relating to sexuality, someone who not only understood you, but could relate to them as well. I'd imagined it would be wonderful to have this shared experience beyond friend-ship. I wished there had been tangible evidence we were ever friends, but now he only really existed in my memory.

My dad had been watching us from our bay window. When I'd gone inside, he'd been sat in the living room with his hands clasped and his head hung; the bones and veins in his neck had been hideously pronounced. I could feel how angry he was even before I'd put my key in the lock. I'd stood at the door for a few seconds before he'd looked up at me and said: 'Harley, we cannot do this.' When I asked him what he meant, he'd grunted and slammed a hand on the coffee table, shaking the miniature Bible he kept on there to the floor. He subscribed to the idea that any kind of queerness belonged to white people, so when he'd seen Darren and me hugging, it had sent him spiralling. It had been as if everything I'd been saying to him since I was sixteen was suddenly taking on a shape he could recognize, or a language that'd suddenly been translated into something he could now understand. 'I won't allow you to do this disgusting thing,' he'd continued. '*Be* this disgusting thing. Do you hear me? I will not have it.'

I'd never thought heartbreak allowed for much nuance, that one iteration of it was more violent or superior to another. But familial heartbreak really was different, I'd realized. It was nothing like I imagined the romantic kind was, where it was the vulnerability that did you in, that made you susceptible to emotional terrorism. You didn't have to be vulnerable for familial pain to ruin you; its power to do so transcended walls you'd built, or the emotional distance you'd put forth because you'd begun to suspect that sometimes love wasn't all that unconditional. I didn't have anyone without my dad; he'd raised me entirely on his own, so this kind of heartbreak really meant steeling yourself and allowing your heart to withstand all that vitriol. Because no retaliation on your part, no outburst, could disguise the fact that the one person in the world who was obligated to love you, simply didn't, at least not as you were. It was like being braced inside a rusty bear trap, your skin gashed, veins of blood pooling into little floods around your foot. And the only person that could help you was standing there, considering your life, assessing if it was a life worth saving.

He'd told me then that he'd prayed for me, that he'd been praying for me for years.

'Look at your life, Harley,' he'd continued. He'd been speaking mostly in Twi by now. 'You want to be sodomite, eh? *Chaa. Dad, I am a gay. Dad, I am a gay.* Me? I thought it was a joke. I didn't pay it no mind. Why would I? My son is not a weak man, a sodomite, a homosexual. The devil has got you, and he has cradled you in his arms, so he can control your life. But, still, I try to help you. Because I don't want you to see hell.'

I'd known I was crying but I hadn't wanted to draw any attention to it by wiping my face. Even though he'd been crying too, it had cemented me as the weaker person. Still, he'd insisted that I attend church with him and be prayed for.

But over the last two years, I'd begun the process of piecing myself together, making myself make sense for no one else but me. Being prayed for wasn't an option, so I'd left, taking none of my possessions with me.

I'd had a shift at Regal in the morning and I'd figured if I was going to be homeless, then I could give myself one more day of normality; I'd be wearing the same clothes anyway. I'd walked through Crayford and Dartford for most of the night, watching as kebab shops and supermarkets and houses turned into hills and planes of empty grasslands. Eventually, I'd ended up at the Regal building where I'd stood for the rest of the night. As luck would have it, Chelsea had been opening up the cinema in the morning. I'd been in a daze; my reflection in the window had been weary and unkempt. She'd looked at me for a moment, confused, and then she'd hugged me. She'd opened the doors, and taken me into the office where she'd made me a cup of tea.

Five

It was Finlay's idea for us all to go to the pub that Thursday night. Muddy finished his shift two hours before I finished mine, and waited for me in his car so he could drive us down to the Shakermaker's Arms in the town centre. Chelsea was doing a thirteen-hour shift because Eddie had been training her for a potential deputy manager position, so she said she'd join us later.

There was loud rap music blaring out of Muddy's car when I came out to meet him. He was slowly eating a sandwich with a confused expression on his face. When he saw me approach his car, he smiled, turned off the music and saluted me with two fingers.

As I sat beside him, he went through his glovebox and held up an album called *Hard Core* by Lil' Kim.

'Ey up, pal,' he said. 'I thought I'd give some hip-hop a go, didn't I? I found this in one of them second-hand places in town for dirt cheap yesterday – fifty pence. Thought she looked quite fit on the cover, so I thought why not. And you did say you were really into them female whatsits, didn't you? You heard this?'

I was thrilled that our conversation the other week hadn't simply been small talk, that he'd followed through.

'It's a classic,' I said. 'What do you think?'

He made a face. 'Well,' he said. 'I've only done the first three songs.'

'Not a fan?'

'Nah, it's not that,' he said, 'the first one's just a bloke havin' a wank in a cinema or something, isn't it? And then after that – well, she don't half love going on about cock, don't she?'

I laughed. 'Yeah, that's pretty much the gist of the album,' I said. 'It's about sexual autonomy.'

'What's that mean, then?'

'It basically means she's taking back ownership of her sexuality.'

'Was it stolen or something?'

'No,' I said, turning my body to face him. 'I mean, in hip-hop, sexual references towards women are used to either objectify or to control. So, she's basically saying: I'm gonna fuck whenever and whomever I so choose.'

'Right, right,' he said, 'well, good on her and everything. But it still just sounds like she's goin' on about cock a lot, to be honest with you, pal.'

I laughed again. 'If you can't get past all the sex stuff, then from a production standpoint, it's just a very excellent album.'

'I'll give you that, mate,' he said, 'it did get my hips movin'.'

I told him about the Oasis album I'd bought in Bluewater. He gasped, clamping his hand on my shoulder, and called me a legend. I told him that, somehow, I'd heard most of the songs before, even ones that hadn't been released as singles.

'Of course you have,' he said, still holding my shoulder. 'We're talking twenty million records sold, four top-three hits here, pal. You had to be livin' under a bleedin' rock to have missed any of it, mate.' He then told me about the summer of 2002, when he and Finlay had seen the band in Finsbury Park, and how Finlay had ditched him for a girl in a union jack crop top, who had been sat on Finlay's shoulders for most of the gig. Afterwards, Muddy had found a group of guys that'd come down from Manchester, with whom he had kept in contact to this day.

'I'll tell you what though,' he said. 'You should come to me first, mate, before you make these kinds of decisions. I could've guided you in the ways of the Gallaghers.' He grouped his fingers and weaved them though the air. 'D'ya know what I mean?'

'I don't think I do.'

'What I'm saying, pal, is you gotta start at the beginning, don't you? You can't just start with the second album like a bleedin' lunatic.'

At the Shakermaker's, Finlay was sitting outside on his own. He was in a polo shirt, navy shorts and white trainers. When he saw us, he got up, clasped hands with Muddy and gave me a nod. He asked Muddy what drink he was having, and Muddy answered, then looked down at me.

'Oh, Chels says he don't drink,' Finlay said.

'Well, he don't have to have a drink, does he, Finners?'

Muddy said. 'He might want a Coke or something. You want a Coke, pal?'

I looked up at him with an eyebrow raised. I felt as if I was being babysat. But still I nodded.

Muddy and I sat opposite each other while Finlay went inside. 'Couldn't tell you what's come over him,' he said.

'What do you mean?'

'Well, he's usually a right tight bastard, him. Pays for fuck all. And now he's getting the rounds in.'

'I guess he's trying to be more mature.'

'Finners?' he said, leaning back and squawking with laughter. 'Mature? The bloke in there? Pull the other one, pal. He wouldn't know mature if it slapped him across his pretty little face.'

Finlay returned, placing our respective drinks in front of us, and sat next to Muddy. He slapped him on the back and asked if Noria was still giving him a hard time about the skincare set.

'She said she won't do a bloke with dry and ashy skin,' Muddy said, dragging his hand down his face and then looking into his palm. 'And now she's havin' a go about the bleedin' gym.'

Finlay laughed. 'Might wanna take her up on that,' he said, squeezing Muddy's stomach. 'You know, a couple hours with me on the treadmills, a few sit ups—'

'Oi,' Muddy snapped, smacking his hand away. 'Piss off, you. You said you'd stop taking digs at my weight after you got me them little dumb-bells for my birthday.'

'Only if you start using 'em, mate.'

'Not a bleedin' chance,' Muddy said. 'Look, pal, I've got a belly, me, and I fuckin' love it, so back off.' Finlay chuckled, holding up his hands in surrender. 'And Harley loves it 'n' all,' he continued. 'Don't you, mate?'

They both looked at me. 'You what?' Finlay said, lifting Muddy's shirt. 'You love all of that, do you?' I smiled and nodded with a little shrug.

Muddy winked at me and slapped Finlay's hand away again. Finlay crossed his arms and said: 'Well, that's not fair. When I had a gut, everyone was fuckin' horrible to me.'

'Yeah,' I said. 'I'm sure *that's* why everyone was horrible to you.' He put two fingers up at me. I looked at Muddy. 'Why don't you just use the face creams?'

'Because it's a load of old bollocks, pal,' he said, pulling out a little orange tub from his pocket and placing it on the table. I slid it closer to me. The label read: Moisturizer for Dull, Tired, Grumpy Skin. 'There's all sorts in the box she got me, mate,' he said. 'There's even a bleedin' face mask. Now, when am I ever gonna use a fuckin' face mask? And you know what, actually, when did water and a bit of soap suddenly stop doing the bloody job? I feel like I'm being left behind here, pal. You got all them, whatsit, metrosexuals knockin' about now, haven't you? And good for them and everything. But me? I haven't got the bleedin' patience. It's all just a load of faff, isn't it?'

'You're one weird bloke,' Finlay said to him, 'a bit of face cream, for a bit of muff, and you don't even wanna hear it.'

'I don't know if I'm feeling it, to be honest with you,' Muddy said. 'I don't care if she don't wanna do me.'

'How've you got a sort like Nor on your arm,' Finlay said, 'and that's the shit you're coming out with?'

'I just have to feel it before I can get into anything,' Muddy said. 'D'ya know what I mean?'

'What?' Finlay said. 'Even into her? That's bollocks, that. Remember Crackhead Kenny's gaff. Didn't you have Cassie Davies down the bushes by the park? Can't imagine you were sober enough to feel anything then.'

'Oh, leave off,' Muddy said. 'I was bleedin' seventeen. I'd like to think I've done a bit of growing up since then. Jesus.'

They went on like this for a while, with Finlay unearthing pieces of Muddy's history, which he viewed as contradictory to the man he was now. 'You *never* pass up free muff, lads,' Finlay said with finality.

Muddy and I both looked at him. 'Are you all right?' I asked him.

'No, he really isn't, pal,' Muddy said. 'He's got a bit of his brain missing, doesn't he? But even people with less brain than he has don't chat nearly as much shite.'

When Chelsea and Noria arrived, I was inside, sitting on a stool, watching Muddy and Finlay playing darts. They kept jumping on each other's backs whenever the other was trying to steady a dart in the air. Muddy and I went outside to greet them, and Finlay went to the toilet.

'Chels, I swear, you're obsessed,' Noria was saying. 'Just calm it down a bit, yeah?'

'No, no,' Chelsea said. 'Here me out, hun. I already told you, I read that it's gonna happen again.'

'And where'd you read that?'

'In a paper or something, I dunno,' she said. 'But it's gonna happen again. And none of us are safe, babes.'

'Nothing is gonna happen,' Noria assured her, and then when she saw me and Muddy, she said: 'Can someone please get this girl a drink please? She's having a moment.'

'What's all this, then?' Muddy said as he hugged them both.

'She's still going on about what's happened up in London,' Noria said, 'she made us walk all the way down here, you know.'

Muddy looked at Chelsea. 'I mean, we're all a bit freaked out, but fuck me, Chels—'

'No, I'm serious, guys,' she said. 'I'm never jumping on a bus again. Actually, I think I'm done with public transport all together. I'm not even joking. You never know who's gonna hop on with you and think: "Actually, fuck it." Mud, hun, you're gonna have to give me some driving lessons.'

Muddy laughed and held her shoulder. 'I think what you need first is a drink, love,' he said. 'What are we all havin' then?'

Chelsea and Noria said they wanted a bottle of red wine to share and then they sat on either side of me at an outside table. Before Muddy went back in, he looked into the pub, eyeing the karaoke machine a few feet away from the bar.

'Does anyone wanna have a go on the karaoke with me?' he asked. He grinned as he waited for an answer. His hopeful look made me feel light, like, if I didn't have this habit of clinging onto things – the leg of a chair, the edge of a table – when I didn't know what to do with my hands, that I might've simply floated away on a cloud of my own affection for him.

'You're like a dog with a bone with this, aren't you?' Chelsea said, and then turned to me. 'He always asks this when we come here.'

'Well, why won't no one go up there with me?'

Noria laughed. 'Go up by yourself.'

'But that's no bleedin' fun, is it Nor,' he said. 'You know, guys, I've always thought it might be a touch to have, like, a duet or something. Like a bit of back and forth. Some Sonny-and-Cher shit or whatever.'

Noria lowered her eyelids. 'Mud, babe,' she said tiredly. 'You'll have to miss me with all of that, okay? I came here to drink.'

'Fair enough,' he said. He clicked his fingers and pointed at me. 'What d'ya say, Harles?' I stared at him blankly; I just couldn't unfasten myself enough to do it. 'Sod the lot of you, then,' he said. 'I'll be back with your drinks.'

'Oh, he is cute, isn't he?' Chelsea said when he left.

'The cutest,' Noria replied. 'I feel bad. But I'm *never* doing that.'

When we had a full table, Chelsea told us that Eddie had been so impressed with how well she'd been doing the managerial shifts this week, that she was being asked to act as deputy manager at another site in Central London. Muddy winked at her, nodding, smiling, holding up a hand for her to slap; Noria had her chin cradled in her palm, grinning across to her with doting, fluttery eyes. I felt such a surge of excitement for Chelsea then; there was something enchanting about seeing a friend succeed.

'I don't know how I feel about going up to London every day though,' she said, looking down at the table.

This was the first time I'd attributed this dread not to simple fearmongering but to genuine anxiety.

'Ah, it'll be fine,' Finlay said, in what I suspected was an unintentionally flippant way, reaching across the table and ruffling her hair very hard, messing it up, saying how proud he was of her.

This made Noria perk up and dart her eyes between Finlay and Chelsea. 'Uh, did he just—?'

Chelsea sighed, shaking her head at Noria with her eyes closed, smoothing her hair back down. The table went quiet as we all looked at Finlay, who was confused at the sudden shift in mood.

'What?' Finlay said, looking at Muddy, who was now a little drunk. 'I can't even touch her now?'

'Mate, you can't just touch her hair, can you?' Muddy said. 'I put my nose in Nor's hair once – didn't I, Nor? Because she'd made it smell all sweet, like. And she was like: absolutely not, Mud.' He jabbed his finger in Finlay's arm, his eyes all heavy-lidded. 'You don't touch the bloody hair! If you can't help yourself, mate, you can get your hands in mine. Go on.'

'Oh, fuck this,' Finlay said as he left the table with his pint.

Still fixing her hair, Chelsea asked if Noria would take her place and accompany me to my dad's on Sunday, because since she had to be in London this week, she was going to be staying at her parents, who lived much closer, in Bexley.

'Ah, I'm sorry, Harles,' Noria said. 'I said I'd go to church with my dad this week. You know, I praise the Lord for a couple hours and he gets off my back about the rent. It's the kinda tit for tat that keeps the peace. And I *need* this peace to be kept.'

Chelsea looked at Muddy next, who was picking his nails with a concentration that made his tongue fall out of his mouth. 'Mud?'

'What can I do for you, my love?' he answered without looking up.

'How's your Sunday looking?' she asked. 'Harley has to see his dad then. Can you go with for moral support?' She looked at me, grazing her fingers across my knuckles. 'If that's all right with you, Harley, obviously? I know you just met each other, but I'd rather you weren't on your own.'

His eyes widened. 'Of course, pal,' he said. 'I'd be happy to drive you over. What time do you have to be there? I'm on 'til one, but I can be at the flat straight after.'

'Oh, don't worry about that,' Chelsea said, 'I'll take you both off the rota, make sure you both still get paid.'

'Get *in*!' Muddy said. 'Some time off, and a nice little family reunion. Happy days.'

'No, not happy days, Mud,' Chelsea said. 'It won't be that kind of reunion.'

'No?'

Noria put her hand on my shoulder. 'What does your dad want?'

'I don't know,' I said. 'He called me. A few times, actually. He sounded like he *really* wants to see me. Obviously, I'm sceptical but he just sounded so happy on the phone. Maybe he's been lonely.'

'Or he's dying,' Noria suggested.

'You think?'

'Maybe,' she said. 'If my parents ever said to me the things he said to you, I'd be on some Mariah Carey shit and *emancipate* myself from that mess. Straight away. And I'd only be back to pull the plug. *Trust* me.'

I knew Noria's parents very well and was often intrigued at how the rules of their African-ness seemed less hostile than my dad's, even though their religion and church was just as integral to the fabric of their family. Her dad had once asked me if I had a boyfriend and I stiffened in fear, until I eventually said no, and he laughed and said that there was someone out there for me. After that, I did wonder if maybe he was cool with it because I wasn't actually a part of their family.

'Ah,' Muddy said, 'didn't mean to stick my foot in it.' He got up and stretched. 'I'll be ready for you whenever on Sunday, pal.' He smiled at me; I smiled back. 'Now, let me go see where my little troublemaker's got to.'

Chelsea and Noria had another bottle of wine and got drunk very quickly. Noria had her fingers in my hair and was talking about braiding it again. Chelsea asked if Noria would braid her hair for her, and Noria said Chelsea could braid her hair if she wanted, but she'd have no part in it. Later, Chelsea toyed with the idea of breaking up with Finlay, which seemed to put her in a good mood.

'But you see what I mean?' she was saying. 'He's an absolute state. I've been in two minds about keeping him around for ages. And, yeah, I get it, he's a cutie. But I couldn't give a fuck. I don't wanna shag a bloody clown.'

Noria swirled around the last bit of wine in her glass. 'If you stay with him,' she said, slurring. 'You know what you have to do, don't you?'

'Oh my god,' Chelsea said, slurring too, 'what do I have to do?'

'You're gonna have to start weaponizing the pussy,' Noria said, jabbing an acrylic nail on the table. 'It's the only way you'll get what you want.'

'What, like, shove a gun in there?' Chelsea said. 'I don't know if I'm into that sort of thing.'

'No, babe,' Noria said, 'I'm saying threaten to fuck his dad. Tell him if he don't start acting right, you're gonna be on the next train up to Scotland. Fuck, I'll even have my dad drive you, if fare's an issue. And when you get there, you're gonna be like: "Hey, Mr Mackenzie. Well, that's a nice kilt you got on there. What's it look like around your ankles?", innit?'

Chelsea laughed, almost tumbling backwards on her chair. I steadied her and said: 'I don't think you should sleep with his dad.'

Noria laughed too. 'Yeah, you're right, Harles,' she said. 'He has an older brother, Wallace. He's sexy too. I saw the pictures on his Myspace once. Come, let's join hands.'

'Why?' I asked.

'Because I don't have any of my quartz crystals on me. So, we need to join hands if we're gonna manifest good dick running in that family. You know, so it's not a wasted journey up to Scotland.' I stared at her. 'Harley, come on, give me your hand!'

Later that evening, it was just Muddy and me stood at the bar. Chelsea and Noria had called it a night and Finlay had disappeared too. Muddy was repeatedly asking the barman if he could put on 'Shakermaker' by Oasis, and the barman was looking at him as if Muddy requested this every time he came in. Eventually he told Muddy that he had no control over the playlist.

I had gone quiet by then, and Muddy turned to me. He asked me how I was finding my time back at Regal and I told him that it was all right, if a little lonely. He suggested that I speak to Eddie about doing a couple of shifts with him on deliveries, and I said that I'd never handled the stock before.

'Oh, it's a piece of piss,' he said, 'you'd be fine. When's your next shift?'

'Day after next,' I said. 'Yours?'

'Tomorrow,' he said, laughing. 'They're trying to keep us apart, they are.' He kept on looking at me, with concern growing in his eyes. 'You *are* all right, aren't you, mate?'

I laughed. 'Yeah, why?'

'Don't know what kind of mate wouldn't check in,' he said. 'You know, ask the question . . . So, I can only assume that you hate my fuckin' guts.'

I laughed again, closing my eyes briefly, shaking my head. 'How are you, Muddy?'

'I'm bleedin' hungry,' he said. 'That's what I am, pal.'

He ordered a plate of chips and called his granddad. They

were talking about birds, and I could hear the muffled and excitable voice on the other end of the line. Muddy held the phone at my mouth and asked me to say hello to him. When I did, his granddad said: 'So, who's that then, son?' And then Muddy threw his arm around me and said back: 'It's my new mate, Harley!'

Muddy had started to lie to him about the rare birds that he'd seen around recently, birds that had been red listed in Britain. After the call, he said it was just comforting that his granddad could experience the sightings of these birds through him, even if it wasn't true. In fact, the lies, he said, made him more determined to actually spot them.

Just after we'd decided to leave, a group of drunk, loud women came in and crowded around the karaoke machine. They were in boas and tiaras and comically oversized glasses. Muddy squeezed my shoulder and said: 'Fuck yes, pal. These are my kind of people!' They were shouting through an assortment of Spice Girls songs, and I honestly thought it was the most excited I'd ever seen Muddy. He told me that he was going over and asked if I wanted to get involved, but I shook my head.

Oh, I just loved how self-consciousness didn't seem to take root in him. He walked over so assuredly, arms open, assimilating into the group as if it were nothing, as if he'd been expected, invited even. There was a lot of screaming, and during 'Say You'll Be There' some of the women even started to touch him inappropriately, as if he were the entertainment. He sang and danced and seemed aloft with happiness. He loved life and life seemed to love him. *What was that like?* I thought. To have life on your side, to be able to accomplish anything, however trivial, and consider nothing, to know nothing of apprehension, of unease, or at least to never allow yourself to fall into their depths?

I couldn't stop looking at him. I clasped my final Coke of the night and watched him move through his tailored world, in which happiness was actually happiness and not simply an absence of sadness. It was such an active, potent form of it that I wondered if it was something that could be taught, a skill I could learn and maintain, like riding a bike. Could I one day inspire happiness in others, the same way he seemed to do in me?

Six

I hadn't slept properly since the night at the pub. I'd been sick with fear over the last two days as the meeting with my dad neared. It was Sunday morning, and I actually threw up as I was brushing my teeth. Outside, Muddy stood in front of his car with his hands in his pockets. He was in navy shorts and a flannel shirt, with a white T-shirt underneath. He smiled when he saw me and said: 'Your chariot awaits, pal!'

I was quiet for most of the journey. Muddy had the radio on, and was singing along to 'Why Does It Always Rain on Me?' by Travis, swaying his head from side to side. I think he must've thought the song was making me sad, so he changed the station before the second chorus and sang along to 'Feel Good Inc.' by the Gorillaz instead, after which he filled the silence with a little rant about how he didn't like Damon Albarn in Blur, but he could make an exception for him in the Gorillaz. I only spoke when I was giving him directions. As we drove into Crayford, dark veins of anxiety etched their way through me. I even considered giving Muddy the wrong directions, so we'd never make it.

My dad had called the night before to confirm I was still coming and to decide on a time. I'd spiralled into a black hole of self-assessment by the time the call was over, wondering if I truly had a forgiving nature or if I was simply being a pushover. How desperate had I been for this connection to be repaired, that I'd let myself be deceived into thinking that the past had simply never happened? How amazing were the restorative qualities of the heart, and how proficient were the healing capabilities of time, that a few years and some nice words on the phone had been enough to fix everything?

I was finding it hard to breathe as we drove through Crayford. Muddy looked across to me and asked if I was all right. I put one trembling hand over the other and said quietly, my voice jittery: 'I'm terrified.'

'If you want, pal,' he said, cupping a hand on my shoulder. 'I could come in with you. Might be a touch awkward since I don't know the bloke, but you know ...' I was scared about what my voice would sound like if I started speaking so I said nothing. 'You know what?' he said then, 'let's hit the brakes for a bit.' He pulled onto a quiet road, turned off the engine and faced me. He craned an arm across the metal bars of my headrest. 'If you wanna have a little cry, mate,' he said, 'don't let me stop you. Don't have any tissues for you though, so we might have to use my shirt or something.'

I had already started crying. But I was laughing too. 'I couldn't do that,' I said. 'I really like your shirt.'

'Must be wearing the heck out of it, then,' he said. 'Didn't even iron it or anything.'

'Oh, I thought you were talking about the flannel.'

He laughed. 'You get any tears in my flannel,' he said, 'and we'll have big problems, me and you.' But he did end up taking it off. I'd swept a hand over myself and now my entire face was wet. He started dabbing the thick fuzzy material under my eyes and on my cheeks. 'Let's get you lookin' all beautiful again, shall we?' he said. 'First my handkerchief, and now my flannel, you're takin' advantage of my good nature, you are, Harley.' He bundled the shirt into a ball afterwards and threw it into the back seat. He looked at my face again, smiling, leaning his back against the door, and fastening a hand around his lap. I was thinking about how he had just called me beautiful and wondering how much sarcasm or comedy he'd packed into the adjective. I bit the insides of my cheeks to stop myself from smiling.

'Do tell me to piss off, obviously,' he said, 'but what's going on with you and your old man?'

I gave him a brief history and he called my dad a bastard and then promptly apologized. 'You know, once he tried to set me up with a fourteen-year-old girl?' I told him.

'He what?'

'Yeah,' I said. 'I was seventeen. He would do this thing where every time I came out to him, we'd have dinner a few weeks later and he'd be like: "I want you to come to church and meet someone." And sometimes it would be some fifty-year-old woman with two kids, but on that occasion, it was this fourteen-year-old. He'd say: "I'm not saying come and sleep with the girl. I'm saying come to church, befriend her, get to know her, and then when she's ready and when she's of age ..."'

'That is fucked, pal,' he said. 'Chels did tell me why you started living with her in the first place, but just, like, said you and your old man didn't see eye to eye or something.' We fell silent for a while. 'How are you feeling now, mate?' he asked eventually. 'Now that you've got my flannel all damp – you feel any better?'

I laughed. 'Yeah,' I said. 'Thank you. Let's do this, I guess.'

Muddy parked around the corner and walked with me to the house. There was a curious number of cars parked on the road, and all the curtains in the house were drawn. We never used to draw the curtains, even at night, really. The door went unanswered for ages after I knocked, which didn't surprise me. I'd been back only once before, with Chelsea, and he hadn't opened up at all then. I started to feel sick again. It felt as if I was being pulled apart, every piece in its own direction. Muddy was behind me, leaning on the gate. I looked back at him, and he was smiling, all wide-eyed, giving me two cheesy, supportive thumbs up.

When my dad opened the door, he looked at me and then at Muddy. 'Who is that?' he asked.

Before I'd replied, Muddy shouted: 'Hi, Mr Harley!' My dad slowly held up a hand in greeting to him, perhaps hoping that the gesture might make Muddy go away, but he stayed and even shouted, as I went inside, that he'd wait for me right there. I feared that my dad might think he was my boyfriend.

He didn't comment but I did wonder what kind of man he would've pictured me with, had he not been so clouded by his prejudice.

Inside, he looked at me properly. 'Hello, Harley,' he said. He was in a stripy blue and white shirt, jeans that frayed at the hems and brown sandals. To my astonishment, he smiled at me; it was bizarre. The expression wasn't very suited to his face, which was all hard lines and square. Not to say that the man didn't smile, but I didn't remember it being so wide and toothy. It made me feel an unfamiliar flavour of happiness; I could feel the nuts and bolts configuring inside me to accommodate the feeling. He lifted up my chin between the scratchy surfaces of his thumb and forefinger and said: 'My boy. He's back.' I exhaled hard. God, the relief was overwhelming, I wanted to hug him, even though we'd never really done that. When he stopped smiling, I determined that his face hadn't changed all that much, but somehow it did look happier and more relaxed. He used to have such an unnerving, disgruntled way about him, the vestiges of which you could still see, if you were intent on finding them. 'It's so good to see you, Harley,' he said. 'Don't you know how much I've missed you? You have been away for so long and you come back from university, and you won't even visit your own father. *Ah. Ah.*'

I smiled at him, baring my teeth. He really did want to see me; he really had been happy to see me. I could see it in his face, his disposition. The idea that my presence now harnessed the ability to make him happy was preposterous. When I was younger, I'd often felt that if I could make him happy, then I wouldn't feel so ashamed to be alive. His happiness that Sunday felt like a gift, and he had given it to me, just like that.

I hoped he really wasn't dying. I was delighted I wasn't dead either.

When he gestured me into the hallway, I asked if someone was having a party. 'It's only twelve,' I said.

'No,' he said. 'No parties. Why?'

'Oh,' I said. 'It's just all those cars parked up on the pavement. What's going on?'

He didn't say anything. The house felt strange suddenly. I couldn't tell if it was because I'd been away for so long, or if something was truly off. I started to go upstairs because I wanted to see my old room, even though I knew nothing would be there, but he cut across me and stood in front of the staircase. He gestured me into the dining room, which had its door shut.

Something weakened in me the moment I touched the door handle. There was a group of black men huddled around the dining table; there must have been ten or so of them. They all had Bibles, some had them open, some closed in their palms, some secreted under their arms. I looked back at my dad, who was standing by the door, still smiling, urging me to walk further into the room.

'Come in, Harley,' one of them said, 'come in, don't be scared. Come and sit down.' I deduced that they must have been pastors from my dad's church and its affiliates. I had hated pastors when I was a teenager, the ones that populated my dad's life at least. I had become disillusioned with their sanctified lives, the way they moved through it in that uniquely arrogant way. As I sat down, the room swelled with their deep, coarse voices, beginning a seemingly endless prayer that had started in English before morphing into Twi, and then into tongues. Once I realized what was happening, I felt like an open wound, helplessly susceptible to these incoming infections. They believed so ardently that they were helping me, that they were saving me, that there was a purity so potent in their prayers that it was healing me, not once considering it might've been poison.

I made my hands rigid, clinging so tightly to the table that I feared I might leave impressions in the wood with my nails. I supposed I was praying too, that I could leave unscathed, that whatever defences I could produce in this moment would protect me. I resisted when someone grabbed my arm. As they continued to pray, their voices circling vulture-like above my head, the table was pushed away from me, scraping across the carpet and towards the wall. I slackened my arms and allowed myself to be taken; I was pulled up and the chair was taken away too, but the intention wasn't to stand me up but to force me onto my knees. When they guided me down, there were hands touching different parts of my body, shoving me in different directions, hands all over my hair and face and back, clamping, squeezing, digging, scratching, until I started to feel little flourishes of pain. They all had their eyes shut, some even had tears rolling down their cheeks. *This demon*, they were saying now, *release him. This abomination, deliver him. Ohhh Lord, deliver him now. In the MIGHTY name of Jesus.*

There was nothing for me here. Since I'd come back from uni, I'd expected something bad to happen, so much that I thought I'd almost willed it. It was hard not to think of this as my own doing. I hated myself for staking anything at all on this reunion, for making and accepting those calls and allowing my apprehension to change into optimism.

Perhaps my anxieties and trepidations could be as protective as they were destructive. Perhaps they kept me from certain places and from certain things because I was simply not meant to experience them.

Prayer doesn't end, not really. Not for my dad, not for the pastors. And not for me, either. There was a knock at the door, a hard, desperate knock that made the pastors return to themselves, like apparitions transitioning back into skin and blood and water. My dad opened the door.

'Hi ... Is, um, is Harley all right in there?'

Hearing Muddy's voice was like a verbal sanctuary. I stood up, manoeuvred past everyone, and exited the room.

'Mate!' he shouted when he saw me in the corridor, wiping the tears away from my face. 'Apologies for interrupting yous. I know it's not my place, but it sounded like someone was bein' murdered in there.'

Long after I'd got back into Muddy's car, I still could hear the pastors' voices in my head. When Muddy spoke, I had to tune the memory of them out just so I could hear him properly. I told him what had happened, and then he put an arm around me and brought me into him, my cheek pressed to his chest.

He hugged me so tight that I could feel the blood rushing to my face; he propped his chin on my head and I could feel him breathing, his chest rising, falling, his breath washing over my face.

Eventually, I looked up at him. 'Please don't tell Chelsea.'

He loosened his hold but left a hand on my shoulder. 'I won't say a word, pal.'

We drove back to the flat in silence. After he parked, we didn't undo our seat belts; we just sat there for a long time, staring out of the window. Eventually, I thanked him for accompanying me.

'No worries,' he said, and then, jolting upright: 'Oh, I nearly forgot about this.'

'What?'

'I think I have something that might cheer you up, pal,' he said. 'Or get you thinking about something else, at least.'

I wiped my face. 'What is it?'

He opened his glovebox and retrieved an album, holding it with both hands in front of his face. 'Thought I'd give this a bit of a listen, didn't I?'

'Oh wow.'

'Well, I was round Nor's last night,' he said, 'and I was havin' a little look through her collection, you know, a little rummage. And I saw this here, and thought, well this looks pretty bleedin' wild.'

It was an album by Noria's favourite rapper, Trina. On the cover, Trina was in a sexy nurse's outfit, holding a pair of white defibrillators, straddling an unconscious man with a bloodstained bandage around his head.

Muddy lay the album in his lap and crossed his arms, looking at it curiously. 'Now, mate,' he said. 'I know you said about the whole female empowerment thing last time. And I do get it, don't get me wrong. But this bird's on one – she's goin' on about fuckin' married blokes in their front room, on her period, while his kids are still in the bleedin' house . . .'

I watched him vacantly. 'You know what, Muddy,' I said. 'You've got me there. I don't have a good explanation for that one.'

'Couldn't believe my ears.'

'I think if you're going to listen to any more rap, you should let me pick your next thing.'

He laughed and patted my shoulder. Still, there was a sadness in his eyes, or concern, something I hadn't really seen since I'd first met him in the woods. I thought I'd got away with what had happened then, that I'd never have to deal with the repercussions of it. But really, I'd never moved past it, and Muddy probably hadn't either. He would never truly believe that I was okay; something was always giving me away.

Seven

One of the first things Noria had ever leant me was her copy of *The Miseducation of Lauryn Hill*, which I ended up keeping. We'd been in her room one evening discussing the fact that I rarely ventured beyond the few black singers who were featured on various *NOW That's What I Call Music!* compilations, and, since then, Noria's presence in my life had informed not only my hair but also my taste in music.

The album had gone on to score many of my moments of contemplation. I used to wish that I understood my dad better; I'd wish, so desperately, that I knew why he was the way he was. I'd wish our relationship had comprised of more honesty and less vitriol.

When I lived with him, I liked inventing different versions of him, different personalities in which he had taken a certain joy and pride in loving me, in having me as a son. Versions of him that had discussed with me how we were all, of course, shaped by our history, but the masculine ideals that had made him feel like a man in his youth, every ideal that had been imposed on him, the kind of man society demanded him to be, no longer held as much weight. After I'd moved out, I'd listen to a hidden song on *Miseducation* called 'Tell Him', and imagined that one of these invented personalities was saying these words to me, was trying to understand me, was telling me that he'd needed me, that he'd loved me, that everything was going to be all right.

Conversely, when I'd thought that I might've been in love with Scottish Darren from work, I'd listened to Lauryn's cover of 'Can't Take My Eyes Off of You', repeatedly. One afternoon, we'd both taken our lunch break at the same time and we'd sat in the breakroom, while he chatted about an audition that he'd had that week for an advert for safety razors. He'd then talked about the exhaustive list of things he wanted for his future. He'd spoken enthusiastically, using his hands expressively, and he'd had such wonder and excitement in his eyes. As someone who had been fearful of every facet of life – the future, the present and the past – I'd found it fascinating to be in the company of someone who seemed to enjoy this minimum wage job, but was equally excited for what was to come, whatever it was; someone who was seemingly unscathed by any hostility shown towards him. I wanted that for myself. If dating hadn't been on the cards, then friendship had been equally pleasurable, I'd supposed. It hadn't stopped me from valuing him for the things he could teach me.

To distract myself from the disappointment with my dad, I spent the following day re-reading what I'd written about the album on my blog, wondering if this could be the first proper recommendation that I could give to Muddy. Chelsea was still at her parents' in Bexley because the Regal site in Central London was short-staffed and needed management. Finlay had come over that afternoon to play video games with Muddy. I was sitting in the kitchen with my laptop, and I could hear them in the living room shouting things at each other. I felt weird about Finlay being in the flat after Chelsea had, albeit drunkenly, expressed her desire to break up with him, so I contacted her on MSN Messenger saying just: 'Finn?' And she replied: 'I'll tell you about it later. It's embarrassing.'

Muddy and Finlay both came into the kitchen later. Muddy fist-bumped my shoulder and Finlay tapped my cheek, standing behind me and looking at my laptop screen. 'The Verve?' he said, looking back at Muddy, who was taking two beers out of the fridge. I had the band's iTunes page up. I'd looked up some rock albums that'd been popular in late-nineties Britain and previewed some of the songs, wondering if Muddy might've been into them. 'You've proper made him your little apprentice now, haven't you?'

Muddy sat up on the counter and chucked a can over to Finlay. 'Yeah,' he said, winking in my direction. 'I'm quite influential, me. I bet you've gone for *Urban Hymns*, haven't you?' I nodded at him. 'Absolute blinder of an album, pal!'

Finlay leaned against the wall, opening the can. 'Well, why ain't you asked what I'm into, then,' he said to me. 'I've got way better taste than he has.'

'Bollocks,' Muddy said, 'don't listen to him, pal, he's chattin' absolute shite.'

'You what, mate?' Finlay said. 'I'm a classic rock kinda guy!'

Muddy laughed. 'Yeah, but don't classic really mean: old as the bleedin' hills, you fuckin' pensioner.'

'Oh, pull the other one, Mud,' Finlay said, 'I'm only *three* years older than you.'

'What was that, granddad?' Muddy said, shaking his can at him. 'Need your pills, do you? Need some of this to wash it down?'

'I'll knock you out, mate.'

'I'll fuckin' batter you, pal,' Muddy said, 'you wanna go, do you?'

'What, you think you're hard?' Finlay said, flinging his arms open and shifting to Muddy's side of the counter. 'Come on then, big man!'

'Christ,' I said, 'do you two need a room?'

'Yeah, right,' Finlay said, 'like he could get a bloke like me.'

'You should be so bleedin' lucky,' Muddy said, 'it'd be the best shag you ever had, mate.'

Before Finlay returned to the living room, he clicked his fingers at me and said: 'Stop listening to him, right? And get on some Def Leppard. It'll change your bloody life, mate.'

I looked at Muddy, who shook his head with his eyes closed, as if to say: Nah, stick with me, pal. He sat next to me afterwards and asked me how I was.

'I've been okay,' I said. 'Thanks for asking.'

'Of course,' he said. He was about to say something else when my phone vibrated on the table. 'Ah, who's that, then?'

I let the screen dim. 'No one,' I said. My tongue felt huge in my mouth. 'Just a friend.'

'Well, anyways, pal,' he said, 'I wanted to ask if you wanted to see the birds with me? You know, for real this time.'

'Like, go birding with you?'

'Yeah,' he said, 'thought it might be a good time. I know you said you didn't wanna talk about it, and obviously I'm not gonna make you. But honestly, mate, what happened with your old man the other day just weren't on, was it? And I'm thinking a couple of hours out lookin' at some birds with me might do you some good. What do you say?'

I smiled at him. 'Yeah,' I said. 'That sounds good.'

'Nice one.'

'Will it just be us?'

'My mate Ian might tag along,' he said. 'No doggin', I promise you.' He laughed and then continued: 'If not then, yeah, just me and you, pal.'

In the morning, Muddy got someone to cover his shift at Regal and we drove to some woods in Ashford. It was an hour-long drive along the M20. I watched the trees and hills blur past as Muddy sang along and thrashed his hair about to 'Dakota' by Stereophonics on the radio. In the woods, Ian was waiting for us in the clearing. As we approached him, Muddy fastened his palms to my shoulders, slanting down to me, and said: 'Ah, there he is, mate. Just look at that shit-eating grin of his.'

Ian was a very tall guy in thick-rimmed glasses with a very visible Adam's apple. He had a bumbag around his waist and a little silver camcorder strapped to his hand. Muddy had told me that he'd always thought Ian looked a little like Stephen

Merchant, so when he waved at us, Muddy shouted: 'Oi, oi, Steve!' And Ian put his middle finger up, looking decidedly unimpressed.

Muddy asked if he was all right and Ian looked at me and then back at Muddy.

'Who's this?' Ian asked drily.

'This is my mate, Harley,' Muddy said. 'He's comin' to see the birds with us.'

'Since when have you got a mate called Harley?'

'You what?' Muddy said. 'I got mates all over the place, me. Called all sorts.'

'Don't he speak?'

Muddy looked at me. 'Oh yeah,' he said. 'I probably shoulda warned you, pal. He's a bit of a wrong'un, him. You'll have to try your best to excuse his rudeness.'

'Hi,' I said to Ian, curtly.

'Oh, I'm not rude,' Ian said. 'I'm just curious. When did you two get so acquainted?'

'He's my new flatmate, isn't he?'

'And you've already got him down in the woods?'

'It's where we first met, actually.'

'Out dogging again, were you?'

'You know me, Ian,' Muddy said. 'If I'm not fuckin' in the bushes, I'm not fuckin' anywhere, am I?' Muddy threw his arm around me. 'Didn't get too many complaints from him, though. We had us a great old time. Didn't we, pal?'

'Yeah, I bet,' Ian said. We walked further into the woods. We followed a narrow trail, falling into single file with me in the middle. At one point, Ian asked Muddy if he'd listened to the new Oasis album yet, and when Muddy said he had, Ian talked about how crap it was and how even though Blur hadn't released anything in two years, they remained the superior, more relevant and more artistically impressive band.

Muddy didn't reply to him, instead he nudged me and said: 'Told you, pal, didn't I? Absolute wrong'un.'

Ian laughed and asked me if I was a birder. I shook my head instead of actually answering him. When we arrived in another clearing, he retrieved a little black notebook from his bumbag and said: 'Got one of these? Let's have a gander.'

'A life list?' I said. 'No, I don't.'

'You don't keep track of anything?' he said. 'Well, how do you know what you've seen and what you haven't? I've got nearly everything I've seen in here. And in eight other volumes. Now, imagine if I—'

'Oh, pack it in, Ian,' Muddy said, 'he don't wanna hear it, mate.'

'I've got nearly fifty different species,' he said, 'in this one alone.'

Muddy looked at me. 'Yeah, he says that. But when he's counting buzzards three separate times in the same bleedin' year—'

'Mud, I told you,' Ian said, 'each of them have their own unique—'

'Nah,' Muddy interrupted, jabbing his finger at him. 'I'm not havin' any of that, mate. You're a fuckin' cheat, and you know it. There's nowt in that book, and there's nowt you can say that's gonna change the fact that it's the same bloody species. You're a menace, you are!'

Ian shrugged. 'Get yours out then,' he said. 'Let's have a look.' Muddy slid off his backpack, opened it up and handed his notebook to him. 'You don't half love these drawings,' Ian said as he flicked through the pages. 'What, you can't spell?'

Muddy snatched the book back. 'You know I don't do too good with words.'

'Ah, illiterate, are we?'

Muddy laughed. 'Fuck you, pal.'

As we moved through the woods, I asked them what this strange hostility was all about. Muddy said it was because Ian was a wrong'un, and Ian said if Muddy said that again Muddy would start to hurt his feelings.

'Well, pardon me all over the bleedin' place,' Muddy said, slapping Ian's back, 'didn't realize you had feelings, mate. You should've said something, shouldn't you? Why d'ya keep it a secret?'

Eventually they both started putting their binoculars to their eyes and looking up into the trees. They crinkled their faces, staring contemplatively at nothing, their ears almost twitching with attentiveness, and walking in all different directions. I asked Ian twice what he was doing with the camcorder. The first time he told me to be quiet, and then he explained he was working on a project tentatively entitled Project Retrace, where he planned on going through all eight volumes of his life lists and attempting to re-create each sighting on video on its equivalent day. I asked him what he would do with all the footage, and he just shrugged. 'Today's an easy one,' he said, 'I saw a flock of fieldfare around here three years ago.'

We were there for nearly an hour. I couldn't stop smiling at Muddy's eagerness; it felt as if I were being flooded with so much bright, iridescent colour, watching him get excited at every bird he saw, even ones that he'd made note of in his life list time and time again. I wondered how such an ordinary activity could inspire this much joy in him, a thought that also made me wonder how someone seemingly as ordinary as he could inspire so much joy in me. He made a note of a chaffinch high up in between some branches. It had a trilling, high-pitched call that made him twist his head around with his binoculars up, trying to locate it, as if he were a bird himself. He heard a brambling that Ian identified for him, much to his irritation, before he actually saw it himself. And when he spotted a redwing in the trees, he started jumping up and down like a child. He said he'd seen them just a handful of times and that it was actually the nickname for his car; he even put his binoculars to my eyes, but his hands were so shaky with excitement that I couldn't see anything.

We lost Ian eventually, and I asked about going to find him. But Muddy said that's how these outings usually ended, and at this point he'd just go back to his car and head home. But since I was here today, we could keep walking if I was up for it. He put his binoculars back up to his eyes again, clutching them with both hands, looking around idly. Sunlight was filtering and shimmering through the branches and the air was so cool. A pleasant quiet fell between us. Life seemed to take on a certain shape when I was in his company: all smooth edges and equal sides. For that moment in the woods, beneath the leaves, beneath the entanglement of branches, beneath that portion of bright sky, I felt so flawlessly good. Life could still feel wonderful, I thought, even if it really wasn't.

We bought two baguettes from a local café and had them on the steps by the water fountain in Victoria Park. I'd told Muddy about my thing about eating in front of other people, and he said that if I didn't finish my baguette then he'd do it for me. He leaned back, placing his hands behind him, crossing one leg over the other, and looked into the sky. His life list was lying open between us and he occasionally flicked through the pages, talking nostalgically about his granddad. Muddy said his granddad, in more lucid days, had once participated in something called a Big Day, where he and his entire birding group had tried to spot as many species as possible in one day, and that he'd seen a house sparrow.

I asked him what was so special about house sparrows, and he said: 'Well, like my precious starlings, they're on the red list, aren't they? They're on their way out. So, you can imagine his surprise when he only went and blimmin' saw one. I was fourteen or fifteen at the time, and I still remember him jumpin' up and down like a bloody nutter in the front room with his little camera.'

I smiled. 'Have you ever seen one?'

'Only a handful of times,' he said, 'I like to draw the ones I probably won't ever see much of. Here, look—' He flicked to another page and showed me a lovely sketch of a house sparrow, with its grey bib and dark chestnut-coloured wings. 'It's a little baby one,' he said, looking up and grinning at me.

'How comes you didn't get that one tattooed?'

He chuckled. 'Who says I didn't?' He showed his back to me, lifting up his shirt. 'You see that, pal? You'll have to excuse all the fuzz.' There were two small birds twisting around each other near his shoulders. 'You got a house sparrow there with a nightingale.' He looked back at me. 'Obviously, don't look as good as the one on my arm but I'm not actually a fan of the old needle, to be honest with you. I had to grin and bear it for these three.' My phone vibrated on the ground, about five times in a row. 'Cor, you're a popular bloke today, aren't you?' He craned his head towards my phone. 'Why haven't you got their number saved, then?'

I looked away from him. 'They're not that kind of friend,' I said.

Eight

In my teenage years, I'd developed a habit of talking to myself. I'd ask myself a question and then answer it. I'd known I was only doing this because I was convinced that I'd never have any friends, so I had this idea of being one to myself. I could be honest and loyal and supportive. I could listen to myself and make myself laugh. But when life grew cold, I couldn't exactly be honest. I'd had to tell myself lies to function: everything would be okay, so I would be too.

But in the good days – and there *had* been good days – my own company had been my most treasured possession. How satisfying, I had thought, how reassuring, to know you could save your own life from loneliness. I'd built a foundation on which I could stand. I could reap the fruits that life bore when it was aware that you had someone in your corner, someone who loved you. But in the bad days, I'd felt compelled to believe how pathetic this all was. I would feel the loneliness as if it were an ulcer on my soul. Sometimes I'd wonder if my dad – mostly having me for companionship and seemingly having no desire to get remarried – ever felt this kind of searing loneliness. That is to say, I knew he was lonely, but I wondered if our respective types of loneliness shared any of the same qualities.

We had been at church once, on New Year's Eve. It was one of the few occasions I'd accompanied him in my mid-teens. I'd always enjoyed the live music there, how loud, and joyous it was, even how passionate the keyboardist and the choir could get. I'd danced. It wasn't like me, but I had. I'd felt the elation thrum through me and immediately understood what it was about this place that made its congregation so happy. My dad had been watching me the entire time, however. He'd been dancing too, but not as enthusiastically as me. And I hadn't realized how much this had ruined his evening until afterwards.

'What were you doing?' he'd asked on the drive home. I'd looked at him and told him that I'd been dancing. He'd kissed his teeth. 'Like *that*?'

He hadn't said anything for the rest of the journey, and neither had I. I suppose I'd understood then that the kind of happiness I'd taught myself to generate was somehow illegitimate. His frustration at my dancing, which hadn't been anything salacious or particularly feminine, had mutated.

We'd had dinner that evening where, out of nowhere, he'd accused me of killing my mother.

'You know what you did,' he'd said, stabbing his finger in my direction. 'How you can just sit there and . . .' He'd let the subsequent silence linger, perhaps in the hope that I might defend myself and give him a reason why I believed I'd had nothing to do with her death. Even though, I guessed, I had. But I didn't say anything. He'd said then that the person that I'd become, and the person he'd feared I'd be in the future, was the reason she was dead. It had been difficult to place just what kind of bad person I had supposedly been becoming (a bad dancer?). He'd stopped shouting and begun to cry. There are only a few things you can do when a parent cries, the most effective of which I couldn't imagine he'd wanted me to do, so I'd just sat there, keeping my hands to myself and watching his tears roll down the backs of his hands. That evening, I conjured up a version of him who had sat on the edge of my bed, placed a hand on my shoulder and whispered: 'Happy New Year.' He then kissed me on my forehead, assuring me that this year, things would be better.

I'd been beginning to understand then that the issues that had plagued our relationship hadn't been about religion or church or faith. They had really been about *me*. There seemed to be something lethal about associating with me; to know me, to be responsible for me had meant prioritizing misery and death above love and joy. And my mum's death had been a testament to that. She'd passed away as she gave birth to me, and my dad had been right to resent me for it. I'd figured the least I could do, instead of sitting there with blood on my hands, was try to compensate him with some normality, the kind society legitimized: with real friends and heterosexuality and masculinity, the tough, black kind that I often assumed my dad had had imposed on him in childhood. I was bad farmland that had been sold to him, land which grew nothing worth harvesting, nothing he could present at market; whoever had sold him this land had scammed him, had promised him things that it would simply never deliver.

I guessed it was this memory that had made me decide to text Paul when Muddy had brought me home from my dad's. In trying to be this exceptionally self-reliant person, I'd forgotten that there was something to be said for someone else – someone real – desiring you in ways in which you hadn't thought possible or appropriate.

My association with Paul had initially been supposed to be a mutually beneficial affair, but quickly it had become inequitable. He was complimentary, which I liked very much. He lived alone and he'd told me he had some job in property and didn't like furniture; his flat was as desolate as a crack house. He didn't like me using the front door, so when I'd gone over, I'd go through the alleyway, climb up the fire escape of his duplex, jump onto his little balcony and knock on his back door.

While I had been seeing him, I'd found myself assembling little theories as to why he might've enjoyed treating me the way he did. Perhaps he viewed white supremacy as a kind of cake, a piece of which had never been extended to him, so he'd decided to bake his own. He looked to me like someone for whom life had failed in many ways, to whom it had made promises on account of his whiteness (money, success and other luxuries he'd seen his peers attain) that had simply never been delivered on. He also seemed like someone who had become increasingly disgruntled at the triumphs of people he felt should've been poorer and less happy than he was. So, I guessed, every time he'd done something bad to me, it had been as if he were doing something bad to everyone who had made him feel inadequate, made him feel as if his whiteness in a white country hadn't been enough.

Initially, we hadn't had sex. The first time he'd invited me over, he'd simply instructed that I take off my clothes and lie on his bed. He'd stood beside me, in the dark, fully clothed with his arms crossed over his potted stomach and stared at me in silence. I would turn to look up at him, wondering if perhaps I was the one that needed to initiate something, but then he'd snap his fingers and direct my eyes back ahead of myself. Eventually, he'd started making comments about my body, about the colour of my skin. He'd commented on the darkness of it, the denseness of it, the black blackness of it, and, I remembered, the beauty of it. You expect quite a few things with engagements like these: a sense of shame, that any amorousness will certainly deplete once it starts, that you'll know the entire time that this (the anonymity of it and the seediness of it and the recklessness of it) is a terrible idea, but something tough and desperate inside you will urge you on regardless. But you don't expect that you'll be called beautiful. I'd never been able to place my blackness, and who I'd been as a black teenager and as a black man. But he seemed to be able to. He'd say complimentary things about me until I could see his erection curving up against the fly of his jeans. I'd started using his erections as a measurement of self-worth.

In the beginning, he really would just stand there, until he'd started masturbating, with his bloodshot eyes wide

open, saying all these complimentary things, until he'd come
into his palm. After that he would lie beside me on the bed,
raking his fingers gently through my hair, asking me to come
too. Eventually, the verbal admiration had morphed into fore-
play and then into sex. I'd been aware that there was nothing
behind this, that I was merely a vessel through which he
could fulfil a fantasy. But the truth was, when I looked across
the canvas of my life, the moments with Paul were where
I felt I'd mattered the most. My blackness seemed to mean
something to him, in a way it never had to me; he understood
something about it, and it probably wasn't anything Lauryn
Hill was talking about on *Miseducation*. But he captured
something about it that I never could. Afterwards, I'd always
feel embarrassed and despondent but still, on some level, he
was someone who wanted me, who truly desired me, and had
made me do nothing to earn this desire, except to simply live
in my skin. I'd started to believe then that his function in my
life was to save me from loneliness.

He still lived in Gravesend, but he'd moved out of his
flat into a semi-detached house with pebbledash walls and
a bay window. I started going over a few days a week after
work. Sometimes Muddy would offer to pick me up after a
shift, and I'd tell him I was going for a walk; it would always
result in him asking if he could go with me, and me insisting
that he couldn't, and then we'd go back and forth until he'd
say: 'All right then, pal, see you back at the flat, then.' But
he'd still text, wanting to know where I was, where I was
taking these walks and why I kept taking so many of them.
He once texted saying that if I ever got tired and needed

a lift back, all he had to do was jump in his car and meet me. What had happened at my dad's had heightened the overprotectiveness in his nature. It started to annoy me. I wished he would channel some of that energy into someone else, maybe Noria. I appreciated his concern, how much he cared, but I'd never asked to be coddled. Still, it was hard not to feel as if I was cheating myself somehow, sabotaging something. The decision to get back in contact with Paul didn't make a lot of sense, even to me. But doing so made me feel as if I had a chance to repair the disappointment my dad had sown. This had been a normality for me once, and it could be again.

The first time I had gone back to Paul, it had been a hot evening. I'd taken a train to Gravesend and walked along Wrotham Road before turning onto Cobham Street. I'd walked up the steps and stood beneath the dark alcove. He'd opened the door before I knocked, and greeted me standoffishly. After he'd gestured me in, he peered outside, looking both ways before he closed the door. The inside of his house smelled like cigarettes; he was in loose jeans and a white polo shirt. He was still bald and clean shaven.

'Glad you could make it,' he said, though not as warmly as the words themselves suggested. 'Been a while, ain't it?' I smiled and told him I liked his new place. It was fully furnished and warm and could pass for a family home, even though the walls were completely bare. 'It's not mine,' he said, not elaborating further, and I didn't ask.

My nerves swelled. He led me into the kitchen and opened the door to the garden. 'You see that there?' he said, pointing to the thin, arched gate at the end of the narrow walkway. 'You see that? That's you next time.'

He tapped my shoulder and headed back down the corridor. He then went upstairs and I followed him. Just like that first night, we didn't have sex. He made me undress while he kept all of his clothes on. There wasn't a whole lot of talking; he just sat on the edge of the bed and ran his trembling, clammy hands across my thighs. The quietness frightened me; my thoughts were too loud. What part of this whole thing had been worth keeping Muddy at arm's length? How, exactly, would it repair what my dad had broken? It had been such a stupid idea. He'd come into his palm and wiped it onto a towel on the floor. He hadn't asked me to do anything myself, he'd just told me to get dressed. I'd assumed I'd disappointed him somehow, but as I was walking back to the station, he'd texted, not saying whether he'd had a good time or anything, but instead asking when I was going to be free next.

Nine

Noria was finally going to do my hair. I'd gone to her house in Northfleet one evening after a particularly terrible shift at Regal. I liked boarding the train knowing that this was the same line to Paul's, but I'd be getting off one stop before Gravesend, so, if I happened to meet someone I knew, I'd have no anxieties about telling them where I was going.

Noria's bedroom was one of my favourite places to be. It was warm and low-lit and smelled of lavender. She had a curtain of purple fairy lights draped across one of its walls and a huge picture of a cyberpunk cityscape separated into three portions on the back wall, creating the illusion that this dingy but iridescent world truly lay beyond her room.

After she'd shampooed and conditioned my hair, I sat cross-legged on her carpet, looking through a stack of albums. She was in a fluffy pink crop top with thin silver chains for straps, white track shorts and knee-high socks. Her hair was in a long, slick ponytail that I could see trailing off the bed as I sat between her legs. There was a bottle of Hennessy on her desk that she kept pouring into a small glass with three pieces of ice; her dad had brought up a glass of lemonade earlier that I clung to as she detangled my hair, fitting the metal spikes of the comb though the ends and towards my roots. She'd tasked me with selecting the next thing she'd have on in the background after *Maxwell's Urban Hang Suite* ended.

I saw the Trina album that Muddy had borrowed and held it up to her. 'So, Muddy gave this back to you, then?'

She laughed. 'I was shocked when he said he wanted to listen to it, 'cause he's so, like, into his rock and stuff. But I'm happy he's finally taken an interest in my shit. I was starting to think he couldn't be bothered with anything I liked. He can be so stubborn about trying new things.'

I raised an eyebrow. 'What did he say about it?'

'I think it confused him, poor boy,' she said. 'You know what's funny? He asked if I wanted him to do any of the stuff Trina was saying on the album.'

'What did you say?'

'I said if he wanted to try and make me come three times in a row, he was welcome to give it a go.' She laughed again and then continued, despondently: 'It's actually awkward talking about that stuff with him. Anyway, he gave it back and took one of my Missy Elliott CDs instead.'

I wondered why Muddy hadn't told Noria the real reason he'd taken an interest in the music she liked. Somehow, it felt cruel to tell her the reason was me.

He'd driven me home that afternoon. I'd had a panic attack on shift. It had been busy, and the queues had reached the back of the foyer. Eddie had taken me into his office, with my heart racing and fingers trembling, and sat me down, demonstrating what calm, steady breathing looked like, and eventually I'd fallen in sync with him. He'd told me that I was just having a panic attack, that all I needed to do was breathe, that I was going to be all right.

I told Noria about the bad day, but not the full extent of it. It didn't seem fair to trouble her with it. I even deflected when she asked me how it had all gone with my dad. She had been out job hunting earlier, handing out CVs at various retail places in Bluewater. She was saying how she suspected that her line manager at her current store, Jennifer, was secretly a racist because she was always asking Noria why she looked so angry all the time, always telling her to smile or asking why her hair was so wild, or why her nails were so eccentric, or why she talked in *that* way to the customers, or why her make-up was so aggressive, when her colleague, Annabel – who wasn't white but could certainly pass for it – received no repercussions at all for her big emo hair and dark emo make-up.

'If you're looking for another retail job,' I said, 'why don't you just apply for Regal? Ed's a pretty good manager. And you'll have me and Muddy, then.'

'No,' she said, 'all you guys do is stand around cleaning up other people's shit, innit. I'm not tryna do that, Harles. And I don't think working with Mud would be good for me anyway.'

'As in not good for the relationship?'

She cackled. '*Relationship,*' she repeated. 'Good one.' When I asked her what she meant, she said: 'He is sweet, don't get me wrong. And I appreciate that he's trying now. You know, I saw a Lil' Kim album in his glovebox last week; like, seriously, I don't know where this sudden interest in rap came from, but I am loving it, it really does make me feel like he cares about me. But still, he can be so, I don't know, wishy-washy? I don't know what it is. Sometimes I feel like there's no energy there. Or even, he's got energy in loads of places, like with his birds and stuff. It's just not where it needs to be. He's not giving me anything, like, literally. Harles, I've been horny as *fuck*, like on some nympho-type shit. Imagine looking this good and I still can't get no dick?'

'Such hardship,' I said. 'I'm so sorry.'

'It's not funny,' she said, laughing anyway. 'I'm a pretty-ass bitch.' She lowered her head down beside mine. 'Am I not a pretty bitch?' I took a sip of lemonade and confirmed that she indeed was. 'Exactly, thank you. I wasn't built to be running around chasing these men for some dick. It's not in my nature, or in my spirit, or in my soul; it's not what my life is supposed to look like, you know? Especially not from Muddy, who is *supposed* to wanna fuck me into one of them comas where you wake up speaking another fucking language.'

I looked up at her as she tugged at my hair. 'Maybe it's because you keep going on about his dry skin?'

'I mean, would it hurt the man to moisturize?' she pleaded. 'I made *one* joke, like weeks ago, about not sleeping with him until he started using some of the skincare stuff, and he's clung onto it for dear life. I even told him I didn't care anymore. You know what we do when he comes over? Cuddle.'

'I mean, that's kind of adorable, right?'

She sighed. 'Yeah, but not all the time, though, damn.' We decided to put on Erykah Badu's *Live* album next, and by the time she was reciting the final track, 'Tyrone', using my head as a microphone, she was finished with my cornrows. She held a little mirror in front of me. My face looked brighter, and the shape of my head was more discernible. I smiled at my reflection and thanked her. I thought I looked very handsome. She put the mirror down and turned me around to face her. 'Oh, look at you, Harles.' I smiled bashfully at her. 'You absolute *king*.'

Noria's mum and brother were in Nigeria for the summer, so it was just the two of us and her dad in the house. Later, we sat in the living room and clicked through the music channels, stopping on MTV Base when we saw the video to 'He Wasn't Man Enough' by Toni Braxton. We'd started singing the lyrics to each other when her dad came into the room, dancing with his hands and pretending to know the words. Noria rolled her eyes and said: 'Dad, please!' And he replied that he was paying the electricity bill that allowed her to watch the telly, so he could dance to the sound it produced if he wanted to.

I smiled and waved at him. 'Hi, Mr Ajayi.'

He stopped dancing, looked at me and then called me handsome. He reached out his hand and pulled me to my feet and looked at Noria saying: 'You did this? Well done. It looks dope.' Noria thanked him, told him not to say the word dope, and asked him to leave. He grinned at me. 'Harley, look at this disrespectful girl.'

I looked at Noria too and said: 'Right? So rude.' And she kissed her teeth.

As he left, he pointed at me and shouted: 'Handsome boy!' again.

During the adverts, I asked Noria why Finlay was under the impression that she thought he was a twat. She laughed and said: 'Is that what he told you?' I nodded. 'I never called him that. But I *do* think he's a massive man-child that treats Chels like a pet, and she deserves so much better.'

'He told me he was trying to be more mature for her.'

'He did?' she said, scoffing. 'Well, you can tell him that I may not think he's a twat, but I do think he's delusional. And if he ever fucks up my girl's hair again, he's getting punched in the throat. I'm not even joking, I'll fight him. You see that over there?' She pointed to a tall, pink cylindrical object on the console table in the hallway, explaining that it was a raw crystal that sucked all the bad energy out of the room and replenished it with good ones. 'I moved it down here while my mum was away; she thinks it's witchcraft. But it helps me manifest shit. Like, Chels seeing the light and letting that man be someone else's problem.'

'I thought you were manifesting that he had good dick running in his family?' She pretended to retch and asked when she had said that. And I laughed and said: 'Never mind.'

When Chelsea came back from London the next afternoon, she knocked on my bedroom door, concerned. Eddie had told her about the panic attack, and she'd been sending me texts all morning. I'd replied to them saying that I was fine. Her eyes widened when she saw me. 'Oh my god,' she said. 'Your hair.'

'I know,' I said. 'I'm well happy with it.'

'Ah, wow,' she said, sitting on the edge of my bed. 'You look so different, hun. It suits you.' I asked her how the new position was going, and she said it was stressful, though she loved the chaos. But she also wished that Eddie would stop messing her about and just give her the title of deputy manager and the correlating pay, since she was pretty much doing the job now. 'I heard he's interviewing people for the position,' she said. 'What's that all about?'

'It's probably just procedure,' I said, 'to create the illusion that they're giving everyone their fair shake.'

She sighed and said, 'Yeah, probably,' and then she suddenly straightened her back, touching my arm, and asked how it went with my dad. I just shrugged and made a face, and she called him a bastard under her breath. She remained sitting on my bed, going quiet for a moment. 'Are you really all right, Harley?'

I looked at her. 'Yeah,' I said. 'I already told you, I'm fine. I just got a bit overwhelmed because it was such a busy shift. I was all over the place.'

'I don't know,' she said curiously. 'It's not just that. I feel like you've been a bit off since you got back from uni. Did anything happen there?'

I stiffened. 'What do you mean?' I said, irritated. 'Nothing happened. The course just wasn't for me.'

'Yeah, you said. But you *are* still into music and stuff,

aren't you? Have you thought about doing any internships or anything? My dad might have some contacts, if you're interested?' She put her hand on my back and I felt compelled to shift away, but I willed myself to stay still. I thanked her for the offer and said, flatly, that I'd think about it. 'Anyway,' she continued, 'I had a chat with Eddie yesterday and I said I'd speak to you about putting you on a buddy system.'

I made another face. 'What?'

'Oh, don't look like that,' she said. 'I think you're gonna like this actually, hun. We're putting you on deliveries.'

'With Muddy?'

She nodded. 'I know you've been finding it tough being back,' she said, 'mingling with the rest of the team and everything, so I thought a couple of shifts with him might be good. For the foreseeable, he's gonna be like, I don't know, your person or something like that.' She looked through her bag and pulled out a piece of paper. 'Here's your new rota for the week.'

I scanned the list of names. Mine was highlighted green, along with the name Harry Barlow. I pointed to it and showed her. 'Who's that?'

She giggled. 'Muddy.'

'What?' I said. 'His name's Harry? Why do we call him Muddy, then?'

'Oh, I don't remember,' she said, 'something about a pig farm in Leeds. You'll have to ask him.'

That afternoon, Chelsea and I sat in the living room while Muddy and Finlay got ready for their rugby match. They both came into the room, looking ruggedly attractive in their white and navy kits, with their trainers banging on the floor, to say goodbye. When they saw me, they both excitedly said that I had very sexy hair and looked 'well different'. Muddy tapped me gently on the cheek and said: 'That's us off, then.' And then to Chelsea said: 'Eh, look after him, you.' I looked away, embarrassed but smiling. Finlay kissed Chelsea on her forehead, and she looked up at him, biting her lip. My eyes widened in confusion. I waited until I heard the front door shut before I said anything.

'What was that?' I asked. She looked at me like: What? 'Stop it – what was that, just then?'

She blushed and threw her head back. 'Oh, god,' she said, running a hand through her hair. 'I said I was gonna tell you, didn't I?'

'What is it?'

'Well, I was still feeling a bit weird about going up to London every day,' she said, 'and he was resetting some toilets on a uni campus in Southwark. Anyway, when he was done, he came round my parents' house, you know, just to see how I was.'

'You introduced them?'

'Yeah,' she said, 'they needed their drain piping done once, so I asked him if he could come round and have a look. But yeah, he comes over and he's looking all scruffy in his little worker gear, and, Harles, I don't know what it is about that, that just fucking does it for me. And obviously the body he has on him don't help. But yeah, hun, we ended up doin' it.' I stared at her. 'And I wanna keep doin' him.'

'So, you don't think he's a clown anymore?'

'No, no, he still is,' she said. 'I think I might've been hate-fucking him.' I raised an eyebrow. 'You know what I mean, don't you? Hate-fucking. I can't stand the bloke, but I don't mind the odd shag. Or frequent shags. Harles, what I'm saying is I don't mind keeping him around for a shag.'

'And how does he feel about that?'

'Well, that's the other thing, hun,' she said. 'He told me he loved me. Like, during. I mean, on the one hand I get it. It was great. When I admitted to myself that I just don't fuckin' like the bloke, it made it so much better. Probably the best shag I've ever had. There was all sorts of shit going on. Like, I don't even wanna look down there, see the bloody state of it. And stop looking at me like that.'

'Well,' I said, my face unchanged, 'I'm not sure if I'm grasping this whole hate-fucking thing. You didn't, like, hurt him, did you?'

'I'm not even gonna lie, Harles,' she said. 'You'd have to ask him. I grabbed his dick really hard and sucked it like it was gonna spunk out my salary bump or something.'

'What did you say when he said he loved you?'

'I just looked behind me like: you what?'

'He told you he loved you, and you gave him a: you what, mate?'

'Yeah, what I should've asked him was: why? I've been a right arse to him for weeks now. Honestly, it got to the point where I'd look at his little mug and it would just piss me off.'

'He did ask me when we were in Bluewater why you were being so off with him.'

She laughed. 'What did you say?'

'Basically, I said you wanted him to be more mature.'

'I did think he'd been a bit weird lately,' she said. 'But we're past that now. I don't want him holding my hand or trying to get me to sit on his lap. It's not really about him being a big kid anymore, really. I'm just not into him like that. I guess we could do the whole friends with benefits thing, but he's saying all these weird things now, ain't he?'

'How do you mean?'

'He just wouldn't stop talking after,' she said. 'He used to just roll over and have a kip, and now he's going on about marriage and kids and the future. Him of all people, talking about bloody offspring and mortgages. This is the same bloke who used to wiggle a finger across my fanny and make baby noises when I asked him to go down on me.'

I laughed, and then she said it wasn't funny. 'So that time I was talking about how fit he was,' I said, 'and you said he was only all right, you were just—'

'Bullshitting, yeah.'

'You should tell him about all of this,' I said. 'He might be into it. How did you and Muddy break up? If you don't mind my asking.'

She smiled. 'We were just sat here one night watching the telly, and it got a bit awkward, and it never was between us. He went to put his arm around me, and we just looked at each other like: what are we doing? And we just laughed off the whole thing. Only lasted a few weeks. I still do just bloody love him, though.' She went silent and sighed. 'Finn also said he was going to cook me dinner this weekend.' She groaned, putting her head in her hands and pretending to cry. 'Look what you've done.'

I gently patted her back and apologized, pretending to be sympathetic. But I really was. Often, I felt comforted by how shallow her problems seemed. Arrogantly, I suppose I always had this idea that Chelsea's issues were quite lightweight in comparison to my own. Being involved in her life this way offered something of a reprieve from things. Her world felt like tranquil waters; life's darker facets were merely diluted when they fell into her depths; her story was an upward trajectory, and I always imagined that things like sadness and anxiety and depression were like seasons for her, that she passed through unscathed. It was consoling to be associated with this kind of privilege. Her family, to my knowledge at least, was well off; her dad not only owned this flat, but many others, and had his fingers in many other industries. Still, I appreciated, more than I could ever tell her, her generosity, for letting me live here for as little rent as I paid, and the fact that she'd never held this over my head or expected some constant parade of gratitude.

I would never tell her about Paul or about what had happened with my dad or what I'd planned to do when I'd first met Muddy. I had this fear that if these parts of my life were to infiltrate our friendship in any bigger capacity than they already had, they may not simply dilute her tranquillity, but instead darken and overwhelm it completely.

Ten

Muddy was ecstatic when Chelsea told him about the change in positions at Regal. The evening before our first shift together, he knocked on my door.

'Hi, pal,' he said, leaning against the frame. 'Chels says you're gonna be with me on deliveries at work now.'

I sat up in my bed. 'Yeah, you're gonna be my person,' I said. 'I'm sorry.'

'Oh, don't apologize,' he said. 'I'd be honoured to be your person. Have a nice sleep, mate. See you in the morning.'

I had been so pleased with how brightly this change had impacted my mood that I woke up early and made break-fast. Muddy had been up hours before, lying across the sofa in the living room on the PlayStation. When he heard the toaster go off, he shouted: 'Put a couple in for me, would you, please, mate?'

Two minutes later, when the bread popped up, I shouted back, asking if he'd like them buttered. But he was standing at the kitchen door now, in a vest and boxers. 'You know, pal,' he said, yawning, scratching himself and sweeping hair away from his face. 'I quite like it when you talk all dirty to me.'

I told him to butter his own toast.

On the drive to work, Muddy sang along to 'Shiver', by Natalie Imbruglia, on the radio. It was the most fun I'd ever had going to work. He kept trying to act out the lyrics of the chorus, doing these elaborate gestures with his arms. I watched him, smiling. 'Filthy/Gorgeous', by Scissor Sisters, came on next and, for this one, he made his voice very high-pitched and used his shoulders and hair for the performance. He made me laugh so hard that I snorted, and then he said, nudging me with his elbow: 'Proper showman, me, aren't I?'

When we hit some traffic, Muddy remembered that he'd recently bought a new copy of *Definitely Maybe*, to replace his broken one. He went through his glovebox, popped the disc in and said: 'So, this is where it all begins, mate.' I saw the Missy Elliott album he'd borrowed from Noria, but I decided not to say anything about it. He started telling me about his personal affiliation with these songs, like how his dad had seen the band at the Boardwalk in Manchester in the early nineties before they were huge. It was the first time he'd mentioned his dad to me, so I asked him if he lived back in Manchester, and he shrugged and said: 'Fuck knows, pal.'

I felt happy and confident as I walked into work with him. In the breakroom – which I often tried to avoid, opting to have my lunch on the benches just outside the building instead – Emily and a few other people were there; she was sitting on a chair in the corner, eating a sandwich and reading a hardback book without a dust jacket. Muddy saluted her with two fingers and said: 'Ems, Ems, Ems, how are we doin' today, then? You all good? How's the old foot?'

Emily stuck her foot out and tilted it from side to side. 'It's better, thanks.'

'You gotta be careful down them stairs, don't you, girl?' he said. 'You silly thing.'

Emily laughed and said: 'Oh, fuck off, Mud.'

I was standing awkwardly beside Muddy as he hung up his coat. 'You not gonna say hello to my mate Harley then?' he said.

I felt so pathetic. I anticipated she might respond with something like: *Well, Mud, how about he just says hello to me? He has a mouth, doesn't he?*

Instead, though, she just looked at me and said: 'Shit, sorry, Harley, how are you? Nice hair.'

I wanted to ask how she was too, wanted to know what book she was reading, about her accident on their stairs, but instead I just said I was fine and made as if I needed to use the toilet. I just wanted that interaction to remain unblemished by my incompetence.

After we'd pulled two transportation cages out, Muddy and I stood outside while the delivery truck reversed into the loading bay. He got us black fleeces from the storage room because it'd suddenly turned cold. He whistled and rolled back and forth on his heels with his hands in the pockets of his shorts. The delivery guy, who was called Larry, but who Muddy called Lazza, stepped down from the truck and handed him some bits of paper to sign. Muddy then handed them to me, saying that I was replacing Geoff, who usually dealt with all the administration stuff.

When Larry opened up the back of the truck, Muddy leaped up inside. 'Will you stop taking the piss, you twat,' Larry yelled. 'There's a bloody forklift.'

'Don't need the bleedin' forklift, Laz,' Muddy said. 'Got my hands and my mate Harley here. We'll be all right. Go and have a smoke or something.'

Larry shrugged and then went to lean against the tractor door where he lit up a cigarette. I looked up at Muddy, who had dragged a few items to the edge of the truck. The delivery was mostly boxes of crisps, sweets and syrup for the fizzy-drinks dispenser. We spent about twenty minutes piling everything into the cages and pushing them inside. Afterwards, Muddy unhooked a blue pen from one of the pockets on his shorts and gave it to me to sign the papers for Larry to confirm the delivery had been made. Before Larry drove away, he and Muddy clasped hands and touched each other's backs; Larry then punched him in the chest, winding him and making him go slack. He hovered a finger in Muddy's face and said: 'Fuck off jumping in my truck,' before climbing back into the driver's seat. When Muddy walked back to me, hunched over, I asked him if he was all right and he started coughing and laughing, his eyes slightly watery. 'Yeah, pal, great guy that Laz.'

There were two more deliveries throughout the day, things that arrived on long wooden pallets wrapped in plastic film. Muddy got out a checklist from another pocket on his shorts and handed it to me, saying: 'Not too good with words, me.'

'What do you mean when you say that?' I asked.

'You what?'

'Not being good with words,' I said. 'You said the same thing to Ian that time.'

He sat down on the rusty silver bench by the fire exit and began ripping away all the plastic from the pallets. 'Means I don't like 'em, pal.'

'How comes?'

'Because they don't like me.'

'Like you can't read them?'

He looked up at me, moving a lock of hair from his face. 'You saying I can't read, mate?'

'What?'

He laughed. 'No, I'm only needlin' you,' he said, 'come on, sit down. Help me get this stuff off.' I sat beside him, and he looked at me, continuing: 'Just don't get on with words, pal. You know, you put a word or something down on the page, you know it's wrong, but you also know you got all the right letters and stuff, but the order's fucked. It's a ball ache, mate, and I just can't be arsed.'

'Oh,' I said. 'Like dyslexia?'

'That's the one,' he said. 'Why the interest in my scholastic abilities then?' I asked him if this made it difficult to do all the birding stuff on his life list. 'My handwriting's still a bit shite, mind,' he said. 'But I been managing for years, pal, so don't you worry about me.' He laughed and then said: 'Have my granddad's fridge magnets to thank, don't I?'

'Fridge magnets?'

'Yeah,' he said, 'when I was a little'un, he used to sit me in front of the fridge, and we'd build all these words together and stuff. And then we'd mix 'em up and go again.' I smiled at him. The absence of his parents in this anecdote made me want to pry. 'That does remind me, though, I need to get Ed to give me some days off so I can go up and see my folks.'

About an hour later, after we'd both been to the foyer two or three times to pack everything away, and me calling out the items on the checklist to Muddy to ensure everything had been delivered, we were finished inside. I came out the back, where Muddy was sat back on the bench, humming 'You're Beautiful', by James Blunt, bundling up all the plastic wrapping into balls. He shifted some over to me with his foot, humming the chorus louder. I smiled at him as I sat down.

'So,' I said, 'Harry Barlow, eh?' He darted his eyes over to me. 'I would've wondered who Harry was when I saw it on the rota,' I continued 'but then I don't really speak to anyone, so I guess it could've been anybody. Why do we all call you Muddy then?'

He laughed. 'Okay, Parkinson,' he said, 'you're really grilling me today, aren't you?' He straightened his back. 'I lived on a pig farm when I was a little'un and I used to throw myself in the mud all the time. You know, for a laugh and stuff. But there was one time where my grandad, because he's a bit of a shite, chucked me in one of the mud puddles with the pigs. But he'll deny it if you ask him, because he's a lying bastard. But the name just stuck, mate. Not unlike the mud my nan had to wash out me arsecrack afterwards.'

'You were doing it naked?'

'Yeah, pal,' he said. 'There's pictures 'n' all'

'That doesn't sound right.'

'Nah, it was all right, that,' he said. 'Pigs were like family, weren't they? Until we killed 'em and sold 'em off, obviously. But, yeah, you should come up to Salford with me sometime; I'll show 'em to you.'

'What – the pigs?'

'No, mate, pig farm was in Leeds,' he said, 'and they're long gone. I meant my naked pictures.'

I laughed. 'I mean, as tantalizing as that sounds, Muddy—'

'What,' he said, 'you wouldn't wanna see me naked, pal?'

'Maybe not when you were little.'

'Yeah, I am a lot cleaner these days, to be fair,' he said. 'I should probably get folks to start calling me by my real name.' He put his arm around my shoulders. 'Harry and Harley,' he said. 'Quite similar, isn't it? What's your last name, then?'

'Sekyere.'

'Ah, never mind then.'

'Well, it wasn't going to be Barlow, was it?'

'You never know, do you?' he said. 'Thought we might be proper little bros, me and you. Of course, a little bro of mine would let me tag along when he went on his little walkabouts, wouldn't he?'

I looked up at him nervously, but he was smiling, looking

sideways at me. He rubbed my back very gently, the motion lasting longer than I'd expected.

That afternoon after work, I ignored a text from Paul and went with Muddy to a massive country park in Maidstone, near where Finlay lived. Muddy said his granddad had been bedridden for the last few days, which meant he hadn't been able to get out of the house to see any birds. So, Muddy had borrowed Ian's camcorder to film some in the area, and then, after Eddie approved his time off, he would drive up to Manchester with the footage to show him.

Our feet crunched across the grass as we trudged up a slope. It was getting colder, and the sky was a pale blue; we stayed out long enough to see soft plumes of orange slowly wash it out. At one point, in his eagerness, he walked so far ahead of me that I could no longer make out his features, just his bulky silhouette. He had on his usual shorts and safety boots, and a patterned shirt with the sleeves rolled up. He stood at what seemed to be the highest point of the hill with his hands rolled into fists on his hips, looking out over the crest into the sky. He turned around and arched a hand across his forehead to look for me. He gestured at me, shouting something I couldn't hear, but he sounded happy and excited. The wind got fairly blustery the closer I got to the top; his shirt had blown up behind him, and his eyes had watered at the force of the gusts. He put an arm around me and said: 'Would you look at that, pal!'

It was a gorgeous view, with the sloping hillside crisp with colour, our immediate view existing in only blues and greens and browns. I could hear birds singing. He took off his bag and knelt down, taking out the camera. I looked into the distance ahead.

We walked down the hill and followed the narrow trails. Muddy soon dodged into a cluster of leafless trees, following a sound. 'Fuckin' chaffinch!' I heard him shout, and then I followed his voice, like he'd followed the bird's. He had the camera aimed at the branch; a bird with an orange face and grey, white and black wings shrieked at the sky. According to Muddy's life list, he had seen so many chaffinches that he'd stopped noting them down, but from the smile on his face, you'd think it was the first time he was seeing one: the excitement was in no way diminished. I looked at it too, unsure whether the reason I was smiling as well was because I could feel Muddy's enthusiasm, as if I'd been injected with it, or if birds now genuinely brought me a similar joy to the kind they brought Muddy, even though I still couldn't tell them apart. Muddy started to whistle, in an attempt to mimic the chaffinch's shrill, sporadic call. He rotated his head in all sorts of directions as he heard more birds singing.

He turned the camera on himself. 'All right, old fella,' he said, 'I know you haven't been well, so I thought I'd come out here for you, didn't I? See what's what; see what we've got knockin' about and all that good stuff. Now, I know you're always worrying that I've been a bit of a Harry-No-Mates down here, but, right, look ...' He swung the camera around to me. 'I got my mate Harley over there. Say hello, pal.' I waved at the camera with a timid smile. 'I haven't just got Finn. I know Nan thinks he's a bit of a knob. Now, we haven't seen much. Granted we haven't been out here that long, but ...' he turned the camera back towards the trees. 'We have seen that beautiful blimmin' chaffinch. *Look* at that. I know you've probably seen a million of these, haven't you? In your centuries on this planet. But in my humble opinion, they don't get any less beautiful, no matter how many times you find 'em. Of course, not as beautiful as the starling I saw the other day. Oh, Granddad, it was a bleedin' sight, that. Shame you weren't here.'

We walked around while Muddy slowly panned his camera across the scenery, talking to his granddad about times they'd spent birding or exploring various nature reserves in Manchester. Like when they'd gone to Moston Fairway, and his granddad had watched him playing in mud and climbing trees, and when Muddy had tripped over a root, face-planting in the dirt, his granddad had laughed at him before he picked Muddy up; like when Muddy had noted down one of his first ever bird sightings: some swans drifting across a lake in Reddish Vale Country Park, and his granddad had used it as an opportunity to help Muddy spell a shortish word. 'Well, anyway, old man, get well soon, will you? We got so much more of the world to see yet.'

We walked in silence for a bit after the filming. 'You're a wonderful liar,' I said eventually.

'Yeah, I'm not too bad, pal.'

'I genuinely hope you do get to see more starlings soon.'

'Cheers,' he said. 'Me too. They're supposed to be knockin' about all year, so in theory, they could pop up anytime.

Which means you'll have to be with me *all* the time, mate, in case we actually see 'em.'

'I don't think I'd appreciate it as much as you.'

'Bollocks,' he said, 'you bloody well would appreciate it as much as me. You just don't wanna say where you've been sneaking off to every day after work.' He put his arm around me and brought me into his side. 'But Chels says I'm your person now. And I don't mess about with her instructions, me. So, we're both seeing this bloody starling together.'

I laughed, looking up at him. 'Fine,' I said.

'Good stuff.'

Eleven

My dad asked me once why I didn't believe in God. This was a few weeks after the second time I had come out to him, when I was seventeen. We'd been having dinner – plantains, eggs and a shared bowl of spinach stew – and I'd tried to explain to him that it wasn't that I didn't believe in God, but rather that the God he believed in, and the religion through which God's powers pervaded, didn't value me.

He hadn't really known what I was saying. But his confusion seemed to be the one thing to occasionally pull us back together as we'd started to grow further apart over the next year. We'd watch *Pop Idol* together and during the adverts he'd randomly say something like: 'But God, he can really help you become a better man!' Which I supposed was his own way of acknowledging my coming out. He'd catch me on the way to the kitchen or the bathroom, or whenever I'd have to go into his room to ask for money, and he'd put to me that same question: why didn't I believe and why was I unwilling to?

As I got older, I realized that I may have understood my

reasons for why I didn't believe in God, but I didn't have any answers for the other whys in my life. I felt like a big conglomerate of whys. I'd started to wonder how important it was to make sense to yourself, if there was any merit in it, since I imagined the only reason you would want to under- stand yourself was so other people could understand you. But I hadn't had other people, so it had never felt essential to understand why I, for example, felt so much anxiety and depression, why my moments of failure magnified them- selves so largely in my head that they could prompt a suicidal thought. Failures were so insubstantial, so repairable, so easy to amend towards a triumph, yet they still harnessed the power to render my life unbearable.

The next time I went to Paul's, a few days after looking at the birds with Muddy, I thought about another why. I won- dered why I'd decided to go. I knew I didn't want to go over, not really. But he'd sent an onslaught of salacious texts and I was starting to feel guilty for ignoring them. After work that afternoon, Noria had met Muddy, and from across the street at Regal I'd seen them kiss; neither of them had seen me. Muddy and I were supposed to drive back to the flat after our shift, but she'd texted him during lunch and now he was going over to hers. He'd invited me too, but I was aware then that Noria was trying to salvage their relationship.

Earlier that day, I'd purposely steered my conversation with Muddy to some of the music he had borrowed from Noria, in the hopes that he would repeat some of this to her to make her happy. Still, I did wonder if some petty part of me was actually jealous: jealous that they had each other, and I'd given myself Paul; jealous that Noria could look at Muddy and call him hers; that whatever had been tenuous about their relationship was becoming stronger.

I felt as if I was punishing myself for this pettiness. If I couldn't have something good, then I'd simply torture myself with something infinitely worse. It felt as if the darkness that usually loitered in the centre of my stomach, all nebulous, was starting to take shape and settle inside me, inflating itself into my arms and legs and the rest of my body.

Paul and I were doing almost everything we had been doing a year ago now, even down to the compliments. I'd have my head in his lap and he'd glide his palm across my body. At times I'd catch myself looking up into his icy blue eyes, and he'd turn my head away; I remember telling myself once that I wasn't going to do that anymore since it was obvious that he didn't like it. Before I'd had cornrows, he'd fit his fingers into the tight curls of my hair, and I'd force myself to settle into the pain because I'd known he enjoyed doing it. Now, he just trailed his fingers along the thin paths.

This night he was naked except for a football shirt that he'd kept on, which draped around his sheathed erection. He always kept the condom on, even after. Once he'd said: 'I don't wanna catch anything, do I? I do like you, mate, but I have heard about your lot; I've done the research and those diseases are fucking rampant with yous, aren't they? You ain't gonna have me taking my last breaths on a hospital bed, sucking soup through a bloody straw.'

I just smiled at him, and processed the humiliation accordingly.

I'd gone over pretty late and turned my phone off because I was sure that Muddy would call. After we had sex, Paul sat beside me and didn't move. We were both silent in the dark, tempered only by the glow from a streetlight outside. His hands got caught in the bright strip of light. I asked him if he had been married once, because there was a mark around one of his fingers. I didn't know why I'd asked, or what I thought it might lead to. I wasn't even sure if I wanted to know him beyond the person he presented himself to be.

'Where did that come from?' he replied, followed by what might have been a laugh, but could just have been a cough; he didn't laugh much. I mentioned the imprint and then he didn't say anything for a while. He still wasn't looking at me. I assumed that if our eyes met, this would impel him to confront something that he simply couldn't. 'I was married, yeah,' he said eventually, 'to a woman before you say anything.'

'I wasn't going to say anything.'

'Good,' he said, 'you can't just go about letting people think you're some kinda poof, can you?'

'How do you mean?' I asked. I must've had an injured expression. I didn't mean to. He told me he didn't mean anything by it. Then he leaned over and put his hands around my waist, picking me up and placing me between his legs so I was resting on his stomach as he lay back. He was breathing really hard. 'You really have beautiful skin,' he said. 'You know that, don't you? Tell you all the time, don't I? Fucking beautiful, mate.' He actually laughed this time. I laughed too; I felt as if I had to. He kept repeating these things about my skin like a mantra. He then pulled off the condom and told me to sit up so he could come on my back.

I couldn't stay too long after that. After he allowed me to clean myself up, I left and walked back to the train station. Standing on the platform, I became so aware of that particular patch of skin on my back. I then started to feel little plinks on the backs of my hands and realized that I was crying. After a while, I started to cry harder, making a fist and clamping my teeth down on it hard, hoping it might pierce the skin, or that the pain from the impression would hurt for a long time, just for the distraction from the evening.

I tried to sift through the rubble of the night, in an attempt to mine something good from it. I'd grown so accustomed to the misapprehension that Paul was saving me from something. At one time in my life, I'd only ever wanted to be wanted by someone, and Paul was there, and he wanted me. When this idyll soured, when it became clear that there was nothing here for me, that I'd been stupid, I'd still hoped that Paul signalled something good, like I was bargaining for happiness. Something stubborn in me wouldn't let myself disentangle from the relationship until he had completed the task: until he'd fulfilled an expectation, until he'd done something with my life to make it less pathetic and made it worthy of something.

Twelve

As a show of maturity to Chelsea, Finlay decided to cook a roast for everyone the next day. When I woke up, it was already late afternoon and it was just him, Muddy and me in the flat. He was making a lot of noise in the kitchen; I would've stayed in my room until it'd stopped if I hadn't been so hungry. I was aware that I'd been crying all through the night, however, I hadn't realized the extent to which the tears were evident on my face. There were long crusty streaks down my cheeks and my eyes were all puffy and red.

Muddy and Finlay had got back from a rugby match an hour or so before and were in the kitchen in their kits. Finlay was by the counter retrieving things from the cupboards and Muddy was sat at the table, drawing in a notebook. When they saw me, Finlay started to say hello but Muddy got up and walked over to me at the door, looking deeply concerned. 'You were out pretty late, weren't you?' he said, leaning over until his eyes were almost level with mine. 'Tried calling you and everything.' I didn't say anything. His eyes softened, moving all over my face. 'You been crying, pal?' I brushed a hand over my face and said no. 'Ah, come on, mate,' he said, 'you got trails on your cheeks. You've been crying, haven't you?' I still said nothing. 'Mate, if something's happened, you can just say, and we'll—'

'What's this?' Finlay said, appearing beside Muddy, holding a roasting tin. 'Who's done something to him?' Muddy straightened up and now they were both looking down at me. 'What's going on?'

I didn't like having my word questioned, irrespective of how much concern came with it. I told them, irritably, that I was fine. They exchanged looks with each other, looks I didn't understand, a widening of the eyes, a tightening of the lips, both grinning at one another. 'You know what we have to do, don't you, Finners?' Muddy said.

'Yeah, mate,' Finlay replied. 'I got you. We gotta find out who made the boy cry, don't we?' I started to interrupt when Finlay clicked his fingers at me and said: 'Eh, adults are talking here.'

Muddy took his car keys out of his pocket and jangled them in the air. 'I'll have the car running.'

'Get us a few bin bags,' Finlay said.

'No,' Muddy said, 'got a few in the trunk, haven't I?'

'Rope?'

'Only one,' he said, 'but it's long.' Muddy motioned garrotting someone. 'Won't take long.'

'A couple of towels for the mess.'

'No mess,' Muddy said. 'I'm a professional, me.'

'Professional killer, are you?'

'I love it, mate.'

'An in and out job, then?'

'In and out, pal,' Muddy said, 'bang bang, mate.'

'Bosh bosh, pal.'

They both looked down at me again and Finlay said: 'So where's Mud driving us then?'

I smiled. 'What was that all about?'

Muddy laughed and put his hand on my back. 'Me and Finners watched *Love, Honour and Obey* again a couple of days ago, didn't we? And now we're a pair of hard nuts, who don't fuck about, and do what needs to be done to whoever it needs to be done to.'

He squeezed my shoulder then and said he was getting in the shower. I stayed in the kitchen with Finlay while he prepared everything. He put Chelsea's floral apron over his kit and said: 'All right, little man. You're gonna be my sous chef for a bit.'

I stretched, yawning, rubbing at the crust in my eyes. 'I don't want to.'

'Too bad,' he said, handing me a whisk, 'now take this, might need you to whisk something in a bit.'

'Whisk what?' I said. 'You haven't done anything.'

He gestured to all the things he'd accumulated on the counter: the big slab of beef, the salt and pepper shakers, the bowls. 'Open your eyes, mate,' he said. 'I've done loads.'

'All you've done is make a mess,' I said. 'And now we're gonna get it in the ear from Chelsea, so thanks for that.'

'Oh, come on, mate,' he said, 'what are you doing to me? I'm just trying to cook a roast for my girl and her mates.'

I felt bad then. 'I'm sorry,' I said. 'You really shouldn't talk to me before I've brushed my teeth and put some lotion on my face. What do you need?'

I ended up whisking the mix for the Yorkshire puddings, one of only two things I did, really. He was making everything from scratch and got annoyed when I said he could get a bag of Yorkshire puddings from Iceland for a quid; he already had the eggs and flour and block of Britannia beef dripping out, so I got the milk from the fridge (the other thing I did). I sat at the table and watched him wash his hands and drizzle oil over the three pounds of topside of beef and then season it with salt and pepper, and then with some olive oil, garlic and mustard. After he put the beef in the fridge to marinate, he brought Muddy's stereo into the kitchen, along with a greatest hits album by Toto, which apparently was one of the few places that his taste in music overlapped with Muddy's.

He made me track-skipper and then started chopping up some potatoes by the sink. 'So, I heard you got Mud listening to songs about cocks now,' he said. 'You trying to turn him or something?'

'Well, first of all,' I said. 'I didn't make him do anything. And second, why would I try and turn him?'

'Well, why wouldn't you?' he said, oddly defensive. 'He's a good-lookin' bloke. Not a patch on me, obviously. But he does all right.'

I laughed. 'You really think you're better looking than Muddy?'

He turned around. 'Leave it out, mate,' he said. 'Course I

am. Now grab a knife, will you, and help me chop up some of the 'taters.'

I stared at our reflections in the window as I helped him chop. 'So, being Muddy's wingman is like a permanent job for you, is it?' I asked.

'Of course,' he said. 'Here, look, you take me to one of your gay clubs or bars or whatever and I'll get you a little fittie too. They'll be all over me obviously, but I'll send 'em your way, mate. Well, the ones that can be bothered to look that close to the ground, anyway.'

I laughed sarcastically. 'Height gag,' I said. 'Well done.'

He pushed all the potatoes into a bowl of cold water. 'No, I'm only joking, mate,' he said. 'I'm sure they've got little fun-sized lads for you to play with in there, don't they? You know, the little midgets they got running about in those gimp masks. Isn't that what they got?'

I rolled my eyes, sighing. 'God, you're exhausting.'

We sat back at the table then. He took off the apron, folded it around his neck and looked at me for a moment. I thought that I could detect a hint of sadness, but then I remembered it was Finlay and a conversation about sadness wasn't one we would realistically have. But he did ask about Chelsea, if she had said anything to me about their relationship. My allegiance to Chelsea was pretty steadfast so I had every intention of lying my way through this entire exchange. I told him she hadn't; I didn't know if he believed me or not. He went quiet again, and then eventually said: 'You ever told someone you love 'em?'

'Not that I can remember,' I said. 'Why?'

'You'd think it'd be, I don't know,' he said, 'magical or something. You gotta work your way up to it, don't you? Well, I did anyway. For a whole week I was like: should I say it or am I just gonna look like a fuckin' mug. But I said it.'

'Really?'

'Yeah,' he said, 'probably weren't the best time or place to do it though.'

I tried to stop myself chuckling. 'Where did you do it?'

He started to say something but then stopped. 'You know, don't you?' he said. 'She told you, didn't she? I bloody knew it.'

'I honestly don't know what you're talking about.'

'Fuck it,' he said, 'I'll ask Nor.'

I made a face. 'Or Chelsea,' I suggested. 'Might be an idea.'

Muddy came back into the kitchen later. His feet slapped against the tiles, and he was dripping wet with a towel wrapped around his waist. He stood between my chair and Finlay's, and I looked up at his broad furry chest as he spoke. 'So, what are we doing for our big day then?' he was saying to Finlay. 'You've said nowt about it, and it's only next month.'

'I don't know, mate,' Finlay said. 'Pub? Get some of the lads round, I suppose. Isn't that what we do every year?'

'You two have the same birthday?' I asked.

'No, he's the day after me,' Finlay said, 'but we always do something on mine.'

'Why?'

'It's just a better cause for celebration, ain't it?'

Muddy laughed. 'Have it at Shakermaker's, would you?' he said. 'No one wants to trek down to bleedin' Maidstone. And I wanna have a go on the karaoke. Oh, and make it fancy dress or something; don't be a Same-Shit-Sheila. Oh, and make it all eighties, like! You love the eighties, don't you?'

'Fancy dress?' Finlay said, grimacing. 'Mud, you absolute bender.' He looked across to me. 'No offence, Harley.'

'Ah,' I said, nodding idly. 'That takes me back.'

Muddy clipped a wet hand on Finlay's shoulder. 'You better apologize to him,' he said. 'I'm not having any of that bollocks.'

Finlay knocked Muddy's hand off him. 'Do you mind?' he said. 'You're fuckin' drippin', mate.'

Muddy shook his hair vigorously on him like a dog, flecks of water flying everywhere. Finlay tried to yank Muddy's towel off, but Muddy stepped away, giggling, just before Finlay grabbed the fabric. 'Careful there, pal,' Muddy said, as he left the room. 'Unless you really wanna see my twig and berries.'

'Like I ain't already had the misfortune of seein' 'em,' Finlay said. 'I'm sure Harley wouldn't mind, though. Look at him. He's gagging for it.'

'Piss off, Finlay,' I said abruptly.

I decided to drink that evening. I'd spent the rest of the afternoon with Muddy and Finlay, and the happy anticipation of the five of us having a meal together around the kitchen table had made me feel warm; I hoped alcohol would prolong that feeling.

Long before dinner was ready, Chelsea and Noria had been in Chelsea's room with their music blaring. When they came into the kitchen, Noria stared Finlay down. Her hair was in

long braids now with little golden clips around each strand,
which co-ordinated with her black lipstick and spaghetti-
strap top. I'd been setting the table with Finlay, who was
now dressed in a polo shirt and jeans; Muddy had been out
getting some more drinks. Finlay looked up at her and said
she looked nice, and when Noria continued to stare at him,
he asked her what she was looking at.

'I wanna see what those hands are doing all night ...'
Noria said.

'You what?' Finlay replied.

'... or there's gonna be some issues.'

'Oh, is there?'

'Nor,' Chelsea said, 'this isn't what I meant by be
nice to him.'

'I'm just letting him know, babes,' Noria said. 'Just 'cause
we've said we like him now, don't mean we have to take our
feet off his neck.'

Finlay smiled at this and winked at me. And I looked at
him like: Good for you. He looked back at Noria and said:
'Lucky for you, Nor, I'm into that shit.' Noria rolled her eyes
and laughed, and Finlay went over to her, putting an arm
around her shoulders, and asked her to help him bring in two
more chairs from the living room for the table.

For dinner, I sat next to Noria and Chelsea on one side of
the table, opposite Muddy and Finlay. I kept reaching for the
beers that Muddy had grouped in the centre; Chelsea's eyes
would trace my hand each time I grabbed one, but she didn't
say anything, and I appreciated that a big deal wasn't being
made about it. At uni, I'd never really drunk to cushion the

anxiety. There'd always been the potential horror of seeing how alcohol could alter a mind that barely functioned the way it should sober. But, still, I'd felt happy that afternoon and wanted to manipulate the feeling into staying.

Finlay was a good cook, and I felt so chatty this evening that I couldn't help but constantly look across to him and tell him so after every bite, narrating how tender the beef was, how succulent, how flavourful. I found myself talking incessantly, not really having a grip on what I was actually saying, but everyone kept laughing. I wondered if anyone else thought it was as weird as I did that I'd placed myself at the centre of attention, that I seemed to be guiding the conversation, my opinions governing every subject we discussed, be it television, movies, celebrities, recent news and even sports. When Muddy and Finlay started talking about some football match, I shifted the topic to how attractive the players – the ones I knew at least – were. I felt so good, and I wanted to spread this feeling and have everyone else feel this good too, so I drunkenly encouraged people to drink more.

After dinner, we played truth or dare, during which someone asked who the fittest bloke at the table was. Later, I would remember answering and everyone laughing again. Assumedly looking at either Muddy or Finlay, I'd said: 'No, no, you really are handsome! And don't let anyone tell you otherwise!' There was more laughter, and someone (probably Muddy) said: 'See, he loves me, he does.'

The evening petered out after that. I leaned back in my chair and let the inebriation wash over and out of me. I watched Chelsea and Nora talking to each other; Muddy and

Finlay having a game of cards; Muddy messing up the cards
every time Finlay lay them on the table, and then looking
at me, smiling mischievously as if this was something we'd
planned together. Later, Finlay pulled a box of cigarettes
from his pocket and shook them at Chelsea. Muddy looked
up at them and said: 'Rotten habit, that.' To which Finlay non-
chalantly responded with a middle finger while he tapped
around himself for a lighter. As he and Chelsea were leaving,
Noria pointed to a small mark on Finlay's neck, all red and
pink and purple. Finlay looked down at her and laughed
bashfully. Laughing too, I looked at Noria and said: 'Must be
all that hate-fucking Chelsea's been giving him.'

Chelsea's eyebrows shot up. 'Harley!' she said curtly. My
eyes widened, and I apologized; she told me to stop talking
and Finlay looked at us confusedly, which was followed by
a wounded expression.

'No, no,' he said. 'Go on, Chels. What's he on about? Hate-
fucking? What's that then?'

Muddy was looking up at him now. 'Mate, don't kick
off,' he said. 'He was only having a laugh.' He looked at me.
'Weren't you, mate?'

Noria looked across to Muddy and said wistfully: 'Wish I
could get some of that.'

'You what?' Muddy said.

'Nothing,' she replied. 'It's just your best friend is getting
all this hate-fucking apparently and I'm just sat here wondering if a girl can get more than a hug and a handshake.
That's all.'

'But isn't it you that said: "Oh, Mud, let's go slow. Don't

want this to be some one-night hook-up thing." And wasn't it you that said you didn't wanna do a bloke who didn't like a bit of face cream. I'm going by your wishes, love.'

'Now, I know your arse is lying,' she said, pointing at him, 'that was weeks ago. How slow do you wanna fucking go? You look like you wanna do Harley more than me for starters.'

Muddy and I both said: 'What?'

Finlay headed into the corridor and Chelsea followed him out.

'All I'm saying is,' Noria said, 'I'm not trying to be your best gal pal, Mud. And, yeah, I like that you've been taking more of an interest in the things I like. But I want something more than whatever this thing is that you're passing off as . . . what? A relationship? I don't even know what this is. I mean, if this is such a chore for you, then, you know, just lose my number and we can be done, innit.'

Chelsea and Finlay were arguing in the corridor; Chelsea kept placing a hand on his chest, and he kept removing it. Noria brushed by them and opened the door, and Finlay followed her out. After that, I heard Muddy slam his door behind me, and then it was just Chelsea and me in the corridor. I didn't know what to tell her, to atone for what I'd done. I was angry that alcohol hadn't done anything to protect me against my own incompetence. She crossed her arms and walked into her room, the door slamming shut behind her.

Thirteen

Around midnight, Muddy knocked on my door. I hadn't been able to sleep. I'd lain awake, preparing apologies in my head for the following morning; at one point I'd run into the toilet to throw up. Muddy now stood at the doorframe in a plaid shirt, cinched by the straps of his backpack, and said: 'You fancy a drive, pal?'

It was a cold night, and we were the only ones on the road. He hadn't said where he was taking us, but we were driving down the M2. He had the radio on, and the windows rolled down on both sides. We were listening to a station playing nineties R&B throwbacks and 'Sweetness' by Michelle Gayle was on. Muddy was rolling his hips to the shoop-shoo-doops of the chorus and smiling at me. But when I didn't respond to his silliness, he turned it down and we drove in silence.

I looked across to him eventually. 'Muddy,' I said. 'If you're driving me out to the middle of nowhere to kill me and dispose of my body because I messed up your relationship, I just want you to know how sorry I am.'

'Well, first off, pal,' he said, 'if I were gonna kill you, I would've taken you out back at the flat, and then wrapped you up in some bin liner and put you in my trunk. But here, look, you're in my passenger seat, aren't you?' He laughed and looked across to me, but I just stared back him. 'What? Oh, mate, you're not serious, are you? I just thought a little drive might cheer you up, that's all. It was a bit of a shite night. Finn's been on the phone to me for the last couple of hours. I imagine Chels and Nor have been going back and forth. And then there's you. And I'm your person, aren't I? You shouldn't have to be miserable on your own.' He nudged my arm. 'You thought I was gonna kill you? Come on, mate. Have you seen me? D'ya know what they'd do to a bloke like me in the nick?'

'Well maybe not kill me,' I said, 'but I thought you'd be mad at me.'

'I'll tell you what, mate,' Muddy said, 'if it makes you feel any better, it takes a lot to get me all riled up. So, you don't have to worry about that, ever. But if I am gonna be mad, I suppose I should be mad at myself.'

'How comes?'

'Well, what happened with Nor,' he said. 'It was my own fault, weren't it? I weren't being honest with her. I weren't interested and I should have just told her that instead of dragging it out. But you know, when you got bloody Finn in your ear, giving it all: *why ain't you got a bird, mate? Why ain't you fucking your bird, mate?* You have to do something, don't you? I tell him all the time I'm not looking to get into anything, especially if I'm not feeling it. But he don't wanna hear it, does he? He just calls me a – well it don't matter what he calls me. But you know how he is, he's a bit of a prat, isn't he?'

'Finlay's kind of awful,' I said. 'Why is his opinion so important to you?'

'Ah, he has his moments, pal, he really does,' he said. 'I care about his opinion because he's my best mate. And when your best mate has something to say about you, you have to give it a bit of a look in, don't you? Sometimes he can see something about me that I can't see myself.'

'But surely not when they're trying to force you into a relationship you don't want?'

He smirked. 'Eh,' he said. 'Finn can have his opinion. But I'm my own man, me. It were my choice at the end of the day. He's a persistent little shite, but I was the one that led her on. She wanted to do stuff with me, and I just wasn't feeling it. Not that she isn't beautiful or anything, don't get me wrong, she's a fuckin' stunner, mate. And obviously what bloke wouldn't be climbin' the walls for her to notice 'em . . . just not me, you know. I felt like I was keepin' her prisoner or something. D'ya know what I mean? And sometimes I think Finn's just feeling a bit shit because he went out with Chels after I did, so he's just really desperate for me to get with someone, so he don't feel as bad.'

'Are you gonna call her?'

'She told me to lose her number, didn't she?' he said, chuckling. 'No, I might give her a bell or something in the morning, when she isn't as pissed at me. She were all right, she was. Shame she don't wanna be my best gal pal though.'

*

We drove to the Isle of Sheppey, where we parked on a quiet narrow road marked with potholes, next to a dark expansive field with large tyre tracks outside its perimeter. He turned off the engine. There was an orange sign on the fence that read: Capel Fleet Raptor Viewpoint.

'That time you said about the dogging,' I said, 'this isn't what's happening now, is it? Am I your rebound?'

'Yeah, I'm proper sneaky like that,' he said. 'Right little scoundrel, me. Get you on your own. No one else knockin' about. Can have my wicked way with you now, can't I?' He laughed and I looked down at my hands. 'No, I've been coming up here to see the barn owls,' he explained. 'Best place to see 'em. Apart from the reservation in Elmley. Obviously, we're too late: you're really supposed to come up here about an hour before dark to see what's what. But it's quite nice out here, I think. So I've been driving up whenever I can. Owls or no owls.' He took Ian's camera out of his bag, which he said he'd now bought from Ian, who had found better equipment for his bird project. 'Come on, pal,' he said as he opened the door.

He went outside but I still stayed. He aimed the camera at the sky; his voice was slightly muffled beyond the window as he spoke to his granddad. He turned the camera onto me and gestured for me to get out of the car. I joined him. The sky was dark and seasoned with stars. When he was done touring it with the camera, turning it back onto me at one point so I could wave for his granddad, he put it down. I turned to look at him for a moment and he smiled at me, and then we were quiet again for a long time.

'You were loving the booze tonight, weren't you?' he said eventually.

I sighed. 'Big mistake.'

'No,' he said, 'a bit of alcohol is never wrong, in my humble opinion, pal.'

'Except tonight, obviously.'

'I bet you were a total riot at uni, weren't you?' he said. 'Bet you were the life and bleedin' soul of the party, like you were tonight.'

'I wasn't – I wasn't anything at uni.'

'So, you don't miss it then?'

'Um, I suppose I miss what I thought I'd get at the end of it? If that makes sense. I really wanted that degree. I really wanted to do something in music after; that's what I wanted my entire life to be afterwards.'

'Harles,' he said, 'you're talking like it's all over, mate. How old are you?'

'Twenty-one.'

'Even if you were bleedin' fifty, pal, it wouldn't be over,' he said. 'So uni weren't great for you, there's all sorts you can do to get into music, isn't there? You're always typing away on your little laptop, aren't you?'

I smiled at him. I knew I had options, that wasn't the issue. The issue was me getting in my own way. 'Yeah,' I said. 'I've been trying to build a portfolio sort of thing. And Chelsea was saying about trying for an internship the other day.'

He slapped my back. 'See!' he said. 'Life always picks you back up, pal. You remember that song by Lighthouse Family, don't you?'

'"Ocean Drive"?'

'Nah,' he said. 'Not that one. Ah, what's it bleedin' called?' He started to hum. 'Oh, "High"! D'ya remember that one?' I shrugged. 'Come on, I'm only twenty-three, so if I remember it, you must do too, pal. The bloke goes on about how December might've been dark but the future's gonna be a different colour. That's you, pal. That's *you*. Nothing's the same for ever.'

I could tell Muddy had no intention of taking us home any time soon, and I didn't want to go either. We sat back in the car, and he took out a ham sandwich that he'd crushed into the handkerchief that I'd got him. He gave me a mangled, crumbly section of it, and as we ate, looking into the sky, he asked me what I thought he should do about Noria.

'Muddy,' I said. 'I have a bit of a bone to pick with you.'

He wiped his mouth and looked at me. 'Go on, mate.'

'Noria thinks you took an interest in the music she likes because of her,' I said. 'You made me think it was because of me.'

'Ah,' he said. 'Well, yeah, I wanted to cheer you up, pal. But it made the pair of you dead made up, didn't it?'

'You're right, it did,' I said. 'But I think the intention behind it is important. If Noria finds out that you didn't do it to get to know her better, I think it might genuinely hurt her. Break-up or not.'

Muddy chuckled. 'I doubt anything I could do could hurt Nor. She's tough as.'

'Muddy, I'm serious,' I said. 'Noria's just as capable of being hurt as anyone else.'

He looked at me a moment and then nodded as if to say: Understood. I wasn't sure what else to add about how he should approach the problem. She wanted sex, and he didn't. Something would have to give, and I'd never known Noria to budge on anything. I suggested that he give her a call in the morning so they could have a more rational conversation.

'She sounded like she didn't wanna hear it, though, didn't she?'

'Well,' I said, 'it's like you said, nothing's the same for ever, is it? And also, you probably shouldn't have told her that I loved you. I don't think that helped things.'

'I did say that, didn't I?' he said. He started laughing and chucked an arm around me, jostling me a bit. 'Fuck me, she probably thinks you want a bit of me, don't she?' This made my stomach all fluttery. 'But let's face it though, pal, you probably do want me, don't you?' I rolled my eyes. 'No, no,' he continued. 'It's good to get your feelings out with this sort of thing, mate. If I get you stiff as an ironing board when you see me in my gruds, it's all right, pal. I'm quite a sight to behold, me.'

'Are you now?'

'Yeah, I've been told I have a certain animalistic magnetism about me.'

I laughed. 'I suppose every animal is considered a deity in some corner of the world.'

'You know what, mate,' he said. 'I'll let you have that, cause you called me handsome tonight, didn't you?'

'I don't know,' I said. 'I could've sworn I was talking about Finlay.'

'Bollocks, that,' he said. 'I'm better lookin' than bleedin' Finn.'

'You think so?'

'Of course,' he said, 'just 'cause he's got all that muscle now, don't mean he's better lookin' than me, pal. I could hit the gym if I wanted or start putting them dumb-bells he got me to some use. But I'm not gonna. And I'll tell you why, mate. My gut's a bloody superpower.'

'How's that then?'

'Gives me my powers of seduction, don't it?' he said. 'It's why you're so in love with me, Harles.'

He said he was only joking then, that he knew Finlay was better looking than he was, in such a strangely sincere way that made me want to reassure him of his handsomeness, that it was apparent on its own and not just in relation to Finlay.

On the way home, Muddy inserted *Definitely Maybe* and the penultimate track, 'Slide Away', started playing. He excitedly told me that not only did he think it was Liam's best vocal performance, but also that it was probably the band's best song. He then said that the long outro with Noel always gave him goosebumps. He even showed me his arm when that part of the song came on and I touched it, feeling how dimpled his skin had become.

We stopped at a petrol station in Chatham, where Muddy asked the clerk if I could use the toilet. When I came back out, he was back in the car with some blue shopping bags in the back seat. He smiled nervously when I got in and asked if I was all right.

'Yeah,' I said. 'Why?'

'Your old mate's a right horny bastard, isn't he?'

'What?'

He flicked his eyes over to my phone, which I'd left on the dashboard. 'Sorry, pal,' he said, 'didn't mean to peek at your messages, but it wouldn't stop going off.'

I froze, feeling strangely disassociated, as if Muddy had been speaking to somebody else. 'Um,' I said, swallowing. 'What did it say?'

'You might wanna have a read yourself,' he said. 'It's not stuff I'd ever wanna say to you, pal.' Muddy gave me a hard stare, his eyes widening with concern. 'Harley, mate, do tell me to piss off obviously, but this bloke, who is he, exactly? Because he don't sound like a mate.' A lump inflated in my throat. 'Some of this shit he's going on about, pal, it's a bit . . . If he's fuckin' hurt you . . .'

I'd never been oblivious to the problematic nature of mine and Paul's encounters, but having Muddy witness it forced me to watch all my fragile justifications for it collapse. When he looked at me then, I almost felt like continuing to mine in the rubble of the relationship, just for something good to present to Muddy, to also make him believe in my delusion that Paul had had a positive role to play in my life. I felt tears fall down my cheeks; I kept blinking until I hid Muddy behind a blur. I saw the vague watercoloured sketch of him reach out to touch me, his palm tight around my shoulders for a moment, before he pulled me towards him and hugged me. I wiped my face and apologized, saying how all I seemed to do was cry on different bits of his clothing.

He laughed. 'It's all right,' he said. He inhaled deeply. 'So, what's goin' on then, mate? How did you get involved with him then? Is he, like, some kinda racist or something?'

After a moment's consideration, I took Muddy back a few years and tried to explain, as best I could, why I'd sought Paul out in the first place; how at some point, in my late teens, the loneliness I'd felt had been so unbearable, that my own company hadn't been enough anymore, that I hadn't known what to do to fix it; that I'd felt that perhaps there were certain things you had to sacrifice when you'd been lonely for so long, in order to be wanted by somebody; that I knew there was no relationship here, that I hadn't been fantasizing about some forbidden love with an older man; but that I did think that in handing over these pieces of myself, I could sustain his interest in me, that maybe one day this interest would blossom into him seeing me as more than just a submissive body with brown skin.

Muddy was a great listener. And as I was talking to him, I felt this overwhelming surge of gratitude in my chest. His eyes were fixed on mine, and I felt so connected with him that as more tears fell, I found myself telling him things that I hadn't dared to admit to anyone, especially not Chelsea. Stories that, in the telling of them, did unspeakable things to my self-esteem, but somehow, told in Muddy's company, there was surprisingly less darkness. I could tell he was trying not to look too horrified though, and I appreciated the effort.

'Once,' I said, 'he came on me while I was sleeping at his. Like all over my back and stuff, and he took pictures, just to show me when I woke up.' When Muddy asked me why Paul had done this, I just shrugged and made a strange shape with my mouth.

'What a fuckin' freak,' he said. 'See, me? If I were gonna come all over you, but you were asleep, I'd obviously wake you up first, and be like: Harley, pal, do you mind if I rub one out on your face. And if you said no, I'd hold my hands up and be like: fine. And go find myself a sock or something.'

'Thank you?'

'No worries, pal,' he said, 'it's only common courtesy, isn't it? No one should have to wake up to a face full of spunk, unless they really want it there.'

'Seems like you've got the whole ideology behind consent down,' I said. 'I'm proud of you.'

'Yeah, proper equalist, me,' he said. 'Those hip-hop birds you got me listening to wouldn't have it, would they?' His eyes softened. 'You weren't crying because of him this morning, were you?' I looked at him a moment before I nodded. There was a tense silence. He started to say something: 'He's not why you …?' and then he stopped and shook his head. 'Ah, Harley, pal, seriously. You're a smart bloke, aren't you? You don't have to keep seeing someone that does that to you. You deserve better, come on. We're not havin' this, mate.' I smiled at him. I didn't know what to say. I didn't know why I found this concept of self-worth so difficult; I almost felt compelled to ask him, how could I know if I actually deserved better? And was it really up to me to decide?

'You know what,' Muddy said. 'Just get bloody rid, mate. Never speak to him again. Never go over to his again. From here on, pal, if you feel lonely? You come and see me. I told you when I first I met you, didn't I? You need anything, I'm just across the hall from you. Don't you bleedin' hesitate.'

He smiled at me. I smiled back.

'Please don't tell anyone,' I said.

'It's all I'm good for these days, aren't I?' he said, laughing. 'Keeping your bleedin' secrets.'

Fourteen

Muddy's talent for remaining friends with the women he'd
dated was remarkable. A few days after that night drive, I
met Noria in Bluewater to assist with her next round of job
hunting and handing out CVs. As we walked through the
shopping centre, she enlightened me to aspects of Muddy and
Chelsea's relationship that I'd had no clue about.

For weeks I'd thought their foursome had established
itself because of their various romantic connections. But as it
happens, post break-up, Muddy still drove Chelsea into work
whenever Finlay was out on a job; sometimes he'd pick her up,
and they would go shopping, and he'd sit and wait outside
her changing room with all her stuff; they had coffee mornings, walks in the park, trips to Shakermaker's. Of course,
all of this had been happening less now that Chelsea had
become part-Londoner. I supposed it made me happy that
there had been something about their friendship that could
survive the erosion of something romantic.

Noria looked deflated that afternoon. After we'd gone

through various shops, which had all given her some variation of: 'We're not hiring right now', I decided that we should browse in HMV, which I hoped would at least make her smile. We were in the pop and rock section; she picked up a copy of *The Velvet Rope* by Janet Jackson and asked me if I'd ever listened to it like she'd requested of me once. I shook my head and she handed it over, saying she was getting it for me. We stayed in the shop for a while.

'You know what gets me, yeah,' she was saying when we ended up by the DVDs. 'If I came into work and I didn't say shit, Jennifer would get on me and be like: "Why are you always in a mood, this is a customer-facing job, you're supposed to be sociable." But the minute I decide to speak, it's suddenly all these weird looks, and, "Noria, keep your voice down, it's a customer-facing fucking job." I feel like I can't win with anything. And I'm not even trying to say that I wanna be left alone, because I don't. I'm not a grumpy bitch. I actually like people. But sometimes I feel like I have to pick between what I'd rather be criticized for, you know? I'm not even joking, every time I walk in there, I literally think: am I even gonna say good morning to these people, just for Jen's annoying arse to come charging round the corner to tell me to stop talking and loitering? Or am I just gonna keep to myself, mind my own business, get paid this minimum wage and fuck off out of there ...'

'I'm sorry,' I said, 'I hate that she's making you so dispirited. You haven't made a dick joke all afternoon, and I think I miss it.' She smiled at me, shaking her head. 'This is a big place,' I continued, 'I'm sure you'll find something. And if not, we can start looking at Lakeside.'

'I'm not trekking all the way to Lakeside for minimum wage.'

'Fair enough,' I said. 'Well, hand your CV to the guy and let's get some food.'

After HMV, we sat on the bench in the middle of the shopping centre sharing a box of Krispy Kreme donuts.

'How much time do you think I'll get for arson?' Noria asked, picking at the icing at the corner of her mouth with her thumb.

'Do you really wanna be a statistic for Jennifer?' I asked. 'Come on, Noria.'

'No,' she said. 'I'm not gonna set her on fire.' She paused and side-eyed me. 'Just her car. No one has to die then. But if someone *does* have to die . . .' she smiled at me now. 'Then I'm with it, I'm not gonna lie.'

'Noria,' I said, laughing. 'Why would someone have to die? I think there's a future in which Jennifer is still alive and you're happy and successful and without a criminal record.'

'You have a lot of faith in the future.'

I put my hand on her shoulder. 'I have a lot of faith in you.'

She grimaced. 'Ew,' she said. 'Absolutely not. Never do that again.' I chuckled and asked if Muddy had called her. 'No, actually,' she said, 'but Finn did.'

'Really?'

'Yeah,' she said. 'I think he's confused.'

'How so?'

'Well, I think he's so obsessed with being Muddy's wingman that he doesn't actually care what Muddy wants,' she said. 'I think he just wants to set Muddy up, and Muddy just goes along with it. You know, Finn's honestly the biggest bullshitter I've ever met in my life. He said that Muddy wanted to give it another go and that he wanted to make it up to me. And obviously that was such bullshit. And I know it was bullshit because I called Muddy myself afterwards, and he apologized for leading me on, and said he was never actually looking for a girlfriend, and he didn't want to be in a relationship. And I was like, Mud, if you'd just been honest about your shit and told me that in the beginning, then we wouldn't have wasted all this time. Stop being such a pushover for Finn.'

I looked at her like: That's fair.

'I thought we were going out for weeks,' she said. 'Turns out I was just trying to fuck my "friend" the entire time. I need, I don't know, I need some compensation, some reparations, a fucking refund, something. I'm gonna have some tough-arse questions for the next guy. Because, me? Be in a relationship all by myself? With an indecisive half-arsed guy? I promise you, no one is gonna see that girl again. She's dead. Arson. Her family have been informed. Her will's been read out. And no one's getting shit. It's done.'

'You think you guys will be friends still?'

She shrugged. 'Maybe, I'd be open to that if he was gay,' she said. 'What do you think?'

'Do I think he's gay?'

'I mean, it would explain some things,' she said. 'But also, he don't really seem gay to me, you know? The way I had to force the face cream on him.'

'Well, that's the thing about us gays,' I said, 'we do tend to vary in our respective gayness.'

'If he is just looking for a friend, I guess I can get over him making me look like a dickhead. I do like being around him; he's just good people, you know. I know he's a Virgo, but he seems more like a Sagittarius to me.'

'What do you mean "like a dickhead"?'

'Yeah, like when we first started going out, sometimes I'd try and kiss him, and he would slyly move away like I'd just seen him in the street and tried to jump him or something. I mean, it did get better, like there were moments where I felt like he was into it. But nah. He was never really about me like that.'

'So, is this you saying that being his best gal pal is back on the cards?'

'I wouldn't mind,' she said. 'I think I'm gonna hit the club again with Chels though. Find myself a nigga this time, you know what I'm saying? Don't know how well that's gonna work in Kent. And I don't know how I feel about clubbing up in London. But still, I'm gonna cut back on the white boys again.' We both laughed and then she leaned across to me, circling one hand around the other, licking her lips in a mock attempt at seduction. 'So, what you saying, then? You sure you're gay?'

I laughed. 'Don't insult me by pretending you think I'm attractive.'

She pinched my cheek and yanked it, saying in a patronizing baby voice: 'Oh, Harles, of course I think you're attractive.'

'Oh, get off me.'

'You should still come with though,' she said. 'You can help me scout.'

'I'm not, nor will I ever be, your gay best friend.'

'But you're Chels's though.'

'Exactly, Noria,' I said, 'I already have responsibilities.'

'I haven't seen her in ages, to be fair,' she said, 'you know, not since you laid her business out like that.'

'That's not what happened.'

'Harles, you closed off a street, set up a stall, drew a crowd, used *two* megaphones and told the people this is how Ms Chelsea Taylor likes to get down. If anyone ever exposed me like that . . .' she kissed her teeth and laughed.

'Like anyone would ever have to,' I said.

That afternoon, Finlay sent Noria a strange, misspelled text, asking her to come to Shakermaker's because Muddy, who was there too, wanted to have a chat with her. So, when we got back to Dartford, we went straight over. But when we arrived we were curiously horrified to find the pub empty except for Muddy and Finlay and the rest of their rugby lot, who were all wearing their stereotypes quite comfortably: loud and rowdy and drunk and in various stages of undress.

We stood at the window and watched them.

The guys had arranged some of the tables into one unbroken line and poured beer all over them. It seemed some of them had been dared to strip down to boxers and use the tables as a makeshift slip and slide.

'What is going on?' I asked Noria, who was waving, trying to get Muddy's attention.

Muddy had been downing a pint of beer at the far end of the tables, before we watched him hoist himself up and glide down on his bare stomach, thudding onto the carpet. As he rolled around, laughing, trying to get back up, some of the guys were shoving him back down, cackling maniacally at him. When he noticed us at the window, he pushed everyone away and stood up, waving excitedly. Finlay was sliding down the tables too now, with a pint in his hand, before he pummelled into Muddy, spilling beer all over Muddy's back.

I'd imagined that my place in Muddy's life was so separate from *this*, that if the two worlds should entangle, he would simply not acknowledge me. And I'd allowed myself to be fine with that; it wasn't as if he owed me access to any other parts of his life. I also imagined that there should've been something exciting, or even arousing, about seeing the both of them this close to naked. But the context was so overpowering in its idiocy that it was impossible to extract anything sexy from it at all.

Noria and I sat at a table outside. We were joined shortly afterwards by Finlay and Muddy, who'd found and put on the bottom half of their kits. Muddy smiled as they sat down opposite us, his hair falling over his face. They both looked so wet and sticky. Muddy offered to get everyone some drinks, but Noria didn't answer and instead asked Finlay why they smelled like piss. He explained that one of their mates, Liam – he pointed Liam out in the pub – had pissed in a pint glass and they'd had to douse themselves in it because of how the match had gone this afternoon. Noria kissed her teeth at Finlay, as did I, and then Muddy laughed, slapping him on the back.

Their friends started to scatter eventually, so drunk that most of them hadn't even noticed that Finlay and Muddy weren't with them anymore. Inside, the staff were cleaning up.

'You disgraceful, dutty goats,' Noria snapped, scowling at the two of them, 'you should be cleaning up, not them.'

They both looked at each other with blank expressions and then Muddy stood up. 'You're right,' he said.

Finlay yanked him back down. 'Oh, sit down, mate,' he said, 'don't listen to her.'

'You're such a dickhead,' Noria said, which only seemed to make Finlay laugh.

'You heard from Chels?' he asked her.

'I'm not telling you shit.'

Muddy asked Noria if they could go and have a private chat. When they left, Finlay looked at me, his eyes heavy-lidded, with one arm slung around the back of his chair.

'So, *you* heard from her then?' he asked.

'You stink of piss, Finlay.'

'Stick to the topic, will you?'

'Well, that's not hard,' I said. 'The topic never really changes, does it?'

'What you on about?'

'I'm just saying we only ever talk about Chelsea,' I said, 'and now you're not even together anymore.'

Chelsea had called from London the day after the dinner to quell any worries I might've had about her being furious with me; she'd said she'd come into my room the previous night to talk to me, but I'd gone off with Muddy. She'd told me that Finlay hadn't seemed as annoying to her after the dinner, that the things about him she'd thought were infantile were actually adorable. I'd asked her if she was serious, and then she'd told me a story about how once he'd had all his rugby lot over at his flat and had showed everyone how he could make his farts sound like Donald Duck. She'd said that this used to make her sick, but now she'd realized it was unique. But now he wasn't answering her calls.

Finlay laughed in agreement. 'Yeah, we do only ever talk about Chels, don't we?' he said. 'You know what, mate, forget I asked.'

'No, I'm only joking,' I said. 'I know you've been ignoring her calls and texts, so obviously you can't be too bothered.'

'I don't know,' he said. 'Thought it'd be nice to see how she was, without, you know ...'

'Without her knowing you're thinking about her?' He nodded. 'Ah,' I said. 'I'm sorry, Finlay.'

'What?'

'I can't really help you there.'

'Why not?'

'Because I like Chelsea a lot more than I like you,' I said, 'so I probably won't be that much use to you as an intermediary. If she tells me not to tell you something, I for sure won't tell you a thing.'

'Well, look at you,' he said, smirking, 'you get a little new hairdo, and you think you're some kind of big man. Even though you're—'

'Even though I'm practically four foot,' I interrupted. 'Yes, Finlay we've heard this one before.'

'Fine then, mate,' he said, 'how's this for a change of pace, then?' He leaned forward and lowered his voice. 'What you think of Mud then? Do you think he might be one of your lot?'

'What?' I said. 'Do I think he's gay?'

'Yeah, why don't you talk a bit louder, mate?' he said. 'Yeah, so, thoughts, opinions, what've you got?

'I've got nothing for you,' I said. 'Why don't you ask him?'

'No, mate,' Finlay said. 'I'm not doing that. Anyway, it's just lately, he's been a bit, I don't know. I told you before, didn't I? He's always been a bit weird with women. Maybe that's the reason it never works out with them. And he's started getting into all that face cream shit lately. And he don't even get to get off with Nor anymore.'

'He's actually wearing it now?' I asked. 'Also, didn't you basically beg him to put it on?'

'Yeah,' he said, 'but that was when I thought it meant he'd get to slip her one. Now he's wearing the stuff because, what, he likes it? Explain yourself, mate, what have you done to him?'

'Will you stop being a prick for, like, two seconds, please,' I said. 'I'm still working through your homophobia. So, if you're so fragile that you can't even stomach Muddy putting on a bit of face cream without sex being the intention, then that's just a lot more work for me, isn't it? You know, being your friend is actually a lot of mental paperwork for me, Finlay.'

'Homophobia?' he said. 'Oh, behave. There's nothing

homophobic about me. Offered to take you out to a gay bar the other day, didn't I?'

'Oh, then I'm sorry,' I said, 'the next time you call someone an "absolute bender", I'll just remember that time you said you'd let me play with some fun-sized men at a gay bar.'

Muddy and Noria were walking back now.

'Fine, that was out of order,' Finlay said. 'Just bad habits, I suppose. I apologize. But be a mate and use one of them gaydars on him that you lot are supposed to have, would you? And let me know what you find out.' He patted me on the head, grinning. 'Good boy.'

'What have you two been chattin' about then?' Muddy asked as he sat down by my side.

I didn't reply and just smiled at him. Finlay raised an eyebrow and said to me: 'Why ain't you said nothing to him about smelling like piss, then? He had to do it too.'

'Well, he's someone else I like a lot better than you, isn't he?'

Muddy looked at Finlay and laughed loudly, holding up a hand for me to slap. 'Atta-fuckin-boy, pal!' He threw a cold and damp arm around me. 'I told yous,' he said. 'He bleedin' loves me, he does.'

I looked up at him, grinning, my pupils almost pushing up behind my eyelids.

Sometimes I felt as if my anxiety was so permanent, so robust – that it had seeped so deep, and for so long – that my feelings were so indiscriminately sensitive, that I would probably not recognize genuine fear if I ever experienced it. But that wasn't true. Whatever limits had been imposed on

my life when it came to fear simply didn't exist, there was
always more distance to run.

It was nearly 10 p.m. and Noria had long taken up Muddy's
offer of drinks. She had then started telling Finlay things
about Chelsea: that the real reason she was still staying at
her parents was because she was trying not to see him, that
she had begged Eddie to let her stay on at the Regal branch
in London, that Finlay had said some awful things to her in
the corridor that evening that made her feel like total shit,
but yet she still somehow ended up feeling as if she had done
something wrong. Noria called him delusional for thinking
he was owed any kind of apology.

It was then that I felt this harsh stitch of terror. A group
of men had walked into the pub, half of them sat at the table
behind ours and half of them went inside, all homogenous –
middle aged, with varying degrees of receding hairlines and
baldness. My skin started to prickle, and I suddenly found it
difficult to breathe. I'd gone so silent and so still that Finlay
clicked his fingers at me and asked what was wrong. As I
was about to reply that I was fine, I saw Paul coming out of
the pub with a pint and ended up saying nothing at all, just
nodding at Finlay with a forced smile. I had often wondered
what Paul's friends would think if they knew what we did
together, if they heard the things he said or made me say.

Muddy, Finlay and Noria started laughing about something; it was apparently so funny that Muddy threw his arm
around me and started tapping my chest, letting his head
fall until it touched mine and some of his hair was resting on
my cheek. I looked at him and forced myself to laugh before

turning back to Paul, who had an eyebrow raised at me and a strange glassy expression on his face. I felt such a swell of guilt that I became desperate to move Muddy's hand off me. But in his elation, Muddy kept tightening his grip and bringing me closer into him and rubbing my arm. When Muddy realized that I was trying to get him to let go, he said: 'You all right, pal?'

I swallowed. 'Yeah,' I said. 'I'm fine. I'm just gonna go to the toilet.'

I didn't know how long I'd been stood at the sink, staring into the mirror, before I heard the door open and saw Paul's reflection; he was standing there with a drink in his hand. I turned to face him. In the light, he looked viciously angry. I thought about how I'd never seen his face well lit before; there was a hostility there that I'd never noticed. Or perhaps I'd simply never wanted to notice. He'd still been sending me texts recently and I'd been deleting them. For a fleeting moment, this had made me feel powerful.

'What you doin' here?' he asked slowly. His voice was low and coarse. I didn't know how to answer without sounding sarcastic, so I said nothing. 'I got my mates out there,' he continued, biting down on each word. 'What d'you think they're gonna say when they see me in here with the likes of you?' He slammed a fist into one of the cubical doors. 'Hmm?' I receded into myself. I felt like an animal with a categorial awareness of how low on the food chain I was. 'What d'you think they're gonna say when they see me in here with a gay, black bastard, eh? Say something then? You bloody poof. What d'you think is gonna go through their fuckin' heads if they see me in here with the likes of you.' His eyes became bulbous and veined with red. I realized that he couldn't see me, not really, that, for him, there was simply an empty space where I thought I'd existed. On some level, I'd always sensed that I didn't really matter, that there was something insignificant about my existence, but it was a different sense altogether to have it confirmed so resolutely, to not only speculate but to know that there was something that happened to things that were associated with me that made them spoil. How long would it be before whatever this disease I seemed to spread around, like some kind of fucked up Sandman, would drift further and further and more forcefully through the air, engulfing anyone who considered me a friend?

I tried to leave. As I was walking past him, he dropped his pint and I flinched at the sound of the glass shattering. He took a step towards me and pinned me against the wall, lifting me high and holding me in place with the length of his arm. His face was so close that I could smell the cigarettes and alcohol on his breath and it made me feel sick. 'You told anyone?' he asked.

I shook my head, somehow managing to say: 'No, no, I haven't.'

'You sure?'

'I am,' I said quickly, using the little bits of breath he was allowing me to take. 'I haven't told anyone, Paul, I swear.'

'Don't say my name,' he growled. 'You *never* say my name. Do you understand me? You little faggot.' He pressed his forearm into my neck a little harder, and although I was choking, I was still trying not to cough. 'You're a little liar, aren't you?' He looked behind himself, at the orange liquid veining between the pieces of broken glass. 'You've cost me a pint, you have. What are you gonna do about that?'

His erection was rigid against my thigh; my heart was beating so fast. *Destroying me would be so easy*, I thought, *like removing the legs from a spider*. There were always going to be repercussions for the crime of trying to feel anything other than loneliness. I understood this now. He threw his head at me and busted my bottom lip. The blood fell and soaked into his shirt which angered him further. The world before me – the white tiles, the urinals, the exposed pipes – began to blink in and out. I felt so weak that I considered if I might actually let him kill me. Perhaps I would have. It was unfortunate that I couldn't breathe. I at least wanted the chance to beg for my life.

The door opened again. I couldn't see him, but I heard Finlay's voice. 'What d'you think you're doing, mate?' he shouted. 'Get off him now!' I saw his arms come around from behind Paul and yank Paul back. I thudded to the ground, coughing hard, my palm wrapped around my throat. The pain from my split lip had started to come through. Paul tried to headbutt Finlay too, but Finlay took a step back, hopping on his feet, his hands rolled into fists, jabbing them before him like a boxer, and Paul missed, slumping onto the ground.

Muddy, red-faced and furious, stood at the door. He

watched Paul slap at the glassy, beer-soaked floor as he tried to get back up. And when he did, Muddy grabbed him, a hand on each of Paul's arms, and yelled in his face: 'You wanna go, do you? Come on then, mate. Let's fuckin' have it, then!' Muddy slammed Paul into a cubicle door; Paul tried to charge at him, but Finlay hooked his fingers into the collar of Paul's shirt and launched him out of the toilet before going after him. The door hit the frame several times before it settled shut.

Muddy rushed beside me whilst I touched my lip curiously, inspecting the glob of blood on my fingertip. He crawled into a cubicle, ripped off a few sheets of tissue and gently dabbed at the cut.

'So, is that the guy, then?' he asked.

I nodded. 'Good timing.'

'Well, you looked like you'd seen a ghost or something, pal, didn't you?' he said. 'He watched you come in here, he did. He looked like he were ready to kill someone. So, I says to Finn: "Mate, something isn't right here." And Finn's been rarin' to go all night, he has. Especially since we lost the match today and we had to douse ourselves in Lairy Liam's piss. So, Finn goes: if we're gonna do someone in tonight, might as well be a fuckin' racist.'

'Thank you,' I said, 'I really mean it, Muddy, thank you so much.'

Gently, he placed his palm on my shoulder, then moved it across my back. He pulled me closer to him until my head was lying on his chest. I could feel him watching me, could feel him smiling. I looked up at him, his eyes were trained on mine; the bright lights made the browns of them seem as if they were glowing.

'Well, pal,' he said, inhaling deeply. 'I gotta look after you. I'm your person, aren't I?'

PART TWO

PART TWO

Fifteen

In early August, about a week after the assault, Muddy renewed his National Pool Lifeguard Qualification. He handed in his notice at Regal to work on a team of lifeguards at a leisure centre in Maidstone. He'd worked as a lifeguard in Swinton, back in Manchester, when he was sixteen, and had joked about missing the water. But really, he said, he wanted to be on ten quid an hour, instead of six, and wanted free access to a pool whenever.

On his first shift, he was going to be the only member of staff closing the pool, so he invited the four of us down. Chelsea had partly moved into Finlay's flat in Maidstone by now, so that evening, I met up with Noria in Northfleet and we got the train down to meet them.

Muddy was standing with Chelsea and Finlay in the carpark, in his new uniform: a yellow polo shirt and red shorts. When Chelsea saw Noria, she screeched and reached into her gym bag, pulling out a yellow swimming costume; Noria screeched back, reaching into hers and pulling out a matching one in pink. And as they ran towards each other, I went over to Muddy and Finlay.

Muddy gave me a two-fingered salute and Finlay fist-bumped my shoulder.

'So, Finners, why haven't we got matching swimwear, then?' Muddy said, nudging him. 'Look at 'em. They're proper chuffed about it.'

''Cause we're not a pair of girls, mate.'

Muddy pulled at the waistband of his shorts and then let it snap back, looking down curiously, and then tried to do the same to Finlay. 'What colour boxers you got on?' he asked. 'Mine are blue. Maybe we're already matching.'

Finlay slapped his hand away. 'Piss off.'

'Finn,' Muddy said, chuckling. 'When you don't share stuff with me, it makes me feel a bit neglected, mate.'

Finlay wet his finger and jammed it in Muddy's ear. 'How's that, then?'

Muddy laughed, patting at his ear, and called him a rotter. He then put his arm around me. 'I swear to you, pal,' he said, 'you've never met anyone who's harder work than Finn.'

'What?' Finlay said, 'I'm chill, mate.'

'About as chill as a bleedin' volcano, you,' Muddy said, and then called out to Chelsea and Noria: 'C'mon, girls, let's get a shuffle on.'

The leisure centre was deserted. In the changing rooms, Muddy and Finlay got naked immediately, while I bashfully took off my clothes; I'd already been wearing my trunks. I then sat on the bench fixed to wall and watched them. Finlay neatly folded his clothes and placed them beside mine, but

Muddy towel-whipped everything off the bench, and then towel-whipped Finlay on his bare arse.

Finlay glared at him. 'Mud, you're a bellend, you know that?'

'That's payback, that,' Muddy said, 'for every time you've done it to me.'

Finlay looked as if he might get his own towel and retaliate, but then he just shrugged and said: 'Fair play, mate.'

A few days ago, Finlay had accompanied me to report the assault at Shakermaker's because Muddy had had the interview for the lifeguard job. Before we'd gone to the police station, I'd shared with Finlay some reservations I'd had about reporting the incident, how I hadn't wanted it to be a bigger deal than it was, how I could just avoid going to Shakermaker's now, how I'd just wanted to move on. 'That might work with Mud,' Finlay had said, 'but no chance with me, mate. We're reporting it.' He was right: I'd also suspected that Muddy would've allowed me to avoid the police, if I'd pleaded my case to him. But Finlay had lectured me about how I was always going on at him for being a homophobe, so now, how could I let this person get away with assaulting me?

Unlike that evening at Shakermaker's, I actually enjoyed watching them be silly while naked. Since the assault, I'd been struggling to smile – at least genuinely – but watching Muddy attempt to rile Finlay up by towel-whipping him again, and Finlay taking Muddy's green swimming trunks and dangling them over the next cubicle, had brought me as close to an authentic smile as I'd had in a week.

As Finlay slipped into his red trunks, he said: 'You can take a peek if you want, mate. I know you want to.'

I rolled my eyes. 'Oh, stop assuming I find you attractive.'

Muddy cackled. 'You heard him, Finn,' he said. 'He don't fancy you, mate. He's only got eyes for me. Don't you, pal?'

'Bollocks,' Finlay said.

'Nah, he thinks I'm proper fit, me.' Muddy winked at me and started posing like they did in those bodybuilding competitions. 'Remember when he got hammered and called me handsome? He's never said that to you, has he?'

Finlay scoffed. 'Oh, sod the both of you,' he said. 'Let's go.'

Chelsea and Noria were already at the pool when we came out. They were sitting on the edge in their swimming costumes, kicking their legs back and forth in the water, their feet blurry beneath the surface. They were talking about something: Noria softly gliding her fingers through Chelsea's hair with one hand, while gesticulating with the other. Chelsea nodded at her excitedly. When they saw us, they stopped talking, and wolf whistled. I looked up at Muddy and Finlay who both had smug looks on their faces. I smiled at the girls and then Noria shouted back to us: 'That was for you, Harles!'

Finlay put his hand on my shoulder, lowering his head next to mine. 'You're really letting my ego starve today, aren't you?'

'I'm sorry.'

'You're not though, are you?'

'Not in the slightest.'

I sat between Chelsea and Noria, while Muddy and Finlay got in the water and swam, racing each other to the deep end.

'Is it actually all right that we're here?' Chelsea shouted to Muddy. He turned around and just waved dismissively at us like: Fuck it.

Noria started to tell me about the new style she was planning for Chelsea's hair when she noticed mine. 'Damn,' she said, rolling the little strands at the back of my neck between her fingertips. 'I'm gonna have to re-do this for you, babes. It's looking a bit messy.'

I smiled at her, shrugging. She then looked at Chelsea as if to pull her into the exchange. Chelsea put her hand on my back. 'How's your lip feeling, hun?'

I sighed. 'It's okay,' I said. 'I don't think you can see anything anymore.'

'Honestly,' Chelsea said. 'Just thinking about it makes me go fuckin' mental. How can someone see that little face of yours and think: right, I'm gonna smash it up.' She held my face and squeezed it a bit.

'That's what I'm saying,' Noria said, squeezing my face too. 'People really think they can just mess with my little king. I don't think so. You know, this is the kinda shit that makes me wanna get the lighter out.'

I shook their hands off and laughed. 'No one needs to be set on fire.'

'Of course they do, hun,' Chelsea said. 'Nor, you have the lighter ready. I'll be there with some lighter fluid.' Noria made a gesture with her head like: Let's go.

'In some ways,' I said, trying to make light of the incident, 'it wasn't all bad. I had two shirtless rugby players come to my rescue. I like to think that this balances things out.'

We looked at Muddy and Finlay in the pool. Noria screwed her face up and shouted: 'Eh, what are you idiots doing?' They were wrestling each other very intensely in the water. Finlay had lifted Muddy and had his face in Muddy's crotch, Muddy's legs dangling behind Finlay's back with his arms wrapped around Finlay's head. Suddenly, Finlay slammed him back in the pool. And as they both exploded into laughter, bobbing up and down, grabbing at one another, Noria stood up, stepped into the water and waded over to them.

'What children,' Chelsea said. 'I think they're doing a WWE thing.'

'It's all very homoerotic,' I said. 'I love it.'

Chelsea laughed and then we went quiet. 'I know you sorted it in the end,' she began eventually, 'but Finn said you didn't wanna report what happened at first. Why's that?'

I shrugged at her. 'I just didn't want to make a big deal about it,' I said. 'Getting the police involved and stuff.'

'But it is a big deal, Harles.'

'I know.'

There was another silence and she returned her hand to my back. 'Are you okay?'

Since the incident, I'd been trying to appear unfazed, as if it genuinely hadn't bothered me. I'd started making myself tired so I wouldn't feel any of my real feelings. I hadn't slept in ages, and I'd been moving through my days all lifeless and apathetic. There was a familiar darkness attaching itself to my thoughts like a graft of skin, a bleakness I believed would simply unpeel itself if I let enough time pass. But these thoughts were becoming more intense, as if my usual mental narration had been replaced with its evil twin. This character had been so active in its fight against me, that I couldn't sleep even when I'd decided to.

'I'm fine,' I replied, smiling as hard as I could. 'I really am.' She looked at me intently for what felt like a long time, as if trying to verify my answer. But she didn't respond to this, and instead asked if I was getting in the water. Unable to hide my melancholy any longer, I said no.

I watched them quietly, as a cold, hard rush of sadness filled my chest, as if it were being pumped full of water. Noria climbed onto Finlay's shoulders, and he held her legs, looking up at her, laughing as Chelsea climbed onto Muddy's. Finlay said that because they were women, he and Muddy would go easy on them. And Noria pushed his head, saying: 'Finn, if you don't slam me into this water right now, like you fuckin' mean it . . . !' I felt simultaneously envious and grateful for their happiness. Everything they did made me want to cry.

After they stopped with the wrestling, Muddy swam over to me. He rested his arms on the tiles, wiped his hair out of his face and we exchanged smiles. He was so glossy with water, and his hair was flat and dark, looking as if it had been drawn on. I tried to will some of the sadness away by looking at him attentively, at his smiley, plump face, at his lovely long dimples that stretched down his cheeks. He asked if I was okay, and I nodded. He put his hand around my thigh and said: 'Come on, pal. If I'm gonna get a bollocking for this, might as well make the most out of it.'

I feared that if I spoke I might actually cry, so I didn't say anything. He looked at me a moment longer, his gaze softening, seeming to understand something about my silence. He jumped up and sat beside me, and after a moment he put his arm around me; he was all slippery and cold as he rubbed my arm. I closed my eyes just for a second. Finlay looked at us and shouted: 'Oi, get a fuckin' room, you two!' Chelsea laughed and hit him, and Muddy put up his middle finger.

Noria was near the back of the pool. She could only look at us.

It was a mostly quiet ride back to Dartford. Noria was in the front seat with Muddy and I was in the back. Muddy was talking about some Missy Elliott songs he'd listened to, but Noria wasn't really responding, just making vaguely agreeable noises every time Muddy said anything. Muddy dropped her off in Northfleet. He tried to hug her but she shrugged him off with a very blunt: 'Bye.'

'Bit frosty, her,' Muddy said as I moved to take Noria's place beside him. 'D'ya think it's 'cause she thought I was chattin' a load of bollocks? 'Cause I wasn't. I thought Missy Elliott were all right. She has some pretty crackin' songs.'

I didn't have the capacity to think about Noria or anyone else; suddenly, interacting with people, even Muddy, felt incredibly difficult. Historically, depression had never meant that I would feel as if my life would cease to go on; it'd never felt as if I was crawling through a forest that grew increasingly dense and suffocating with foliage, new trees drifting into my path with every movement. But I couldn't respond to Muddy that evening, I couldn't help to rationalize Noria's sudden mood shift. I couldn't do, or be, anything for him. He said something else that I didn't respond to. He sighed and turned on the radio. 'Over and Over' by Nelly and Tim McGraw was on. He tapped his fingers on the wheel, humming quietly, taking quick glances at me, beginning sentences and never finishing them. I rested my head on the window and closed my eyes until we got to the flat.

In my room that night, I sent a few texts to Paul. I told him that I was sorry if I had offended him in any way, and apologized on Muddy and Finlay's behalf. But his number was no longer receiving text messages. Without undressing, I slithered under my bedsheets. In a scramble to trick the universe into brightening, I sent a few texts to my dad, asking if he would care if I were dead, or if the death of gay men didn't hold much weight for him, and if I agreed to be prayed for, would he consider loving me then. My face was illuminated by the glow of my phone. My tears magnified the characters on the screen. When he didn't reply, I called him and let it ring until the automated voice started talking to me. I thought if I could repair at least one thing, then perhaps I could buy back from life one more moment of happiness. Every time I'd felt this small before, there'd always remained at least an ember of hope. I was never so broken that I couldn't be fixed. But the hope was no longer there. Or it had secreted itself so deep inside of me that it needed to see me shrivel before revealing itself.

At around four in the morning, I ran myself a bath. I sat on the cold bathroom floor, watching the water fill up until it started to gush over the edge of the tub. Even then, I didn't remember deciding anything. Subconsciously, I knew I didn't want to be in the woods again, not after last time. I didn't remember retrieving another x-acto knife from the kitchen, but I must've done, because I had one in my hand. I didn't remember deciding that I wanted to hurt myself, but I must've done because I was in the tub, hovering the blade over my wrist. I didn't remember deciding that I wanted to die, or come close to it, but I made an incision and started to draw the blade back, inexpertly, splitting the skin and watching the blood glug out, my mouth slack, my breaths pulsing out, wincing and then writhing and then bleating and then screaming in pain. *Life,* I thought, looking up into the light, tears gliding down my cheeks, *is this enough? Please, let this be enough. Please save me. I don't want to die. I don't want to die. I want to be happy.*

Everything was then reduced to flashes of light, things melting into blurs, hands on me and then long uninterrupted sequences of movement; lights were shifting into darkness and back into light again. Then things began to clarify themselves, the lights came back on permanently. I saw my arms first, the right one imbedded with stitches, about three or four of them running a few centimetres up my arm. My legs were covered in sheets and punctuated by a wooden board. And then, to my side, Muddy asleep in a chair, hair all over his face, snoring.

Whenever I'd thought about my death, it had always been important to me that I wouldn't get in anyone's way. I was never going to do anything that drew a crowd, like throw myself in front of a train or off a building. I'd previously kept cutting in my head, as a sort of private comfort: I liked the idea of its relative simplicity, its access, its secrecy. I'd simply imagine it and often that was enough. I'd imagined it so much that, that night, nothing about it felt too outlandish, too uncharacteristic; it even felt familiar; finally doing it felt as if I'd stepped into this desolate world through which I'd only seen through a keyhole.

'Muddy?' I said, frightened by how coarse and faint my voice sounded.

He juddered out of sleep, smacking his lips together, circling his fists on his eyes. 'Mate!'

He asked me how I was and then told me how he'd heard my screams and found me passed out in the bathroom. He said I'd almost drowned and that we were in Darent Valley Hospital, and that it was now Friday. I could see how terrified he was; he was smiling, but there was so much concern in his eyes. I was terrified too. Things had never been this bad before. I felt as if I'd smashed myself into bits and now I had to piece everything back together again. But back into what? I used to understand myself as someone who only *thought* about death. But now that I'd actually attempted to venture into it, I couldn't understand myself as anything.

Muddy pulled the chair closer to my bed and warned me that he had to tell someone I was awake, that someone had to speak with me. When I asked who, he just shrugged and said he didn't know, a psychiatrist or something. I was about to say something else, when he stopped me and said: 'No, I haven't told Chels or anyone, if that's what you're about to say. But mate, I do have to ask, and I've been kicking myself for not asking when I first met you. I dunno, I just thought it might've been rude or awkward or whatever. But that day in the woods, you were trying to, you know, kill yourself, weren't you? I mean, that's what you were gonna do, with the blade you chucked away when I showed up?' I paused before I nodded at him. 'Jesus!' he said quietly. 'And today?' I nodded again. He squeezed my knee, trying to relax his eyes and the tremble in his lips. 'It wasn't because of Paul, was it?'

I'd woken up so hollow, but there was something about his concern . . . It replenished me.

My defences fell then, as if the bricks and cement I'd used to construct these walls had actually been glue and glass.

'I've never really felt as if I've mattered to anyone before,' I said, 'I thought reconciling with my dad might help. I don't think I'm the first person to think a parent loving them unconditionally would fix everything. I mean, how is that not magical, right? How wouldn't that repair everything? But when that didn't happen, I thought I could use what I used to feel with Paul as a substitute, I guess. God, it was so stupid. He always made me feel like I mattered. And then when he said all those things to me at the pub, I just, I don't know. I mean, he just felt about me everything I often feel about myself, and I thought, well, if someone outside of myself feels it, then, you know . . .'

'So, these are the only times you've thought about trying to um . . . ?' He nodded at me, as if saying the words *trying to kill yourself* again might summon something. I shook my head and told him that, yes, there had been other times, but usually it was just thoughts, that I'd only thought about hurting myself or dying, that I'd be sad for a while, but then things would be normal again. 'So, when you got back from university, in the woods,' he continued, 'that was just thoughts, was it?'

I sighed. 'I don't know what to think anymore, Muddy,' I said. 'I just feel like a failure, all the time. From the little things that everyone should be able to do, like just talking to people, to the big things like trying to succeed at uni. I mean, I've always been prone to these bouts of sadness and sometimes they last longer or hit a bit harder than others, but they do go away.' I was crying now; he moved his hands from my knee and rested his fingers in my palm.

'Going to uni was supposed to be this really big thing for me, so when I became the reason that it wasn't successful, I felt like something began to crumble in me. Even though I was excited, I also thought that deep down, going would make things better; I thought it would make me less lonely, and maybe make me more outgoing, make me a bit happier. I thought being around likeminded people would really do that. But I got in my own way. I tried, Muddy, I really did. I tried so hard to be normal for people. But my head, it just gets so dark sometimes. I don't know what life feels like without constant fear; I don't know what it feels like to have a spotless mind. I sleep to stop myself from thinking, but then sometimes I can't sleep, so I'm just there, wading in all of it.'

That night in the bathtub, perhaps what I was doing was trying to get close enough to the point where I might realize that life was worth living after all; it'd always worked before. I made my move, and life made its move against me; I infused myself with *this* much darkness, and in exchange it gave me *this* much happiness. I was constantly atoning for things I'd accepted as my fault – my mum's death, my dad's rejection. Was I grateful for Muddy's interruption? Maybe I didn't need my life to be saved *for* me, not by my dad or Paul or even Muddy, maybe I needed it to be saved *from* me.

He was gently moving his hand up and down my arm now, looking at me intently, blinking slowly. 'Mate,' he said. 'I feel like I been looking after you since I met you.' There was relief in his voice. 'You know,' he continued. 'I watched you.'

'You watched me?'

'Yeah,' he said, 'I watched you for a while, pal. You were stood in the bushes for ages, looking into your hand. You were so ... still, like. I wasn't sure what was going on. But I had a bit of an inkling, so I tapped you on your shoulder and you leaped out of your bleedin' skin, mate. You looked so scared and angry when I tried to help you out with my handkerchief. Obviously, I never had the bottle to ask the question. But I thought I'd keep my eye on you.' He chuckled. 'That afternoon, I just sat in my room, and kept coming out, knocking on your door. No answer. D'ya know how relieved I was when I saw you in the front room that night? Ah, I just wanted to get up and hug you, and I barely even knew you.' He went quiet a moment; tears had emerged in his eyes. 'Harley, mate, I really tried my best to make sure you weren't on your own. You know, without seeming like your overprotective brother or something. And, I mean, I've seen it myself, haven't I? You've had a bit of a shit go of it lately. And, I don't know, I thought I could try and make you happy, didn't I?'

His friendship had made me happy, and I wished I knew why that didn't seem to alleviate things, why the thought of him hadn't stopped me from moving the blade any further. Had I thought of him? I knew love didn't exactly conquer all, but surely it should've counted for more than it did in that moment.

'And you know what, mate?' he said. 'You've bloody done it, you have. Because I'm gonna be right on you now. You're never getting rid of me, pal.'

I felt so sorry for him. I felt sorry that he had chosen me as a friend. The feeling ran deeper than if I were simply his personal misfortune, I felt that the happiness he seemed to enjoy so resolutely was in jeopardy now. How could some-one risk something so rare and precious for me? I continued to smile at him, hoping to silently communicate some of this, hoping that he might realize what a detrimental trade off this was. He could simply walk away and never speak to me again.

He brought his face really close to mine. 'You deserve to be alive. You do, Harley,' he said, his voice low. 'And fuck anyone that ever made you feel like you didn't.' I wiped my face. 'I've gotta hope,' he continued, 'that means more to you than whatever that Paul bloke was saying to you.'

I turned my head, so we were directly facing each other, and thanked him.

'You're always thanking me, aren't you?' he said. 'But at this point, I don't know what I'd do without you.'

'Muddy, stop it,' I said. 'I'm very sure you'd be fine.'

'No, pal,' he said. 'I'm dead serious. You know, you always look at me, like, I dunno, like I'm the best guy in the world or something. Like I can't put a foot wrong.' There was a glint of embarrassment in his eyes, and he briefly turned away from me. 'You get this little look in your eye, you do. Makes me feel dead good about myself, that.'

'Really?'

'Yeah,' he said, 'you're always smiling at me, you are. What, you haven't noticed?'

I laughed. 'Yeah,' I said. 'I suppose I have.'

'You've got a nice smile, mate.'

I winced. '*Muddy*—'

'No, you do!' he said, laughing. 'I'm not having you on, pal, you do!' We looked at each other in silence for a moment. 'I'm gonna, um, I'm gonna hug you now, mate, yeah? And then I'm gonna kiss you on your forehead, if that's all right with you.'

'Yeah,' I said. 'That's all right.'

He pressed his lips to my head and cupped a hand softly around my face, his thumb slowly brushing back and forth on my cheek. 'Can't let you go, pal,' he said. 'I can't do it. Obviously, I'm never gonna understand how hard it's been for you. But please, mate, I'm begging you. You have to try and keep yourself alive for us ... please.'

The psychiatrist, a pale oldish-looking man, spoke to me later, asking if I knew why I was here, if this was the first time that I'd tried to hurt myself, and why I'd done it. We discussed whether I had a history of self-harm, and I assured him that there had been none, even though I hadn't been able to explain coherently why this had happened now. The whole exchange scared me. I feared I was presenting my mental health in a much worse a state than it really was. The more he talked, the more it seemed I'd be transferred to some kind of psychiatric ward. He mentioned the Dartford Liaison Psychiatry Team, an on-site team of mental health nurses who would provide me with support. He was worried about the severity of the injury, about discharging me and the prospect of me doing this to myself again. In the end, I spent twenty-four hours on suicide watch. We talked about how I'd only imagined hurting myself in the past. 'I think you've suffered from passive suicide ideation,' he said. 'At least at one point. But the fact that you've made an attempt on your life is very worrying.'

I didn't know what would happen to me. When Muddy visited the next day, I told him how frightened I was, about how real it would feel if I were moved to a psych ward and if I were forced into therapy, that it would no longer be something I could keep to myself; that I would no longer be able to judge the severity of things for myself, that everything would be dissected by a professional; how things would no longer be what I said they were; how I wouldn't be able to control the narrative anymore, it was going to be written down on paper and solidified; they were going to prescribe things. People would have an opinion, over which I would have no influence.

Muddy reassured the psychiatrist that if he were to discharge me, I wouldn't be on my own, that he didn't believe that I would hurt myself again, that he'd be with me to sort out whatever help I needed from here onwards. Although the psychiatrist's enthusiasm for doing anything other than discharging me had started to wane anyway, still it seemed as if Muddy's case for my leaving the hospital carried more weight than my own. The psychiatrist strongly recommended that I started seeing someone – listing local mental health professionals in Dartford – officially judging the risk to myself as at least lower than severe. He said he would notify my GP and that was it.

The respite was over. Life would now propel me back into this perpetual game of bargaining, and I hoped I'd pleased it.

Sixteen

Muddy brought me home that evening. I sat on my bed and looked out of the window, into the night and its navy sky, at the soft glow of the streetlights, at the occasional car that crawled down our road, slowly stroking the bandage on my arm. Muddy had been rattling around in the kitchen since we got back, and then he came into my room holding two mugs. He made a loud grunting noise as he sat beside me, handing me one of them. It was lukewarm and had mostly milk swishing around in it, but I decided to take at least one sip at some point to be polite.

We were quiet for a long time before he said: 'I know you worry about Chels sometimes, but the bathroom's all cleaned up now.' I'd felt so awful at the idea of him having to clean up after me, that I kept apologizing to and thanking him. Even after he'd told me it was all right, I hadn't been able to stop, as if I'd been malfunctioning. 'So, I don't think she'll have any questions for you,' he continued. 'We just have to work out what we're gonna say about your little bandage there.' I looked at it, still moving my thumb up and down the fabric. 'I mean, I have a few suggestions I could throw your way, if you want.'

I smiled at him. 'Yeah,' I said. 'I don't think she'll buy me having another accident.'

He tightened his lips. 'So, like always,' he said, 'do tell me to piss off, mate, but why can't Chels know?'

'It's just . . .' I said, sighing. 'It's just better this way.'

He nodded and didn't ask any further questions. He then suggested some things we could tell Chelsea about my bandage that made me laugh, like how he'd completely dominated me in play wrestling, or how he'd tried to teach me how to play rugby, and I'd broken my wrist. And I joked that he'd never seen me run, let alone throw a ball, so Chelsea would never believe it.

'So, that's what we gotta do then, pal!' he said excitedly, patting my back. 'We gotta get you out with Finn on his little morning jogs and then doing some bits out on the field with me. Make it believable for Her Highness.'

'Absolutely not.'

He put his arm around me. 'Well, you say that, but I've been told that I'm quite an influential man, me. And I've got—'

'Muddy, *who* is telling you these things?'

He laughed and then sighed. He squeezed me, rubbing my arm, and then gently laid his chin on top of my head. He put his mug down and put his other arm around me tight. There was a long silence. I could feel his heart beating against my shoulder. 'Ah,' he said. 'I've never been so scared in my bleedin' life, pal. Don't you dare scare me like that again. I'm always tellin' you, aren't I? You feel sad, you feel angry, even if you feel bloody nothing, you come and you see *me*. I'm tellin' you this now, and you better not forget it. *I'm* gonna be there for you, and that's a bleedin' promise.' He looked at me now, his eyes sparkly with tears, his hands clipped on my shoulders. 'Do you hear me, mate? Whatever's going on, Harley, we're in this shite together now, you and me.' He pulled me closer to him. 'I'm not a total idiot. I know just because I'm here, don't mean you're never gonna feel lonely, but, mate, you'll never be on your own, not if I have something to say about it. We clear, pal?' I looked at him a moment, wondering how it was possible for someone to care about me this much, and then nodded. 'Good lad.'

I leaned into him, sinking into the comfort of his pillowy chest. As someone who had always coveted love, it had always felt like this perpetual journey to a place that may or may not exist. But this was when I knew that I was no longer hiking towards some vague destination, that I could see it now, that I had been able to see it for a while, and that he had been seeing it with me.

We stayed in my room for most of the night. Muddy made some comments about how small my room was, and I accused him of stealing mine. He laughed and took several gulps from his mug. I'd gone to finally take a sip from mine too, when he hovered his hand over it and said: 'Nah, don't drink that, mate.'

'Why?'

'It's just for show, pal,' he said, 'I've never been too good at makin' cuppas.'

'Well, you seem to be enjoying yours,' I said. 'What've you got?'

I leaned over to look, and he moved his mug away from me. 'Don't worry about it, pal,' he said, grinning.

'Is that – is that beer?' I asked, after seeing the orange liquid ringed thinly with foam. 'You poured beer in your mug?'

He laughed again. 'Well, I was hardly gonna sit here and drink a shite cuppa, was I?'

'Unlike me?'

'Well, it's just respectful, isn't it?' he said. 'You gotta make someone a cuppa when they're going through something, don't you?' I laughed, shaking my head. He moved his mug over to me. 'Want the rest of this, then?'

'No, you're all right.'

'You sure?' he said, gulping it down. ''Cause when it's gone it's gone, mate.'

The front door opened then, and I froze. We heard Chelsea's voice calling out: 'Hello?' I looked up at Muddy, who looked back at me like: it's all right, calm down, and then he shouted that we were in my bedroom. She knocked on the door and asked jokingly if we were decent. We turned to look at her in her grey tracksuit and with her gym bag hanging on her shoulder; she said she was just stopping by to get a few things to take back to Finlay's.

'Well, you two look cosy,' she said, and then when she saw my bandage shouted: 'What the hell happened?'

'I knocked him over playing rugby, didn't I?' Muddy said.

Chelsea came in and sat on the other side of me, glaring at Muddy as he spoke. 'I know, I know,' he continued. 'I'm a chunky bloke and I need to be careful with him 'cause he's only small. You don't have to say anything. We've been up the hospital; we've had the whole song and dance; he's got his little bandage, and he's fine.' He tapped my back, smiling. 'Next time, I'm gonna be proper gentle with him.'

'Playing rugby?' Chelsea said confusedly, holding my arm, examining the bandage. 'Fuck off, Mud.'

'Nah,' Muddy said, 'he just wanted to come down and see a bunch of big sweaty blokes chuckin' a ball about, didn't you, Harles? Proper horndog, him. And after, I thought why not show him what's what about my favourite sport.'

'Finn didn't say anything about a game.'

'Well, we're not joined at the bleedin' hip, are we, Chels?' he said. 'And the lads don't really like him down there, so we had us a great old time.'

Chelsea looked at me. It was difficult to tell if she believed him at all. 'You're listening to Oasis, looking at birds and playing rugby now,' she said. 'Mud, when's it gonna stop? Next you'll have him in flannel and talking like a bloody Manc.'

Muddy nudged me, winking. 'See, I told you, pal,' he said. 'Influential man, me.'

Before Chelsea left, she told me that she had spoken to her dad about potentially getting me a job as a PR intern at a record label called Amnesiac Records. She said she knew it wasn't exactly what I was after, since it wasn't particularly journalistic, but at least it would get my foot in the door. 'It's like talking to clients, scheduling events, doing press clippings and, like, administrative stuff,' she said. I thanked her as we hugged at the front door. She then told me not to let Muddy pressure me into doing things I didn't want to.

Something strange happened when I decided to have a bath that evening. I stood there, looking at the tub filling with water, overcome with this terrible feeling. After a few minutes Muddy came up behind me, wanting to brush his teeth. He asked if I was okay, and I just looked at him blankly. Like at the pool, he seemed to understand something about my expression. He looked at the tub, then back at me and shrugged. He took off his shirt and boxers and we looked at each other in silence. I attempted to remove my clothes single-handedly, but he laughed and asked me to lift my arms in the air so he could help.

He turned off the taps and we sat opposite each other in the lukewarm water. We had our arms crossed over our knees and our feet on top of each other's. 'Well,' he said, 'this is a bit different, isn't it?'

'Yeah,' I said, 'when you said I wouldn't be on my own, I didn't think you meant it quite so literally.'

'Still, quite nice, this,' he said. 'Don't think I've ever been in the tub with someone else before.'

'Especially not another guy, right?'

He giggled. 'Bet you've been in the tub with loads of blokes.'

'What are you trying to say?'

'I dunno,' he said, 'I was just trying to get a laugh out of you.' I gave him that laugh. 'So, what happens now then?'

I was quiet for a moment. 'I'm not sure.'

'We should probably start thinking about getting you in to see one of them speccy birds with the glasses and the clipboards.'

'And just so we're on the same page,' I said, 'you're talking about a therapist, aren't you?'

'That's the one.'

I was silent again. 'I don't know,' I said. 'I've spent a day on suicide watch. I don't know if I'm ready to think about a therapist.'

'But you will start thinking about it, won't you?' he said. 'Seriously, pal.'

I looked down at my bandage again. I thought about the time I'd tried to be my own best friend and how I'd now betrayed myself. If being a good person began with being one to yourself, then perhaps I hadn't deserved, and still didn't deserve, to be loved or wanted. Eventually the water became clouded with soap, our sponges dripping over on the side after we'd used them. Muddy was singing 'Tubthumping' by Chumbawamba now and drumming the sides of the bath. He then stood up, grunting loudly. He had a thick uncircumcised dick that dangled beneath some dark pubic hair, which he quickly covered up. 'Apologies, pal!' he said. 'No one needs a face full of my todger this late in the evening.'

I laughed. 'When would the appropriate times be then?'

'I dunno, mate,' he said, putting his hands on his hips and looking down at it curiously. 'I'll have to write you up a schedule or something.'

I watched him towel himself dry by the mirror, chuckling at how chaotically he did it, dragging the towel between his thighs, and then rolling it up into a rope and whipping his back to catch the droplets.

We went in his room after that. I sat on his bed watching him change into a fresh pair of boxers and a vest. I asked him how he was finding being a lifeguard again, and he said he loved it, that he just sat on his arse for eight hours a day, telling people to walk instead of run.

He was looking in the mirror now, raking his fingers through his hair, contemplating getting a haircut, his first in months.

'I thought I might get a trim,' he said. 'Go for something a bit more handsome. What do you think?'

I considered this. 'I like your hair the way it is.'

'You don't think I'm too scruffy or whatever?'

'Well, yeah, I do,' I said. 'But I love that about you.'

He smiled at his reflection. 'You love me, do you?'

'I said I love that *about* you.'

He laughed. 'Nah,' he said. 'You said what you said, pal.' He turned around and leaned on his dresser. I smiled at him, coyly. 'I've told you before, mate, haven't I? It's not good to keep this stuff bottled up, Harles. It's not healthy.'

On his dresser, beside his little dumb-bells, was a bottle of black nail polish. I asked where he'd got it from, and he laughed and said he was at Finlay's a few days ago. He'd been bored and Chelsea had left it out, so he'd started painting a few of his nails with it just for something to do.

'I thought it looked all right on me, to be fair,' he said, 'proper sexy, pal. But Finn huffed and puffed about it and said I looked like a poof or whatever. Made me feel dead shit about it, so Chels got the remover out and helped me take the stuff off. Still, she let me keep the bottle.'

He looked sad about this. He sat down next to me, but I got up and picked up the polish. 'You let Finlay talk you out of wearing this?' I said, slowly rotating the bottle. 'Muddy, come on ...'

'Well, you know,' he said. 'He shouldn't have called me a poof, that weren't on. But he has a good point, doesn't he? I don't wanna make myself look silly. People already think I'm a bit of a nutter 'cause of how much I go on about my birds.'

'I've heard a lot of things come out of Finlay's mouth,' I said, 'and a good point has never been one of them.' I couldn't help but feel somewhat disappointed in Muddy for yielding to Finlay like this. 'Didn't you say once that you were your own man? And you did whatever you did because it made you happy?' He laughed nervously and didn't say anything. I looked at the bottle and smiled at him. 'Give me your hand.'

'You what?'

'Give me your hand.' I repeated. I sat next to him again and he looked at me like: Really? And I gestured at his hand with my eyes.

'So, you're just gonna paint my nails, are you?'

'Sure,' I said. 'Why not?'

He held up his hand, inspected his fingers and said: 'All right, pal, go on then.'

He laid his hand in my lap and as I imperfectly coated his nails with polish, I asked him why he let Finlay dictate certain aspects of his life. He didn't agree that this was what was happening, and then I brought up Finlay's forceful matchmaking with Noria, how dismissive he'd been over Muddy's ideas for their birthday party and what he'd just done with the nail polish. He called Finlay a 'lad's lad' and said that Finlay saw the world in a very specific way and for years they'd navigated this particular world together, and that it was too late to change what Finlay considered normal.

'Well,' I said, moving onto another finger, 'it wasn't that long ago you were ranting about metrosexuals. And now look at you.'

'Finn's not so bad, really,' he said. 'He's not an affectionate bloke, but he does have his moments. I had a bit of a health scare some years back. And I'd been a bit weird about seein' someone about it. I mean, Finners don't like it when I bring this up to people, because he stopped being all hard and showed me a bit of heart, so don't tell him I told you. But he's a good guy, him. And, you know, I know a good guy when I see me one. He has a mouth on him, but he shows up when it counts. He cares about people. He just has his own way of showing it, I s'pose.'

There was a brief silence. 'Are you okay?'

'Oh,' he said, dismissively. I must've had a concerned look on my face, because he then said: 'Don't look at me like that, pal. I'm all right. I'm tough as nails, me.'

Seventeen

Muddy had been determined for me to believe, just as much as he did, that Finlay was a good guy. So, on Muddy's instruction, Finlay picked me up after work one afternoon the following week. I'd never been in his car before. It was a blue hatchback and the inside had an overpowering smell of deodorant. Before my shift, he'd sent a text asking me to wait for him by the bus stop outside the cinema.

When I got in his car, I asked him where he was taking me. 'Just get your seat belt on, will you, Midge,' he said. He was in his gym clothes: a dark grey vest that accentuated his pectoral muscles and shorts, and a hoodie was folded in his lap. As I did up the seat belt, I repeated the question. 'You're mine for a couple of hours,' he replied, 'so I thought we'd get something to eat, before I take you home.'

I lifted an eyebrow. 'What do you mean: I'm yours?'

'Mud's idea, mate,' he said. 'He said you were having a shit go of it lately, so here we are. He also said to ask how your day had gone when I picked you up. So, you got three minutes.'

'Well, I wouldn't want to bore you, Finlay.'

'You got two now.'

The day had actually been somewhat triumphant. Since Muddy had left Regal, I'd been moved from deliveries to working in the kitchen, defrosting tiny tubs of guacamole and heating up cheese for the nachos and hot dogs. I was alone for most of the day, but I hadn't felt particularly lonely. But I had been feeling numb since my stay at the hospital.

That morning I'd had a conversation with Emily, whose hair had gone from bleached blonde to black. She'd only come in to give me some silver pots to wash up, but she'd stayed and spoken to me. She'd asked what had happened to my arm, and if I missed Muddy because she certainly did. I'd told her about the fictitious rugby accident and confirmed that I indeed missed Muddy too; she'd patted my shoulder and called me a 'poor little thing'. A few days prior to this, I'd seen she was reading another book in the breakroom, so I'd finally asked her about it. She'd replied at length and I'd smiled as she did so. When she was done, I'd even said: 'You know, I used to think you hated me.'

She laughed. 'Well, I thought you hated *me*.'

I was both surprised and not that she'd said this. I was aware my anxiety made me standoffish, but I knew I'd never hated her. Still, I'd said: 'Really?'

'Oh yeah,' she'd said, 'you always ignored me. And every time you looked at me, you looked like you wanted to kill me.'

'I did?'

'Yeah,' she'd said. 'But then you had your little wobble that time when Ed had to take you into his office. And then

I thought that something must've been going on.' I'd smiled sheepishly. 'And as well, I saw the way you were with Mud. And I don't think he'd hang out with anyone that actually wanted to kill someone.'

I'd seen my reflection in the silver fridge behind her. Muddy was right. I did have a nice smile.

Finlay drove us to a 1950s-American-diner-style restaurant in Lakeside. He put on a greatest hits album by Def Leppard and sang along to 'Pour Some Sugar on Me', tensing his hands on the wheel, throwing his head back and forth. He got annoyed that I wasn't as enthusiastic about his music as I was about Muddy's, and called me brainwashed.

In the restaurant – all checkered floors and shiny red booths – I told him that if this place was really authentic, I wouldn't be allowed in here. As he put his hoodie on, he told me to stop being a smart-arse.

'No,' I said. 'I'm serious.'

'Yeah, I know that obviously,' he said. 'It's just a bit depressing, innit. And if I've brought you somewhere that's making you depressed, Mud's gonna have my head, isn't he? Now, stop trying to get me in trouble and get a smile on that fuckin' face.' I bared my teeth at him. 'That's more like it, mate.'

When we sat in the booth, he talked about how happy he was about Muddy's new job. He said one of the benefits was a free gym membership. He knew Muddy would never use it, so it was essentially his now. After we ordered, he talked, or rather ranted, about Muddy's interest in painting his nails.

'He's done 'em up all black now,' he said, 'you seen 'em? He just did the two last week and now he's gone full pelt.'

'I have,' I said. 'I helped him do it.'

He narrowed his eyes at me. 'You what?' he said. 'What are you turning my mate into?'

I pinched the bridge of my nose. 'You give me headaches, you do,' I said. 'Why is it such a big deal?'

'Well, of course, you'd fuckin' ask that.'

'Finlay, you're such a hypocrite.'

'How am I?'

'You poured another guy's piss all over yourself a few weeks ago,' I said. 'How can you care so much about Muddy painting his nails?'

'Ah, but that's different, isn't it?' he said. 'I was hammered. And we lost a match.'

I looked at him for a moment. 'You shouldn't have made him take it off,' I said. 'That was out of order. And I think he respects you too much to tell you that.'

'And he respects me because I'm his best mate,' he said, 'and I always tell him what's what. And what's what is that he looks like a massive fuckin' pansy with all that shit on his hands. He's gonna be laughed off the bloody pitch, mate. All the lads already think he's a bit, you know, a bit soft.' He leaned back in the booth. 'Did you find out if he is one of your lot, like I asked?'

'I never agreed to do that.'

'Ah, you let me down,' he said. 'Anyway, the whole thing did get me thinking—'

'N'aw did it hurt?'

He laughed mockingly. 'It got me *thinking* that he might not be gay. There's other ones, isn't there? Other things you can be.'

I shrugged. 'It's all a spectrum, yes,' I said. 'If that's what you mean. Why are you so obsessed with this?'

'I'm not obsessed, mate.'

'You sure?'

'Well,' he said, 'if he is something else, I'd wanna know about it, wouldn't I? I'd have to stop setting him up with women and start finding blokes who'd wanna be with him.'

'Has he asked to be set up, though?'

'No one really asks, do they,' he said, 'you just do it.'

'That doesn't sound right,' I said. 'You forced him and Noria together and that didn't exactly work out.'

'Well, you can't win 'em all, can you?'

'Why don't you just stop?'

'I'll never stop, mate,' he said. 'Don't know why you're talking though. I could put in a good word for you.'

'And why would you do that?'

'You know sometimes you look at the bloke like you want him inside you, don't you? I saw it myself at the pub the other week and at the pool.'

'I'm not having fun anymore, Finlay,' I said. 'I would like to go home.'

'Oh, cheer up, mate,' he said. 'I'm only joking. But be honest, he gets your engine all revved up, don't he? I mean, I'll be honest with you, if I weren't the King of Pussy, I'd probably slip him a few inches myself.'

I rolled my eyes. 'He does nothing to my engine.'

'Ah, shame, that,' he said. 'I'll let him know. Tell him he's a shit mechanic.'

In truth, I supposed Muddy did do a lot to my engine. I really liked who I was when I was in his company, and how much he seemed to enjoy being in mine. I liked how he cared about me and how happy he made me; I liked how sharing the things he loved with me brought him so much joy; I liked being held by him. But I didn't feel compelled to explain any of this to Finlay. When our food arrived – hot dogs and burgers and milkshakes – I told him how nervous I got eating in front of other people. I thought he'd laugh but he said: 'That's all right, mate. Just slide whatever you can't finish my way.'

After Finlay had finished eating, he looked at me. 'I'm under strict instructions from Mud to mind my own business,' he said. 'It's why I ain't said a word about your arm. But I thought this Paul bloke was just some prick out for blood that night. So why am I feeling like there's more to the story?'

Muddy was a very easy person to trust. Life simply packaged him up that way. Finlay was different. I felt as if I had to consider how he'd react if I told him about Paul; if he'd be too honest or too dismissive or apply some misguided sarcastic humour that would do more to humiliate than to help me. I went quiet for a while and shrugged. 'Fine,' he said, 'keep your little secrets with Mud then. I mean, it's not like I saved your life or anything. Who came in that toilet all: "Oi, guv, what do you think you're doing, eh?" Who took the first blow? Not Mud.'

I laughed. 'Why does it sound like you want me to pick the better parent or something?'

''Cause the only correct answer is me, mate,' he said. 'I'm the better parent. I was proper gonna do him in for you.'

'Because you care about me so much, right?' I said. 'And not because you lost a match and had to drench yourself in piss?'

'No, but seriously, mate,' he said, leaning forward. 'If you're having a bad time, I wanna know what he knows. That's all. Regardless of who's the better fuckin' parent.'

When Finlay said he would take me home after, I didn't realize he meant his own home in Maidstone. It was an immaculate flat with blue walls and cream-coloured carpeting and meticulously selected furniture.

As we arrived, the smoke detector was going off; his corridor was filled with smoke and we could smell something burning. We heard shouting and giggling coming from his kitchen. Noria and Chelsea were in there; Noria was standing by a pan on the stove with smoke wafting from it and Chelsea was laughing hysterically beside her saying: 'Oh my god!'

'Don't just stand there, Chels,' Noria said. 'Help me!'

'Well, what do you want me to do?'

Noria was tugging at the stove knob. 'Why won't it turn off?'

I stood at the door while Finlay separated them. 'What have you plebs done?' he said as he turned off the stove, lifted the pan, and then waved his hand beneath the little white smoke detector in the middle of the ceiling. 'How the fuck have you burnt pasta?'

Noria and Chelsea looked at each other. 'Well, we sort of left it simmering, like you do,' Chelsea said.

'And then the pasta sort of absorbed all the water,' Noria followed.

'And then it just sort of started burning,' Chelsea continued.

'And then we didn't really notice until we could smell it,' Noria finished.

Finlay looked at them quietly with an irritated expression, and then pointed to the door. 'Get out, now,' he said, turning back to the stove and then muttering to himself: 'That was my favourite pan, as well.'

They left, grabbing each of my hands and laughing as if they'd just been reprimanded at school. We circled into the living room, an open-plan space that bled into the kitchen, separated by a marble island. They sat on either side of me on the sofa and stared. I kept looking back and forth between them. 'What?'

Noria tapped my bandage. 'So, you're playing rugby now?'

Chelsea tapped my shoulder. 'What she said.'

I got nervous. 'Well, I didn't play,' I said. 'Muddy was just showing me some stuff.'

'So how did *that* happen, then?' Noria asked. 'Did he just charge at you or what?'

'Yeah,' Chelsea said, 'because I don't understand how Muddy of all people could just rugby tackle you so bad that you'd hurt your wrist and end up in the bloody hospital.'

Noria leaned forward to look at Chelsea. 'Ooh – you didn't tell me about the hospital part, babes,' she said, and then looked back at me: 'You were in hospital?'

'He was in hospital,' Chelsea answered. 'Mud's lovely, but he's a bad influence. Whenever I see you and you've been with him, you're always hurt.'

I hadn't anticipated this interrogation and felt my nervousness turn into irritation. 'Well, it was an accident,' I said.

'Yeah, but—' Noria began.

From the kitchen, Finlay shouted: 'Give it a fuckin' rest, you two.' He threw a ball of cabbage at Chelsea's head and then said: 'Give Crouch and García a feed, will you?'

In front of the island were two rabbits shifting around in a big black cage. Chelsea looked back at Finlay. 'Fuck off,' she said, as she prepared to chuck the cabbage back at him.

'Do it, Chels,' Noria said, smiling mischievously. 'Aim for the dick.' Chelsea threw it and missed, hitting the cabinet behind him. 'Ah well,' Noria said. 'Maybe you can join Harles, and Mud can give you a lesson too.'

As Chelsea eventually fed the rabbits, Noria touched my hair and asked me to come around to her house whenever I was free, so she could finally take my cornrows out. 'It's looking real crusty,' she said. 'Real, real crusty, babes.'

I remembered then how strange she had been acting when Muddy drove us home from the pool, and I asked her what had been up. She made a face that seemed to suggest that I'd imagined the whole thing.

'No,' I said. 'I could've sworn you were pissed off at me, or at Muddy, or at something at least.'

She shook her head. 'Nah,' she said. 'I don't know what you're talking about.'

Because of my own lies, I didn't feel well suited to press her on this. I also thought she was brave to outrightly deny something Muddy could corroborate.

Chelsea sat back on the sofa and asked me if I'd given any more thought about the PR internship at the record label. Noria raised an eyebrow and said: 'Chels, no.' They both leaned forward to look at each other and I leaned back. 'He needs to go back to uni.'

'Well, he didn't like uni,' Chelsea said. 'What's the point in going back? At least with this he could get his foot in the door.'

'But it's PR, babes,' Noria said. 'He won't really be writing about actual music like he wants.'

'What he *wants* is something music-related,' Chelsea said. 'And that's what this is – isn't that right, Harles?'

'Yeah, it's music-*related*,' Noria said, 'but it's not what you actually wanna do, though, is it, Harley?' They both looked at me, but I didn't say anything. 'See, Chels. Your idea is so clapped it's got him speechless.'

Chelsea laughed. 'But, Nor, what I'm saying is, the doors it would get his foot—'

'The hell kinda door is he trying to get his little feet into?' she said. 'He loves writing about music. What's he gonna be booking bands and talking to clients for?'

Noria had started asking me what it was about uni that I hadn't liked, when Finlay shouted: 'Nor, heads up!' And chucked the remote for his stereo at her, asking her to press play because he was too far away from the system.

'Uh, you dickhead,' Noria said.

Finlay smirked. 'Oh, pipe down, babe,' he said. 'Do what you're told, yeah?'

Noria scowled at him and had started to throw the remote

back when she reconsidered. She got up and went through Finlay's CD collection on the shelf by his telly. Beside the CDs were pictures of his rugby team, all clumped together in a field in their kits; and then there was one of him and Muddy in football shirts, standing in front of a fence: Finlay was in sunglasses, standing behind Muddy, with his arms around him, while Muddy punched his fists jubilantly in the air.

Noria pulled out a greatest hits album by Blur and held it up. 'Finn, is this one of Mud's?'

Finlay looked back at her, shrugging. 'I dunno, probably.'

She then motioned at his stereo and its glass doors separated, unveiling the disc tray, which had a Quiet Riot album inside; she removed it and replaced it with the Blur CD.

When Muddy arrived, 'Country House' was playing. He had on a navy hoodie over his lifeguard uniform and as he pulled it off, exposing his stomach, Finlay wolf whistled at him. Muddy giggled and then stood at the living-room door; he greeted everyone and then clicked his fingers at me.

'There's my little rugby star,' he said. 'How was your day out with Finners, then? What d'ya get up to? Finn, did you ask him how his day had gone, like I asked?'

Finlay was leaning on the island now with a napkin thrown over his shoulder. 'Yeah,' Finlay said. 'I did everything you asked, mate.'

I looked up at Muddy, smiling. 'Yeah, he asked how I was and let me talk for ages. He took me out to dinner and didn't say a single shitty thing, not even a dig at my height. Absolute gentleman, your friend.'

'See, told you,' Finlay said, winking at me. 'He might even prefer me to you now, Mud.' Muddy made a face at me like: I told you he was a good guy.

'Oi, Harles,' Finlay said, gesturing me into the kitchen with his head.

Muddy took my place between Chelsea and Noria on the sofa, squeezing my shoulder as I got up. When he sat down, he put his arms around them both, and crossed his legs on the coffee table. Chelsea and Noria laid their heads on his shoulders.

'Why are you so sweaty?' Chelsea asked.

'I tried to leg it to the kebab shop before they closed up, didn't I?' he said. 'But I didn't make it.' He tilted his head back. 'Finners, get some scran on, will you?' After a moment, he realized what was playing and looked around the room saying: 'Who put this shite on, then? Finn, mate, what gives?'

'Nah, that was all Nor, mate.'

Noria took her head off Muddy's shoulder and glared at him.

Finlay decided to make spaghetti puttanesca for everyone. I stood beside him at the far end of the kitchen, slicing anchovy fillets the way he'd shown me: very finely, he'd insisted. He was chopping up onions and crushing garlic. At one point, he retrieved a bowl of capers from the fridge, selected one and inspected it closely.

'How do you feel about capers then?' he asked. They looked shrivelled and dark, so I made a face. 'Yeah, they do look a bit rank, to be fair. No capers.'

I asked him if he'd always liked cooking. And he said

that his brother, Wallace, who lived in Edinburgh with their mother and his wife, had always been into cooking since they were young, and often made Finlay help him out in the kitchen. 'I thought he could've been a chef or something,' he said.

'What is Wallace now?'

'Fuck knows,' he said bluntly. 'Bloody layabout – here, you know how to chop up parsley properly?' I shook my head. He took a step closer to me. 'Now, don't go getting the wrong idea, mate. I'm just showing you how to chop up a bit of parsley.' He paused and then said in a mocking tone of voice: 'Oh yeah, apparently you don't fancy me, do you?'

'There's no *apparently* about it.'

'Still think that's bollocks, look at me,' he said. 'Anyway ...' He asked me to wash the knife and gathered the parsley into a little hill. 'Hold the knife like this.' He showed me, with his hand over mine. 'One hand. Tip on board. Other on top. And chop, mate.'

He watched me as I finished up on my own, flashing me a smile. I slowed the pace of my chopping. 'Finlay?'

'Yeah, mate?'

'Paul,' I said. 'I knew him.'

'Yeah,' he said, laughing, starting on the tomatoes. 'I knew him too. I see him down at Shaker's quite a bit.'

'No,' I said. 'Like actually knew him. That's what Muddy didn't want you to know.'

I told him about Paul then. I went into a lot more detail than I'd intended and saw Finlay's face cringe at certain parts and his eyes widen at others. When I'd finished, I thought he'd ask me why I'd do this to myself, or why I was bringing it up now, or, worse, pretend as if I hadn't said anything. Instead, he washed his hands, drying them with the napkin on his shoulder and said: 'That's not why you didn't wanna report it, was it? You didn't like, actually love him or some-thing, did you?' I shook my head and then we were silent for a moment. 'So, is that the shit time Mud was on about then?' I nodded. 'Well, I hope you're starting to feel better about it, mate. Same goes for your wrist.'

'Thank you,' I said. 'Please don't tell anyone this.'

He nodded. 'Yeah, sure.'

At the table, I sat between Muddy and Finlay on one side, facing Chelsea and Noria. Everyone was eating except for me and Finlay; he was drinking a beer and talking across me to Muddy about some football match. When Noria had finished eating, Finlay asked her how the job search was going.

'You know what, guys, yeah?' Noria said. 'I think I'm like one more rejection away from giving up and just doing some hoe shit. Honestly, I'm so tired.'

Chelsea laughed. 'You're always threatening to do "hoe shit", hun.'

'So, what's actually wrong with where you are now though?' Finlay asked.

She told him about Jennifer. 'I swear, every day, she's on some passive-aggressive bullshit, literally about everything I do. She's constantly like: why do you always look so pissed off? And, honestly, it takes everything in me to not just be like: bitch, how about you start saying some shit that makes me happy, then we can move forward, innit. She's always on me and literally no one cares. They think I'm being dramatic when I say anything.'

'Just get a job at Regal for the time being,' Chelsea said. 'If you said yes to me right now, you'd have a new job in the morning.'

'Or you can be my little assistant on my plumbing jobs,' Finlay said. 'You know, fetch my supplies and all that stuff.'

'Or you can get some training done and get on the life-guard team with me,' Muddy said. 'It's piss easy.'

'Or you could look into pursuing hairdressing profession-ally maybe?' I said. 'Instead of jumping straight into hoeing?'

Noria looked at us all blankly for a second and then at Chelsea. 'So, babes, I'm gonna need some six-inch heels, some new weave and birth control. I don't know what sugar daddies want these days, but I think I'm willing to start with the basics.'

Muddy raised his beer at her. 'Well, I've got no bleedin' clue what you're goin' on about, Nor. But here's to the hoe shit, and I hope it serves you well, my love.'

Finlay looked across to Muddy. 'Mate, put your fuckin' beer down. She's just messing about.'

Noria laughed, and then prompted Chelsea to tell us that Eddie had finally given her the deputy manager position. Muddy held up a hand for her to slap; I smiled proudly at her; Finlay reached across the table, presumably to ruffle her hair, but Noria smacked the back of his hand with her fork.

'Okay,' Chelsea said, 'the other bit of the news is that there aren't any positions at the Dartford branch, so I'm going to be based in Central London permanently.'

'You're moving back in with your parents, then?' Muddy asked.

'Yeah,' she said. 'But don't worry, I'll talk to my dad about the rent, see if I can still keep it what it is.'

Muddy smiled at her. 'Cheers.'

'Finn, didn't you say you'd just drive her up every day?' Noria said.

'Yeah,' Finlay said, 'she said it wasn't realistic.'

'And it isn't,' Chelsea said. 'We both work weird hours. And it's like an hour drive every day, plus the congestion. It's just not worth the hassle.' She looked at Muddy now. 'I want to take as little as I can to my parents, so, Mud, since you've been getting into all my nail polish lately, you can have at them.'

'You serious, Chels?' Muddy said.

'Of course,' she said. 'Gives me an excuse to go shopping with Nor. And also, you did kind of mess up most of my brushes.'

'Sorry about that, love,' Muddy said. 'But cheers.'

'Oh, come on,' Finlay said to Muddy, 'what's with you and fuckin' nail polish?'

'What?' Muddy said.

'You look like a massive poof, mate!'

The table went silent. 'Yep,' Muddy said curtly. 'Cheers, pal.'

Chelsea and Noria scowled at Finlay. 'Ah no,' he said. 'I didn't mean it like that, guys. I just meant, like . . .' He looked at me. 'Harles, help us out, will you? Tell him, I didn't mean it like that.'

I shrugged. 'That's more paperwork for me, Finlay.'

Muddy looked at me. 'Hold on,' he said. 'What does that mean, then?'

'It's just something I do when Finlay does or says something stupid.'

'When did you start doing that then?'

Finlay laughed, even though everything was still tense. 'He thinks I'm a homophobe, when obviously I ain't, because I've—'

'Finn, enough,' Noria said, 'please, just chill out, yeah? Stop talking.'

Muddy waved dismissively. 'No, it's all right,' he said. 'I know what he meant.' He looked at Finlay. 'No hard feelings, pal.'

'Well, you'll be having a strop in a minute, won't you?' Finlay said.

'Mate, come on, don't be a bellend,' Muddy said, 'I said it's all right, didn't I? Let's move on.'

But we didn't really move on and Finlay gave a few more awkward, unfinished apologies. When Muddy was done eating, he tapped me on my back, and said: 'Let's get goin, pal.'

Finlay looked up at him. 'I thought you were both sleeping over?' he said. 'You said to make up the spare room. I got the spare sheets out and everything.'

'Yeah, change of plans, mate,' Muddy said. 'We're gonna head home now.' He asked Noria if she was coming, and she said Finlay was going to give her a ride home later. He thanked Chelsea for the polish again and left the room, and then I followed him out.

On the ride back to Dartford, I asked him if he was having a strop like Finlay said.

He laughed and nodded. 'Just a little one though, pal.'

'I don't think anyone could tell.'

'I'm a master of deception, me,' he said. 'I'll pull the wool over anyone's eyes.' He looked down at me. 'No, I'm only joking, mate. He just looked so guilty. I'll call him up tomorrow, let him know he's forgiven.'

He smiled as he said this, but I detected a glint of disappointment in his eyes. I felt as if he'd been sacrificing something for a friendship almost incapable of accommodating change, which made me feel disappointed too.

Eighteen

The first time I'd returned to my dad's after I'd left, Chelsea had accompanied me. It was the week after she'd found me outside the Regal building, when I'd spent the night wandering aimlessly through Dartford. She'd let me stay in her flat from that day onwards; she'd made up a bed for me in what was now Muddy's room. My first night there, we'd sat in the kitchen, and I'd tried to explain to her what had happened, about Scottish Darren and the hug and the horrid confrontation with my dad that had followed.

Her horror had far outpaced mine. There was a certain inevitability about the whole thing that had cushioned me. Sometimes life presented itself in ways which I simply couldn't change. Chelsea had replied to all of this with flimsy but well-meaning things like she couldn't believe he'd kicked me out, and that he should just accept me for who I am, and why couldn't I just stand up to him, get him to understand, that he would come around eventually. And I'd considered, before thinking better of it, explaining the complexities that threaded through religion and black people and homosexuality.

'Well,' she'd said then, 'you just need to go back and say, you're here, you're queer, get used to it, hun. That type of thing. It's a different world, isn't it?'

It's not so different, I'd thought. I'd told her that it just didn't work like that, and she'd asked me why. 'Well, firstly,' I'd said. 'He's never laid a hand on me, but if I told my dad that I'm here and queer, he'd choke me out for sure.'

She'd laughed. 'What?'

'Yeah,' I'd said, laughing too. 'Like a proper garrotting. I know I'm laughing but I'm not even joking. He would literally get his church lot to put some money together and send me to Africa, even though I've never been.'

'Why, hun?' she'd said. 'What's going on in Africa?'

'Well, I mean, in general, quite a few things, Chelsea,' I'd said. 'But they'd send me there to be prayed for, or to be killed, or to be stripped and left to the wolves in the wilderness or something. It's like a torture lottery, who knows what'd happen?'

'But surely he already knew?' she'd said. 'I mean, hun, it don't take a bloody brain surgeon, does it?' I'd thanked her sarcastically, telling her then about how I'd come out to him three times, but he'd forced himself not to really hear me. 'Three?' she'd said. 'How the hell did that happen?'

'Well, there's having the power of belief,' I'd said, 'and there's whatever my dad has, where he wants to believe that his view of the world is so true, so badly, that he'll willingly deceive himself. I guess when he saw Darren hug me, he couldn't do that anymore.'

'Really?' she'd said. 'But Scottish Darren hugs everyone. He's a hugger.' I'd nodded agreeably. 'Well, what kind of hug was it? Did he, like, sniff your neck or grab your arse cheeks?'

'No, I don't believe he did.'

'So, what's your dad's problem then?'

'It wasn't the way he hugged me,' I'd said. 'It was the fact that he'd hugged me at all.'

Chelsea and I had had other exchanges like this that week, with her trying to find rationality somewhere in the situation. Finally, just as I'd been leaving for work one day, I'd got a call from my dad. He'd talked at me for about ten seconds, asking that I come over that afternoon. Chelsea had been saying how it would all blow over, but I'd known my dad, and it had been difficult to happily anticipate some reconciliation on account of how miserable he'd sounded on the phone. I'd asked Chelsea to accompany me.

After we'd finished work, we got the ninety-six bus into Crayford. She'd been awash with optimism the entire journey, questioning why my dad would even call if he hadn't had every intention of mending things. 'He's your dad,' she'd kept saying, 'you don't have anything to worry about, hun.' And I'd kept explaining how removed he'd sounded on the phone, and how he hadn't even asked where I'd been staying this last week.

We'd knocked on the door several times, but he didn't answer. Chelsea had slammed her hand on it, shouting: 'Mr Sekyere! Mr Sekyere!' Then she'd asked me what time we'd agreed on, and I said he'd just said this evening. For a moment, I'd had the thought that something bad might've happened to him, that he'd fallen ill suddenly, impeding his ability to open the door. But my dad never got sick, which was either because of luck or genetics or because he woke up at 5 a.m. every morning to pray in tongues very loudly. This thought had disappeared when Chelsea pointed out that our bins were overflowing; she'd walked over and said that it smelled a little like smoke. She'd gone to lift the lid, which was already propped a little way open because of all the rubbish.

And it *had* been rubbish, to my dad at least. But it was also my stuff. I'd never owned much, but apparently it was enough to fill the wheelie bin. There'd been about five or six books that'd been charred, wedged in amongst broken discs and jewel cases and ripped-up album booklets and bits of clothing. There were also photos, or rather, what had once been photos, all blackened and crisped up, except the corner of one, which still had a visible part, as if the fire had been sentient and felt some kind of sympathy. There was a portion that featured a slice of grass, and my bare one year-old leg, as well as my dad's leg. I'd closed my eyes for a moment and the whole untarnished image resurrected itself in my mind. I'd looked so happy in this picture. It had been a gorgeous summer's day in the early eighties. We'd been in our garden, and he'd been holding me, but I didn't known who'd taken the picture. In it, I was holding a tiny bottle which had a little bit of milk in it. It was a chaotic little photograph; I don't think my dad could keep me still because I'd been shaking the bottle so frantically, so elated, my gums bared, my eyes so wide and delighted. Life had loved me then, it had loved me so much. I swear, I could've kept my eyes closed for ever.

'Look,' Chelsea had said then, standing by the bay window. 'There he is.'

We looked through the curtains. He'd been sitting at the dining table with his back to the window, literally statuesque, reading a newspaper. Maybe after we'd knocked, he'd quickly moved from wherever he'd been in the house and sat there so we'd see him. We didn't stay long after that. I'd looked at her, defeated but strangely, briefly happy that we'd both considered the situation and arrived at the same place. She'd looked back at me in silence. I'd felt something shift, something instantaneous, something physical.

From that moment, the anxieties that had shaped my perception of the world seemed to magnify, somehow there hadn't been much stock in simply existing anymore. Those had still been good days, in a way. I hadn't had any suicidal thoughts at that stage, I'd only felt as if I had to try harder to be a person: a person worthy of being wanted, of being loved; a person worthy of asking for things and receiving them; a person worthy of mattering to someone, worthy of being alive. Life had been hard, sure, but back then, I'd never thought it was insurmountable.

During Chelsea's last week in Kent, we went to a different pub in Northfleet called Ye Olde Leather Bottle; it was a lovely, pale-yellow building on a quiet road, with Tudor-style architecture on top of it. Inside, it was warm and dimly lit. We sat near a pool table. She was drinking a passion-fruit mojito and I was drinking a can of Coke; Noria had come over to the flat that morning to take out my cornrows, so I was constantly gliding my fingers through my afro. Chelsea kept talking about Finlay and the strange, transitory place their relationship was in. She just wanted to have sex with him, and he'd said that he wanted the sex to lead to some kind of future. But since sex was a commonality in their wants, she'd decided to just ignore everything else he was saying.

'He says he'll wear me down eventually,' she said. 'He still keeps talking about kids and marriage. And he looks so cute when he does, so I don't want to be mean. So, right now, I'm just smiling and nodding.'

I looked at her contemplatively. 'It's amazing, isn't it?' I said. 'Finn's so hot, and he's great in bed apparently, and he wants a family, and he's obsessed with you, and he's actively trying not to be an arsehole anymore. But you're not feeling it?'

'Is that weird of me?'

'No,' I said. 'It's just interesting, I think. Life gave you something it thought might make you happy, but maybe it read you wrong.'

She laughed. 'Well, I wasn't asking life for Finn,' she said. 'I was asking it for a permanent managerial role and better pay. So, I think it knows me pretty well.'

'So maybe life is just trailing Finn with you, then?' I said. 'Giving you the option for a future with him?'

'Maybe,' she said, shrugging. 'So – what the hell is going on with you and Mud? He's been so weird lately. Like, weirder than usual. You know he asked all of us to be nice to you?

And I was like, that's a bit rich coming from you, hun, after he sent you to the bloody hospital.'

I looked down, smiling. It made me happy that she seemed to believe the story now.

I didn't think I held grudges, but every time I considered unveiling to her a piece of my misery, I thought about a time at Regal when we had both been cashiers. A projector in one of the screens had stopped working and Eddie had asked me to go in and explain the situation to the sixty or so people inside. I'd made an ostensibly flippant comment about being scared and anxious and Chelsea had asked if I didn't think that there was something a little vain about 'all that anxiety stuff'; she'd thought there was something self-serving about people who always whined that they were being watched, when that was rarely the case.

I was sure a candid conversation might've shifted her assumptions, but I'd already internalized what she'd said. Sometimes I got annoyed with her comments even when she was being so generous, like when she'd let me go months paying a laughingly small amount of the rent, and when she had seemed entirely preoccupied with the question of what might've been 'wrong' with me.

When we left Ye Olde Leather Bottle, she was none the wiser about everything that was going on with me. I felt content that I hadn't defiled her life in any way by telling her about the suicide attempt. However, on the way to the bus stop, I thought about how grateful I was that there was someone that knew everything, that for every relationship that I'd infected with my lies, there was at least one that was privy to my truth. On the bus, I was quiet, wondering how handing these pieces of my sadness to Muddy might impact him, if it had been selfish or cruel of me, considering what happened to things that became too associated with me. Could Muddy's enthusiasm to simply appreciate me as a person worthy of life, who had a right to be happy, overcome this? He reinforced everything I'd been so desperate for in lonelier years, and I knew then that I'd been right to want these things. There was a special satisfaction in knowing that the acquisition of companionship, of finding someone who cared so much about you that they'd not only share in your miseries, but their very presence could be the catalyst for moments of intense happiness, hadn't disappointed me. I'd expected that truly mattering to someone would be wonderful, and it was.

When we got off the bus, Chelsea linked her arm with mine and asked if I'd given any more thought to the internship, or if I'd sided with Noria and would just go back to uni. She laid her head on my shoulder and said, chuckling: 'But, you know, it's fine. We all just want what's best for you.'

I was thrilled that a path to work somewhere in the music industry had opened up for me. But I knew I would let myself down. I simply couldn't work in PR ... But then, I'd always thought writing was so solitary and peaceful and required nothing but myself and my thoughts: did the safety I'd often felt in writing really just reflect the fear of doing anything else outside of isolation? Perhaps this was the first hurdle I needed to overcome: following the psychiatrist's advice and honouring what I'd said to Muddy, and see someone. Maybe this was how I could live my life now: one hurdle at a time. And with every success, appreciate the gift that was still being able to breathe, aided by friends who loved me unreservedly.

'You know,' Chelsea said as we walked along Central Park. 'Despite what he did to your wrist, I actually like how close you and Muddy are these days.'

I smiled. 'Why?'

'Well, it's just really sweet,' she said, 'and also when it was just me and him in the flat, I always got the impression he was a bit of a loner.'

'Loner?'

'I mean, he'd third wheel with me and Finn. But other than that, he'd just be on his own in the woods, looking at his birds. Or with his mate Ian, who I don't even think he likes that much really. He used to go back home to Manchester a lot too. I don't know what's going on with you two, but he seems well taken with you.' I was smiling at the pavement now. 'So, do you fancy him then?'

I was quiet for a moment. 'If you're asking if I think Muddy's fit,' I said, 'then of course. I think he's beautiful.'

Chelsea laughed. 'No,' she said. 'I'm asking what I actually asked.' She looked at me. 'N'aw, look at your little face. You actually fully fancy him, don't you? You're in love!'

'I'm not in love—'

'Well, tell that to your face, hun,' she said. 'Your eyes are giving you away.'

I closed them. 'It wouldn't even matter if I was,' I said. 'I don't want to be that gay person pining after a straight guy he'll never have.'

Sometimes thinking about my friendship with Muddy

made me spiral. I'd wonder if it only existed because he'd saved me from myself not once but twice; if what I recognized as affection and love might've been merely sympathy.

'I don't know if he's gay,' Chelsea said. 'But *something's* going on there.'

'Because he didn't fuck you?'

'You bitch.'

'Honestly, he just makes me happy,' I said. 'It would still be nice if that's all it was. Just someone I was happy around.'

'So, is that you saying you fancy him then?'

I sighed and shrugged. 'Yeah, Chelsea, I guess I do.'

Nineteen

The next day, after my shift had finished, Finlay drove me to the leisure centre in Maidstone so I could meet up with Muddy. 'Crazy Chick' by Charlotte Church was playing on the radio. I told him it sounded like something Muddy would dance to, so he changed the station. But then I changed it back and asked what his problem was. As he pulled into the car park he ranted about the fact that Muddy hadn't spoken to him in three days, except to ask him to pick me up.

'You need to tell him to just get over it, mate,' he said.

'He already told you he's fine.'

'But obviously he ain't.'

'Well, what did you have to go and call him a poof for?' I said. 'You were so aggressive with it too. What's wrong with you?'

'I dunno,' he said, shrugging. 'I just said it.'

'I'd say it's like a weird little obsession with you,' I contin-ued. 'But you never really disrespect *me* like that, and you keep doing it with him. And you don't even know if he's actually gay. Why won't you let him be, Finn?'

'I don't fuckin' know, mate,' he said. 'Maybe that's why I do it. I just wanna know what's going on, because this is all a bit too fuckin' weird for me. And I don't know why we're all pretending like it's normal when it ain't. This is the same bloke who used to eat his cereal out of a measuring jug, the same jug he'd had his curry in the previous night and hadn't washed. This is the same bloke who made me pass him one of my socks under a toilet stall so he could wipe his arse. And now he's putting on fuckin' face creams and wearing nail polish and listening to songs about cocks. And you know what, actually, mate—'

I tapped his arm. 'Um, Finn . . .'

'What?'

Muddy was standing by Finlay's open window in his yellow shirt and red shorts. 'Well, actually,' Muddy said, his fingers clinging onto the glass, 'it was my own sock. You borrowed 'em from me, remember? And it wasn't my fault the bog didn't have any loo roll. You can't just go about with a swampy arsehole, can you?' He winked at me and gestured for me to get out of the car. As I did, he clicked his fingers and pointed at the dashboard. 'You know what, that's a bleedin' mint tune, that.'

Finlay looked at me and made a face. I sighed and looked at Muddy. 'Finn told me to tell you to just get over—'

'Uh, no, mate,' Finlay interrupted, 'what I actually said was—'

Muddy put his hand up. 'It don't matter what you said,' he announced. 'I said it's all right. Change the bleedin' record.'

*

Before Muddy had left for work that morning, he'd sat beside me while I phoned the GP to book an appointment. After I'd put the phone down, he'd started singing 'Ocean Drive' by Lighthouse Family, shaking me back and forth, while I'd jokingly tried to push him away from me.

In the changing room now, he sat on the bench while I changed into my trunks. I asked him if he was all right and he said, laughing: 'Christ, it's like a bleedin' disease with you lot, isn't it? I already told you, I'm all right. What's my face doing that I don't know about?'

'Nothing,' I said. 'I just wanted to make sure. I won't ask again, I swear.'

'Good lad,' he said. 'I've told you, haven't I? I'm tough as bloody nails, me. I can handle a couple of comments.' I smiled at him. 'And I mean,' he continued. 'How would that make *you* feel, you know, if I got all fucked off that he called me a poof, like there was something wrong with it. D'ya know what I mean?'

My smile grew wider. 'That is adorable.'

'Oh, piss off,' he said. 'Adorable? I'm as hard as they come, me.'

'He said with his cute black nails.'

He held them up in front of himself. 'They are pretty cute, aren't they, pal?' he said. 'C'mon, let's get going.'

Muddy had been the only lifeguard on shift again and was preparing to shut things down. I sat on the edge of the pool, kicking my legs back and forth. Muddy was walking up and down in his white trainers, looking annoyed. There was a guy in a swim cap and goggles doing laps, who ignored Muddy and dipped beneath the surface when Muddy told him to get out. Muddy put his whistle between his teeth, crouched beside the pool and blew it until the guy climbed out, not taking his eyes off him until he was far down the hall.

When Muddy had finished up his closing duties, he squatted next to me and placed a hand on my back, the other batting some hair from his face. He took off his shoes and socks and hiked his shorts up over his thighs, joining me on the edge of the pool; he draped an arm around me and pulled me closer, his fingertips gently raking my arm. 'Ah,' he said. 'What a day, eh?'

'Been busy?'

He laughed. 'Nah, I've done fuck all, pal.'

We were silent for a while. There was something about the contrast of the bright hall and the pitch-black darkness outside and the glistening, wrinkled surface of the water that made me feel so light and wonderful. Muddy started humming 'High' by Lighthouse Family and I could sense him smiling at me, could feel his breath, warm down the side of my neck. I realized then that one of the hallmarks of my affection for him was always feeling moved to talk to him, even if I had nothing to say really.

I asked him how he'd ended up in Kent, all the way down from Manchester, and he said that when he was seventeen, his granddad – who was also called Harry Barlow – had got ill, so his nan had sent him to live with an aunt in Canterbury. The aunt had been neighbours with Finlay and his mum then.

'So,' I asked him, 'have your rugby lot given you a hard

time about your nails?'

He laughed. 'I hope you haven't been worrying about me,' he said. 'They have, but you know, I suppose it would bother me a lot more if I didn't just look so bleedin' sexy.' He pulled me even closer. 'I know you said you weren't up for it, pal, but I think we should do what we told Chels we were doing. Turn that cheeky fib into something honest.'

'What?' I said. 'You hurting me in the middle of a rugby pitch?'

'Fuck me, Harles, no,' he said, chuckling, 'I meant getting out there in the fresh air, chuckin' a ball about. I could teach you a couple of things, me.'

On days when we'd had PE in secondary school, I'd always come with an excuse prepared for why I couldn't participate; eventually I'd become so synonymous with avoiding sports that none of the teachers could be bothered with me. So, for the hour, I'd sit on the field ripping grass out of the dirt, watching my classmates run up and down the field playing whatever the day's sport had been.

'I'm sorry,' I said. 'The last place I wanna be is around your rugby lot.'

'Ah, mate,' he said. 'They're not that bad, really. They're actually all right when they're not hammered.' I tightened my lips and looked at him. 'Okay, how about this then. I drive you down to the pitch one evening. And then – just you and me, no one else – we have a quick sesh of our own. And then that's more bits of the day when you aren't on your own. Would put my mind at ease, that.'

I sighed. 'But would they want me there?'

He made a face. 'What are you talking about, pal?' he said. 'It's a bleedin' field out in Dartford. We don't have any jurisdiction.'

I laughed. 'You know what I mean.'

'Harles, Harles, Harles,' he sang, 'you gotta be kinder to yourself, mate. You can go anywhere you want.' He jostled me a bit and chuckled. 'And seriously, you gotta stop kidding yourself.'

'What?'

'All this bleedin' beef around you. You love it. Well, I suppose Finn's more muscle actually and I'm more porterhouse.'

'You know, he said something recently that I thought was funny.'

'What was that then?'

'He said he'd slip you one, if he weren't, and I quote, "the King of Pussy".'

'He can get fucked,' Muddy said, laughing. 'He thinks it'll be that easy, does he? He's always been a right tight bastard.'

'I mean, he did take me out to dinner,' I said. 'So, I guess he's not so cheap anymore.'

'Yeah, you're right,' he said. 'I suppose I can squeeze a couple of meals out of him before I let him squeeze a couple of inches into me.' I groaned. 'Oh, you love it, mate,' Muddy said.

*

On the ride home, I looked across at him. His eyes were caught in strips of orange streetlights that turned their browns into little pools of honey. 'Muddy?'

'Yeah, mate?'

'What you've been doing lately,' I said, 'with making sure I'm not on my own and being so . . .' I laughed. 'Being so literal about it. Just . . . thank you.'

He put his hand around my thigh and squeezed it. 'Don't have to thank me, pal,' he said. 'Don't cost nothing to be a mate.' He looked at me a moment. 'So, how you feelin' about your appointment tomorrow then?'

I exhaled hard. 'Good, I guess.'

'You gotta give me more than that, Harles,' he said. 'Want me to give you a bit of "Ocean Drive" again?'

I laughed, shaking my head. As he started to sing, I put my hand over his mouth and told him, enthusiastically, that I was ready for the appointment. He licked my hand and I removed it. I wiped it on my trousers while he said: 'You can't stop the music, pal. You can't stop it.'

I went birding in Maidstone with Muddy the morning of my appointment with the GP. We sat beneath some trees in Mote Park; I was cross-legged, staring at the bright expanse of sloping grass and the enormous brown lake, over which a gaggle of geese slowly drifted; Muddy had his back resting on the tree, with his notebook between his legs, filming the geese for his granddad, turning the camera onto him-self to talk.

After he put the camera down, he took out a ham sand-wich that he'd crushed into his handkerchief again. I was lying on my stomach now, resting my chin on the backs of my hands; he looked down at me and smiled. He offered me the other half of his sandwich and I told him that I was too nervous to eat.

'Ah, pal,' he said with his mouth full. 'I'm proud of you, mate. Tellin' you not to be nervous probably won't be much help, so be nervous if you have to. But you've got this.'

I smiled at him. Seeking help had never registered with me as something someone could be proud of me for.

We went back to the flat to kill some time before the appointment. Finlay turned up before we left again; I opened the door, and he was standing there in a tight polo shirt, black jeans and white trainers. 'All right, Midge,' he said with his arms behind his back. 'Mudzie in?'

'Yeah,' I said, 'but we're just about to head out.'

'Where you off to?'

'Just out.'

From the living room, Muddy asked who was at the door, and eventually appeared beside me. I stepped out of the way and, joyfully, Muddy said: 'Finners! What's up, mate?' Finlay went quiet for a moment before he held up his hands. There was a long silence before Muddy erupted into laughter, saying: 'What the hell have you done to yourself?'

'I'm sorry I called you a massive poof,' Finlay said.

He'd painted, quite chaotically, his fingernails a random selection of bright colours. Muddy's laughter swelled and he bent backwards, one hand on his stomach and the other dragging across his face. 'The absolute state of you, mate,' he said. 'Ah, come here, pal!' They hugged each other. 'Ah, Finn, what've you done?'

'I don't know,' Finlay said. 'I've never put on nail polish before, have I? I didn't know what my colour was, so I thought fuck it, get 'em all on there. Chels is gonna fuckin' fume when she's sees what I've done to her stuff.'

Muddy took Finlay's hand and inspected it closely. 'Did you paint 'em with your feet or something?'

'You'd think I'd be well good at it, mate,' Finlay said. 'I painted this bloke's whole kitchen last week, and I can't even do my own fuckin' nails.' Muddy was still laughing. 'It's fine, right?' Finlay asked. 'The stuff comes off, don't it?'

Muddy was coughing with laughter now, unable to compose himself to explain that it wouldn't just come off. He patted my back. 'Harles, come on, let's get a shuffle on—'

'Where are you both in such a rush to get to?' Finlay asked.

'Just headin' out, mate,' Muddy said, 'see you in a bit. Might pop round yours this afternoon and catch a bit of the match.'

Finlay looked at us both. 'Well, I could do with a day out, myself,' he said. 'Ain't got much on. So, where we takin' our kid, then?'

'Already told you,' Muddy said, 'we're just poppin' out.'

'What – I ain't invited?'

'No, not really, mate,' he said. 'See you in a bit. Come on, Harles.'

'Are you still having a strop?' Finlay said, raising his voice. 'Thought we just patched it up? What is your problem? Painted my nails for you and everything. What are you dragging this out for?'

'Will you keep your bleedin' voice down,' Muddy said,

closing the door, 'we've got neighbours to think about, you king of the fuckin' hyenas.'

Finlay lowered his voice. 'Why won't you tell me where you're going?'

'Because it's none of your business.'

Finlay eyed me curiously. I glanced up at Muddy and told him it was all right. 'He's coming with me to the GP,' I said.

'Oh god,' Finlay said. 'What's wrong with you now?'

In the end Finlay drove us to the practice in Crayford. Much to Muddy's annoyance, Finlay kept asking about why we were going to the GP. Muddy kept telling him to mind his own business and I wondered why Finlay wanted to know so badly.

When we hit a traffic light, Finlay turned around to me and said: 'What? Does Mud speak for you now or something?'

'No—' I started to say.

'Mate, back off,' Muddy said.

The thought of telling Finlay the truth made me seize up with fear. This thing that I'd done to myself had existed in a bubble and exposing it to the open air, to the likes of Finlay and then probably to Chelsea and Noria, made me feel sick. But Finlay was determined to make Muddy and me uncomfortable until we told him, so I did; I told him everything: the blade, the tub, Muddy finding me, the hospital, being on suicide watch and now, presumably, therapy. Muddy was so quiet as I spoke. I could feel how annoyed he was that Finlay had made me tell him. I thought I was perhaps relieving Muddy of some of the burden, but I realized that keeping these secrets for me had been a point of honour for him.

The truth didn't placate Finlay at all. 'So, you've both just been keeping this to yourselves, then? What – you didn't think I could be trusted with this? Or you thought I wouldn't care about you trying to take your own life as much as Mud would?' He sighed. 'Does Chels know?'

I shook my head. 'Finn, please,' I said. 'Please don't say anything to anyone. I'm begging you.'

'Yeah, Finn,' Muddy said, 'I know you struggle with this sort of thing, mate, but for our kid's sake, keep your bleedin' mouth shut, yeah? You heard him. He's even begged you. Keep it zipped.'

'Funny how he's our kid now,' Finlay said, 'but he tries to top himself and you say fuck all to me. How could you not say anything, Mud? Especially after everything with me. How could you keep me out, you bellend?' He looked at me now. 'Obviously, I know it's your issue, right. You can do what you want. But *fuck* me, lads. You shouldn't keep that shit a secret. Not from a fuckin' mate. If you've hurt yourself, Harles, if your mind ain't right, Mud's not the only one who would wanna be there for you, make sure you're all right.' He went quiet for a moment. 'God! You pair of absolute cocks.'

In the reception, they sat on either side of me. Finlay, now calm, picked up a car magazine and flicked awkwardly through the pages, trying to hide his colourful nails; Muddy was destroying a plastic cup he'd just drunk some water out of. As the wait went on, they started playing a game where one of them would reach over me and try to slap the other on the back of the head. I kept looking at them both, scowling, whispering for them to quit it. But they only stopped for a moment, before Muddy started chucking bits of plastic in Finlay's hair and whispering: 'Goal!' and Finlay started fishing them out of his hair and throwing them back, provoking annoyed stares from the, mostly elderly, people around us.

I had every expectation of going in on my own, but when my name was called, all three of us stood up. The stout, white-haired doctor asked if I was all right with them coming in too. And then I looked up at them, with an expression that I hoped conveyed how much I didn't want them to mess about.

In the office, Finlay sat on the chair next to mine and Muddy stood behind me. The doctor, seeming to recognize me, though I didn't recognize him, asked me how my dad was.

Muddy put his hands on my shoulders and said: '*We're* his dads now, actually, pal.'

Finlay laughed and shook my knee. 'Yeah, we're separated but we thought it'd be good to come together for the kid. You know, united front and all that.'

The doctor stared at us, bewildered. I closed my eyes and pinched the bridge of my nose. 'Guys, thank you. But can you both get out, please?'

When they left, I told the doctor everything I'd told Finlay earlier. I told him about the passive suicide ideation the psychiatrist had mentioned. I told him that I was certain that I wouldn't hurt myself again, but this didn't do much to alleviate the fear that, one day, a depression would secrete itself so deeply and so resolutely inside me, that I would be beyond recovery. I also told him about the anxiety, about the panic attacks; I kept going until he suggested that I see a counsellor. He stressed how long the waiting list to see someone would be, especially if I wanted anyone local. He went through some practices, each one further and further away, deeper into Kent. We settled on a practice in Coxheath, a civil parish south of Maidstone, that could take me sometime in the oncoming weeks. He made an appointment and then said I should consider meditation.

We stopped at a petrol station on the way back to Dartford. I stood by the car with Finlay while Muddy went inside the shop to pay for the petrol. Finlay leaned against the car with his arms crossed.

I looked up at him. 'You know, I didn't think we were those kinda friends,' I said. 'I genuinely didn't think you cared that much.'

He glanced down at me. 'I don't think you have to care about someone to want 'em alive, mate,' he said. 'But I suppose I do care about you a little bit, yeah. And no, not just 'cause of Chels and Mud before you start giving it all this . . .' He made a talking mouth with his hand and crossed his arms again. I told him that I cared about him too. 'Oh, piss off,' he said, smirking. 'Well, I'd hope you did care about me a bit, mate. Especially when I'm runnin' about knockin' people out for you and everything.' He went really quiet and then sighed. 'You know,' he said eventually. 'I'm not an idiot . . .'

'I'll have to stop spreading that around then.'

'No, I'm being serious,' he said. He looked into the shop window and Muddy was at the counter, laying down a bouquet of crisps and chocolate bars and bottled drinks. 'I'm sorry I had a pop at you earlier, mate. It's just ... I think you're lucky to have had Mud with you while you've been going through this. If there's one thing that bloke knows how to do it's to be there for a mate. We've been through a lot, me and him.' I asked him if he was referring to the fact that they'd both dated Chelsea and he laughed, shaking his head and continuing: 'He's a fuckin' lad, mate, and I'd probably kill for him if it came down to it. A couple years back, I, um, I hit a bit of a rough patch myself, and I mean, you'll know, that's how it starts, innit? You feel a bit sad, a bit down; it goes away, comes back, lasts a bit longer; goes away, comes back, lasts even longer than before; and suddenly you feel like shit every day, motivation's down the drain, you're sitting there scared for no fuckin' reason, feelin' like the world's biggest sack of useless shite. And, you know, you don't always get someone that'll give you the time of day about it, sometimes you really do have to go at it alone; sometimes you'll have people that'll just keep askin' you *why* when you tell them how you're feelin', and you can't even really tell 'em why, cause sometimes there ain't any fuckin' why, is there?

'It got so bad; I was on the sauce, twenty-four seven, mate. And I was doin' some pretty heavy shit: shit I'd probably never touch again. None of the boys cared, really. *"Oh, there he goes, bein' a miserable git again, just get another pint down him."* And one night, I wanted to show everyone I was all right, you know, still up for a laugh, so we went clubbing and I just did everything, mate. I was passed out, blind drunk by the end of it, on my arse in some alleyway after, and, of course, I knew the boys would think it was absolutely hilarious, but Mud didn't. I woke up at his aunt's, and he was just like: *"What the fuck's been goin' on with you?"* And when I told him, he said if I was gonna be a mopey bastard then I had to be a mopey bastard around him; he wouldn't let me be on my own after that, he kept checkin' on me, kept dragging me along with him to look at his bloody birds; once he even tried to teach me how to get a robin to eat out of the palm of my hand, when I went with him to visit his folks. And yeah, it *was* annoying and very fuckin' boring. But, you know, don't wanna sound like a soppy git, but it's what you want, innit? You just wanna know someone gives a toss about you. And he gives a toss about people.'

I looked at him fixedly. 'I feel like I should hug you now,' I said. 'Should I?'

He rolled his eyes. 'Yeah, go on then,' he said. 'But make it quick, yeah?' I stood closer to him and leaned my head against his side, and he hooked an arm around me; as he did so, he brought his head closer to mine and said, almost whispered: 'I know you got a bit of a thing for Mudzie, which is still pretty fuckin' unbelievable, 'cause I always thought I was the better looking one out of the two of us. But, to each their own. Anyway, I don't know if he is actually one of your lot, but I've seen the way you look at the bloke, and if your eyes went any gooier, I could have them on the side with a bit of ice cream. And don't even try to deny it.'

I took a step back; he still had his arm around me. 'Are you being my wingman now?'

'I suppose I am, yeah.'

I was a silent for a moment. 'Finlay, please don't tell him any of that,' I said. 'I'm serious. I don't wanna make things weird. Things are fine the way they are.'

He laughed. 'Look at you,' he said, 'runnin' about like a little leprechaun, telling people secrets and shit. But you must think he's a total idiot if you think he don't already know. He actually thinks the world of you, mate. And I've—'

'What's going on here, then?' Muddy said, returning from the shop, holding two blue bags. 'Where've *my* hugs been then, Finn?' He started walking towards us with his arms open. 'You owe me bleedin' loads, mate.'

Finlay tore himself away from me. 'You put a hand on me, Mud, and I'll gut you.'

Twenty

A few weeks later, on the morning of my first counselling session, Chelsea sent me several angry messages and nudges on MSN Messenger.

I'd been up all night writing a review on my blog to try and tame the anxiety for the session. It was a review for *The Back Room* by Editors, a new album Muddy had brought into his collection and had recommended I listen to, but Chelsea's tab at the bottom of my screen kept flashing orange so I stopped to acknowledge her fury.

Chelsea says:
Harleyyy! I'm fucking fuming!!! I came back to Finns and he'd ruined my entire nail polish collection!

Harley says:
All of them? Really?

Chelsea says:

ALL OF THEM!!! The bastard took the same brush and dipped it in every bottle. Why the ACTUAL FUCK would he do that? Is he having a tantrum because I said about letting Mud keep some? If that's the case, then the prick should've had it out with HIM, and not come after my collection. They were brand new, Harley!

Chelsea says:

HE DESTROYED THE BRISTLES!!!

Harley says:

HAHA Chelsea calm down. I'm sorry he messed up your stuff, but he didn't do it maliciously. Give him a break!

Chelsea says:

What? How do you know? Are you REALLY sticking up for him?

Harley says:

He painted his nails a few weeks ago to apologize to Muddy for calling him a poof. It was actually pretty adorable.

She didn't respond for a few minutes.

Chelsea says:

Well, I'm still angry.

I sent a wink of an angry stick figure smashing a guitar, and then she sent one back of a woman with a head shaped like a banana laughing.

Chelsea says:
K, I'm angry. But I'm sad I missed it. He didn't even say anything about it.

Chelsea says:
So, when he gets back do I get pissed at him for it, or do I just be like – babe, how've you done up your nails and you didn't even show me?

Harley says:
Definitely, the latter. He doesn't deserve your anger. Beneath all that muscle and 'LOOK AT ME – AREN'T I SUCH A LAD!?!', he's a sweetheart, really.

Chelsea says:
H, are you in love with my bf?

Harley says:
Just a lil bit.

Chelsea says:
Back off.

Harley says:
Make me.

A few minutes later, she linked an article from the *Guardian*, documenting the further attacks in London, in Warren Street, in Oval, in Shepherd's Bush.

Chelsea says:
See H: 'TUBE UNION CALLS FOR MORE STAFF AFTER ATTACKS.' I told you. You said I was fearmongering, but I fucking told you.

Harley says:
Congrats?

Chelsea says:
I'm just saying. They're getting more staff in. Now why would they do that if they didn't think shit was gonna go off again, hun! I told you! It's not over!

Harley says:
It's just preventative measures, isn't it? Not necessarily because it's gonna happen again. You NEED to calm down about this, seriously!

Chelsea says:
NEVER!!! Aaaanyway. How've you been? You jumped Mud's bones yet?

Aside from the nervousness, I felt so good about this new step that I'd taken with the counselling that I felt compelled, and even excited, to tell her about it. But then I ran this hypothetical scenario in my head, curating different responses from her, and kept curating until I made her say something that made me miserable, and so talked myself out of it. If I didn't tell her, then she would remain unburdened by anything that had happened to me recently, and I wouldn't have to risk any of the goodness I felt leaving.

As I started to tell her that I was fine, and that, no, I hadn't jumped Muddy's bones, I realized both Muddy and Finlay were stood at my door.

'Hurry up, Midge,' Finlay said, with his arms folded.

'Stop callin' him Midge,' Muddy said. 'Let's just give him a couple of years. His height is bound to kick in.' He winked at me and gave me a thumbs up.

I rolled my eyes and then followed them out of the flat, leaving the message to Chelsea unsent.

Something brilliant had happened when Noria and I had become friends. Prior to her my only association with other black people had been through infrequent trips to church; associations with other black men had been even rarer. With Noria, it felt as if a certain piece of my blackness had clicked into place. Often, I'd felt so culturally adrift, and then she'd emerged in my life and suddenly I had cultural touchstones to tether my blackness to. She did wonderful things for me; every time I was in her company it was as if these new facets of my personality were developing. But there were other sections of my blackness that felt like a wasteland. And it was in this wasteland that I realized I would never stop feeling this way. I saw my father in every black man I encountered. I felt so inferior to them. Masculinity was worn differently on black men. And whilst I'd never considered myself to be particularly unmasculine, by comparison to what I would project onto every black man I saw, masculinity – the definition I'd curated through what my father represented – was simply an area in which I couldn't exist.

When Muddy and Finlay dropped me off at the counsellor's office in Coxheath, I was expecting the counsellor to be like the person Muddy had described in the bathtub that time: a woman in glasses with a notepad and pen. But, to my surprise, a very tall black guy in a shirt and jeans, with a neatly trimmed beard and a low-cut skin fade greeted me at the door. *In Coxheath, of all places*, I thought. I was overcome by this strange submissive feeling and my heart sank. I'd coloured him with judgements before he'd even let me in the small, dusky room. In that moment I felt embarrassed by my entire existence; I couldn't even look him in the eyes. It was difficult not to imagine, just as I'd started to believe that I could overcome my plights, that this was someone the universe had deliberately imbedded in my life, to usher me towards an uncomfortable conclusion about the day that my dad had essentially tried to exorcize me. I'd had every intention of being candid, forthcoming. How could I do that now?

'It's nice to meet you, Harley,' he said, once we were settled inside. 'My name is Matthew.' His voice was cheery. 'I can see you're already a bit tense there. I just want to assure you that this is a completely safe space and if at any point you feel uncomfortable, just let me know, yeah?' I put my hands in my lap. He smiled warmly at me, which should've prompted me to smile back, but my lips only grew tighter and I became so vigilant of my posture and expressions. He asked if I was okay and I swallowed, nervously replying that I was. From a clipboard on his lap he recited back to me everything I'd told the doctor, and said he understood I'd been feeling badly about myself. He asked me to tell him how long I'd been feeling this way. I told him things had been this way for quite a while.

'Have you sought counselling before?'

'Counselling wasn't really something that was encouraged or even talked about when I was growing up,' I said.

'Yeah,' he said. 'I get that in certain cultures, this isn't really the way of things. Some people turn to things like—'

'Prayer,' I said, quickly, unsure why I didn't just let him finish his thought.

'Exactly,' he said, laughing. 'Like prayer. And how do you feel about prayer? Is that something you've turned to, when you've been feeling bad about yourself?'

'Not really,' I said. 'That's more my dad's thing. I don't have anything against it myself. Well, I mean, the act of believing in God, I don't have an issue with. I just, I don't know, I wish there was room in that field for me to be myself without having to compromise anything.'

'And why do you think there isn't any room for you?'

I cocked my head to the side. This was one of the things I'd immediately decided to veto disclosing when I saw him. But, for whatever reason, I still said: 'Because I'm gay.' I almost pressed my eyes shut after I said it.

'Are you okay?' he asked, chuckling a little. 'Harley, it's

okay, truly. You can relax. Just breathe.' He fanned out his
fingers by his mouth and drew them into a pinch, exhaling.
'It's okay,' he said then. 'So, you're gay. And how does your
dad feel about you getting counselling for feeling bad about
yourself? Is it something you've spoken about?'

'He doesn't know,' I said, 'we're kind of estranged these
days. We sort of parted ways.' He said he was very sorry
to hear that. 'Well, it was mutual,' I said, as he stared at me,
widening his eyes thoughtfully. 'No, it wasn't,' I admitted.
'He kicked me out essentially. He wanted to pray away the
gay, and obviously, I didn't want that, so I left.'

'And have you had any sort of interaction with him
since then?'

A stillness settled in the room; I could hear my own
heart beating. 'Yeah,' I said. 'I dropped out of uni recently
because everything was getting worse, and when I came
back, I thought there might have been a chance we could
patch things up. I mean, he called me up and everything. He
sounded pretty excited about it; we had a few good conversations then actually.'

'Oh,' he said, scribbling away. 'I'd like to come back to that,
if that's okay, about uni. But how did that go, with your dad?
Tell me about it?'

A nervous laugh leaped out of my mouth and I placed
my hand over it as if I'd just burped. I looked everywhere
but at his face. 'Yeah,' I said, 'yeah, no, it didn't go as well as
I'd hoped.'

'What did you end up discussing?'

'There wasn't a discussion as such,' I said, and then there

was more silence, some sighing. 'He just made me believe that he really wanted to see me, and I really did believe it was going to be a reconciliation, that in the years I'd been away something had changed. But . . .' I swallowed, looking down at my hands, entangling them with each other. 'But he just had a few people waiting at the house, a few pastors, to pray for me. There was like, I don't know, ten or so of them, hiding out in our dining room with the door closed.'

'Woah,' he said, shifting forward a little. 'And I'm going to assume that this wasn't brought up at all on the phone call you had prior. This ambush.'

I repeated the word to myself. *Ambush.* I suppose I'd been too upset at the time that I hadn't even bothered to apply a term to it. It was just this ugly smudge of a thing that had happened. 'No, it wasn't,' I said.

'Has this sort of deception been common in your relationship?'

'How do you mean?'

'Well, from the sounds of it, he led you to believe one thing, when there was really something else at play. Has he displayed this kind of deceptive behaviour before?'

As I began to tell him about the wheelie bin filled with my torched possessions, I started to cry. I felt it in my stomach and then in my throat, in my nose, and then Matthew liquified into watercolours. I made my hand into a fist and bit down on my knuckles as the tears fell. He passed me a packet of tissues and told me he was very sorry that had happened. I could only respond with stuttering apologies for all the tears. He asked me then if this was when I'd started feeling badly about myself.

'I suppose so,' I said, dragging my hand across my face. 'I mean, I've always, just generally, had a not-so-great estimation of myself, and this kind of solidified that, I guess.'

'Not-so-great estimation,' he repeated. 'What do you mean when you say that?'

Inside my pit of anxiety the previous night, I'd thought about my mother. I'd wondered what she would've thought of me. I'd even considered if everything I'd undergone was retribution for what I'd done to her. Perhaps she would have blamed me as much as my dad had. She'd always been such a quiet figure in my head – dormant and harmless – it hadn't occurred to me that in carrying the burden of her death, she, from wherever she resided now, could seek vengeance as well, to halt any potential triumphs, to revoke life's most basic tools for survival. She hadn't known me; she hadn't had any reason to want wonderful things for me.

'I just feel like …' I started. 'Sometimes, I genuinely feel like I don't matter, like there's something insignificant about my life. I always feel like I'm being punished for something and no matter how much I apologize for whatever that is, the feeling never goes away.' I paused for a second. 'I never even used to think I was worthy of having a funeral or a gravestone if I really did die. The image of me rotting away in the woods or in a bin bag somewhere didn't scare me as it should.'

He looked down at his notes then and began writing some more. I started to breathe a lot harder, and my eyes were stinging. 'So, I do want to discuss your suicide ideations and your attempt on your own life,' he said. 'I believe it was the first time you'd tried something like this. Is that right?'

I nodded. 'It was the first time,' I told him; I was suddenly conscious of him thinking I was more suicidal than I actually was so I decided not to tell him about the woods. 'But in the past, when things got really bad, it would usually just go away eventually. And even if it didn't for a while, I could still carry on with my life. I could still go to work, do my shifts; and these days, I even hang out with my friends without even thinking about it really. For the most part, the dark thoughts are just that: thoughts.'

'For the most part?'

I paused again. 'Yeah,' I said. 'For the most part.'

'Would you say you still have moments where you lean towards being more active with these thoughts?'

'I mean,' I said. 'I can't imagine I'd do it again. If that's what you mean? Like I said, the thoughts usually go away. But that time, it just got a little darker than usual.'

He wrote some more. 'Well, it does sound to me like you could have high-functioning depression.' When I asked him what that meant he said: 'Well, it's exactly like you said. You've been feeling bad about yourself, sad, feeling this intense sense of worthlessness. But from the sounds of it, usually, you can still be productive. That's high-functioning depression.' I looked at him thoughtfully. He asked me if I minded that he was taking notes, explaining the logic behind it and so forth, and I nodded, not realizing I had a say in the matter. 'These thoughts,' he continued, 'would you be able to talk about what kinds of things, or feelings, bring you to that place? Or the kinds of triggers? Or is it just a state you find yourself falling into, seemingly without reason?'

I paused for a moment. 'I guess sometimes it feels like there isn't a reason. At uni, these feelings of, like, I don't know, uselessness, loneliness, kind of crept up on me. But when I ended up in hospital, it was because I was seeing someone I shouldn't have been seeing and it hadn't ended well. There was an altercation, and some things were said, and I guess they took me over the edge.'

'Do you have any friends you can confide in when things are this bad?' he asked. 'Or a boyfriend or anything like that?'

A smile slowly stretched across my face; it seemed to make him smile too. 'I do, yeah,' I said, 'have, um, friends.'

'They make you feel better about yourself, don't they, Harley?' he said. 'I can see it in your face. It's great you have people there for you when things get bad. Were any of them there when you were admitted into hospital?' I nodded at him, trying to reel in my smile. 'I guess,' he said, still smiling, 'going back to what you said earlier, it's nice to know that you matter to someone, and to really feel that.' He wrote some more things down, making plans for what we'd discuss at the next session, and then he explained the medication I could be put on. I'd been hoping to avoid it, though I didn't know whether it was appropriate to tell him that now. I didn't want him to think that I wouldn't be taking these sessions seriously.

Outside, with all the windows rolled up, Muddy and Finlay were singing in Muddy's car, jabbing their hands in the air as 'Lola's Theme' by the Shapeshifters blared. They were eating burgers and occasionally utilizing them as microphones, pointing to the bonnet as if there was an imaginary audience.

When Finlay saw me, he nudged Muddy who unlocked the door. The car was hot and smelt like McDonald's and sweat. Muddy turned down the music and asked me how it had gone.

'Well,' I said, as I slid into the back seat. 'I'm still alive.'

Finlay, with sauce around his mouth, looked at Muddy. 'The kid's still alive,' he said, excitably. 'That's a touch, isn't it?'

'I know,' Muddy said, 'we're killin' it, mate.'

Finlay wiped away a fake tear. 'He'll be off to nursery soon, won't he?' he said. 'They grow up so bloody fast.'

Muddy put his hand on Finlay's thigh. 'Ah, c'mon, mate, let's have another.'

'No chance,' Finlay said, 'the one kid's enough. Look at him. Bet he fuckin' loves being an only child – all this attention he gets from us.' He looked back at me, reaching to pinch my cheek as I shielded my face. 'Don't you, champ?'

It was Finlay's idea to drive down to Folkestone for the rest of the morning. Before we left, we stood outside Muddy's car with the doors open to air it out. Finlay mapped out how the day was going to go. When Finlay stopped talking, Muddy saluted him and said: 'Sir, yes, sir!'

By the time we got to Folkestone, the weather had turned cold. We went into a small chippy and Finlay and I waited outside while Muddy ordered. For himself, Muddy bought two portions of chips and a chip butty; and for Finlay and me, he got two battered sausages. On the walk to the sea-front afterwards, Finlay, who was wearing a grey tracksuit, laughed at Muddy for being in shorts.

We sat on a bench by a long strip of grass. Before us was a burgundy fence with lots of little poppies tied to the railings, and beneath was a glorious view of the beach and the rolling bright-blue waves. Muddy shared his chips with me but put his arm up to block Finlay every time he reached across him to take one. Eventually Finlay slapped him on the back of his head, but instead of retaliating, Muddy said he'd give Finlay some chips if he could catch them in his mouth. Finlay immediately stood up in front of us, rubbing his hands, legs hip-width apart, crouched over a little and said: 'C'mon then, lads, let's have it!'

Muddy laughed and threw a few, steadying each one in the air as if they were darts; I threw some too, though less expertly; Finlay swerved his head from side to side, jumping all about, catching nearly every one. When Muddy ran out of chips, Finlay punched the air with both fists triumphantly, just like Muddy had done in that photo of them in Finlay's living room.

We sat there for the next several hours as it got colder and the sky darkened, watching people moving in clumps over the sand down on the beach.

Finlay leaned back and put an arm across the back of the bench, looking at Muddy. 'Mate, you seen the date?' he asked.

'Can't say I've been paying much attention,' Muddy said. 'What is it?'

Finlay shoved him and then Muddy shoved him back, asking what that was for. 'August twenty-fifth, you pillock.'

'Oh shit, yeah,' Muddy said. He hooked a thumb in the waistband of his shorts and boxers and pulled it back, looking down and giving a thumbs up. 'Cheer's for behavin'.'

I leaned back to catch Finlay's eye. 'What's so special about the twenty-fifth? And why is Muddy talking to his penis?'

'He's actually talking to his balls, mate,' Finlay said.

Muddy looked at me. 'Remember I was tellin' you about my little scare.' I pointed to his crotch, arching an eyebrow and he nodded. 'A couple of years back, I found this big fuck-off lump on one of my nuts, didn't I? Kept gettin' bigger and bigger, until I said to Finn one afternoon after training: "What's it mean when the lump on your bollock starts gettin' bigger?" And he was like: "There ain't supposed to be any lumps, mate. And if there are, they ain't supposed to be gettin' fuckin' bigger."'

'And obviously,' Finlay said. 'Because I'm a top bloke, I had a bit of a gander.'

Muddy laughed. 'Bollocks,' he said. 'I had to beg him just to take a look for me. We got back to his place, and he made me sit on the toilet and then he got a pair of rubber gloves out. He was gonna have a little root around my pair, but he didn't have to in the end—'

'It was *ma-hoosive.*'

'Thought I was gonna die, mate,' Muddy said. 'Thought I had that testicular cancer. I called my grandparents, told my aunt, thought it was all over. Like I told you, Harles, I felt a bit weird about going in the hospital – and what was it you said, Finn?'

'Well, mate, I just was like: you can't go about with a lump the size of a bloody grapefruit on your nutsack, can you? Stop getting all worked up about what people are gonna say and—'

'No, that's not it,' Muddy said. 'You said if it got any bigger, we could use it as a bleedin' rugby ball.'

'Well, I was just trying to lift the mood a bit, wasn't I?' Finlay said. 'Stop you moping about. I still came in with you to do the ultrasound, didn't I?'

Muddy grinned at him. 'You held my hand, didn't you?'

'Oh, leave it out, mate.'

Muddy looked at me. 'I told you, he don't like it when I talk about this bit, but tough. Finn held my hand, he did. Said he was gonna be with me every step of the way.' He went to pinch Finlay's cheeks, who slapped him away, grumbling.

'So, what happened?' I asked. 'Was it testicular cancer?'

'No,' Muddy said. 'Just a bit of fluid, pal.' I looked at him, confused. 'Yeah, all that panic for a bit of fluid in my balls.'

'I nearly felt him up, and held his hand in front of everyone,' Finlay said, 'just for a bit of fuckin' fluid build-up in his ball-sack membrane or something.'

'Well,' I said to Finlay, 'what's wrong with holding his hand?'

Muddy turned to face him too. 'Yeah,' he said, 'and what's wrong with feeling up my balls? Thought we were mates, Finn? If you'd ask me to feel your balls, I'd be *right* in there.'

'Yeah, course you would, mate,' Finlay said. 'But like you'd ever get the fuckin' privilege.'

On the way back to the car, Muddy said the anniversary wasn't an anniversary just for himself, but also for all of his friends, including Finlay. He hated how embarrassed he'd been about telling them, how terrified he'd been that, even after the all-clear, the fear had burrowed itself so deep that it'd mutated into something that not only concerned himself but his friends as well. So even though they'd laughed, even though they'd taken the piss, and called him a queer and a fairy and a bender and a faggot because of his sudden interest in their testicles, he'd still urged them – on the twenty-fifth, just a few hours after he'd left the hospital with Finlay – to take more care with themselves: to inspect their balls more, to get checked out if anything was amiss, to know that he would be there for any one of them, a gesture that extended beyond a scare of this nature, and towards everything. He was tired of there being something shameful or unsettling about the blunt expression of friendship, of the simple desire to be there for someone needing to be mocked before it could be respected, of the fact that caring about a friend and wanting the best for them didn't hold the same value as money, when it was just as essential, if not more so.

Twenty-one

The following week, I came home from work to find Muddy on his phone, pacing around the kitchen in a grey hoodie. He was clutching at the back of his head looking deeply distressed. I sat at the kitchen table, picking at the Italian pasta bake Finlay had made us the previous day with the fork we'd left in the bowl.

I waved at Muddy, and he held his hand up like: One second.

'All right, yeah, yeah,' he was saying, 'I'll be up. No, no, Nan, I'll be up.' When he got off the phone, he joined me at the table.

'What's wrong?' I asked.

He stared at his hands before he told me that his granddad had been taken into hospital again, explaining that he'd been diagnosed with early onset dementia a few years ago, and now he was having more bad days than good. He ran a hand through his hair. 'He managed to get out of the house about an hour ago,' he said, 'and someone found him collapsed out on Clarendon Park.'

'Oh god,' I said. 'Is he all right?'

'My nan sounded a bit all over the place on the phone,' he said, 'but from what I understand, he might've done his leg in.'

'What are you gonna do?' I asked. 'Are you gonna drive up?'

'I am, yeah,' he said. 'I think I might go now actually. I'm just gonna bum off work for a couple of days. I couldn't give a fuck, to be honest.'

'I can come with you if you want?'

'You sure, pal?' he said. 'You not worried about Eddie?'

'If you're not worried about work,' I said, 'then I'm not either. If it comes down to it, I guess we can be unemployed together.'

He laughed. 'What about your sessions?'

'I need to be back by Friday,' I said. 'But if you still need to stay, I can get the train or a coach or something.'

'Don't be daft,' he said. 'We'll be back by Friday.'

As I headed out of the kitchen to get dressed and pack an overnight bag, Muddy said: 'Thanks, pal. I don't think I could bear the drive on my own.'

In the car, Muddy was so worried that he chose not to play anything. We drove in silence, and he kept looking over at me, smiling in his usual, warm way and then looking back ahead to the road, his hands so tight on the wheel that faint flourishes of pinkish red appeared in the space between his thumb and forefinger. At the petrol station, he asked if I wanted anything for the four-hour drive. I said I was all right, but he bought some crisps and chocolate bars and drinks anyway, in case I changed my mind. His hands shook as he handed over the money to the cashier. By the time we drove into Manchester, I'd long been asleep. As he lined up the car in the car park at Salford Royal Hospital, he shook me gently, whispering: 'Wake up, sleepy.' I rubbed my eyes and smacked my lips, rolling my tongue across the roof of my mouth, feeling like a terrible passenger. I asked him if we were there and he said: 'Well, I bleedin' hope so, mate. I've parked up and everything.'

His nan, Mabel, was a petite woman, just a little taller than me, with short brown hair in tight curls. When we saw her in the reception area, Muddy ran up to her so fast it looked like he might take her down, but he hugged her gently. For a moment she was a frenzy of criticisms, about how long his hair had got, about his black nails and about the sweat patches stamped beneath his arms.

'It's good to see you too, Nan.'

'Look at you, you come all this way,' she said, sliding her fingers down the drawstrings of his hoodie. 'You want a brew?'

'No, I'm fine, thanks,' he said. 'Is Granddad all right?'

'Oh, he's fine, your granddad,' she said. 'It was all a bit of a scare at first, if I'm honest. Seafood Sheila found him, didn't she? Put me in a right mood, that has. She was out walking that feral creature of hers: still no muzzle, the cheeky cow. She comes knockin' our door, making a big song and dance about something. She says: "Your Harry's out on Clarendon, on his arse, Mabel." And I was like: "You what, Sheila?" thinking she's trying to start something. You remember what she's like, don't you, she'll say anything for a bit of attention, her.'

'Yeah, I remember, Nan.'

'And she hasn't bleedin' changed neither,' she said. 'I'm thinking Harry's still in the house, so I call his name, 'cause the last thing I'm gonna do is take that deceitful mare at her word. So, I go upstairs and he isn't there; and then I'm like: "All right, Sheila, so it's not just the stink of fish that comes out your gob then, I'll give you that, well done." So, I get my robe on, she takes us across to the park, it's pissin' it down, and low and bleedin' behold, there he is, on his arse with his legs stretched out, looking up at us going: "Well you took your bloody time, I sent Sheila to get you ages ago."'

'Well, why didn't she call an ambulance or something?'

'Prehistoric cow,' she said, 'she hasn't got a mobile, you see. She hasn't even got a bleedin' landline. Not after phone company had her disconnected because the tight cow's been fuckin' off her bills, hasn't she? She come round ours once, askin' to use the phone. And I said to her: "You can make *one* call. But don't take the piss because the whole street's heard about you and your tight ways."'

Muddy laughed. 'Nan, why are you going on about Sheila, when Granddad's fighting for his life?'

'Oh, he's not fighting for his bleedin' life,' she said, 'it's only a little more than a sprained ankle. I'll have to put a bell on him or something in future, keep track of him. He did have a bit of a shit go of it today though, started talking to himself in the mirror again. But we've been here before, haven't we? And he always finds his way back to himself, don't he?'

Muddy smiled at her and put his hand on his chest, breathing slowly.

'Oh, and Sheila?' Mabel continued. 'Mud, you couldn't ask for a worse neighbour. She does my bleedin' head in, she does. Always in your business, always chattin' absolute shite, always wants something for nothing. She's a bloody menace, she is. And her little mutt fuckin' stinks and all. I swear to god, the stench ponging off of that thing, it'd burn off your fuckin' nose hairs. And she's not far off smelling like it too, since the council's only gone and turned her bleedin' taps off.'

'Right, okay, Nan,' he said, 'can I see him then?'

'Oh, not today, love,' she said, 'they've just got done faffing about with his leg. He needs his rest. You'll have to come back in the morning. I'm sorry, darling.'

He sighed. 'That's fine,' he said. 'I'm just glad to hear he's all right.'

Mabel looked at me. 'Is this the little black lad you were on about earlier?' she said. 'You've let me run my mouth for god knows how long and haven't even introduced him.'

'Well, you didn't exactly give me a chance, Nan,' Muddy said. 'Bangin' on about bleedin' Sheila. This is my flat-mate, Harley.'

'Aw,' Mabel said. 'Lovely to see you, love. Nice of you to come all this way with our Mud. Must've been a dreadfully long drive.'

'It's nice to meet you too,' I said.

'He fell asleep on me, didn't he?' Muddy said, laughing.

'Well, you do have a tendency to drone on a bit, don't you, love,' Mabel said. 'I've been tellin' you since you were a little'un, not everyone is gonna care about the birds as much as you. You and your granddad might be obsessed, but other people have lives, don't they? But speaking of the birds, your granddad's feeders—'

'Oh, no worries, Nan,' Muddy said. 'Leave it with me.'

Muddy drove us back to their house, a brown-bricked terrace wedged at the end of a cul-de-sac off Liverpool Street.

When we went in the kitchen, Mabel said: 'Now, Mud, put the kettle on and back away. I'm still recovering from the last dodgy cuppa you made me.'

'Oh, leave off, Nan,' Muddy said. 'My cuppas aren't that bad. Made one for Harles a while back. And he bleedin' loved it.' He nudged me. 'Tell her, Harles.'

'Did you, love?' Mabel asked.

'Uh, yeah,' I said. 'It was great. Not too milky at all.'

I sat at the table with Muddy, while Mabel got some mugs from the cupboards. While we waited, Muddy informed Mabel of his new job and how, yes, Finlay was still a twat, and no, he wasn't going out with Chelsea anymore, but that Finlay was with her now, and no, he wasn't looking for a new girlfriend, and maybe he'd think about cutting his hair. Mabel then told the story of the last time Muddy had brought Finlay up. They'd gone out to a nightclub and Finlay had brought a girl back, with whom he'd had sex in Muddy's childhood bedroom. Mabel had walked in on them and Finlay had politely asked her to close the door.

'You know,' she was saying, 'I still get bleedin' nightmares about that.' When she noticed Muddy's nails again, she said: 'So, what's going on there then, love? What've you done to your nails?'

Muddy held them up to her. 'What do you think?'

She took his hand and inspected it closely. 'Well, you haven't done a good job, have you, love?' she said. 'So, is this what the kids are doin' now, is it? Didn't take you for the type, mind. Makes you look like one of them lot you see hangin' about the Lidl car park these days. You seen 'em? Pale as fuck, hair so spiky it could cut you in half, conjuring up their little spells.' She sighed. 'But you will get that stuff off before you see your granddad in the morning, won't you?' Muddy gave her a wounded smile and took his hand back.

Before Mabel went to bed, she said if I felt too uncomfortable sleeping on Muddy's floor, even with all the extra blankets, then I could always sleep on the sofa.

We went up to his old bedroom. The walls were covered with posters of sports stars and rock bands, including one of Noel and Liam Gallagher in blue Manchester City FC shirts with 'brother' written on their fronts.

There was an empty CD rack, and next to it a desk cluttered with framed pictures which Muddy excitedly gestured to, saying: 'That's me and my granddad outside Maine Road.' He was eight or nine in this one – he couldn't remember – stood outside the stadium in a woolly blue hat and scarf, grinning at the camera, while his granddad had one hand on Muddy's shoulder, punching the air with the other.

'That's me and him in the woods—' he sighed. 'I dunno why he thought we were gonna see some starlings or a bloody murmuration or something. I remember he bigged it up the whole day and we saw fuck all.' Muddy was ten or eleven in this, with a pair of binoculars around his neck; his hair was short and spiky, and his face pale and freckly; his cheeks were still plump and dimpled. Even then, he had such a warm and friendly face, that I wished that I'd known him in childhood. I wondered what my life would've looked like, what my history would've been, what memories I'd have now, if I had.

'Me and my nan,' he said, pointing to another photo. In this one, he was about five. His nan was sat in a green chair, and she was steadying him on her lap; he was covered in mud, and they were looking at each other, beaming, noses pressed together. 'She was ...' Muddy began. 'Shit, what's wrong, mate? You all right?' I hadn't realized I was crying. He placed his hand on my back and brought me over to the single bed in the corner. 'My nan did always say my waffling could bring someone to tears,' he said, laughing. 'I'll keep it zipped now, pal, if you want.'

I didn't tell him why I was crying and tried to awkwardly change the subject. There was a cassette player on his window ledge that I pointed to and said: 'Wow, that's old school!'

Muddy's eyes widened and he replied: 'Oh shit, mate. My nan found that last time I came up. Have I ever told you about my old Oasis days?' I shook my head. He laughed and got the cassette player. 'Ah, honestly, pal, I was pissin' myself laughing listening to this last time. I was such a bleedin' twat.'

He took out the cassette and showed it to me. 'Muddy Gallagher Interview #2,' I read, chuckling, still wiping my face. 'What is this?'

He put the cassette back in and clicked play and a very young, very squeaky Muddy started talking in a much thicker Mancunian accent than he had now. 'Yeah, yeah, Mud Gallagher here,' he was saying. 'Yeah, I'm all about the music, me. I make music for the people, innit, d'ya know what I mean? None of this artsy fartsy shite that's been knockin' about. I'm proper mad fer it, me! It's all about the rock and rooolllll! C'mon, let's 'ave iiiiitt!!!' 'Roll with It' suddenly started playing in the background and young Muddy sang along.

I couldn't stop smiling and when the cassette ended, I said: 'I know you keep saying you're tough as nails. But I genuinely think you're the most adorable person I've ever met.'

'Well, back then, yeah,' he said. 'But I'm a proper hard nut now, aren't I? I tell people what's what and give 'em the business if they wanna start something.'

I rolled my eyes, laughing. 'How many of these are there?'

'Interviews one through ten probably,' he said. 'But I think only this one survived. Proper fuckin' star, I was.'

When we decided to turn in, Muddy was adamant that I wouldn't sleep on the sofa. So when were in our boxers and vests, we lay down on opposite ends of the bed. Muddy was looking up at the ceiling with one hand across his chest, the other behind his head.

'Apologies if my feet stink, pal,' he said.

'Yeah, same.'

'Nah, they're all right.' I remained silent. 'That bad, eh?' Muddy continued. 'You know what? This is ridiculous. We've shared a bleedin' bathtub. Get up here, you.'

'Really?'

'Yeah,' he said. 'This is silly.'

I crawled to his end of the bed. 'So, are we going back-to-back, or . . . ?'

He laughed. 'No way,' he said, stretching an arm out. 'Get in here, you.' I smiled at him and slowly lay down by his side, resting my head on his upper arm as it hung off the bed. I was so rigid, my arms planked by my side, legs entirely straight. 'Mate,' he said quietly. 'Is it all right if I put my arm around you and hold you, like this?' I started to sweat as if we were suspended above a pit of fire. I told him it was fine, and he tightened his arm around me. 'You're so stiff, pal,' he said. 'You can do the same if you like.'

'You sure?'

'Of course,' he said, 'go on, Harles, get your arm round me.' I laid my arm across his chest. I could feel his heart beating on my wrist. 'Cheers for comin' up with me.' I looked up and smiled at him; he smiled back and then gently stroked my arm with his thumb. He yawned and then said in a sleepy voice: 'So, what was with the tears earlier, then?'

I was quiet a moment. 'It's just,' I began. 'Um, that picture of you and your nan, it was really nice.'

'So nice it made you cry, did it?' he said, smiling, now rubbing my arm a little harder. I started crying again, nothing hysterical, but I did apologize. He shifted himself upwards and now my head was lying on his stomach. He hunkered over with his arms around me possessively. I decided to tell him that my mum had died giving birth to me. 'Ah,' he said. 'That's fuckin' rough, pal. I'm sorry.' The tears did eventually get hysterical, embarrassingly so. I told him that it had been my fault and even my dad had agreed. I told him it wasn't even an idea that my dad had quietly put in my head, but rather an actual conversation that we'd had, where he'd accused me of killing her and I'd simply owned up to it.

'Harles,' he said. 'Your old man actually told you that? You're havin' a laugh, aren't you?' There was a silence. 'Look at me, mate,' Muddy said, confused. I wouldn't face him. I was trying to dry my face with my vest, promising him that one day I'd stop crying on him so much. 'Come on, pal, look at me, will you?' We sat up and faced each other, crossing our legs on the bed. He put his hands on my shoulders and brought his face close to mine. 'What happened to your mum, it's not your weight to carry. And if your dad's made you feel like it is, then no offence to the bloke, but he's a prick.' He touched my face. 'Ah, pal, someone should've told you ages ago that your mum wouldn't have wanted you to carry this with you. Someone should've told you that she would've been proud of you.'

I looked down. 'I don't know if I've done anything she'd be proud of.'

'Where you off to Friday, then?'

I looked up. 'My session,' I said. 'Why?'

'And why are you going to your session?'

'Mud—'

'No, come on, Harles,' he said. 'I can't have you talkin' about yourself like you haven't accomplished anything. What I'm trying to say to you is, she would be proud of you, no doubt about it. In my humble opinion, pal, there's nothing as admirable as someone who sees that something isn't right and says they're gonna do something about it; someone who listens to a mate when they try to help 'em.' He smiled at me. 'Not only would she be proud of you, Harles, but she'd have so much respect for you 'n' all, like I do. Honestly, knowing you need a bit of help and asking for it, there's nothing worth respecting more. So yeah, she'd be proud of you. And I s'pose it's fine if you don't believe it now, I'll believe it for you. But you gotta promise you'll join me soon.'

I fell asleep lying on one side of his chest, with my hand on the other, feeling his heart beat into my palm.

Muddy's grandparents' garden was small and bordered with berry-covered shrubs. Its centrepiece was an eclectic arrangement of bird feeders, an entire feeding station, really. There wasn't any food on the bird tables or ground feeders or in any of the tubes, so in the morning, we drove to a nearby retail park off Trinity Way. At the pet store, we bought a five-kilogram bag of niger seed. When we got back to the house, Mabel had already left for the hospital and Muddy called to say we'd be over once we were done with the feeders.

In the garden, he put the bag of seeds by my feet and retrieved an empty tube with lots of little holes and metal rods piercing the centre of its body. He handed the tube to me and said: 'Let's feed some bleedin' birds then.' I unlocked the metal mechanism and lifted the lid up, while he poured in the fine black and brown seeds. Afterwards, Muddy hung it up on a wooden post. 'That's the goldfinches sorted then,' he said. In the kitchen, he looked through all the cupboards and found a heavy-duty zip bag filled with sunflower hearts. 'Ah, the robins bleedin' love 'em,' he said, handing me the bag, instructing that I empty it out onto the little trays on the ground. I reminded him then that there were five trays. 'Ah, won't be enough, will it, pal?' he said. 'Well, just do the one for now, and we'll pop out again later.'

While I was pouring the seeds out, Muddy was on his hands and knees in the kitchen, looking through the cupboards, calling out to me about how empty they were and potentially doing a big shop before we headed off home. Then I heard a loud thudding sound, followed by lots of swearing. I turned around and saw Muddy standing up, holding the back of his head with a pained expression on his reddened face. As I hurried back into the kitchen, he held his hand out to me and said: 'Lifted my head up too quick, didn't I? Squeeze my hand, would you?' I looked at him, confused. 'Just do it, mate, please,' he said. 'Really bloody hard, if you can.' I took his hand and squeezed it and he said: 'Harder, mate.' I squeezed it until his hand had turned as red as his face. And when I let go, he clasped the edge of the counter with his eyes closed, sucking in air through gritted teeth.

I assembled a makeshift icepack with some ice cubes from the freezer, and a plastic food bag I found in one of the drawers. We sat out on the grass afterwards, and I held the ice pack on the back of his head. 'Ah, feels nice, that,' he said with his eyes closed. He was steadying an empty mesh feeder between his legs, attempting to pour in a whole bag of shelled peanuts. When he was done, he quietly watched the cloudless sky with this far-off look in his eyes, idly dragging his thumb down the mesh of the feeder. Apropos of nothing, and still looking up, he said: 'You ever tried to tame a robin before?'

I looked across to him. 'I think we both know I haven't.'

He smiled. 'My granddad used to ask my nan to get him some cheese whenever she popped out for a shop,' he said. 'Every Wednesday, from the local, she'd come back with a big block of it, and he'd get a butter knife and cut some of it up into little rice-sized pieces. He has quite shaky hands, my granddad, so I'd cut it up for him sometimes. Whenever we'd see a little robin bouncin' about by the bushes, he'd quietly put the cheese down on that little round table over there, and we'd stand a few feet away and just wait. They'd be hiding up in the branches, and sometimes they'd take ages to come down. So, over a few days, I'd put a bit of cheese on the table, and I'd stand closer and closer until one day I put the cheese in my palm and the little bugger flew down and ate it right from me. My granddad would say: *"It's a gradual process, pal; it's a gradual process."* And it was; it took bleedin' ages, but it was nice.' I smiled back at him. 'I could show you sometime, if you want,' he continued. 'Tried to show Finners once, actually. But he got bored and left me to go wind up my nan.'

I laughed. 'You and Finn keep trying to teach me things like you're actually my dads,' I said. 'It's like you actually believe what you told the doctor.'

'You what?' he said. 'I think we've been great dads to you, pal. Only thing we haven't done is take the ball for a bit of a chuck about. But that aside, I think we've smashed this, to be fair. Gonna need you to fill out an evaluation or something. Let us know how we've done.'

'An evaluation?'

'I'm only joking,' he said, 'but I am always thinking about what you told me back in the hospital, about feelin' alone and stuff. So, I s'pose the evaluation would go something like: Have we made you feel less alone? Have we made you feel as if you matter to someone? Yes; Not very much; or, You did fuck all, Mud.'

He stared at me.

'Oh,' I said. 'Do you actually want answers to that, like now?'

'A couple of answers would be good, yeah.' I smiled; my heart felt so incredibly full. 'See,' he said. 'That's that smile I was going on about, mate. Makes me all bleedin' giddy, that. I s'pose that means we've done a good job then. Well, me mostly, right? Finn could probably use some anger management classes or something.'

We visited his granddad, Harry, at the hospital later that morning. He had a little smiley pinkish face and white wispy hair. I imagined this must've been one of his good days. Muddy was showing him the footage of the birds he'd taken on his camera and every time Muddy came into shot, Harry pointed at the screen and said: 'What's your old man doing on there then? That's where he's been all this time, then. Down in the south with you. Can't imagine it's too safe for you, with the bombs goin' off twenty-four seven.' Muddy smiled nervously and said: 'No, Granddad, that's me.'

'Cor, you don't half look like him, lad.'

Mabel, who was sat beside him, reached over to touch Harry's hand. 'Let's not dwell on that, love.'

Harry had been perplexed about what had happened the

previous night, though he didn't agree that he had wandered out of his house idly. He claimed he'd been deliberately going for a little walkabout and didn't appreciate the fuss over him doing something so arbitrary.

When Muddy introduced me to him, he shook my hand with both of his and said: 'You're the lad on the video, aren't you?' He looked back at Muddy but pointed at me. 'Here, look, there he is. It's so nice to meet you, lad. Our Harry never brings anyone up to see us. We were startin' to think he'd gone down south and become a Harry-No-Mates.'

We were warned that there were too many people in the room, but Mabel told the nurse to give it a rest, that we'd be out of their hair soon.

'So, what happened to that girl you were talking to last month?' Mabel said to Muddy. 'What was her name? *No-Riah* was it?'

'Noria,' he corrected. 'There's nowt going on with that anymore. We're just friends now.'

'Well, how are you gonna find anyone if you keep turnin' 'em all into bleedin' friends?'

'Oh, pipe down, Mabe,' Harry said, 'leave the boy alone. He's only young. He don't need to find anyone, does he? Let him be. Let him bloody live.' Muddy asked him what had happened to him last night. 'Well, I go on my little walka-bouts, don't I?' Harry answered. 'Have to get out the house; get some fresh air. Can't be cooped up all day watching the bloody omnibuses.'

'But that late though, Granddad?'

'It was only the bloody afternoon, Jesus,' he said. 'I used

to go hiking, me. Walked for fuckin' miles, and now I can't even leave my house without ambulances carrying me away.'

'That's because you had an accident,' Muddy said.

'Wouldn't have been any accidents if they hadn't put those big bloody rocks in the way. I'm only grateful lovely Sheila came along when she did, bless.'

'You what?' Mabel said, visibly disgusted. 'Lovely Sheila? Oh, shut up, you. Seafood probably had something to do with it 'n' all.'

'Oh, leave off, Mabe,' Harry said. 'And you gotta stop callin' the woman Seafood bleedin' Sheila to her face. It's not nice. Just because her breath could probably strip the grass of its bloody colour, don't mean she deserves the name.'

'Well then,' Muddy said, 'I guess you're gonna have to watch where you're going more, if you're gonna go out on your own.'

'Oh, pack it in, son,' Harry said, 'I do watch where I'm going. It's the bleedin' council, you see. They don't take into consideration men of a certain age, and of a certain physical ability, and what someone like me might require, when I'm going out on my little bloody walkabouts! You little'uns might be able to duck and weave round all those boulders they got cluttering up the gaff. But me? I need room. I need fuckin' space, don't I? I can't be runnin' into bleedin' rocks. I don't have the time. I only got a couple of decades left, me.'

'You shouldn't be so proud, Grandad,' Muddy said, laughing, 'or we'll have to put you in a home to keep a better eye on you.'

Harry scoffed. 'Me? In an old folks' home?' he said. 'Sat in a semi-circle with all the old girls? Clapping along to Cliff fucking Richard, with a shit-eating grin on my face, stewing in my own piss? I don't think so, pal. Not me. I'm in the prime of my life, me.'

'Oh, don't be so ridiculous,' Mabel said.

'You hear that, lads?' Harry said. 'All I'm trying to do is go for a bit of a walkabout without being thrown to the bleedin' elements, and *I'm* being ridiculous.'

Later, Harry and Muddy showed each other their updated life lists. According to Muddy, Harry hadn't updated his in years, but he still talked about it as if he'd only just recently jotted everything down. When Harry mentioned that he hadn't seen a starling recently, Muddy showed him his tattoo. And even though Harry had seen it plenty of times before, he said: 'That's class, that, son. When you get that done, then?'

Before we left, Muddy went to the toilet. Mabel and I waited for him, sat on the chairs in the corridor.

'Harley, you're not gay, are ya, love?' she asked. I looked across to her, wide-eyed, not offended, but certainly shocked at the casual and random nature of the question. 'Oh, there's nowt wrong with it, love. I just thought I'd ask, 'cause when I checked in on you boys this morning, you and our Mud looked pretty cosy. I'm always walkin' in on all sorts in that bloody room.'

'Oh,' I said, laughing. 'I am, yeah. But Muddy just didn't want me to sleep on the sofa or on the floor.'

'Yeah, but, you know,' she said, 'he's started doin' his nails up and everything now, hasn't he? I've never been one to judge. But it has had me thinking. Barbra who lives down the road has a gay son, but he's nothing like our Mud. Nothing like you, to be honest ...' She gestured at her face as if to indicate that the person she was referring to hadn't been black. 'I've often thought I had an inkling 'bout these sorts of things, but he's never struck me as the type. If he were hiding something, you'd think I would've cottoned on, you know, found filthy magazines tucked away in the back of his wardrobe, or something. Well, I suppose he did have all those men on his wall.'

'You mean the football players?'

She nodded. 'And, like I said, he did look awfully cosy with you, didn't he? Had his arm wrapped around you with that cheeky little grin on his face. You don't meet too many people that sleep with a great big smile on their face, do you?'

'You watch people sleep often, do you?' I said, surprised at my own casualness.

'You cheeky blimmin' sod,' she said, laughing.

I had no intention of speaking on Muddy's behalf, especially not on speculations about him. So, when she asked whether I thought he was like me, I told her that I honestly had no clue, and she said: 'Really, love? You can't tell?'

On our last day in Manchester, Muddy and I went to the Kersal Wetlands, an expansive grassy floodplain surrounded by the River Irwell. He'd been so excited to see some wildlife, that he'd even given me a pair of binoculars too, little ones he'd used in childhood. I'd been so used to just watching him look into the sky with these things, that I was excited to actually participate.

It was late afternoon, and the weather was very warm. He

was in a grey shirt, navy shorts and worn-out Converses. He
had on a backpack into which he'd thrown a notebook, a pen,
some sandwiches and a rugby ball. The place was quiet and
felt very isolated from the rest of the city; we slowly walked
along the trails, holding the binoculars to our eyes. He identified every bird that we came across: buzzards and jays and
sparrowhawks and woodpeckers, and a couple of swans.
He'd tap my shoulder and point in a certain direction, and
I'd quickly look. I asked him to tell me how he knew what
species a bird was just from looking and listening, so when
we saw a kingfisher hovering over the water with its shrill,
penetrating whistle, Muddy said: 'You hear that?' And then
imitated it. 'You can't miss 'em, Harles. And look at their little
blue and orange bodies.'

In the evening, we went to a nearby field where Muddy
insisted we have our first rugby session. Muddy took off
his backpack and then his shirt. He must've sensed that I
was nervous about playing any kind sport, even in private,
because he started shaking his stomach at me, saying: 'Could
feed an entire village for weeks with this: like a plate of jelly,
my belly.' I laughed like I imagined he wanted me to, but I
didn't enjoy him doing this. One of the things I liked most
about him was his inexplicable talent of putting himself up
on a pedestal without seeming conceited. And sometimes,
almost like a father hoisting their child onto their shoulders,
he helped me see myself from that height too.

The first time he threw the ball, it went over my head, and
I went after it. When he asked me to throw it back over, I just
managed to get it halfway; he ran up to the ball to pick it up,

smiling. 'Okay, pal,' he said, taking my hands. 'You want your hand here on the ball and the other here. Your left hand is just to guide it; your right is doin' all the work.' He turned me around and said: 'You wanna always pass it back. So, I'm gonna be right behind you and you're gonna take a little jog and chuck it back.'

'Okay,' I said. I started to jog and then threw it back to him. After he caught it, he said: 'Not bad, pal, not bad. But you wanna turn your body into the throw. D'ya know what I mean? Like this.' He held the ball and slowly rotated his body. 'You see that, Harles? You wanna turn with the ball. Look in the direction the ball's goin'.'

I wasn't listening to anything he was saying. I was just marvelling at the hair that started off lightly around his shoulders, then grouped darkly in the centre of his chest; the way he kept spreading his stocky thighs apart to demonstrate whatever technique he was showing me. I stared at him long after he'd finished speaking.

'What's on your mind, pal?' he asked.

I smiled at him. *You're beautiful*, I thought. 'Nothing,' I said.

He made me show him what he'd just taught me. I suppose I must have taken something he was saying in, because he was very happy and impressed with my next, more enthusiastic throw. He ran towards me and put an arm around me, quietly but eagerly chanting my name.

After that, we sat on the grass. The sky was a gorgeous dark navy and the surrounding trees were in silhouette. He threw over a second ham sandwich he'd packed for me, and when I caught it, he winked at me, smiling.

'So,' I said as I chewed. 'In theory, at what point during this would you have broken my wrist?'

He shrugged. 'I s'pose I could've rugby tackled you. Charged after you while you had the ball and just took you down straight.'

Eventually, we fell quiet, but I couldn't stop looking at him. He put his shirt back on and lay down on his back with his hands behind his head, and I sat cross-legged beside him. I was thinking about that Oasis tape he'd made when he was little.

'I really wish I'd known you when I was younger,' I said, looking into the distance. 'I can't help but wonder what my life would've looked like if I had.'

He chuckled. 'Nah, you were better off, pal,' he said. 'I was a proper nightmare, me.'

'Really?'

'Nah,' he said. 'I was a fuckin' treat, not gonna lie.'

'What was your childhood like?' I asked. 'Aside from, you know, jumping in mud puddles and pigs and Oasis.'

'Well, I had my paper round, and scouts—'

'And friends?'

'Yeah,' he said after a pause. 'Not the best ones, I s'pose. I was a bit of a shit at one point.' There was another pause and then he sat up. 'I'm not even jokin', mate.'

I laughed. 'How bad could you have been?'

He sighed. 'Well, I used to know this kid, right?' he said. 'Ben, his name was. Everyone used to call him Speccy Benny 'cause he had these massive glasses that made his eyes look fuckin' huge. And my mates at the time used to give him tons of shit for it. Like it was proper over the top stuff, considering some of 'em wore glasses themselves. But one day we see Ben at the gates before school and my mate Archie goes: "Mud, go on, get his glasses, would you?" And, you know, I do it, thinkin' it might make the lads laugh a bit and I'd give 'em back. But then my other mate Ollie comes out from nowhere and smashes 'em in front of the little lad.'

'What did you do?'

'Well, I joined in, didn't I?'

I looked at him. 'What?'

'Yeah,' he said, solemnly, 'I didn't want 'em to think I was a massive loser or whatever. I'd actually forgot all about that until recently.' He turned to look at me. 'I was tellin' you before how you're always lookin' at me like I can't put a foot wrong, but I've put plenty wrong, mate.' He went quiet for a second. 'I've been a right arsehole to people. And I can be a proper pushover sometimes.'

I smiled at him. 'If I'd told you that story, you'd probably tell me to look at the person I was now, how much I've changed, how much I cared about people, and so on.'

'Yeah, well, pal,' he said. 'People *are* tellin' me how bleedin' insightful I can be.'

Before we went back to Kent the next morning, we visited his granddad again. Muddy played 'Songbird' by Oasis on the way there, whistling, and tapping his lap rhythmically.

In the hospital, Harry was energetic and talking a lot, though I wasn't sure about what. But eventually, he took a breath and said to me, but pointing to Muddy: 'You know what we used to call him, don't you?' My eyes widened with interest. 'We used to call him: Dirty Little Mudlet.' I laughed. 'Aw, he was a chunky little thing, he was. When we lived on the old farm in Leeds, he used to roll around in the mud with all the pigs like he was one of their fuckin' own. Aw, he was a happy child. Right in his element, he was.'

'Oh, Harry,' Mabel said, 'you're always remembering that wrong.'

'How do you mean, love?'

'He never liked to roll around in the mud with the pigs.'

'Course he did,' Harry said. 'He was all about the mud and the little piggies. We still bleedin' call him it now, don't we?'

'No, he wasn't,' she said, 'he was pushed.'

'Aw! Leave off,' Harry said. 'A likely story, that is.' He looked at Muddy. 'Now, listen, son, don't go about makin' up lies. Your old dad, wherever he's fucked off to, wouldn't want you being dishonest. If you wanna roll around in the bleedin' mud with a bunch of pigs, then you go right ahead and you make yourself comfortable behind that trough, and don't let no one, not even your nan, tell you any different. It's the twenty-first century, son, and the rules are bloody changing. If you wanna run with the fuckin' swine, then you—'

'No, he really was pushed,' Mabel said.

'Course he was,' Harry said, 'look, you've got him all embarrassed now.'

'But you're the one that pushed him.'

'Me?' Harry said. 'Push over our little Mudlet? My own flesh and blood?' There was a silence. Harry squinted his eyes and shifted his lips. 'Oh yeah, that's right. I did push you, didn't I? Sorry about that, pal. Chucked you right in there with the little piggies. You were five, weren't you, you said you wanted to go to the zoo and see the pigs or something, and I said: what do you wanna go to the zoo for, we got pigs here.'

Mabel was laughing. 'No, Harry, you were just bullying him.'

'Oh, come off it, Mabe,' Harry said. 'I'm not a bully. I'm fuckin' lovely.'

Muddy laughed too. 'No, Granddad, you were a bit of a bully. Sorry to tell you.'

Harry looked at both of them. 'Was I?'

'Well,' Mabel said. 'You said the pigs had more poise and decorum than our Mud, and that he could learn a few things from 'em. Do you remember now? We were havin' dinner and Mud was shovelling everything in his gob so fast the poor fella couldn't even breathe.'

'Ah right, I did, yeah,' Harry said, looking at Muddy then. 'So, you learn anything, lad? Any of it sink in?'

'That was fifteen years ago, Granddad,' Muddy said.

'Plenty of time, pal,' Harry said. 'I wasn't bullying you. I was giving you free lessons in how to eat without choking yourself.' He looked at me. 'You see, son? You try and give 'em the best future you can, really try and prepare them, you know, and now look, you're a bully because you chucked one of them in with the bleedin' pigs. That's the last time I try and help out one of my own. I've been doing everything for him since his dad fucked off.'

Before we set off to Kent, Muddy sat in his car in silence and stared blankly out the window. This strange blankness didn't change for some time, even when a tear fell down his cheek; he simply dragged his knuckle beneath his eye. After a brief hesitation, I put my hand on his shoulder. He looked at me, his eyes glossy with tears now, and smiled, putting his hand over mine.

'Sorry,' he said. 'I made a big song and dance about being tough as nails and here I am blubbering.'

'I mean, I'm not gonna judge you for crying – to your face, anyway.'

'Gonna take the piss with Finn behind my back, are you?'

'Of course,' I said. 'You're the Liam to our Noel. We just find you unbearable.'

He laughed. 'Well as long as I'm Liam, then it's happy days.' He paused for a moment. 'I love my granddad. I just wish he wouldn't go on about my dad so much.'

'Am I all right to ask what happened with your parents?'

'Nah,' he said. 'A bit personal, that. We gotta have boundaries, you and me.'

'Okay.'

He cackled and tapped my shoulder. 'Um, well,' he said, 'my mum had troubles when I was a little'un, like in her mind and stuff, so she couldn't look after me, so she went off to live with my grandparents on her side, and I'd see her like once every few years, so it was just me and my dad. But he had big dreams, my old man. Really wanted to make something of himself. I don't know what he wanted to be, but he couldn't exactly be trapped here with me. So, one day, he packs up all my stuff, it's all very exciting, drives me up to the farm in Leeds, says I'm gonna be staying with Harry and Mabel for a bit, that he'll be back in a few days. And then he just never came back. Never saw him again.'

'I'm so sorry.'

'Oh, it's fine,' he said. 'Obviously, it's not nice when someone you love doesn't want you. But I don't let it get me down. It has taught me something over the years, actually.'

'What was that?'

'Well, it made realize that we all have things that are important to us in life and stuff, right? And, you see, my thing is that no mate of mine should ever feel as if they're not wanted. Obviously, I can't be everything to everyone, but I can be a mate to someone who needs it. Don't take much to ask someone how their day was, to smile at 'em, give 'em a hug if they're so inclined.' I grinned at him. 'You know, I might never go to uni. Might be on minimum wage all my life. But I don't know, there's just something about making a mate happy: out on the pitch with Finn, havin' a coffee with Chels, letting Nor mess about with my hair, out and about looking at birds with my mate Harley . . .' He nudged me and winked. 'That just, I don't know, for me, nothing compares to it, pal.'

Twenty-two

A few days after Muddy and I came back from Manchester, I got a text from Chelsea saying that Noria had finally got a new job. It was the beginning of Chelsea's week-long stretch of annual leave, and she was still figuring out what she wanted to do with it. The text was a drunken one with lots of exclamation marks and random characters. Shortly after this, I got one from Noria which was even more illegible, but ended with about five question marks, asking me to come over.

Noria's dad opened the door to me. 'Hi, Mr Ajayi!' I said.

'Handsome boy!' he replied in his thick Nigerian accent, pulling me in for one of those hand clasps that turn into a back-tapping hug. 'Harley, the women have taken over my house. Your white friend came over and I haven't known peace.'

'Hi, Harles,' Chelsea said, appearing from behind him, holding a small glass filled with a dark orange liquid. 'White friend, here.'

He smiled at her. 'There she is!' he said. 'You know, this one – all she does is give me headache.'

Chelsea giggled. 'Oh, you love me really, hun,' she said, 'go and have a paracetamol.'

Noria's dad was such a lovely man; he had the right sensibilities for a suburban dad. I liked how he'd take an interest in my life without seeming as if he were interrogating me. Sometimes I deeply envied Noria's privilege of being able to be so playfully annoyed by her dad's congeniality. She'd roll her eyes whenever he'd bring up sandwiches to her room and comment on whatever she was doing at the time. Once, she'd been playing the explicit version of 'Nann', by Trick Daddy and Trina, very loudly, and he'd stood at the door with a mortified expression, saying: 'Noria Ajayi. So, this is what you are listening to, eh? Pussy this, pussy that; sex this, sex that?' And I was crying with laughter beside her, and she'd buried her head in her hands, begging him to leave.

It was difficult not to compare our dads. Noria did things that would've made any other God-fearing African parent find a wooden spoon or a belt, but I suppose she was playing a different game with life than I was. Perhaps she had better things to barter with than I did. Maybe there was something about her that was comparatively more lucrative, so life simply arranged itself differently around her.

I had never moonlit as Chelsea's wingwoman at a club, promising various men that Chelsea would kiss or dance or have sex with them if they bought me a drink. I had never dragged Chelsea to my mother's Pentecostal church because there had been a rare sighting of, not just a white guy, but, a cute white guy, and then left my number and a sexually explicit message for him on the back of an envelope in the collection pot, which was subsequently read out by the pastor to the entire congregation. Yet my dad disliked me very much, and Noria's was just in awe of her.

In Noria's room, there was half a bottle of Hennessy on her desk, and she had Mary J. Blige's *No More Drama* album playing. She was in a zebra-print bomber jacket and hoop earrings, and had her hair in a long, braided ponytail, diamonds of black and orange feeding into each other. Chelsea sat on the floor by the stereo, swishing her glass around, singing along to 'Rainy Dayz', while Noria cheered her on, shouting: 'Chels, you better hit them notes!'

When Noria saw me, she screamed. 'Congratulations!' I said.

Chelsea looked at us. 'Oh my god,' she said. 'Have you told Harles what you said to your old manager?'

Noria took my hand and we sat on the bed. 'Okay, so after I got the new job, I was like: Jen, you've been trying me ever since I started. And you've been calling me out of my name. My name is *No-ri-a*. Not weave queen or the loud girl or the one with the arse.'

'She called you weave queen?'

'I told you, Harles,' she said, 'she's awful. And you were like: we *shouldn't* set the hoe on fire—'

'Because I'm scared you might be a pyromaniac and I don't want to encourage you.'

'Anyway,' she said. 'I was like fuck you, Jen. And fuck your references. You can choke!'

Chelsea crawled over to us. 'She's not even exaggerating. She literally said all of that and then some.'

'And then some?' Noria repeated, taking a huge gulp from her glass. 'What else did I say?'

Chelsea stared at her a moment. 'I don't remember, babes.'

'Shit, neither do I.' They cackled loudly at each other. When they stopped, I asked Noria where she was working now. 'L.K. Bennett,' she said.

I stared at her. 'What – isn't that next door?' I said. 'Noria!'

'Honestly, right,' she said. 'Just handing out CVs is a bunch of bullshit. So, I went into L.K. Bennett and said to the lady: here's what it is, and here's how it's gonna be, so what we saying?'

'And she just gave you a job?'

'No,' she said, 'she took my CV and said she'd get back to me whenever. But on my way out I did tell a customer that if she bought that ugly-arse dress she was eyeing up that she would've just wasted two hundred quid; her eyes might've been saying yes, but her body was screaming: absolutely not.'

'And they *still* gave you a job?'

'Actually, they tried to have me removed from the store. But I was like, just hold on a minute, *that* dress is doing absolutely nothing for you, but *this* dress, this four-hundred-quid dress, is doing everything.'

'Was it actually?'

'It actually was,' she said. 'She looked *amazing* in it. But obviously, I would have lied if I had to. You think I won't run a scam for rent money?' She kissed her teeth, and Chelsea held up her glass to her, asking if this meant that she'd stop cussing out Jennifer now. Noria giggled, hiccupping, and said: 'But you guys get what I'm saying, right? She can call me weave queen behind my back. But if I were to choke her arse out, I'd be the "bad" person.'

'Yeah,' I said. 'It's crazy how violence gets you in trouble.'

'But she was violent too!' she argued. 'Just differently, with her words.' She went silent and then sighed. 'I can't believe I was gonna look for a sugar daddy.'

'Yeah, neither can I.' Chelsea said.

'What do you mean?' Noria said. 'Are you actually saying you wouldn't have joined me? Bitch, we do everything together! If I'm selling coochie to some sixty-year-old man, then so are you.'

'Okay, *sure*,' Chelsea said, reaching for her glass, 'gimme!'

Noria held the drink away from her, her eyelids falling. 'No,' she said. 'Think of the money we would've made!'

'I applaud the entrepreneurship,' I interjected.

'Exactly,' Noria said. 'We're already two different flavours.'

'You could've even called yourselves Cookies and Cream,' I said.

'C'mon Chels,' Noria slurred. 'Cookies and Cream!'

Just then, Chelsea's phone rang. She looked at Noria and said: 'Well, here's one of *many* reasons why I won't be seducing old men with you any time soon.' She answered the phone and exclaimed: 'Finn! ... Yeah, I'm just with Nor and Harles ... No, I'm not drunk ...'

'Uh, Chels,' Noria said. 'Come here a sec.'

'One minute, Finn,' Chelsea said, putting the phone on the floor and looking up at Noria.

Noria put her hands on Chelsea's shoulders. 'Chels, babe, look at me – what am I always telling you?'

'Um ... don't be out here fuckin' for free?'

'No, not that.'

'If he doesn't act right, fuck his dad?'

'No.'

'If his dad won't go for it, try his mum?'

'Chels, no—'

'Well, hun, you say a lot of stuff, okay?' Chelsea said, 'I can't always keep everything straight.'

Noria grabbed the phone and stood up. 'Don't let him make you feel like you have to lie,' she said. 'Yes, Finn,' she said into the speaker, 'she's drunk on Henny. And what?'

We could hear Finn laughing on the line as Chelsea grabbed the phone back and left the room.

I shook my head at Noria. 'Why are you teaching her all that foolishness?'

'I only have the best intentions for that girl.'

'It's corruption.'

'It's love.'

When Chelsea returned later, she pointed at me and said: 'Finn says he's taking you running. And that he doesn't care if you're annoyed about it because it's happening anyway.'

'Damn,' Noria said, side-eyeing me. 'Rugby and jogs. What is happening to you?'

'I've been asking myself the same question for weeks,' Chelsea said. 'They're trying to turn him into them. You know what it is, Nor? We've given the boys too much control.'

'You know what,' Noria said. 'You're right, Chels. If Mud

has you doing rugby shit and Finn has you out running, then you have to do something me and Chels like.'

I groaned. 'I don't like rugby. I won't enjoy jogging at six in the morning. And I won't enjoy drinking and being in a small, sweaty room dancing to trance music. Why don't you all do something I like for once?'

'Like what?'

'I don't know,' I said. 'Like bowling or something.'

'But you don't bowl,' Chelsea said.

'Exactly,' I said. 'And neither do yous. No one will be in their element then. And you can all take the day off and not feel compelled to teach me anything.'

After Chelsea left, Noria and I watched *Girlfriends* on Trouble TV in her living room while she sobered up. She was quiet during the whole episode, and then in the advert break, she looked at me with sad eyes and said: 'Why did Muddy choose you over me?'

I looked at her, bewildered. 'What?' After a long pause, she repeated the question. 'You think he chose me over you?' I said.

'Yeah, I do.'

There was another silence. 'I *knew* you were pissed about something,' I said. 'That time at the pool—'

'I wasn't pissed,' she said. 'I was just processing.'

'Processing what?'

'How you're probably in love with him and how he probably loves you back.'

'I'm not in love with him.'

'Harley, stop it,' she said. 'If that's not love in your eyes whenever you look at him, then I swear this is the biggest scam a man has ever run.'

'Okay, fine,' I said. 'I'm not in love with him. But we've just been through some things together recently and—'

'Wasn't he the reason you were in the hospital though?' she asked, looking at my arm.

'What – no, he wasn't,' I said abruptly.

'So, he didn't really hurt you then?'

She seemed entirely sober now and I was trying not to look at her. I had no intention of telling her anything, but I knew that if I cried, I'd have no choice. She would probably want an explanation that justified these tears, and no lie I could muster up now would suffice. But tears started blotting the fabric of the sofa anyway. For a minute, she didn't do anything. Then she placed her fingers beneath my chin and lifted my head. She looked at me silently and then put a hand on the back of my head, laying me on her chest, softly gliding her thumb down my neck.

'Harles, you've been hurting, haven't you?' she said. I nodded. I felt like a child. Why did the simple fact of my existence demand so much from my friends? None of them seemed to need as much as I did. None of them seemed dependent on anyone else. None of them seemed to require as much kindness and generosity and forgiveness. Instead, they offered these things to me. As she held me, I thought about how complicated I'd found the idea of friendship when I was younger, but how simple it all seemed now: there really wasn't much to it except for sharing.

As I began to tell her the truth about why I'd dropped out of uni, about Paul, about the two suicide attempts, about the therapy sessions now and how Muddy had been trying to ensure I would never be alone, she held me tighter and tighter. I felt something shift in our relationship. I knew she could feel it too. Bearing witness to my secrets made me look and feel different. Unburdening myself was liberating, like I was destroying a barrier of my own making, exposing this sad and starved and decrepit person that had resided behind these walls. We stayed silent for a long time.

'Harley?' she said eventually, wiping my tears away with the back of her hand.

'Yeah?'

'You can have him,' she said. I laughed. 'No, he's all yours,' she insisted.

She told me how jealous she'd been that he seemed to like me over her, that even though she'd broken up with him, she had even tried to force an interest in his music.

'Is that why you put on that Blur album at Finn's that time?' I asked. She nodded. 'Wow – you were way off the mark with that one.'

'It's all the same shit, innit.'

'It really isn't.'

'Really?' she said. 'Well, still, I don't understand why he got so angry about it.'

I laughed and then looked at her. 'Please don't tell Chelsea.'

She looked confused. 'What? Why?'

'Just don't, please.'

'Harley, you're insane,' she said. 'Of course I'm gonna tell her. How have we been sat here, like a bunch of idiots, going back and forth about how you should go back to uni, or if you should do this record label thing, and the whole time you've been going through this shit. And you haven't told anyone except, who? Muddy?'

I looked away from her. 'Well, and Finlay.'

She recoiled. 'Nigga, what?'

'Oh, stop it.'

'You told Finn, though,' she said. 'Finn!' There was a strange contemplative look on her face now. 'Oh my god, you told him before *me*. I'm actually gonna cry, you know.'

'He's an angry and adamant, but surprisingly kind-hearted, person,' I said. 'You're actually quite similar in a lot of ways.'

She put her hands on my shoulders, holding her face directly in front of mine. 'Harley, babe, look at me,' she said, her voice low. 'If you *ever* say that to me again, I will not be responsible for my actions.'

She pulled me into a hug. 'Noria, you're scaring me,' I said.

'That's because I'm fucking scary, Harles,' she said. 'You should remember that the next you wanna start keeping secrets.'

We pulled ourselves apart. 'Please don't tell,' I said. 'At least, let me do it myself.'

She stared at me for a long time. 'Fine,' she said. 'But then don't tell her you told me though. Because if you think I'm protective, you don't wanna know what she'll do. She's gonna go *off* on you. Especially for telling Finn of all people before her, and I'm not tryna be caught up in that, 'cause she'll go off on me too for not telling her. And that's not the vibe I'm tryna take into autumn.'

I laughed. 'Fine.'

She stared at me once more. 'Oh, come here!' She hugged me again. 'You know Mud called me up, asking me to be nice to you.'

'You too?'

'Yeah,' she said. 'I told him if he ever said any shit like that to me again, I'd shave him bald. How is he gonna tell me to be nice to you, like I don't already love you?'

I wasn't upset anymore, but to change the mood, we switched channels to MTV Base, where we sang along to nearly every song that came on. Further into the evening, there was a nineties throwback section, and the video for that Trick Daddy and Trina song she loved came on. She screamed and said we should do our respective parts like we used to, where I was Trick Daddy, and she was Trina; she rapped Trina's verse with her eyes closed, consumed by the same elation I'd seen on the faces of the congregation of my dad's church.

I saw her dad in the doorway while she was rapping. We made eye contact for a second. He shook his head, smiling; and I smiled back, shrugging. Then he walked out of view.

Twenty-three

Before Chelsea returned to London the following week, she told Finlay about the bowling, who then told Muddy. It took practically the full week to co-ordinate our schedules with Finlay, who had been spending his days in the boiler room of a thirty-two-floor office building in Canary Wharf, replacing some rotten piping. On the last day of the job, he picked me up from the flat and we drove down to the Hollywood Bowl in Maidstone. I'd gone home after my shift for a shower and a change of clothes, and Muddy was already down in Maidstone with Noria.

When I opened the door to Finlay, he was in a black bomber jacket, a white shirt and jeans. And so was I, except my jacket was navy.

He looked me up and down and chortled, bending backwards in elation. 'Take that, Mudzie,' he said, throwing an arm around me. 'Who's fuckin' influential now?'

'Oh no.'

'Oh, yes!' he exclaimed. I went back in the flat, pretending as if I were going to change, but he pulled me back. 'Nah, Harles, this is good, this. You got any white trainers you could put on – so we've got it spot on? That'll really get his back up.'

'Absolutely not,' I said. 'Let's go.'

On the drive down, he talked about how terrible that job in Canary Wharf had been and how he could feel his back getting messed up. 'But I'm looking forward to this, though,' he said. 'Ain't been bowling in yonks.'

'You any good?'

He laughed. 'I'm fuckin' brilliant, mate. Thrashing the lot of you is what's been getting me through the day.'

After we parked up, Finlay reached into the back seat and retrieved some body spray. 'Harles,' he said, smirking. 'Do me a favour, would you?'

'What?'

He shook the can. 'Let me spray some of this on you.'

I grimaced. 'Why?'

'Just let me spray a little bit on you, c'mon.'

I sighed. 'Is this to wind up Muddy?'

He shook with laughter. 'If you walk in there dressed like me, smelling like me, he'll go fuckin' mental, mate. C'mon, Harles. I can't pass this up. It's gonna be brilliant!'

I lowered my eyelids. 'Okay, fine,' I said. 'But if he asks, you forced this on me, which is essentially what you're doing anyway.'

He started spraying. 'Whatever you wanna say, mate.'

When we walked through the arched pink doors and into the brightly lit foyer, Finlay had his arm around me, grinning.

Muddy was stood by the desk in a pale green hoodie and black shorts, taking off his Converse shoes and handing them to the cashier. Noria was by the vending machine; her hair was in a little curly afro now, cinched with leopard-print hair clips.

When Muddy turned around and saw us, he made a face and shouted: 'Oh, fuck off!' Finlay started screeching with laughter as we walked over to him. 'Nah, I'm not havin' this,' Muddy said. He looked down at me, his nostrils flaring at the volume of the body spray wafting off me. 'Christ,' he said. 'Finn put you up to this, didn't he?'

I pretended to be hysterical. 'Oh, Muddy it was awful, he said he was gonna kick me out of the car if I didn't let him spray me down.'

Muddy pointed at him and scowled. 'You bleedin' what, mate?' I smiled up at Finlay, who quietly shook his head at me. Muddy then took off his hoodie and held it out to him. 'Give me your jacket.'

'Piss off,' Finlay said. 'I'm not putting on your minging hoodie.'

Muddy smelt it and then held it out to him again. 'Nah, it's all right,' he said. 'Now – off!' Finlay grumbled as they swapped clothes.

Noria walked over holding two packets of crisps. 'Harles!' she said, and then looked at Muddy and Finlay. 'What are yous doing?'

'I'm making things right, that's what,' Muddy said as he put his arms in the sleeves of the jacket, running his hands down it, asking us how it looked; Finlay, whose head hadn't yet reappeared from putting on Muddy's hoodie, said that it looked shit. But I made an approving gesture at him, touching my thumb and forefinger together. 'Ah,' Muddy said, sighing happily. 'All is right with the world.' He put his arm around me. 'C'mon, guys, let's get bowling!'

Muddy got some chocolate mini eggs from the dispenser across the foyer, while Finlay and Noria stood by the line-up of bowling balls. I was sat on the end of the long line of green chairs, sending a text to Chelsea about how Finlay seemed to be behaving himself so far. When Muddy came back, he sat next to me and poured some mini eggs into my palm. He then slid one arm along the top of the chair, stretching out his legs, twitching his red and white bowling shoes.

'So,' he said. 'How are you on the ole lanes, then?'

I smiled at him. 'Oh, complete rookie,' I said. 'How about you?'

He threw a few mini eggs in the air and tried to catch them in his mouth, but they all rolled down his chest and into his lap. 'I'm not too bad,' he answered, before trying again. 'Not as good as Finners, mind; he's a competitive little so-and-so. Look at him.' Finlay was explaining to Noria how to hold the ball properly as she took her turn.

'Um,' Noria was saying, 'I know how to hold a bowling ball, Finn.'

'Go on, then,' he said. 'What's your technique?'

Noria rolled her eyes. 'You're such a bastard.'

'A curious bastard,' he said. 'Let's see.' Noria took a ball, jammed her fingers in the holes and furiously, but seemingly expertly, flung it down the lane, knocking down eight of ten pins. She smirked at Finlay. 'Nah,' he said. 'You're doing it all wrong.' He picked up a ball for his turn. 'So – you've got your conventional grips, right? And you got your fingertip grips and the pressure you apply—'

I looked at Muddy. 'What is wrong with him?'

He was still chucking mini eggs in the air, with his tongue on his chin, looking utterly delighted, even though he'd yet to actually catch one. 'Couldn't tell you, pal,' he said. 'Poor Nor. But she'll have to save herself, mate. When Finn thinks he's better than you at something, you'll never stop him trying to prove it.'

After Muddy had had his turn – knocking down five of ten pins; half-dancing back to us, punching in the air, singing the chorus of Oasis's 'Rock 'n' Roll Star' – I was up. I missed every pin on my first frame and then again on my second, with every ball rolling down the gutter. When my turn came around again, Muddy stood behind me, massaging my shoulders as if he were prepping me for a boxing match.

'Harles, listen to me, pal,' he said. 'You got this!'

I laughed. 'Do I?'

'Of course you do, mate,' he said, 'You just—'

Finlay shouted at us to just throw the ball and Muddy turned to him, saying: 'Zip it, you. Takes time, this.' He looked back to me. 'Okay, chuck it, pal. Show 'em what's what.' I took a step back and rolled the ball.

Muddy dropped to one knee and flung his arms out, narrowing his eyes and pursing his lips. He slowly moved his

hands as if he could control the journey of the ball by teleki-
nesis. In the end, it hit only two of the pins. I turned around
and Muddy stood back up, pulling up one of my arms, and
nodded his head at everyone like: Look at him go! and I
shielded my face in joyful embarrassment.

Throughout the evening, Finlay and Noria both consist-
ently bowled strikes in their frames, while Muddy got at
least half in his. I continued to knock down one or two pins
or miss entirely, amassing the least number of points by the
end of the night.

During our last frames, Noria and Finlay started arguing.
'Your technique's shite, mate,' he told her.

'You know,' she said. 'I'm about two seconds from chucking you down one of these lanes if you don't shut up. You're
just pissed I'm probably gonna win.'

'Bollocks.'

'Why are you talking to me like I won't fully fight you?'

Finlay laughed. 'Go on, then, girl,' he said. 'Let's go. You
can have the first shot.'

Muddy stood by them, moving his paper cup between
them, offering some of his mini eggs. When they both
ignored him, he looked back at me and shrugged. He then
threw another mini egg in the air and finally caught one in
his mouth. He smiled, winking at me. I nodded at him like:
Good for you.

Finlay and Noria were still arguing when we went for
dinner after the game. We sat at a table behind the sequence
of lanes; Muddy and I sat opposite them. There was a plate
of loaded nachos in the centre of the table, surrounded by

burgers and hot dogs and chicken tenders. Finlay was going on to Noria about who the better bowler was. 'Yeah, you got strikes,' he was saying, 'but you were just chuckin' it down, weren't you? In any old bloody way.'

'And what were you doing that was so special?' she replied. 'And how are you even talking right now when I won? Boy, shut up!'

'I'm talkin' because I've got technique, I've got—'

'Finners!' Muddy shouted, throwing a chicken tender at him. 'Pack it in, will you? You've been mithering her all night about your bleedin' technique. You're doin' our fuckin' heads in, mate. Just take the loss on the chin. I mean, look at our kid.' He pointed at me. 'He weren't very good, was he? But here he is, happy as a bleedin' clam, gettin' that burger down him.' He gently patted my stomach. 'Nor didn't just beat you, she beat all of us. So, maybe your technique's shite and my technique's shite and our kid's technique is shite. Maybe you should've been payin' attention to whatever she was doin' all night, shouldn't you? Instead of runnin' your massive gob. But guess what, mate? None of it fuckin' matters. Because I came here for a good, happy time with my mates, so shut up and get a smile on that fuckin' face before I chuck another chicken tender at you.'

There was a brief silence. 'Nah, but what I'm saying is,' Finlay said. 'I'm just trying to teach—'

'But, Finn, nobody wants to be taught by you,' Noria insisted.

'I'm just—'

Muddy picked up another chicken tender. 'Just congratulate

her and keep it movin', yeah?' he said, and then started singing the chorus to 'Keep on Movin'', by Five, nudging me to join him. And I did, very enthusiastically. We put our arms around each other, and we swayed from side to side until we were done singing.

Noria and Finlay looked at us blankly and then at each other, slowly breaking into smiles. Finlay then put his arm around her. 'Sorry,' he said. 'You did good, Nor. Congratulations.' She rolled her eyes, leaning against his side as he rubbed her arm; Muddy and I smiled at them.

After the burger, I didn't really touch the rest of the food, which made Muddy ask if I was all right. The question seemed to trigger something at the table, making everyone go quiet and look at me.

'What?' I said.

'Nothing,' Finlay and Noria replied.

Muddy looked around the table. 'Everyone stop bleedin' lookin' at him.'

'Oh god,' I mumbled ashamedly, excusing myself to go to the toilet. Finlay joked that he and Muddy should probably come with me, especially after what had happened at Shakermaker's last time. I felt as if my dignity was being clawed out from inside me. I became very aware that everybody at the table now had access to the darkness that I'd tried to keep from contaminating them. The liberation I'd felt in telling them was beginning to turn into guilt and irritation. The playful babying of me had begun to feel real. Had I really become someone who was unable to use a public toilet by themselves? I was overcome with such an intense rush of embarrassment, as if what I was beginning to understand as vulnerability was actually this innate pathetic quality rooted deep in my nature.

When we got back to Dartford, everyone wanted to go to the pub, but I wanted to go to my room. I told them this knowing that it would make them worry, especially Muddy.

He and I were stood in the hallway. 'I appreciate the concern,' I told him. 'But I think I just want some space.'

He had his hands in his pockets, looking at me. There was such worry in his eyes. I realized that I hadn't thought enough about how much Muddy finding me in the tub would've affected him, how much having to be around me every day would remind him of it. I wondered if he had nightmares about it, perhaps dreams in which he had been too late in finding me, and I'd bled out and drowned. I wondered how practical our friendship could be if my prevailing function was to serve as a symbol of his torment, a reminder of everything he had to conceal – the worry, the fear, the anxiety – for the task of being my friend. Maybe he wasn't happy as often as I'd thought he was. Maybe he needed time away from me to breathe and recharge.

He peered into the living room, where Finlay and Noria were. 'Guys,' he said. 'You can go ahead. I'm just gonna stay back here with Harles.'

'Muddy,' I said, holding his arm and pulling him back into the hallway. 'No, don't do that. Go. Have fun. You not doing what you wanna do because of me is only gonna make me feel bad.'

'What I wanna do is stay here and make sure my mate is all right.'

'Well, that's bullshit,' I said. 'Because I know what you really wanna do is go out and have a couple of drinks.' He grinned at me. 'See!' I slid my hand down his arm. 'And you look pretty sexy in Finlay's jacket, and I think more people should see it.'

He took a step back, dramatically flinging the jacket open and posing with a hand on his hip and a serious look on his face. 'I do, don't I, pal?' I smiled at him. And then he looked at me a moment longer, sighing very hard. 'Fine, Harles,' he said. 'But keep your bleedin' phone on, yeah?'

I'd wanted to spend the evening updating my blog with a new album review; I was going to go into Muddy's room and take something from his collection. But reflecting on his concern for me had made me feel warmer, less self-deprecating. I put on *The Miseducation of Lauryn Hill,* skipping all the way down to the cover of 'Can't Take My Eyes Off of You', and lay back on my bed, looking at the ceiling, smiling, thinking: *I am worthy of concern.*

Perhaps my dignity wasn't being pried from me, it was actually being returned. There was a dignity in being cared for, in being fussed over, in being loved. I let the song's jaunty composition inhabit me and I closed my eyes, nodding my head in agreement with the lyrics: Muddy often had felt too good to be true, I often couldn't take my eyes off of him, it often felt like heaven when he held me, love had indeed arrived, I was thankful he was alive and I loved him. By the end of the song my head felt so clear, and my heart so heavy with joy.

I played it again.

I spent the rest of the evening answering calls from Muddy, from Finlay, from Noria, all asking if I was fine; the latter two agreed Muddy was doing it too much. Muddy would try and keep me on the phone for ages, and I could hear Finlay in the background saying: 'Mud, put the fuckin' phone down and leave the kid alone!' He called me again during my sixth listen of 'Can't Take My Eyes Off of You', and again while I was watching telly and again while I was brushing my teeth. Before I went to bed, I made some toast, and while I was waiting for the bread to pop up, he called again. At this point, it felt like a joke, so I ignored it. Another call followed, which I ignored too.

As I was getting into bed, there was another. I picked it up without reading the screen and said: 'Muddy, seriously—'

'Mate.' It was Finlay's voice. 'Why ain't you been picking up?' he asked. 'Do you think you can get down to the hospital? Something's happened. I'd pick you up, but I'm taking Nor home.'

'What do you mean something's happened?' I asked. 'To who?'

'To Mud,' he said. 'He's in a pretty bad way, mate.'

I stayed silent.

'Harles, you there?'

At the hospital, Muddy lay in a bed with patches of dried blood around his mouth. His left eye had swollen into a shiny red lump speckled with little bits of purple. When he saw me he tried to smile, and his teeth were stained red. I couldn't tear my eyes away from him, even though I wanted to. I felt such a surge of anger the longer I looked at him, thinking about who had done this to him and why. It felt as if someone had broken into my home and defiled a precious possession of mine and had attempted to destroy something I loved.

Finlay was on his way back from taking Noria home, so it was just Muddy and me.

'Harley, is that you, pal?' he said, his voice cracking.

'Yeah,' I said, sitting in the chair beside his bed. I was speechless for a moment before, finally, I said: 'What the hell happened to you?'

'Oh, you know,' he said, grunting as he sat up. 'Just got myself in a bit of trouble, didn't I? It's no big deal. Dunno why I'm even here to be honest. All I need is a couple of painkillers in my gob.'

'What do you mean?' I said. 'You look awful. It looks like someone tried to smash your face in.'

'Oh, leave off, pal,' he said. 'Awful? I'm still bleedin' sexy even if I can't see out both eyes.'

'Muddy, what happened?'

He sighed, wearing a distant expression. 'What do you think of Spice Girls, mate?'

'What?'

'You know, Spice Girls.'

'Mud, be serious, please—'

'No, it's important to the story, this.'

I sighed. 'Fine, I don't think of them much. What does that have to do with anything?'

'Well,' he said, 'I'm partial to a bit of "Spice Up Your Life", you see, when I've had a few. I had a bit of a go on the karaoke tonight, thought I'd spice up my fuckin' life a bit, and give everyone a show. And you know me, don't wanna disappoint the people. But I suppose some of the lads down there tonight didn't care for it much.'

'Did you get beat up?' I asked. 'Because you were singing?'

'Well, no,' he said, 'they were singing 'n' all.'

'Okay? Then why?'

'It was probably the wig they had an issue with.'

'Wig?'

'Baby Spice wig,' he clarified. 'They had one just lying there behind the bar and I looked pretty crackin' in it. Had my shirt tied up and everything, belting my little heart out. But after, one of the lads followed me into the gents, didn't they? Givin' it all: "You sure you in the right place, mate? Ladies are down the hall." And you know me, I laughed and told 'em to stop mithering me and to let me have a slash in peace. And I thought that was the end of it, but no. I said goodbye to Finn and some of my new gal pals I'd made tonight, and started making my way back home. But some of the lads were waiting for me in the ginnel, weren't they?'

'Waiting for you in the what?'

He chuckled. 'Ah, apologies, pal – alleyway,' he said. 'You can take the boy out of the north and all that. But yeah, they jumped me. Didn't see it coming, obviously, and next thing I knew, I was on the floor and a couple of them were kicking away at my face. They were all: faggot this, faggot that. What kinda pillow-biting Mary wears nail polish and all this, and I was like: hurry up lads, some of us got places to be. You need help or something?' He looked at me and smiled. 'Now, obviously, Harles, when you're being pounded to a bloody pulp, you don't wanna say that out loud, might give 'em the wrong impression about how good you think your chances are in the situation. But you better believe I was thinkin' it.'

Muddy was about to say something else when I hugged him. I rested my head on his chest and caged my arms around him tightly, which made him cough. Neither of us moved for a moment. I felt him inhale, and his chest vibrate. He put a hand on the back of my head, and I told him quietly, still clinging onto him: 'I'm so glad you're all right.'

He put his other hand around my face, and slowly lifted it up to meet his. He smiled at me again. 'Course I was gonna be all right, pal,' he said. 'I've been telling you, haven't I? I'm tough as nails, me.'

Finlay returned later with two Lighthouse Family albums and a Walkman. He put them on the bedside table and stood next to me. His face was red, and his fists were clenched. 'We ever see these cunts again, Mud, you point 'em out, d'you hear me, mate?' Finlay said. Muddy laughed sleepily. 'I'm not even joking. Next time we see 'em, it's gonna be a fuckin' slaughterhouse.'

Muddy chuckled, coughing again. 'Gonna have the car runnin', are you?'

'Bin bags and ropes in the fuckin' trunk, mate,' Finlay said. 'And knuckle dusters.'

'Bloody hell,' Muddy said, 'new one, that.'

'Yeah,' Finlay said, 'gotta step it up. We're doin' all the heavy artillery, mate.'

'Guns blazing,' Muddy said.

'They won't see it comin',' Finlay added, smiling.

'Knock 'em out easy,' Muddy said, 'with your blimmin' knuckle dusters. Bing bang.'

'Drag 'em out to the middle of nowhere,' Finlay said. 'Bosh bosh.'

'And into the river they go?' I said. 'Is that right? Bosh bang?'

After Finlay had driven me home that evening, I stood in the bathroom watching my reflection; the glass was all peppered with water spots and paste marks. The flat was so silent that it amplified the sound of the tap dripping, of my breathing, of the hum of the heater. Whenever the anger I felt from having seen Muddy in that state began to wane, I'd blink and see him lying there, all beaten and bloodied, and the anger would flare up again.

I scanned my face carefully, attempting to understand once and for all what it was about me that dispensed so much misfortune; why did the people who associated with me seem to suffer? Was it something I could physically remove? Did I have to pray it away? I really *had* been a weed: strangling the healthy plants that surrounded me. It wasn't enough to simply wish happiness upon my friends, perhaps I needed to go away; maybe, at the end of the day, happiness and I were simply incompatible. I couldn't be trusted to be there for Muddy the way he had been for me. The longer I stood there, the more I felt my world being punted off its axis, the more I felt these new things that I'd welcomed into my life, to make it better, slip out of place, sliding down their shelves and shattering to pieces; I was never meant to have these things, I realized: friends and optimism and therapy, none of it. There was a reason for my loneliness and, in the end, no matter how far I veered away from this place, life always brought me back; it might've looked different, but it still felt the same.

I decided to go into the woods across from the flat that night. Without Muddy, without Chelsea, I could be sure that I wouldn't be interrupted. I walked the trails, plunging myself further and further into darkness, seeing only jagged patches of dark sky and moonlight. It was a cold evening and I kept accidently walking off the trail and tripping over clusters of branches.

I came to a stop in the clearing. It was so quiet. I took a deep breath and let the fear of being entrenched in the darkness fill me, letting it percolate in my chest, wading in the unease of something terrible happening to me. I heard this sharp, high-pitched call then. It was beautiful and wistful, and its lovely notes seemed to float down to me – gentle and comforting. I felt my way around my surroundings until I touched what I was sure was a tree; I slid down it and sat there, listening, smiling into the dark.

I didn't know what I'd wanted to find in the woods, but I knew right then that I wanted this. I wished Muddy had been there to tell me what bird was singing, but it had to be a robin, surely; I'd heard him replicate these sounds in a shrill, stuttering whistle so many times. I tried then to revise what I thought it meant to be a friend to someone. I of course appreciated the joys Muddy had brought me, even the smallest ones. But they hadn't stopped life from growing cold. Friendship didn't insulate you from affliction, but it did make the path to some sort of recovery feel worthwhile and almost pleasant, it allowed you to experience the most wonderful things, even in the dark.

Twenty-four

The next morning, before my counselling session, I visited Muddy in the hospital. He was being discharged at the end of the day. The swelling on his face had gone down, but he had also sustained an injury to his shoulder, so he had to have his left arm in a sling for the next few weeks. When he saw me, he smiled brightly; I loved seeing his dimples deepen. He looked delightfully scruffy, even more so than usual, but a little tired. 'Ah, give us a hug, pal,' he said.

'It looks like it might hurt.'

'Didn't stop you last time,' he said. 'Get over here, now!'

I smiled as I walked over to him, and he tightened his right arm around me. On the table, there was a tiny pot of face cream, Finlay's Walkman, a few more CDs and an empty white tray with remnants of gravy and vegetables. 'You know, Harles, people always chat shit about hospital food. But I've had jacket potatoes, omelettes and a bleedin' roast. I've had the time of my fuckin' life, pal.' He told me that Finlay and Noria had just been round, and Chelsea had called him several times from London, but he hadn't told his grandparents that he was here.

Eventually we fell quiet and he looked at me earnestly and said: 'Harles, can I ask you something, pal?' I nodded. 'Bit of a weird one, this. But when did you first know you were a queer?'

I laughed. 'A queer?'

'Oh, sorry, mate,' he said, 'you don't like that? I meant gay.'

'No, it's fine,' I said. 'I was ten, maybe? It wasn't anything particularly earth-shattering. I remember I liked our neighbour's son; I used to get really excited when I'd see him from my bedroom window. Sometimes he'd be in the garden with his friends having a drink or he'd be trimming hedges. One summer, when I got older, I saw him sunbathing shirtless with his girlfriend and I think I just had to admit that I was a bit different.' He went silent, seeming to consider this. 'So, why do you ask?' He looked at me but still didn't say anything. 'Is it because those guys called you a faggot?'

He nodded and then went quiet yet again. Eventually, he said: 'So that gaydar thing you lot are supposed to have ... that legit?'

'Of course,' I said. 'Signal can be a bit shit sometimes, but it's usually foolproof.'

'Go on, then.'

'What?'

'Use it on me.'

'You think you're gay?'

'I dunno,' he said. 'Not really. I'm not sure.'

'Well, I guess the first thing to establish is if you've ever been sexually attracted to another guy?'

'I don't think so,' he said. 'I mean, obviously you see a good-looking bloke, and you're like: yeah, that's a good-looking bloke. But I've never thought: yeah, that's a good-looking bloke, let me go over and slip him one real quick. D'ya know what I mean?'

'Yeah,' I said. 'So . . . if you've never been sexually attracted to men, why do you think you're gay?'

'Well, that's the thing, pal,' he said. 'If you don't wanna sleep with blokes, then you're s'posed to wanna sleep with birds, aren't you?'

'No, not really,' I said. 'But go on?'

He was silent a moment further before he said: 'Well, I don't really want that either, mate.'

'Really?' I said. 'You don't wanna sleep with women?'

'No,' he said. 'Not really. I dunno, the whole thing makes me a bit . . .' He made an odd shape with his mouth and then a strange noise. 'If I'm honest.'

'You've never wanted to?'

'No,' he said, 'can't say that I have.'

'Is that why you didn't wanna do anything with Chels and Nor?'

He nodded. 'I've been out with other girls, and I've slept with 'em. But you have to, don't you? You can't be in a relationship and not wanna do your missus. People would think you weren't normal or something.'

I chuckled. 'When have you ever cared about being normal?'

'Oh, come on, don't do that, pal,' he said. 'You make it

seem like I don't care about anything. I care. Course you wanna express yourself and stuff, be your own person. But you still wanna feel normal, don't you? Accepted, loved, the whole lot.'

'I'm sorry,' I said. 'It's just you said once that as long you were happy, what other people thought didn't matter. And also that you were tough as nails.'

He laughed. 'Well, mate,' he said. 'You can get them shit nails as well, can't you? The ones that can't do owt.'

I laughed too. 'You're not a shit nail, Mud,' I said. 'So, how was it with those girls, if you didn't like doing it? I'm assuming this includes the thing you did in the bushes at, what was it? Crackhead Kenny's house?'

He laughed again. 'Finn likes to big me up, he does,' he said. 'Nowt actually happened. Well, at least not what he thinks. Cassie just sucked me off by the bushes; I didn't even come or nothing, pal; barely got myself hard. But I told Finn we did all sorts, because he was so proud, you see. But I have had a fair few, me. But that was just because I'm a bloke, you know, and that's what you're supposed to do, isn't it? But I've never been the type to go: "Corr, I really wanna have a go on that one, let me have at it."'

'How did you feel afterwards?'

'Didn't feel anything really,' he said. 'Like, if I'm being honest, if I never had to do it again, I'd be like: yeah, all right then.'

'Never again?'

'Is that weird?' he said. 'I just don't feel it, mate.'

'No,' I said. 'I don't think that's weird at all.'

'Is it not?'

'Nope.'

Another silence fell between us and then Muddy said, in an unusually flat tone: 'Do you think it's weird I like my nails painted?'

'Maybe it's a bit unorthodox,' I said. 'But I don't think it makes you weird.'

'Is that what I am then?' he said. 'Thorodox.'

'*Un-ortho-dox.*'

'Back off, pal,' he said, giggling. 'You mumble, you do. My ears are fuckin' huge and even I can't bloody hear you sometimes.' He touched my shoulder and smiled at me. 'So, what's your little gaydar saying then?'

'Well, let's forget the gaydar stuff,' I said. 'I think it's perfectly fine to be someone who just doesn't want to have sex with anyone.'

'You sure?'

I paused. 'No,' I said. 'It's all bullshit. You need to fuck someone and fuck them right now. Literally, the next person you see.' I brought myself closer to him and hung my face directly in front of his. 'The *very* next person you see.'

Over the next few weeks, Matthew and I discussed my anxiety and depression at length. I took an almost embarrassing delight in talking about things of this nature with another black man. Every time he asked me a probing question and then smiled at me, I felt like crying. Just like with Noria's dad, I felt so happy about being respected by another black man. There were plenty of people in my life now who cared what I had to say, but this was different somehow. There was a different kind of weight in him listening to me and responding in that thoughtful way he did. I realized it was his job to make me feel comfortable and that everything he said could've been disingenuous, but I appreciated it more than he would ever know.

The next few sessions became an assortment of suggestions and coping mechanisms: cognitive restructuring and journaling and interoceptive exposure. I'd been holding off on disclosing how uncomfortable I'd been about being put on medication, but I did tell him eventually. He asked what my concern with it was, and I tried to explain the best I could that I didn't want to have to rely on medication; that I didn't want to feel as if I was so far gone that counselling wouldn't be enough, as if I'd waited so long, I now needed pills to prop me up and pull me through my day, as if medication was some kind of punishment for thinking that I could save myself alone. If high-functioning depression meant I could still live my life, albeit with this dark undertow, then perhaps being on medication, or even being on the journey to finding the right medication, might force me to gamble away the bits of brightness life had been kind enough to give me.

'But if we were to put you on medication,' he said, 'it definitely wouldn't be a case of you just relying on them. I don't want you to worry about that. It would be taken alongside this counselling.' I didn't look convinced and started to play with my hands. He smiled then. 'Think of it as *one* ingredient, Harley,' he said. 'It's not the whole thing.' I smiled back now.

'In my opinion,' he continued. 'I think it should be something to consider. I think an antidepressant will be beneficial, particularly for your symptoms of depression, but not really for the root cause of it, which is why you'll never have to rely on them. It'll always be taken in tandem with these sessions. But I do understand. And for the time being, we can see how you get on, the more of these sessions that we have.'

We'd already talked about the anxiety, about work, about uni; I'd explained to him how it'd impeded my ability to make friends in both environments: to thrive in customer-facing roles, to function in social settings. He'd asked just how much anxiety had played a part in my dropping out of uni, if there was anyone that I could've spoken to so that dropping out wouldn't have been the only option; I'd told him that I'd never looked into it, and that, looking back, I couldn't see myself making the effort, getting out of bed to seek out that kind of help.

Now he was saying: 'Would you consider going back, if you could handle the anxiety better, if we continued to discuss medication and techniques?'

I looked at him. 'I'm not sure,' I said. 'I guess I have been thinking about it. A friend recently proposed the same thing.'

'Well,' he said, cradling his pen into the spine of the notebook, 'from what I've understood, Harley, you didn't go on a whim; the opportunity offered you a chance to get something you wanted from life, it offered you a chance to apply something you really enjoyed to something academic. And it's a shame that your anxiety and depression put up a roadblock. I don't get the impression that leaving is something you genuinely wanted to do. Of course, if it was then we can leave it, but this experience feels very unresolved to me. What do you think?'

I sighed. 'How would it be any different?' I asked. 'Like, really?'

'Well,' he said, chuckling a little. 'I like to think that if you really didn't believe you could be any different – and this extends to everything, Harley: depression, anxiety, suicidal thoughts – then you wouldn't be here. But ultimately, I think you should at least give yourself the opportunity to try. You think you can do that?'

Matthew then suggested we try something called 'pleasure activity scheduling'; he explained it was a technique that could be helpful for depression. 'Don't worry,' he said, chuckling again, noticing how worried I looked. 'It's simple but effective. We're just going to discuss activities you can schedule for yourself for the near future: things you can look forward to.'

'Oh, right,' I said, 'okay.'

'Your friends make you really happy, don't they?' he said. I nodded at him. 'Can you think of anything you might do with them, or you have been doing with them, that you can look forward to?'

I went silent for a while. 'Well, Muddy got a new job at the leisure centre in Maidstone, and he's been sneaking us in for a swim just before he shuts it down. No one knows if he's allowed to do that; he won't tell us. Um, I played a tiny bit of sports for the first time since, like, secondary school days recently.'

'Oh, really?' he said. 'What was it?'

'Rugby,' I answered. 'We also went bowling recently, and sometimes Finlay likes to cook for us. He lets me help in the kitchen; I've never been much of a cook, as in, I never did it at all, so that's been a nice change of pace.'

'That's cool,' he said. 'And Finlay's the one that—'

'That's a bit of a dick,' I said, 'but I love him anyway, yeah.'

He laughed. 'And how is Muddy doing now?' he asked. 'Is he on the mend?'

'Yeah,' I said. 'He was discharged a few weeks ago. I mean, apart from his sling and the bruises on his face, you wouldn't know anything had happened to him. He's so ... well I don't know to explain it, really. He's just being very *Muddy*.'

He laughed again. 'So – you and Muddy, are you just friends then?'

I arched an eyebrow. 'Matthew,' I said. 'What are you insinuating?'

'I'm just saying that it's nice hearing you talk about him,' he said. 'Is a relationship something you've thought much of? If not with Muddy, then with someone else?'

I shrugged. 'I've never cared about getting into a relation-ship, really. It's honestly not a priority for me. But I do like Muddy a lot, yes. And, I don't know if it sounds stupid or whatever, but I just like being in his company. It makes me happier than I could possibly explain to you right now. I don't need it to be, you know, labelled or anything, I just want it to, I don't know, I just want it to exist. I just like knowing that he's there and he cares about me. That's it.'

'Would you *look* at that smile,' he said. 'Christ, does your face hurt at all?'

I laughed. 'Matthew, stop it,' I said. 'I'm serious.'

'Okay,' he said, closing his notebook and sliding it by his side. 'It doesn't sound stupid at all, by the way, what you just said.' I smiled at him. 'Go on then, Harley, tell me more about him. What does he look like? What is he like? What is he into?' Still laughing, I asked him why, feeling a little pathetic at how happy the thought of talking about Muddy made me. 'Because I'm worried you'll never frown again if your cheeks don't relax!' And so, I did tell him. And after I did, I confessed that entertaining the possibility of returning to uni meant being apart from Muddy. And as I was speaking, I started to fear that Matthew might immediately diagnose me with separation anxiety, as if I was bouncing my way across a bingo card of anxiety disorders. But instead, he said, picking his notebook back up: 'Well, I like to think good friendships have a way of lasting for ever, even if those friends aren't always physically together.'

'Ah, but that's really cheesy, though, isn't it?' I said. 'Sounds like something Muddy might say.'

'Then I guess you have nothing to worry about, do you?'

That evening I sat in Muddy's room on my laptop waiting to talk to Chelsea on MSN. Muddy was in bed, lying on his back with pillows on each side and his arm across his stomach. His hair was in a ponytail now because even though he had decided not to cut it, he was tired of brushing it out of his face. He was saying how ready he was to get rid of the sling and get back to work. I laughed because I knew that, out of boredom, he'd been turning up to the leisure centre anyway with a whistle to blow at people running alongside the pool.

'So, what's Chels sayin' then?' he asked. 'Haven't heard from her in a while.'

It was 8 p.m. now. I'd messaged her that morning saying that I wanted to talk. I wasn't sure how many of my issues I was going to reveal, but as each week had slipped by, I feared Noria would lose her nerve and spill everything out on my behalf. Chelsea had told me she was working late and that we could talk afterwards, in an unusually blunt way that made me regret bringing anything up. I'd waited anxiously for her to come online, staring at our chat window for literally hours.

As I waited, Muddy was asking me what I had going on tomorrow, and if I fancied going down for a walk in the park and checking out some birds. He then joked that he meant the animals and not the ladies. I was too preoccupied with waiting for the little dot next to Chelsea's name to turn green to laugh. He nudged me saying: 'Get it, mate? Birds?' I waved him away and looked back at the screen to see that she was now online.

Harley says:
Hi Chelsea

I waited for her to reply while Muddy was still talking to me. He kept grabbing my shoulder and saying: 'D'ya get it, pal? D'ya get it?' And I nodded absently.

I slowly typed things out, erased them, and then started typing again: So, I haven't been okay. I know I told you that my injuries were because I was out looking at birds with M or because I was playing rugby, but actually—

Chelsea says:

H, come on.

Chelsea says:

What is it?

Chelsea says:

You're such a slow typer.

Chelsea says:

Goodddd.

Chelsea says:

???

I closed my laptop and turned back to Muddy. 'Sorry, Mud, what were you saying?'

'Nah,' he said. 'It's all right, pal. I'm only over here, all slinged up. Poorly. One of my eyes fucked. I've been unorthodoxly attacked, me! But it's fine. You just get on with your evening, pissin' about with Chels. And I'll just be over here, gaspin' for a bit of bleedin' hospitality, wondering why my mate won't give me the time of day.'

I smiled. 'Mud, your eye is fine.'

'I know,' he said. 'But I just want the attention, don't I?' He stretched out his arm and beckoned me. 'Just get in here, will you, and let me hold you for a bit, yeah? C'mon!' I pretended to be annoyed by this and when I lay down next to him, he let out a loud grunting noise and rubbed my arm. 'Oh, get that look off your face, mate. You bloody love this.'

Twenty-five

The next day, Muddy and I went for a walk in Darenth Country Park, just behind the hospital where he had stayed. It was a warm day; the sun glazed the walkways in bright buttery streaks. Every time Muddy heard a bird sing, we'd walk to the edge of the field and lean on the fence. He'd given me his binoculars and I was holding them tight, panning my head back and forth. When he was done trying to identify them, he'd pat my back and we'd keep walking.

Eventually we sat on a lone bench at the side of the park. Muddy was trying to get me to play a game of naming any birds we heard in the vicinity, explaining it was something he and his granddad used to do.

'I don't know anything about bird calls,' I said.

'Course you do, pal,' he said, patting my back again. 'Now get those binocs up.'

'Okay.'

'Good lad.' We sat there in silence for fifteen or so minutes while he looked up, twitching his head in every direction it could go. Finally, we heard a descending series of light notes, as if they were being played on a triangle. He looked at me, smiling, and said that I had ten seconds.

'Why the rush?' I asked.

'Because I don't want you naming every bird you know and getting it right by accident. Serious business, this. So, yeah, ten seconds.'

We listened to the repetitive, delicate notes, not saying anything, Muddy looking at me, tight-lipped, his eyes widening in excitement, his hands and legs all fidgety. At least a minute went by and eventually, I saw a little green bird fly out of a nearby tree. I put the binoculars down and said: 'Chiffchaff?'

'Well, they are pretty recognizable,' he said. 'I guess it could've also been a widow warbler.'

I groaned. 'You're such a bird snob.'

'And you took your time.'

'Oh, let me have this one,' I said. 'I probably won't get another.'

'Fine,' he said. 'I'm always doing you bleedin' favours.'

We had lunch in a kebab shop in town. Muddy knew the guy behind the silver counter, calling him Hamzie. He ordered two greasy doner burgers and a portion of chips to share. When Hamzie brought over some tiny packets of salt, Muddy, who now had bits of burger sauce in his stubble, looked up at him with his thumb up and said: 'Proper table service this, isn't it?'

I tried not to look as uncomfortable as I felt. The shop was filthy and the chairs we were on had had their vinyl ripped to shreds.

'What's that look on your face for then?' he asked.

'It's filthy in here,' I replied.

'Ah,' he said, 'didn't realize you were so posh, pal. You should've said something. Would've taken you out to one of them fancy places, wouldn't I? With the wine and the steaks and the candles and the, um, what else they got, mate ... tablecloth.' I laughed. 'Nah, mate,' he continued, 'I'll take you out, I will. Take you out, hard. Hold the door open for you and everything. Pull your chair out, get the kitchen to put a ring in your soufflé, the whole lot.'

'What and ask to marry me?'

He laughed. 'Now, what's that look for?' he said. 'I hope you're not tryna say you wouldn't wanna marry me, mate. I'd make a great fuckin' husband, to be fair.'

'You can't be my dad and my husband.'

'Yeah, you're right,' he said. 'Would have to divorce Finners first. Poor bloke. He won't take it well. He acts all hard, but it'd break his little heart.'

On the way back home, the sun started to go down. The sky was warm, in soft shades of orange. As we cut through Central Park, Muddy thought he might've heard sounds that could've been a starling. He even made us sit down on a nearby bench so he could concentrate. He mimicked the noise, with little scratchy throaty noises that made him sound completely unhinged. But, in the end, he'd mistaken a blackbird for it. 'Ah, just wishful thinkin', I s'pose,' he said.

'What is it about starlings?' I asked.

'I dunno, pal,' he said. 'They're my granddad's favourite bird.

They haven't got that many marks next to 'em on my list. And when you see something so beautiful that rarely, you're always itchin' to see it again, aren't you? Apart from that, they just have my heart, mate. It's not just the way they look, but in what they do too. They, you know, do everything together. They build their nest and protect it ... they just bloody get it, don't they?'

'Get what?'

'That we're just not meant to be alone, are we?' I smiled at him, and he looked down at me. 'What's *that* look for, then?'

'I guess, I'm just in awe of how positive you can be when life throws shit at you. I wish I had that.'

He laughed. 'Oh, come on, mate,' he said. 'I'm not a bleedin' robot. I can have my moments of melancholy.'

'Settle my curiosity?'

'Well,' he said, 'when I first moved down from Salford, I weren't too optimistic then. When my granddad kept getting chucked back in the hospital, gave me a touch of the old anxiety, that. Oh, and obviously, when those lads gave me a good beating, that weren't too nice.' He put his arm around me. 'The night I brought you back from the hospital. *God*, that night, Harles. I don't know if I'll ever forget it, mate. Even now, even today, I'm so happy and grateful and relieved you're still here. Sometimes, I just have to look at you, pal. Don't have owt to say to you, really, but I just have to look at you, just to, I dunno, remind myself you're still alive, still my mate, that I still get to see you every day. You know, I did something really silly that night, actually.'

'What did you do?'

'When you went to bed, after we'd had our little bath ... I

sat outside your room for ages, didn't I? I only got up when I heard you get out of bed for a piss.'

'Really?'

'Yeah, I was in a bit of a mess, pal,' he said. 'I thought if I just stayed there, stayed put, kept my eyes on you, then I could . . . I dunno, make sure I'd see you through to the morning or something.' He smiled at me. 'Harley, I bleedin' love you, I do. I hope you know that.'

We were silent now. The sky was getting darker. I thought about how fulfilled I'd been by his friendship, how worthy of love he'd made me feel, how my place in the world felt so significant now, that it was something I'd be able to feel even when I wasn't around him. I liked who I was when I was with him, and now I could see, quite clearly, a future in which I liked myself unequivocally without him. The way I looked in his world was beautiful, and I couldn't wait to transpose that person to my own world, step into his skin and occupy his body.

'What's on your mind, mate?' he asked. 'You look really deep in thought or something. You all right?' I felt my fingers go numb and my heart slam against my chest as if it were a bit of malfunctioning machinery. Strangely, I didn't recognize this as anxiety; I wasn't sure what it was, but things were happening inside me that I couldn't exercise much control over; it almost made me feel sick.

'Muddy?' I said as he was about to get up.

'Yeah, pal?'

'Can I kiss you?'

He looked at me blankly at first, tilting his head a little, every painful second slipping by as he said nothing, the knots in my stomach tightening. But then he smiled. 'You wanna kiss me, do you?' he said. 'Ah, come here, pal.' The knots unravelled. He threw an arm around me and pulled me close to him, cupping a hand on my face and pressing his lips onto mine. I could feel him inhaling, could feel the air sweeping across my upper lip in a gentle wave, could feel his stubble bristle against my chin, could feel this bright rush of energy pulsing through me. I could've almost collapsed beneath the weight of the relief, of the warmth, of the intensity, of the vast sensation of simply being wanted by someone like this. I breathed in so deeply and let him inhabit me, and it was as if we were secreted in the woods again. I put my hand on his chest then and felt his heart beating. When we pulled ourselves apart, he smiled at me and said in a low voice: 'How was that, then?' The only thing I could do was smile back. 'That bad, huh?' he joked. 'I haven't actually ever been told I'm a good kisser, so apologies if I'm—'

'Muddy, it was fine.'

'Fine?'

'Yeah.'

'Bollocks.' He puckered his lips at me. 'Come on, let's go again, pal. *Fuckin' fine*. You're having a laugh, aren't you?'

I laughed. 'It was more than fine.'

'Happy days, then,' he said, patting me on the back and looking back across the distance. 'Happy days.'

Twenty-six

The best thing about joining Finlay on his morning run later that week was the fact that he wore a tightly fitted vest and running shorts that barely covered his muscular thighs. At one point, he stopped by a bench, where he stretched his legs on the armrest and took off his vest, wringing out the sweat. He then tucked the vest into his shorts and continued running.

The worst part was everything else. I trailed behind him, limp and out of breath, stopping every so often, bending over with my palms around my thighs, begging for a break. We were out in Mote Park for so long that my phlegm started to taste like blood. Eventually I sat on the cold grass, and he ran back to me.

He clapped. 'All right, pick it up, Midge.'

'I thought Muddy told you to stop calling me that.'

'Eh,' he said, 'when I'm lookin' after you, what I say goes. And when we get back, you're chuggin' a beer. None of that soft drink bollocks.'

When we got back to his flat, he had a shower and I sat at his kitchen island, looking down into his rabbits' cage, watching Crouch and García dawdle about eating bits of cabbage. I then idly flicked through a newspaper on the table while I waited for him to return. He came back down shirtless, just in some grey joggers. He asked me if I was up for a bit of food tasting; he was preparing something for Chelsea: for an occasion that he would not disclose to me yet. I said of course, and then he started making fluffy banana pancakes. He was like a hot TV chef, explaining everything he was doing, like how to elevate the pancake. He was going to cook some pancetta and make some homemade golden syrup. He put brown sugar, vanilla essence and lemon juice on the counter.

'So, what is this for?' I asked.

'I want you to try the food first.'

When he was done breaking eggs and whisking and frying and flipping, he presented to me a tall stack of pancakes sat in a puddle of the luxurious-looking golden syrup. He stood in front of me and peeled a banana, cutting it up and placing five slices on top. He asked me what I thought, and I said it looked good.

'Good,' he said. He retrieved a fork and stabbed through a bit of pancake, pancetta and banana. 'All right, mate, open up.' I ate it and told him it was tasty, just like I expected it to be. 'Great – what do you think Chels will say?'

'How am I supposed to know?'

'Because you know her, don't you?' he said. 'You know what she likes—'

'Finlay,' I said. 'What is this about?'

'Okay, fine,' he said. He left the kitchen and returned a few minutes later with a little black box and placed it in front of me, grinning. I looked up with a confused expression. He flipped the box open, revealing a tiny, shimmering ring cradled in the centre.

I was silent a moment. 'Absolutely not,' I said. 'It would never work. I don't know if I'm there yet. I don't know if I'm ready to be Harley Mackenzie.'

'Fine then, mate,' he said, laughing. 'I'll give it to Chels instead.'

I smiled at him. 'You're really gonna ask her to marry you?'

'Oh, yeah!' he said. 'So, I got this whole day planned, right. It's gonna start with a banging fuckin' breakfast in bed, a cracking lunch, a tasty fuckin' dinner. I'm thinking probably steaks or something. And that's when I pull out this bad boy and be like: so d'you wanna marry me or what?'

'Right,' I said. 'Get her so full she can't be arsed to get up and run away.'

'Stop pissing about, Harles, or you're grounded, mate.'

I rolled my eyes, laughing. I picked up the box and inspected the ring. 'Okay, carry on.'

'I'm gonna make her suspicious all day,' he said. 'When we have these pancakes in bed, I'm gonna be all: Chels, I got something to ask you, it's really important. And then ask her, I dunno, if she minds if I throw away some of her shoes, because they're takin' up too much space. And then do the same at lunch, and then the same when we go for a little walk in the park. But then at dinner, actually pop the bloody question. I think she's gonna be well chuffed. How romantic is that?'

I rolled up the newspaper and batted him on the head with it. 'Bad Finlay!' I said. 'Bad, bad Finlay!'

He rubbed his head, giggling. 'What?'

'Your definition of romantic is cursed,' I said. 'You will *not* be threatening to throw away her shoes, Finlay. Especially not in a lead up to a marriage proposal.'

'Oh, it's just a joke, mate.'

'Well, it's not though, is it?' I said. 'It's not a joke to you, and it won't be one to her. Just think about it. I'll help you out. What do you think is gonna go through her head, if you spend the entire day asking her stupid questions, putting her on edge and threatening to discard her possessions? If you popped the question to me after all of that, I'd for sure tell you to fuck off, regardless of how great of a cook you are. Or how great you look shirtless.' I gestured vaguely in his direction. 'Which, by the way, I'm enjoying very much, thank you. Apart from the run, it's been a great morning.'

He laughed and then said, flexing one of his arms: 'ah, you think I'm fit, don't you, mate? I bloody knew it.' He then rested his palms on the table, sighing hard. 'Okay, mate,' he said. 'Hit me, then. What should I do?'

'Keep the food stuff,' I said. 'I think being her personal chef for the day is a really cute idea. But everything else is horrible. It's like you've based it entirely on provoking her. Instead, just ask her more thoughtful, genuine things throughout the day. You can try and make her happy? Put her on a cloud, and get her to say something like: "Oh

wow, what a great day this was," at the end of it, before
you ask her.'

'Yeah, you're right,' he said, nodding.

'Muddy is your best friend,' I said, 'how has none of his
sentimentality rubbed off on you?'

'He'd probably have me paint my nails or something.'

That afternoon, Finlay made me taste test a sauce he was
making for a spaghetti carbonara, and then we watched the
telly, eating prawn cocktail crisps out of a bowl between
us, both of our legs crossed on the coffee table. I told him
that I was proud of him for seeing this whole maturity
thing through. He flashed me a very cute smile, put his
arm around me, and tapped my chest, leaving crumbs
on my shirt.

'So, honestly, mate,' he said. 'Is this actually a good idea? I
don't wanna look like a pillock.'

'I mean,' I said, 'you've spent more time with her recently.
I'd hope you'd have thought the whole thing through, and
were sure it'd be something she'd respond well to. Have you
talked about it? Or has she dropped hints?'

'Well,' he said, 'not hints about marriage exactly. But it
wouldn't be much of a proposal if she knew I was gonna do
it, would it? And she has said something about kids.'

'Doesn't sound like her.'

'No, really,' he said, 'she has. She did this thing on this
website, right, where you put in a picture of two people and
it gives you a picture back on what your baby is gonna look
like. She did it with us and she was fuckin' obsessed. She
loves me, mate. I'm sure of it.'

There was a joy in his eyes that I hadn't seen before. I didn't have the heart to tell him that there was something flimsy in this evidence, so I just congratulated him.

'Cheers,' he said, throwing his arms across the top of the sofa and turning to me. 'So, how's things with you then, geeze?' he asked. 'Anything you wanna share?'

I looked at him curiously. 'No,' I said. 'Why?'

'You sure, mate?'

'Yeah.'

'Well, that's funny because Muddy told me you kissed.'

My back stiffened. 'Lies.'

'You what?'

'We did no such thing.'

'So, Mud's a liar, yeah?'

'Yup.'

He looked at the clock and then got his phone out of his pocket, dialling a number. 'Hello, Mud?' he said, putting it on speakerphone.

'All right, Finners!' Muddy said cheerily on the line. 'How you doin' – how can I help you, mate? Be quick though, I only got ten minutes left on my break.'

'No, yeah,' Finlay said, side-eyeing me. 'Just a quick one. What was it you said you did with Harles the other day?'

'You what?' Muddy said, and then laughed. 'Is he there with you? Yeah, I kissed him, mate. I thought I was a bit shite, to be fair, said I wanted to give it another go, but he didn't wanna hear it.'

Finlay chuckled, looking at me. 'Oh yeah,' he said, 'while I got you, mate, for our birthdays next week, you remember your whole eighties idea? I think I could get on board with that.'

'Nah, it's a bit naff, that, actually.'

'You what?'

Muddy laughed. 'No, I'm only joking,' he said. 'Thanks, pal. Let's do it!'

'So, how do you feel about Run DMC?'

'Like what? Dress up like 'em?'

'Yeah,' he said. 'You, me and Harles. Tracksuits, chains, trainers, hats, the whole lot.'

'Ah, you're talking my bleedin' language, pal,' he said. 'Sounds good, mate. Look, I gotta go, but chat more about it, yeah? Talk to you in a bit. Tell Harles I said hi, if he's still there.'

He put his phone away then and looked at me smugly. 'Why lie?'

'You know,' I said, 'there's just something about you that still gets my back up sometimes.'

'How do you mean, mate?'

'I don't know,' I said, 'but I guess you can help me figure it out by telling me what you said when Muddy told you that we kissed.'

We stared at each other for a long time. 'Okay, fine,' he said. 'You got me. I thought it was fuckin' weird, didn't understand it, like, the ergonomics of it; he's like six foot and you're what? Four—'

'Five foot three, actually.'

'Did he, like, lift you up or something?' he said. 'Or did you climb up onto his shoulders?'

I rolled my eyes. 'Well,' I said, 'as long as you didn't give him shit when he told you.'

'Look at you, then,' he said. 'All protective over him and stuff. Of course, I didn't give him shit.'

'What do you mean "of course"?' I said. 'You're usually the first in with the pejoratives, even if nothing gay is actually happening.'

'Look, mate,' he said, 'we had a chat, didn't we?'

'You did?'

'He came down to watch the match a few nights ago, and on the way home he started puffing out his chest in the car, telling me to back off setting him up with people all the time. He said he wasn't sure what he was, but all he knew was that he didn't wanna sleep with anyone, and that I was out of order for always forcing him, and that it wasn't on anymore. I'll tell you what, though, really put me in my place, that.'

I smiled. 'Good for him,' I said. 'I wish I could've been a fly on the wall for that conversation.'

'What? You think I kicked off?'

'Didn't you?'

'No, mate,' he said. 'I told him that we were brothers, that I loved him no matter what. Then he said some shite about how we were like Liam and Noel, and I told him not to take the fuckin' piss.'

'If you love him, then why have you been such a dick?'

'I just wanted the bloke to be happy, Harles,' he said. 'I thought I fucked it when I started going out with Chels, so I thought I'd do everything I could to fix it, make sure he had someone in his life, so he wouldn't hate me for taking his bird.

He'd say he didn't care, but I thought it was bollocks. Because if someone took my bird, I'd come after 'em, all guns blazing. Turns out it weren't bollocks. The bloke just doesn't wanna fuck anyone.' He looked at me fixedly then. 'But he's up for snogging you apparently.'

'He probably only did it because I asked him.'

'You *asked* him?' he said, laughing. 'You're so bloody polite. I already told you the bloke thinks the world of you.'

'And if that's what consent looks like to you,' I said, 'then I guess that's just more paperwork for me to deal with, isn't it?'

'Oh yeah,' he said, 'and it should go without saying, mate, keep it zipped about Chelsea.'

'I won't say anything to her,' I said. 'I swear.'

Twenty-seven

When Chelsea came to evict us the following week, Muddy and I both stood in front of her in the corridor like two misbehaving school children, looking down at our feet, hands behind our backs, trying to explain why the bins were overflowing with takeaway packaging, and why the bathtub had these grainy brown stains all over it. She called us a pair of pigs, and then delivered the news that her dad had told her that morning he was selling the flat.

'You what?' Muddy said. 'When?'

'I don't know, hun,' she said, sighing. 'But I think he's already setting up viewings and stuff. So, I think very soon. I'm so sorry, my lovelies.'

Muddy nudged me. 'It's all over, pal,' he said. 'We're gonna be turfed out, given the old heave-ho. I'll keep an eye out for any underpasses on my way to work, or a tunnel. Oh! Or a ginnel that has two big fuck-off wheelie bins that we can make a home in between. Could be quite cosy, I s'pose. Worst comes to worst, we could stay in my car.'

I looked up at him. 'Or we could just look for somewhere else to live,' I said. 'Unless your heart is really set on living by an underpass.'

He gripped my shoulder. 'It's the adventure, pal!'

'Actually, it's the homelessness, Muddy.'

Chelsea giggled. 'You two!' she said. 'Anyway, I will try and push back until you guys can get somewhere else sorted. Whether it's a flat or, yeah, an underpass. I suppose it would be cheaper and you'd have tons of boxes from the move to curl up into.'

'Well, don't do us any bleedin' favours Chels,' Muddy said, putting his arm around me. 'I'm gonna spend my wages on a massive tent, and Harles and I are gonna go live out in the woods and live off the fat of the land.'

I took his arm off me. 'We're not doing any of that, Muddy.'

'Ah, c'mon,' Muddy said, 'we're getting back to nature with this.'

'Well,' Chelsea said, 'how about you get to an estate agent first.'

That afternoon Chelsea and I went to the local Tesco Express to stock up on a few things. We walked down the brightly lit maze of aisles and I held the basket while she linked her arm around mine. I was thinking about how I still hadn't told her everything that had happened, how something as inconsequential as a blunt message had stopped me. She was somebody I loved, the same as the others, so it had become imperative that she know what they did. But the prolonged secrecy had made the whole thing seem so seedy somehow, like on top of everything, I'd also done something so evil, so sinister, that unburdening myself to her would do nothing but incriminate us both.

'So,' Chelsea said as we walked down the confectionary aisle. 'I've decided to concede.'

'How do you mean?'

'With Nor, I mean,' she said. 'I see where she's coming from about uni. If there's an opportunity there to do what you really wanna do, I think you should go for it. I didn't want it to seem as if I was forcing the PR job on you or anything. It's just, I thought since you had a tough time at uni, that it would be an easy way to get back on track, you know?'

'Yeah,' I said. 'I get that.'

She looked at me quietly. It was as if she wanted to ask me something but couldn't quite bring herself to. She looked down at my wrist and gently lifted it up, inspected it closely – my stitches had long disappeared – and then she dropped it. She still didn't say anything and then neither did I.

'Um, so, how do you feel about going back to uni?' she asked eventually.

'I have been thinking more seriously about it,' I said.

'You remember when you came back,' she said. 'And you said about the anxiety and depression – you were being serious, weren't you?'

'I mean,' I said nervously. 'Yeah, I wasn't joking. But, you know, we don't really discuss those kinds of things, do we?'

She looked at me, confused. 'What do you mean?'

'Nothing,' I said. 'It's just not what we talk about, is it?'

'Then what do we talk about?'

I shrugged. 'I don't know,' I said and then laughed. 'You?'

She tapped my arm, feigning shock. 'So, how bad was it?'

'How bad was what?'

'Harles!' she said. 'The depression and anxiety and whatever else—'

'What do you mean "whatever else"?'

She looked at me again. 'You know what, hun,' she said. 'Forget it.'

As we walked around the store, I kept looking down at my wrist where my stitches had been. I thought about how much easier this would've been if they were still present. I could've just shown Chelsea the evidence, rather than having to explain everything. I was so acutely aware that so much of what she knew of my life was a lie. My miseries had written their stories on my body but now I walked around as if these stories had never existed. Now she could look at my wrist and see only a glint of a line that was fading; she could look into my palm and see nothing at all. She could look at my face and see no fear or loneliness in my eyes. Just standing in front of her, I presented only a partly formed version of myself. So much of what I liked about myself now, so much of the internal happiness to which I had so recently gained access, had been because I'd tried to overcome things she had been oblivious about. How much history did a friendship need to be infused with to be valid?

We had paid for everything and were on our way out of the shop when a hand landed on my shoulder. I froze, and then looked across to Chelsea, who was staring up at someone. Slowly, I followed the long brown fingers splayed out on my shoulder to the sleeve of a dark grey jumper, then all the way up an arm until I saw my dad's face. He was smartly dressed in a navy tie.

'Hello, Harley,' he said.

I stood there, seized with fear. 'Dad?' I said eventually. I realized then just how fragile emotional progress could be. In the space of a few seconds, I felt as if I was regressing into a foetus. 'You work here now?'

He looked at Chelsea. 'Is this your girlfriend?'

'Hello, Mr Sekyere,' she said. 'You don't remember me? We used to work together. Or, actually, you might remember me from that time me and Harley came down to your house, after you kicked him out and you shoved all his shit in a bin, and then didn't open the fucking door when we knocked, even though you're the one that asked him round.'

He was looking at me now. 'What is she talking about?' he said, sternly, turning back to her. 'Shut your mouth. Disrespectful girl.'

I put my hand up at him. 'Dad, please don't talk to her like that.'

He scowled at her. 'You are going to let this girl say these things to your father?'

The longer I looked at him, the longer I let him speak, the more it seemed as if all the progress from the past few weeks and months was being erased.

'Say what?' I said. 'The truth? I mean, you did do all those things, didn't you?' He went silent. 'Didn't you?'

He looked at me, really looked at me. It was as if the boy he had seen over our years together had evaporated for good and been replaced with me: the boy he'd caught only a glimpse of while I'd hugged Darren, the one he'd disowned, the one he'd tried to manipulate back into his life with prayer. I was so stubbornly and resolutely placed before him now. He couldn't be the reason why I'd fall apart again; he couldn't be the reason why I'd find myself in the woods again; he just couldn't.

Chelsea, all red-faced now, said: 'Well, then?'

'Chels, stop—' I said.

'No, Harley, I've had enough of this,' she said, looking back up at him. 'He's your son, literally your only one, and instead of just fucking accepting him for who he is, you've got him in therapy, you've got him trying to fucking take his own life, you've made his life so difficult, and all you had to do was bloody love him!'

'Chelsea, for god's sake,' I said. 'Please, just stop!'

'What, Harles, I—'

'Chels, no.' I looked up at my dad.

My dad looked back at me. 'What?' he said. 'What is she talking about?'

I was quiet for a long time, studying his face. I was embarrassed standing before him. I felt strangled by the ghosts of every humiliation I'd ever suffered in his presence. I felt physically sick.

'I've been so sad for so long, Dad,' I said. 'I've spent so much of my life trying to understand why you spent so much of yours acting as if my existence was something to apologize for, something I had to be ashamed of. Dad, I don't suppose you know what it's like to feel embarrassed to be alive? To feel your life simply doesn't matter? It's a genuine question. Because I've also tried so hard to understand you. Everything you've done over the years felt so purposeful, so intentional; every moment you could take advantage of to hurt me the deepest, you took. You destroyed my things; you blamed me for Mum: you cried at me like it was genuinely something I'd done. You made me believe that this guilt you'd forced on me was justified.

'You know, I don't think you were cruel because you didn't know any better, or that you were just stuck in your ways, or that it was some misguided way of showing affection, or that there was some lesson to be learned. I think you were cruel because you hated me. And that's fine, it really is. I know that family doesn't guarantee love. And I know you don't like that I am the way I am, and that's okay. There are people who do. People who love me, even.' I glanced over at Chelsea. 'I think life has compensated me quite nicely for what you made me feel I had to beg for. And no,' I finished, 'she's not my fucking girlfriend.'

Chelsea and I stood outside afterwards with our shopping bags by our feet. She had her arms folded, staring at me, her eyes soft with tears.

'How did you know all of that stuff?' I asked.

'What?' she said. 'That you're seeing a therapist? Or that you tried to kill yourself? Or that you were seeing that bloke that beat you up at the pub, and he was doing all this disgusting racist shit to you?' I just looked at her blankly. 'Well, Finn has a big mouth. He likes to be trusted, but then he gets so excited that someone's actually trusted him, that he can't keep his mouth shut. I told him I wouldn't tell you anything he told me, because he didn't want you to be pissed at him. And, you know, don't be because—'

I sighed. 'I'm not pissed off at him.'

'Well, I am at you,' she said. 'I'm so fucking angry at you. And if I weren't so happy that you're all right, I'd bloody strangle you.'

'What?'

'When I said I was glad you and Mud were this close, I didn't think that what you were keeping from me was *this* bad. Why did you let me think everything was all right? Do you not trust me anymore or something? You literally told everyone, and I bloody knew you way before any of those lot. I mean, for fuck's sake, Harley, you told Finn!'

I took a long, shaky breath and shrugged. 'Look,' I said. 'I've just always felt as if I can't tell you certain things.'

'Why not?'

'Your life and mine,' I said. 'It's just different.'

'Well, yeah,' she said. 'But that don't mean you can't tell me things, what the hell, Harley? Ain't I been there for all the shitty things that've happened? I've *always* been there. How can all this other stuff happen, and it don't even cross your mind to think: Hmm. Maybe I should say something to Chels.'

'That's what I mean,' I said. 'In your eyes, my life's just been a series of shitty things you've had to help clean up. I've just been wary of darkening your world with all my stuff.'

'Darkening my world?' she said, confused. She disentangled

her arms and started pointing at me. 'You better start making some fucking sense, Harley, I swear to god. What are you on about?'

'Do you really not understand?' I asked. 'I've never felt as if I can just come up to you and tell you that I'm suffering from anxiety, or depression, or suicidal thoughts. Your life just isn't – well, it's not that, is it?'

'What, because I never get anxious?' she said. 'Or feel sad or depressed? You don't own any of that stuff. Or get to assume I don't experience any of it.'

'I didn't say that,' I said. 'But you have made some comments in the past that's made me not wanna talk to you about this kinda thing.'

'What comments?'

'You know,' I said. 'You said people who suffered from anxiety were narcissists.'

'Never used that word in my life.'

'Well, you said something similar.'

'Well, that's not fair,' she said. 'You can't just make up conversations in your head, and then project them onto me. That's insane.'

'You *did* say that though.'

'Okay,' she said. 'I might've said some shit – but that was probably ages ago.'

'Fine,' I said, solemnly. 'But comparatively, your life is easier. And I didn't want to be the one that got in the way of that.'

'Well, first off,' she said. 'Bullshit. My life *could* be easy. I could sit on my arse and let my dad fund everything for me, but I don't. And secondly, fuck you. It's not as if I haven't worked my arse off to make things happen for me. You don't get to talk about my life like I'm some lazy bitch who's done fuck all, just because her parents have a bit of money. Just because I don't mope about, saying how sad I am all the time, don't mean I don't have it hard sometimes, like I don't have my days. You don't have the foggiest how dark, or not dark, my world is. You haven't even asked the bloody question, and you're acting like you have the answers. You can be a judgy little shit, you know that?'

There was a silence. I shifted my eyes about awkwardly. 'So, how are you?'

She laughed. 'I'm fine, thanks.'

I sighed. 'Is that what you think I do?' I said. 'Mope about? I'm not hurt, I'm genuinely asking.'

'That was a bit out of order,' she said. 'You can express any emotion you like, however long you like, just like I can. I just deal with my stuff differently to you. But it shouldn't mean that you can't talk to me. I love you!'

'I love you too,' I said. 'And I don't think you're a lazy bitch. I adore you.'

She smiled at me, picking up all the bags. 'I'm glad you're seeing someone about your issues though,' she said. 'Finn says it's going well.' She hugged me. 'You're not leaving us, Harley. No way. My heart literally sank when he told me. And fuck you for not letting me be there for you.'

In the elevator up to the flat, Chelsea asked if I'd told Muddy that I was thinking about going back to uni.

'I haven't,' I said. 'I'm still not one hundred per cent about it. I don't know if I wanna say anything just yet.'

'I mean, hun, you heard him earlier. He thinks you're about to get a new place together. Or that you're gonna be living under a bridge anyway . . . You should probably tell him soon, let him know where your head is at. You know how overenthusiastic he gets about things.'

I looked at her. 'Do you know we kissed?'

She sighed. 'Yes, Harley,' she said. 'Everybody knows you kissed. He won't shut up about it. He told me, he told Nor, he told Finn. I'm pretty sure he's even told people who haven't even bloody heard of you.'

'You think?'

'Knowing him,' she said, 'probably.'

Twenty-eight

Finlay dropped by the next week, on Chelsea's dad's behalf, to see if the flat was ready for viewings. Muddy and I had promised Chelsea that we'd make it look presentable, but we hadn't done a thing. In fact, it had gotten messier. Perhaps, subconsciously, we'd wanted to delay things.

'What a shithole,' Finlay said when Muddy opened the door to him. 'So, is this how you lads have been treating the place while Chels has been away, yeah?' He walked into the living room, the kitchen and the bathroom, and then met Muddy and me standing in the hallway. He clapped his hands together. 'Right then, boys,' he said. 'Let's get the brush and the mops out. Let's get this crack den spick and span.' Muddy and I just stared at him. 'What are you looking at? You got viewings next week. Chop-chop, boys. Let's get crackin', c'mon!'

He went through the cupboards in the kitchen and retrieved a selection of dustpans and brushes and mops and sprays, assembling them before Muddy and me. He threw a yellow sponge and a spray bottle over to me and told me to start in the bathroom, he then kicked the red Henry Hoover over to Muddy and told him to get sucking.

In the bathroom, Finlay kept coming in every ten minutes and saying things like: 'Pull your finger out, Harles; I've curled out turds cleaner than this.' And I kept showing him my middle finger.

When I was done, I went into the living room, where Muddy and Finlay were dusting, vacuuming and picking up rubbish: crisp packets, bottles and wrappers that had probably been there for weeks, ensnared in thick clumps of hair and dust. Even though cleaning had been Finlay's idea, at one point, he tipped the mess he had in his dustpan over Muddy; Muddy retaliated by lifting the lid off the Hoover, pulling out the dust bag and puffing it into Finlay's face. They both laughed in the moment, but Finlay got angry afterwards, batting at his own face, accusing Muddy of being a child who needed to grow up; and Muddy accused him of being an uptight grouchy shite.

The place never really got clean, and Muddy and Finlay spent most of the afternoon playing games on the PlayStation. When Muddy went to get more beers for them, I asked Finlay why he had told Chelsea everything I'd asked him not to. 'Why am I even keeping your proposal a secret, if you can't even give me the same courtesy?' I said.

'Ah, I'm sorry, Harles,' he said. 'But this is different, isn't it? She knew something was up with you and she asked me about it; she said you were ignoring her messages on MSN; and I was feelin' a bit smug, 'cause usually people don't tell me stuff. And it just sort of came out.' I gave him a disapproving look and then he opened his arms wide. 'Ah – let's hug it out, mate.' I didn't move. 'Weird. Hugs usually go down a treat with Mud. What are you into, then? Kisses?' He puckered his lips, putting a hand on the back of my head and pushing me towards him, trying to kiss my forehead. I laughed as I wiggled out of his grasp.

'Oi,' he said. 'I heard you're thinkin' about going back to uni. You told Mud?' I shook my head. 'Let me give you some advice, mate. Man to man. Dad to offspring. You gotta stop keepin' secrets from people.'

'Fuck off, Finlay.'

I didn't know how to tell Muddy that I'd been thinking about returning to uni. I thought about it so much that it had become its own source of anxiety. Sometimes the fear got so bad, that I started to talk myself out of it. I was so close to reneging on the idea that I considered telling Chelsea to forget I'd even said anything. I considered if I was perhaps sacrificing something in going back. Constantly being around Muddy and Chelsea and Noria, and even Finlay, I felt as if I didn't have to bargain with life for happiness: it was readily available. Returning to uni meant I would be sacrificing people for whom my best interests had been a priority, people whose affection had been tethered to a desire to see me succeed, and it was reciprocated; I would be sacrificing people who also understood that sometimes I became so engulfed in sadness, that I needed help to be lifted out of it, to breathe easy again. I remembered telling my dad at the supermarket that I had friends who loved me for who I was. I hadn't been able to stop thinking about that. There was a kind of luxury in being loved for who you were. And here it was, all for me. I was loved.

One day shortly after we'd 'cleaned' the flat, I sat in my room reading the overview of the course I'd dropped out of. I felt the same excitement I'd experienced reading it the first time: smiling at how enticing it sounded, as if the text had formed tentacles and latched onto my interests. I smiled at all the buzzwords and phrases: 'reporter', 'editor', 'writing for the university's publication and for external clients', 'not only practising music journalism but developing creative projects'.

I put my laptop to the side and stared at the ceiling. I'd stopped going to lectures and seminars back in May; there had been a long week or so where I hadn't left my dorm. I'd been so desperate to separate my life from those months, as if closing a door on them would also shut away the shame and the failure I'd felt for dropping out. I didn't know what I'd missed since then: what assignments, what group projects. I'd been forcing myself to pretend as if those months had belonged to someone else, that all the responsibilities of coursework and exams and attending lectures and seminars hadn't been my own, but some phantom Harley that I'd created and then abandoned.

I wondered then if I wanted to resurrect that person, take Matthew's advice, and give him the opportunity to try again.

At my next session with Matthew, I told him about the confrontation with my dad. In a previous session, he'd suggested that we do something called the 'empty chair technique'. He'd wanted to know how I felt when I thought about my dad, what kind of emotions he brought up in me. And I'd told him I felt stupid talking to an empty chair.

'Even so,' he'd said then. 'I'd like you to go with it. I do think your father is quite a huge reason why you, in your own words, have such a low estimation of yourself. I can assure you that you won't look stupid. I'm only ever gonna do what I think is best to help you. Otherwise, why are we even here, right?' I nodded. 'When was the last time you spoke to him? Like a proper conversation, a real back and forth, sort of thing, where you each express something emotionally significant.'

I hadn't had an answer for him then, but I did now. He nodded proudly at me after I told him what I'd said to my dad at the supermarket. Then he asked me how I'd felt.

'I'm not gonna lie, Matthew,' I said. 'I felt fucking great.'

He beamed at me. 'You see?' he said excitedly. 'It's like what I was telling you before. The way we treat our emotions is so important for managing our mental health. Ah, Harley. I'm proud of you! I really hope you continue finding it within yourself to acknowledge how you feel, keep trying to understand why you're feeling these emotions, and then finding healthy ways to let them go. I just never want you to forget that your emotions – they're valid, Harley; they're very real.'

I almost said to Matthew that I wished he had been my dad. I would've played it off like a joke, but I would've meant it. But instead, I smiled at him, basking in how happy he was for me.

*

Muddy was so excited about the prospect of us finding a place together. And I still hadn't told him about uni; I was hoping that eventually my excitement would dwindle, and I wouldn't have to tell him at all. One day, in a week where we'd both been working mornings, he picked me up from Regal after our shifts and we went shopping for some things for his and Finlay's birthday party. We drove to a retail park in Ashford where we bought bucket hats and cheap green tracksuits; he said he could make chains out of the foil we had in the kitchen. After that, we drove up to Mote Park because it was still so gorgeously sunny. I'd been quiet for much of the day, mostly thinking about when and how I would tell him about uni.

'So, when do you wanna start looking for a new place then?' he asked as we walked down the muddy slopes towards the benches.

I tensed up. 'I'm not sure,' I said.

'Well, I've been thinking about it loads,' he said. 'It's gonna be a bit shite on the rent front since we probably won't get a landlord who'll be as easy-going. But I was thinking a little two-bed; we could start looking in Rochester, or Sheerness or Sittingbourne or even blimmin' Sheppey, but I don't know how I feel about all that marsh or being on the seafront – I like me a bit of water, but, you know, not all the time – or here in Maidstone or Faversham or Whitstable or Canterbury; and if you get your licence sorted, we could even do Margate or Dover or Folkstone or Ashford or New Romney; it's all a bleedin' oyster, mate.' He looked down at me. 'So, how's that sound then? Messy as we'd blimmin' like, takeaways every day, clog those fuckin' arteries up; or switch it up, start eatin' all healthy shite, become completely different people. I'm tellin' you, pal, we can do *anything*.'

'You weren't kidding,' I said. 'You've thought about this a lot.'

'Yeah, pal,' he said. 'I could finally start my little record collection like I've always wanted; you could do one as well; build us a little cabinet and put our stuff in together; get my granddad's old record player down. I could bring my pictures down and all. Oh! And get us a picture of me and you, stick it on the bleedin' wall, make it a proper little home.'

We boarded a massive paddle boat shaped like a goose and slowly pedalled it across the river. A strange melancholy settled itself deep within me then, a sensation that only intensified the more Muddy talked about this prospective flat of ours – which seemed to be located in every town in the county of Kent – what it would look like, and how chuffed he was that we were doing this.

The distance ahead, to the destination of this journey I'd been trailing for as long as I could remember, was clearer than it had ever been. As if I could see pieces of a town that'd previously been in fog. There was a single road through this town, with signposts and houses and traffic lights. Smiley-faced residents lined the pavements – people who had perhaps made the same journey, perhaps people whom life had saved from its own torment – waving and beckoning and whooping and congratulating me.

In recompense for my mum and my dad and Paul and all the things I'd done to and thought about myself, life had rewarded me with this place. This place that realigned my consciousness into a bright, salubrious green the moment I walked through its gates. This place, a vibrant, bucolic island where bits of sadness weren't traded for bits of happiness. This place, where happiness in fact existed in molecules in the atmosphere, and I only had to exist and breathe to take them in. This place, so densely populated with the nightingales and skylarks and cuckoos and song thrushes and house sparrows and starlings that had evaded Muddy's life list for, elsewhere, they had been so rare. This place, where Muddy already lived and stood at the end of the road, beyond the residents, with his arms open wide and a smile on his face.

'You all right?' Muddy asked again, still pedalling. 'Never seen you so quiet, pal.'

I leaned my head against his side. 'I'm okay,' I said.

He held me close, his fingers gently stroking my arm. I listened to him continue to talk about our prospective flat, as the dark water sprawled and shimmered before us.

Twenty-nine

The day before Muddy and Finlay's birthday, I went for a walk through the farmers' market in Dartford town centre, on the lookout for a present for Muddy. I'd been set on buying him another pair of binoculars when I saw two paintings hanging at the back of one of the stalls. The first one said: TITS at the top and had illustrations of bearded tits and willow tits and great tits beneath the text. The other one said: PECKERS and had illustrations of great spotted and golden-fronted and ringed woodpeckers. I bought them both.

The next evening, I stood in his doorway, leaning the paintings against the wall. I watched him in his mirror, dancing to the Jason Nevins's remix of 'It's Like That'. He was in the green tracksuit with pale green stripes down the sides. My tracksuit was green also, a much darker shade, but had white stripes. I'd gone into Chelsea's room and taken a pair of orange-tinted glasses from her drawer to finish off the look. Muddy kept putting on his brown bucket hat, removing it, ruffling his hair, and then putting it back on. On his desk, there was a pair of white trainers next to a vial of green nail polish and the chains he'd made for us in the kitchen earlier, folding bits of foil and looping them around each other. When he saw me, he tilted his hat in greeting.

'What's that you got there, then?' he asked.

I smiled at him. 'Your presents.'

'Presents?' he said, walking over to me. 'You didn't have to get anything, mate. You're always getting me gifts, you.'

'I've only ever got you one thing before,' I said. 'The handkerchief.'

He knelt down to look at the paintings. 'If you think that's all you've given me,' he said, 'then you haven't been paying attention, pal.'

'What do you mean?'

'I'll let you figure that one out,' he said. 'You look great, by the way.'

I thought so too. I'd combed out my afro which seemed to pair well with the outfit.

'So do you,' I said.

He started laughing. 'Ah, that's bleedin' hilarious, that, Harles. Tits and Peckers. It's gonna look pretty fuckin' good in our new place, when we find it.' I smiled tightly at him as I sat on his bed. 'How much this set you back, then? Ed giving you the big bucks now, is he?'

I looked up at him. 'Mud, can you just hug me already?' I said. 'That time Finn came around and gave you those eye-pieces for your binoculars, you literally lifted him up off the ground and spun him around.'

'Ah,' he said, laughing, 'it's why you did this, isn't it? To get a bleedin' hug out of me.' He pulled me in, thanking me in a low voice, directly in my ear. I told him he smelt nice, and he stood up, pulling out from his pocket a new pot of face cream Noria had bought him recently. 'As you can probably tell, pal,' he said, rubbing at his cheeks. 'I've not got a dry face anymore. It's actually pretty blimmin' soft.' I touched him and nodded agreeably. 'So, she's taken me off the stuff for grumpy skin, and now I'm on . . .' he read the label: 'Oils of Life: Intensely Revitalizing Cream.'

'Congratulations.'

'Cheers, pal,' he said. 'Proper proud moment, this.' He looked at me curiously. 'You never have dry skin. What do you use then?'

'Palmer's Cocoa Butter.'

After we put on the foil chains, we looked at our reflections in the mirror. I felt a goodness in me that was tempered by a slight flare of nervousness about the party. It wasn't enough to put me off going, so I didn't chalk it up to anxiety. But still, the tips of my fingers were beginning to prickle, and my tongue was going numb. In one of my last sessions with Matthew, we'd been discussing ways in which I could control the level of anxiety I experienced, particularly in social situations. He'd suggested an exercise called the 'downward arrow technique', where he would guide me through a succession of questions, attempting to target and unravel the particular anxieties I had. Every time I told him what I was scared of, he'd say: 'And, Harley, would it be so bad if that happened?'

Muddy clipped a hand onto my shoulder and said: 'How

cracking do we look, eh?' He spent the next few minutes painting his nails mint green. When he was done, he stood up, shook his hands and then held them up to me. 'What do you think, pal?'

'Lovely,' I said. 'Um, is your rugby lot gonna be there tonight?'

'They sure are,' he said and then saw my worried expression. 'Oh, you're not still worrying about me, are you? Come on, Harles. If I have to tell you all about how tough I am again, pal, I'm gonna have to tattoo it on my bleedin' forehead or something.'

I laughed. 'Fine,' I said, holding my hands up in surrender. 'You're tough as nails, and I'll stop worrying about you.'

'Good stuff,' he said. 'It's gonna be a stonker of a night, mate. And you, my dear Harley . . .' He put his hands on my shoulders and brought his face very close to mine, his brown eyes wide and heavy with excitement, 'you have absolutely no time for worrying.'

Muddy played 'Acquiesce' as we drove down to Shakermaker's, removing his hat, throwing his hair back and forth, explaining that this was one of the rare Oasis songs where Liam and Noel sang together.

There were a lot more people at Shakermaker's than I'd anticipated; it was totally packed inside. We parked a few roads down and walked up to the pub; there was a small crowd of people outside, and amongst them were Finlay, Chelsea and Noria.

'Oi, oi, Freddie,' Muddy called out to Chelsea. Her hair was slicked back, and she had a fake moustache above her lip; she was in some pale high-waisted jeans with a black belt, a tightly fitted tank top and a jewel-studded strap around the top of her right arm.

She walked up and kissed us both on the cheek. 'Aw,' she said, beaming. 'My precious huns. Look at you both! Matching and everything! I love it!' She wished Muddy a happy early birthday and then asked about the house hunt. I shook my head intensely at her with my eyes wide.

Muddy nudged me and said: 'Well, he's leavin' me to do all the bleedin' work, isn't he?'

Chelsea slid her fingers around our foil chains. 'Well, I'm sure Finlay wouldn't mind you guys moving in with him for a bit if you can't find anywhere.'

From way behind her, we heard Finlay shout: 'Piss off!' And then he and Noria walked up.

Noria rested her arm on Chelsea's shoulder and another on her own hip, awaiting her due compliment. She had shoulder-length mullet-styled hair that curled around her face; and she had on dark jeans with white knee pads, and a black T-shirt tied in a knot, exposing her midriff.

I nodded at her, smiling, and said: 'Hello, Miss Jackson.'

'Yes!' she shouted. 'I knew I could trust you to understand the absolute gift that is this outfit. These lot didn't have a clue.'

I laughed. 'Janet in the "Pleasure Principle" video; I love it.'

She started dancing, repeatedly placing her hand parallel to her face and then under her chin, like Janet did in the video. I reached out and twirled her around. Finlay then stood between Muddy and me, in his brown hat, red tracksuit, white Adidas trainers and gold chain. He put his arms around both of us and said he was already quite drunk. He then lifted Muddy's hand, inspecting his green nails.

'You like 'em, mate?' Muddy asked.

Finlay laughed and said: 'Oh, Mudzie, you crazy bastard. I love you so much, man! Happy birthday, mate. Let's get fuckin' wrecked!' He gave Muddy a passionate, vigorous hug and then looked down at me, slapping my back. 'You too, son, c'mon!'

Muddy and Finlay went on ahead, and I walked in with Chelsea and Noria on either side of me. Inside, there was a very poppy eighties playlist going, and there were clusters of people everywhere that seemed to multiply every time I looked up. At the bar, I saw Muddy's friend Ian talking to Larry the delivery guy; Ian was in his usual clothes – he even had his bumbag on – except for a glittery silver glove on his right hand. And Larry had on a high-vis jacket and grey jogging bottoms, with no fancy accessories at all.

As Chelsea was ordering, Noria was telling me about a new guy she'd started seeing, a black guy with dreads and tattoos who was supposedly built like a brick shithouse and was working in the JD Sports in Bluewater. I asked if she'd thought about bringing him today.

'My ex's birthday do?' she said. 'Think about it, Harles.'

'Right,' I said. 'I guess I don't really think of Muddy as your ex, but more as someone you're just friends with now.'

'Absolutely not,' she said. 'I spent money on that man. So, no, he wasn't just a friend, he was *mine*. And just because you stuck your tongue down his throat, doesn't mean he was any less mine, okay? We've *all* been in his mouth. Isn't that right, Chels?'

I laughed. 'Fair enough,' I said. 'So, how is the new job anyway?'

'Good,' she said. 'I'm not cussing people out in my head first thing in the morning anymore. I mean, yeah, when it's quiet they talk about shit I don't care about. But no one gives me grief, and they keep telling me how amazing I am with the customers, and it's just nice to work somewhere where people are always telling you the truth, you know.' I nodded at her, chuckling. 'But yeah, I'm content. I didn't actually realize they paid *that* much more. I mean retail's retail, innit? But I can pay my parents more than half the rent now. And I have a bit left to fuckin' *de-rink* with. Let's get it!' She slapped the counter, getting Chelsea's attention, who now had four shots and a glass of Coke in front of her. Chelsea slid the Coke over to me and then ripped off her moustache, rubbing the skin beneath it.

She asked us if we thought Finlay had been acting strangely. 'No more than usual,' Noria said. 'Why?'

'I don't know,' she said, 'he's just been so weird all day, so shifty, like. He's gonna do something stupid and childish and I'm gonna be mortified, I can feel it. His whole bloody rugby lot's here as well, so that don't bode well.' She looked at me expectantly, and I just shrugged.

I decided that I would drink that night; I drank half the Coke and Chelsea bought a fifth shot to pour into it.

The night proceeded in a prolonged haze of drinking and talking and people multiplying further and arranging themselves in various positions to have pictures taken: Chelsea sticking her fake moustache on me and pinching my cheeks; Noria and I holding each other very closely and dancing to a slow Whitney Houston song in the empty space by the bar; Chelsea and Noria swapping different parts of their outfits and drinking some more; me sitting in between the two of them, melting into songs that made me feel so unquestionably good; Finlay stealing Ian's glittery glove and chucking it across the room; Finlay throwing me over his shoulder to introduce me to his rugby lot, and all of them making loud happy drunken noises at me, and me making happy drunken noises back; the rugby lot asking if I was the gay black lad that Muddy and Finlay were always going on about, and then me giving them a thumbs up, my eyes heavy-lidded, then slanting down from Finlay's shoulder sloppily before he caught me; Noria and Chelsea getting on the karaoke and doing a semi-choreographed performance to Chaka Khan's 'Ain't Nobody'; Muddy and Finlay eventually getting on the karaoke too and singing a terrible, but passionate, duet to 'Especially For You', by Kylie Minogue and Jason Donovan, with their arms around each other, looking into each other's eyes; me slamming my hands on the table and yelling: 'Kiss! Kiss! Kiss!' when they were done and everybody laughing.

When Muddy had finished his last few songs – A-ha's 'Take on Me', screeching the falsetto of the chorus, Spandau Ballet's 'Gold' and Diana Ross's 'Chain Reaction' – he finally let someone else have a turn and sat down next to me. Chelsea and Noria were in the toilet, and I was looking after their bags. Finlay had gone outside to smoke with some of the rugby lot. I dotted my eyes round the place, at the various constellations of people, feeling something both happy and despondent inflate inside me. Muddy was saturated in sweat and had taken off his hat, becoming a mop of dark dripping hair. He leaned back in the chair and slung his arm around me, sighing in delight.

'You look like you've had so much fun tonight,' I said.

He laughed, picking up a bag of pork scratchings Finlay had left on the table. 'I have, mate,' he said, as he threw some into the air, catching them in his mouth on the first go. 'You should have a bit of fun yourself.'

'I've had fun.'

'Night's still young,' he said. 'You could still have a bit more, couldn't you?'

'I guess it depends on what kind of fun you're talking about.'

'I think you know what kind of fun I'm on about, pal.'

'Mud—'

'Harley, come on,' he said. 'Please. It's my birthday.'

'No, it's not.'

'*Paaal!*' he said. '*Come on*, I'd never make you do anything you didn't want to. Except tonight, obviously. Come on.'

He gave me puppy dog eyes, with his bottom lip pushed out. It was the most adorable thing I'd ever seen in my entire life.

'All right,' I said.

When Chelsea and Noria got back, Muddy and I went up to the front and took a mic each while an instrumental of Lighthouse Family's 'High' started playing. Finlay shouted out that this wasn't an eighties song, and Muddy told him to fuck off.

The joyful, triumphant nature of the song and Muddy wrapping his arm around me, making us sway from side to side, made my eyes watery; I looked up at him hoping the tears wouldn't fall. *God*, he looked so happy. He looked at me and smiled, winking, squeezing me tighter as we sang through the entire song, which ended with rowdy, boozy cheering flooding the place.

Towards the end of the night, people started to file out of the pub and were drinking on the pavement and in the street. The five of us sat around one of the tables outside, in varying degrees of drunkenness, surrounded by a wall of both happy and angry shouting. There was a plate of fries in the centre of the table that Chelsea, and Noria, who was sitting on Muddy's lap, were sharing; Noria was wearing his hat and his foil chain now; and I'd given her Chelsea's orange-tinted glasses.

The conversation took on various shapes, shifting haphazardly from person to person. I wasn't listening, but Chelsea would touch my arm, or Muddy and Noria would look at me expectantly and I'd nod. I found myself just looking at them, my heart filled to the brim with elation. I thought about how I'd closed my eyes the first time I'd met Muddy in the woods, hoping that once I opened them up there would be something, some kind of reassurance that I was worthy of love, of life, of being wanted, of being respected. And, finally, here it was. My eyes were wide open and the glorious manifestations of happiness that I'd begged for were dotted around the table.

Later, Muddy slapped Finlay's back and Finlay juddered, reaching into his jacket pocket, his hands trembling, walking around to my and Chelsea's side of the table. He got on his knees between us and presented the ring to her, his voice a stuttering mess of false starts.

Chelsea's face flushed red, she looked across to Noria, who just shrugged, and then turned her gaze to me; I smiled nervously. Finlay, his voice the feeblest I'd ever heard it, told her how much he loved her, how he wanted to spend his life with her, that he couldn't imagine his future without her in it. Muddy winked at him, pressing the tips of his thumb and forefinger together. And eventually Finlay said: 'So, do you wanna marry me, then?'

Chelsea was silent a moment. 'What?' she said flatly.

'I said: do you wanna marry me?'

'No, I heard you.'

'So?'

'No.'

'What do you mean "no"?'

'What do you mean you wanna marry me?'

There was a long painful silence. 'Why wouldn't I?'

'Are you serious?'

'Well, of course I'm bloody serious,' he said. 'I'm on my fuckin' knees, aren't I?'

'God, Finn,' she said, 'I knew you were up to something.

Why would you do this on your birthday? Now I'm just gonna look like a right bitch, aren't I? I don't wanna get married, why would you even think I wanted that? I thought you were happy with how things were. We've fuckin' talked about this.'

'But what about the babies?'

'What fuckin' babies, Finn?'

There was another silence. 'Chels, babe, please,' Finlay begged, his voice shaky again, looking up at her. 'Just ... just give me a chance, alright? Just give me a chance to show you that—'

'Finn,' Chelsea interrupted, touching his face. 'Just get up, will you?'

Finlay closed the box, stood up, and softly said: 'But you're everything to me, babe. I love the fuck out of you.'

Chelsea stared at him a moment, seemingly taking in the sadness in his face, which seemed to make her sad too. She then sighed, folded her arms, and pushed past him down the pavement, and he followed.

This seemed to sober Muddy up, but not Noria who just pulled the plate of chips closer, as well as the rest of Chelsea's drink.

'Well, that was fuckin' rough,' Muddy said. 'Unlucky bloke.'

'I know,' I said, 'he had this whole plan for how he was going to do it. I wonder why he jumped the gun.'

'I s'pose he couldn't wait.'

Noria, still unbothered, asked if one of us would fetch her some more salt and pepper. Muddy nodded and stood up. 'Oi, Harley,' he said.

'Yeah?'

'That's gonna be me and you,' he said, pointing down the way at Chelsea and Finlay, 'if you don't get a move on and help me look for this new place, pal.'

Thirty

For Muddy's actual birthday, he and I drove back to the Isle of Sheppey in the evening, and parked along that long narrow road, beside that dark expansive field with the orange sign. He'd said he'd be looking for owls again, but when we got there he didn't move; he didn't even take out his binoculars. We just sat quietly in the car for a while. The sky was mesmerizingly navy and aglow with stars, almost as if it wasn't quite real, like it had been staged for a film or something. I was unsure what kind of silence this was; it felt simultaneously comfortable and uncomfortable. I hesitantly touched his shoulder. He looked across to me, smiling, although I had the sense there was some dejection in his eyes.

'Mud, are you all right?' I asked.

He didn't answer; he just laughed softly. 'Come on, pal,' he said, 'let's get out there.'

We got out of the car and leaned on his bonnet, staring out into the distance. It had got so cold. He was in cargo shorts, safety boots and a red and black plaid shirt. I rubbed my upper arms and exhaled hard, making an O-shape with my mouth. He looked at me, chuckling, and lifted an arm up, beckoning me closer to him. I moved nearer and rested my head on his side; he embraced me tightly and rubbed my arm. We were silent a moment further.

'So, Harles,' Muddy said eventually, 'is there anything you want to tell me?'

'What do you mean?'

'You know,' he said, 'is there anything you want to say?'

'Um,' I said, 'if you were playing the long game and had really brought me out here to kill me . . . congrats. I fell for it. I really believed you loved me.'

He laughed and then sighed. 'Finners has a big mouth, pal,' he said, 'and an even bigger one when he's hammered. Tells me everything Chels tells him.'

I went silent again. 'Oh.'

'Well,' he said, 'I got the impression, when he told me, that it might've been something you were anxious about saying, that maybe you were just waiting for the right time, or that you just didn't want to hurt my little old feelings, even though I've told you more times than I can bleedin' count that I'm a tough fuckin' bloke. So, I thought I'd just let you tell me yourself . . .'

'Mud,' I said, 'you were just so excited about finding a new place together and—'

'Well, of course I was, pal,' he said. 'Come on, why wouldn't I be excited about living with you? I love you, mate! You make me so bleedin' happy, you do. I don't know if I've ever met anyone who just has to look at me and that puts me on top of the bloody world. I'd keep you around me for ever if I had my way. But, Harles, I do know that's not how life works. My plans aren't your plans. I can't have you with me all the time just because I want to.' He went quiet. 'I think it's great that you're thinking about going back to uni.'

'Is it?' I said. 'The last time I went I literally wanted to die.'

'And look at you now, pal,' he said. 'Look at everything you're doing to sort yourself out. You're on a bit of a journey, aren't you? And I just know it's going to take you to wonderful places, mate, and you're going to do wonderful things.' He was gently rubbing my back now. 'You're gonna go off to uni, you're gonna get your degree. You're gonna go and work at some big-shot magazine place in London or something. You're gonna do everything you ever wanted to do. And, you know, I'll be here, in the woods somewhere, looking at my birds, cheering you on. It's been a bleedin' honour being your person, Harles.'

I'd tried to suppress my tears. 'It really hurts,' I said, my voice quiet and shaky. 'The thought of not seeing you every day anymore. You've given me something that I've been looking for for so long that the thought of you not being there anymore, this close, it ... Muddy, it genuinely hurts.'

'Well, I hate to break it to you, pal,' he said, laughing, 'but you got me in your life for ever. Don't matter where you go, really, I'm sorry. It's just like that Lighthouse Family song says: you, me, for ever.'

I shook my head, smiling. 'Mud, what is it with you and Lighthouse Family?'

'They're just a great fuckin' duo, aren't they?' he said,

'They're legends, they are. They don't make 'em like that anymore. Everyone's too scared to get emotional these days, you see. Not me though. I'll always wear my emotions on the sleeves of all my plaid shirts.'

I laughed, looking up at him. 'Ah, Muddy, I love you.'

'You're gonna be all right, pal,' he said, 'you're gonna be just fine.'

One day in early September, Muddy and I went back up to Manchester. His granddad, despite his protests, was being moved into a retirement village soon, and Muddy wanted to ensure that he'd at least get to see his feeding station bustling with life again: brimming with quarrels of sparrows and mischiefs of magpies and worms of robins and charms of gold-finches. We sat in the garden, while Mabel was lying on the floor weeding. Muddy was in a black fleece and cargo shorts, his hands in his lap, with bits of cheese secreted in his palms. We were quietly looking above the fence, into the branches.

That morning, we'd driven to Castlefield, where we'd walked along the canals and had lunch in Saint John's Gardens. We'd sat on a bench, engulfed in little pink flowers, and he'd leaned back, stretching his arm across the back of it. 'We've had a right old summer, haven't we, mate?' he said.

'Well, technically it's not over yet,' I said. 'I only called up student finance last week, so we still have a week or so together.'

He looked into the sky. 'You got your counselling and stuff sorted over there then?'

I nodded. 'And I have all the proof of the depression and

anxiety and everything to give to them. It's weird, I used to think I'd hate having this written down, that it would cement it somehow, but it's not that bad. It's proof I've done something about it. Did you talk to Finlay about moving in with him?'

'I did,' he said. 'He's making me pay the full rent, and I think he's added some on top just to be a bastard.'

'How is he by the way?'

'He's hanging in there,' he said. 'He told me he's fine, but I don't wanna pry, just in case I piss him off and he chucks me out.' He sighed. 'Ah, he was such a mess after Chels said no. I haven't seen him like that in a really long time, pal. I'm kinda scared he might fall back into his old ways. I don't know if he ever told you, but he used to hit the sauce pretty hard, him. He'd be on his own, chugging it down at all hours of the morning. Life got pretty dark for him. And I never wanna see him like that again, so it looks like I have quite a bit of work to do now. When I get back home, I'm not lettin' him out of my sight, no matter how much I get on his nerves. You know, he's not even gettin' angry at any of my jokes. I said to him, if Chels won't have him, then I would. I even told him how sexy I'd look in a wedding dress.'

I laughed. 'What did he say?'

'Well, he started crying again, didn't he? And then I tried on the engagement ring, and it got stuck on my finger. So, when we got it off, he told me to get out.' Muddy had sighed again. 'He's a bleedin' sexy bloke, he is. They'll be linin' up. Plenty more fish and all that. He'll be all right. Chelsea too.'

Now, back in the garden, we heard some rustling in the

branches over the fence; we both got up. Muddy stood next to me holding the bits of cheese. He put his hands over mine and poured the cheese into my palms; his were starting to tremble in excitement as he let go.

'Is the robin still there?' I asked.

'Yeah, pal,' he said, 'robin's still chillin' up there. Give it time, mate. And if it don't come down, it's all right, we can try again tomorrow. It's a gradual process. Just don't bail on me like Finn did.'

We smiled at each other. I looked up, and I could see the little robin too; I wasn't confident that it would fly down because it had gone so quiet.

All my life I'd known happiness to be this evasive thing, something I'd had to pounce on and hold still even as it evaporated through my fingers. These moments of disappointment, of sadness, of emptiness, had permeated my life, and I'd felt resigned to them. Life, with all its facets, terrified me. Happiness was scary because the loss of it was scary. Loneliness was scary also, but so was losing that familiarity it gave me, that awful sense of home I'd made in it. I'd always felt like a weed growing amongst flowers, competing for light and water: too neglected to be picked, but somehow too weak to be a threat to anything. But, in the end, these flowers had given me something, they'd arranged themselves around me, and made me feel as if I were one of their own. And now, I could see the potential for longevity in these spells of happiness; I could see deeper shades of happiness, more enthusiastic rushes of it, as if what was once an occasional fragrance that had drifted haphazardly through the atmosphere, had solidified, and I could now hold a small piece of it in the centre of my palm like a rare iridescent crystal.

So, the robin stayed still, twitching its head. I looked at Muddy, smiling at me, nodding, winking, and then back up into the branches. It was as if the distance to the bird had collapsed, and everything I saw captured in this close-up had slowed in motion. The robin started to rustle, and then it prepared to fly.

Acknowledgements

I'm eternally thankful to my agent Juliet Mushens for believing in me, for being my biggest champion and, most importantly, for being a friend. This book was born from such a dark place, and it was because of her reassurance and invaluable insight that some light eventually found its way into the story. Thank you, Juliet, sincerely. Lord knows where I'd be without her.

Thanks also to my editors Chris White, Wilhelmina Asaam and Jesse Shuman for their unwavering enthusiasm about the book and for their excellent editorial vision, which made this a better novel, and me a better writer. A special thanks to Wilhelmina for coming up with the title and also huge thanks to the teams at Scribner and Ballantine Books.

I'm immensely grateful to Gulcan Akbal for their untiring emotional support over the years, for reading sections of early drafts and for being a wealth of knowledge. Words will never be able to express how much I appreciate them and their friendship and how much of their time they gave me during this whole journey. Their loyalty, patience and generosity are unparalleled.

Many thanks also to Andrew Huddleston, who was the first to read a full-length manuscript of mine and provided such thoughtful feedback. Thanks so, so, much for being a mentor to me, and for the years of wisdom and encouragement. I truly believe my world is a better place for having met him.

Thanks also to my friends who, over the years, have checked in on me and my progress with this manuscript and simply listened while I talked about what I hoped would one day become a proper novel. Thanks to: Liam Andrews, Thomas Emmans, Pim Wangtechawat, Maria Brookes, Owen Longuet, Chloe Marks, Robbie Carr, Conor McLaughlin, Stevie Dixon, Doug Cowderoy, both Sarah Smiths and Etta Davies.

As ever, I'm very grateful to my family, especially my siblings, Jason and Rianna Mensah for their support.

Thanks also to my English teachers, especially: Erin Woodhall and Carley Johnson for igniting my passion for reading and writing; I can't imagine what my future would've looked like if I hadn't had these women as my educators. I don't think it's an exaggeration to say that my life was thoroughly changed for the better.

And lastly thank you to Terry Miller, whose resilience and optimism in the face of life's challenges is an unceasing inspiration to me. I adore and respect them and it truly is an honour that I get to call them my friend.